CHERUB™

Robert Muchamore
CLASS A

THE GRAPHIC NOVEL

Illustrated by
DAVID COMBET and **BAPTISTE PAYEN**

Creative consultants
ANDREW DONKIN and **HELEN CHEVALLIER**

Hodder Children's Books

HODDER CHILDREN'S BOOKS

First published in Great Britain in 2017 by Hodder and Stoughton

1 3 5 7 9 10 8 6 4 2

This graphic novel is an adaptation of the novel *CHERUB: Class A*,
originally published in the UK by Hodder Children's Books in 2004
Graphic novel adaptation and illustrations copyright © Casterman, 2017
Translation copyright © Robert Muchamore, 2017

Translation by Andrew Donkin and Helen Chevallier

The moral rights of the author and illustrator have been asserted.

A CIP catalogue record for this book
is available from the British Library.

ISBN 978 1 444 93978 1

Printed and bound by Canale in Romania.

The paper and board used in this book
are made from wood from responsible sources.

Hodder Children's Books
An imprint of Hachette Children's Group
Part of Hodder and Stoughton
Carmelite House
50 Victoria Embankment
London EC4Y 0DZ

An Hachette UK Company
www.hachette.co.uk

www.hachettechildrens.co.uk

CHERUB IS A BRANCH OF BRITISH INTELLIGENCE. ITS AGENTS ARE AGED BETWEEN TEN AND SEVENTEEN YEARS AND ARE RECRUITED FROM CARE HOMES ALL OVER THE COUNTRY.

THEY UNDERGO CHERUB'S TOUGH BASIC TRAINING REGIME, THEN CARRY OUT DANGEROUS UNDERCOVER MISSIONS.

THEY LIVE ON CHERUB CAMPUS, A SECRET FACILITY HIDDEN IN THE HEART OF THE ENGLISH COUNTRYSIDE.

NOBODY REALISES KIDS DO UNDERCOVER MISSIONS.

ALTOGETHER, ABOUT 300 CHILDREN LIVE ON CHERUB CAMPUS.

THE EVENTS DESCRIBED IN THIS ACCOUNT ARE BASED ON REAL CASE REPORTS.

JAMES ADAMS
n°0232251145
Twelve-year-old operative. Has a habit of getting himself into trouble.

LAUREN ADAMS
n°0698856521
Younger sister of James Adams. Superior intelligence rating.

KERRY CHANG
n°0021458967
Born in Hong Kong. Expert in hand to hand combat.

GABRIELLE O'BRIAN
n°0001458968
Kerry's best friend. Born in Jamaica.

BRUCE NORRIS
n°0008987511
Karate champion. Born in Wales.

KYLE BLUEMAN
n°0025478569
Two years older than James. Known for his rebellious streak.

THEY CONCERN THE ACTIVITIES OF THE ABOVE AGENTS.

FOR OFFICIAL PURPOSES, THESE CHILDREN DO NOT EXIST.

CHERUBS ARE RANKED ACCORDING TO THE COLOUR OF THE T-SHIRTS THEY WEAR WHENEVER THEY ARE ON CAMPUS.

ORANGE T-SHIRTS ARE RESERVED FOR VISITORS. IT IS FORBIDDEN TO TALK TO THEM.

RED T-SHIRTS ARE FOR KIDS WHO LIVE ON CHERUB CAMPUS, BUT ARE TOO YOUNG TO QUALIFY AS AGENTS.

BLUE T-SHIRTS ARE FOR KIDS UNDERGOING CHERUB'S BASIC TRAINING REGIME. THOSE WHO PASS AND ARE QUALIFIED FOR MISSIONS ARE AWARDED A GREY T-SHIRT.

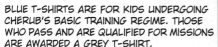

A NAVY T-SHIRT IS GIVEN FOR OUTSTANDING PERFORMANCE WHILE ON A MISSION.

A BLACK T-SHIRT IS THE ULTIMATE RECOGNITION FOR REALLY EXCEPTIONAL ACHIEVEMENT.

WHEN CHERUBS RETIRE AT 17 OR 18 YEARS OLD THEY RECEIVE A WHITE T-SHIRT.

THEY CAN WEAR IT WITH PRIDE WHEN THEY RETURN TO CAMPUS. MOST INSTRUCTORS ON CAMPUS CAN ALSO BE SEEN WEARING WHITE T-SHIRTS.

AWAY FROM CAMPUS, AGENTS DON'T HAVE TO WEAR A REGULATION T-SHIRT AND CAN RELAX A LITTLE.

EVEN DURING THEIR FIVE-WEEK SUMMER HOLIDAY, AGENTS ARE REQUIRED TO REMAIN IN GREAT PHYSICAL SHAPE IN CASE THEY'RE NEEDED ON A MISSION AT SHORT NOTICE.

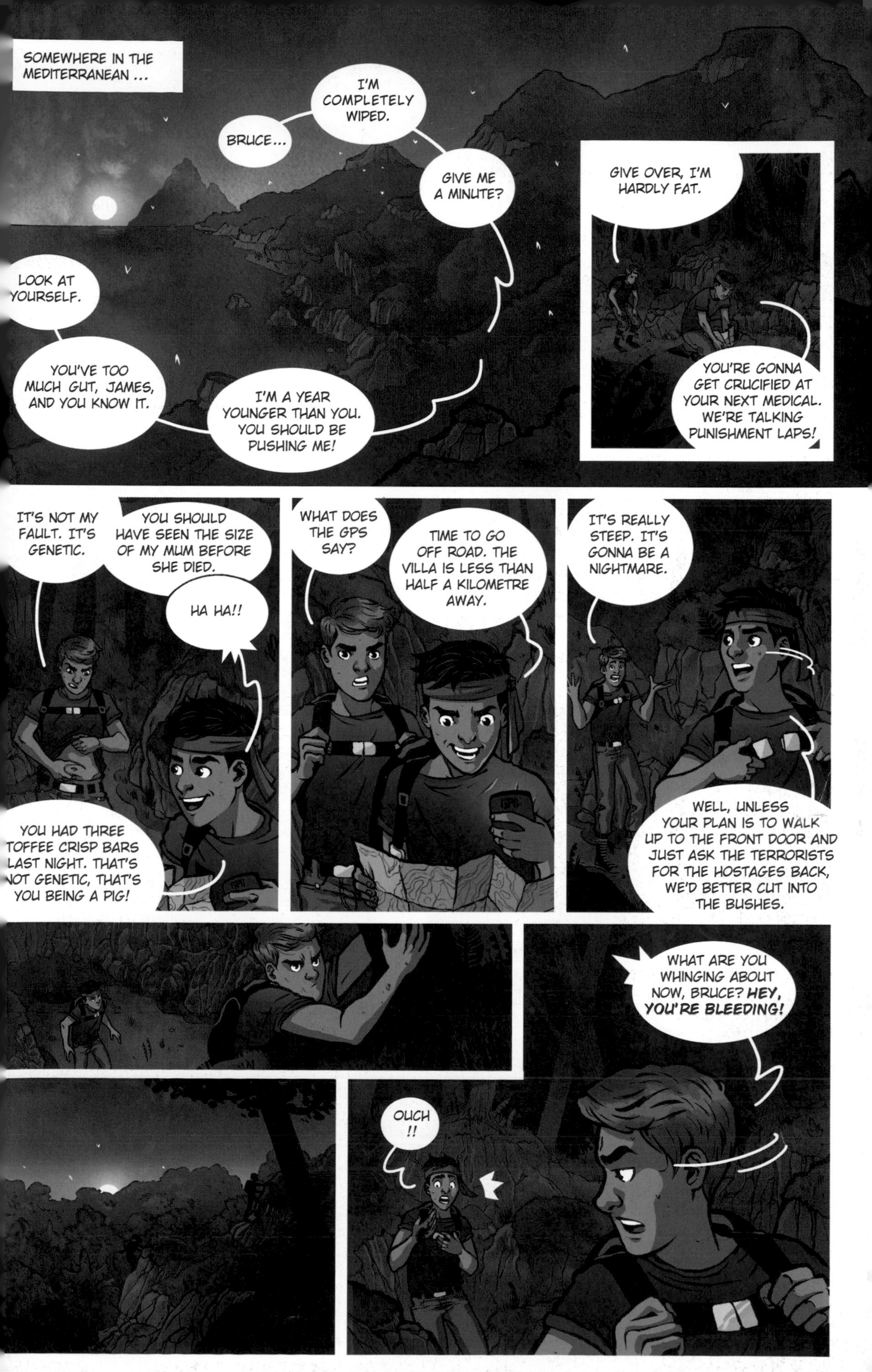
SOMEWHERE IN THE MEDITERRANEAN ...
BRUCE...
I'M COMPLETELY WIPED.
GIVE ME A MINUTE?
LOOK AT YOURSELF.
YOU'VE TOO MUCH GUT, JAMES, AND YOU KNOW IT.
I'M A YEAR YOUNGER THAN YOU. YOU SHOULD BE PUSHING ME!
GIVE OVER, I'M HARDLY FAT.
YOU'RE GONNA GET CRUCIFIED AT YOUR NEXT MEDICAL. WE'RE TALKING PUNISHMENT LAPS!
IT'S NOT MY FAULT. IT'S GENETIC.
YOU SHOULD HAVE SEEN THE SIZE OF MY MUM BEFORE SHE DIED.
HA HA!!
YOU HAD THREE TOFFEE CRISP BARS LAST NIGHT. THAT'S NOT GENETIC, THAT'S YOU BEING A PIG!
WHAT DOES THE GPS SAY?
TIME TO GO OFF ROAD. THE VILLA IS LESS THAN HALF A KILOMETRE AWAY.
IT'S REALLY STEEP. IT'S GONNA BE A NIGHTMARE.
WELL, UNLESS YOUR PLAN IS TO WALK UP TO THE FRONT DOOR AND JUST ASK THE TERRORISTS FOR THE HOSTAGES BACK, WE'D BETTER CUT INTO THE BUSHES.
WHAT ARE YOU WHINGING ABOUT NOW, BRUCE? **HEY, YOU'RE BLEEDING!**
OUCH!!

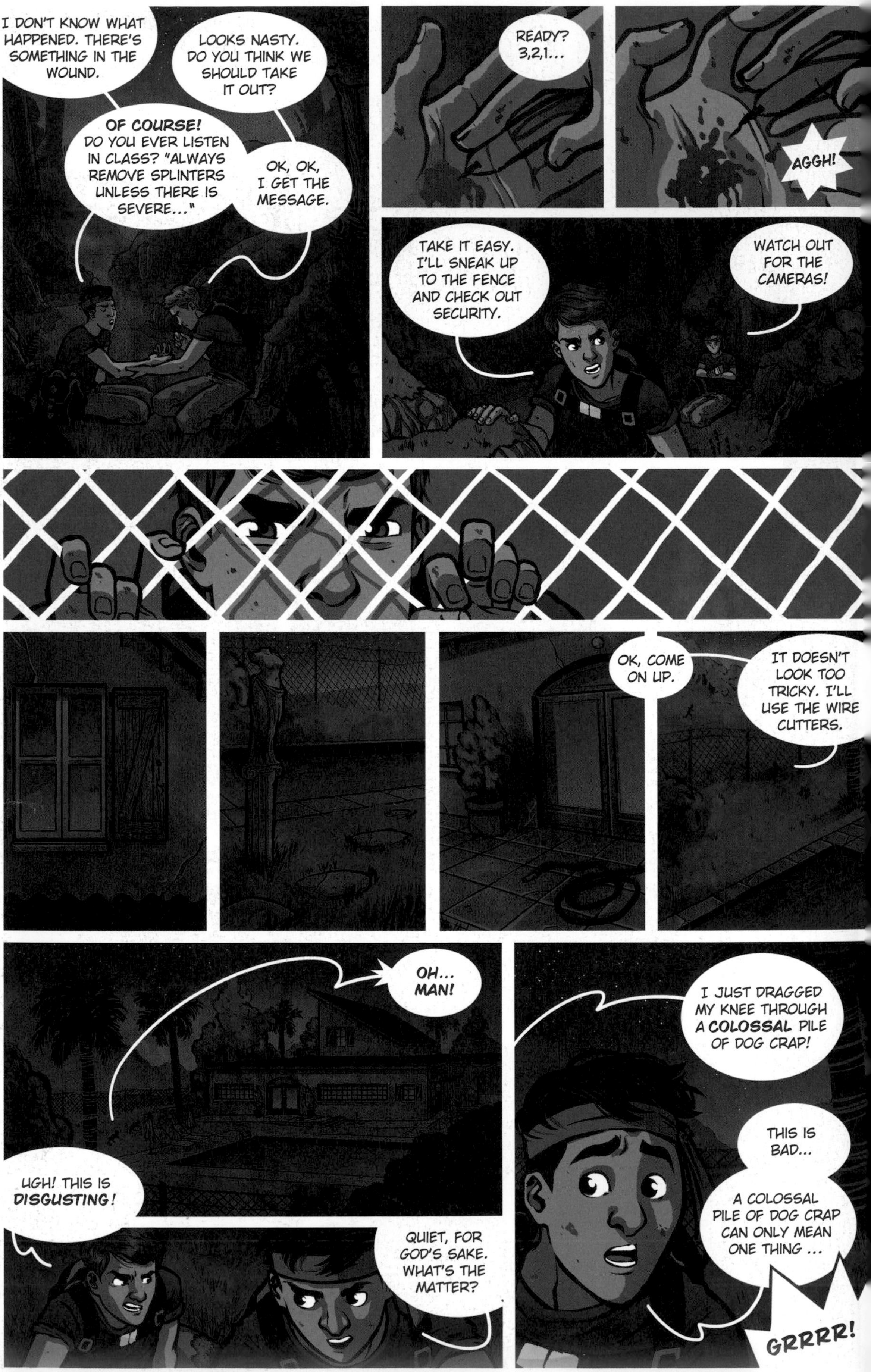
I DON'T KNOW WHAT HAPPENED. THERE'S SOMETHING IN THE WOUND.
LOOKS NASTY. DO YOU THINK WE SHOULD TAKE IT OUT?
OF COURSE! DO YOU EVER LISTEN IN CLASS? "ALWAYS REMOVE SPLINTERS UNLESS THERE IS SEVERE..."
OK, OK, I GET THE MESSAGE.
READY? 3,2,1...
AGGH!
TAKE IT EASY. I'LL SNEAK UP TO THE FENCE AND CHECK OUT SECURITY.
WATCH OUT FOR THE CAMERAS!
OK, COME ON UP.
IT DOESN'T LOOK TOO TRICKY. I'LL USE THE WIRE CUTTERS.
OH... MAN!
UGH! THIS IS DISGUSTING!
QUIET, FOR GOD'S SAKE. WHAT'S THE MATTER?
I JUST DRAGGED MY KNEE THROUGH A COLOSSAL PILE OF DOG CRAP!
THIS IS BAD...
A COLOSSAL PILE OF DOG CRAP CAN ONLY MEAN ONE THING ...
GRRRR!

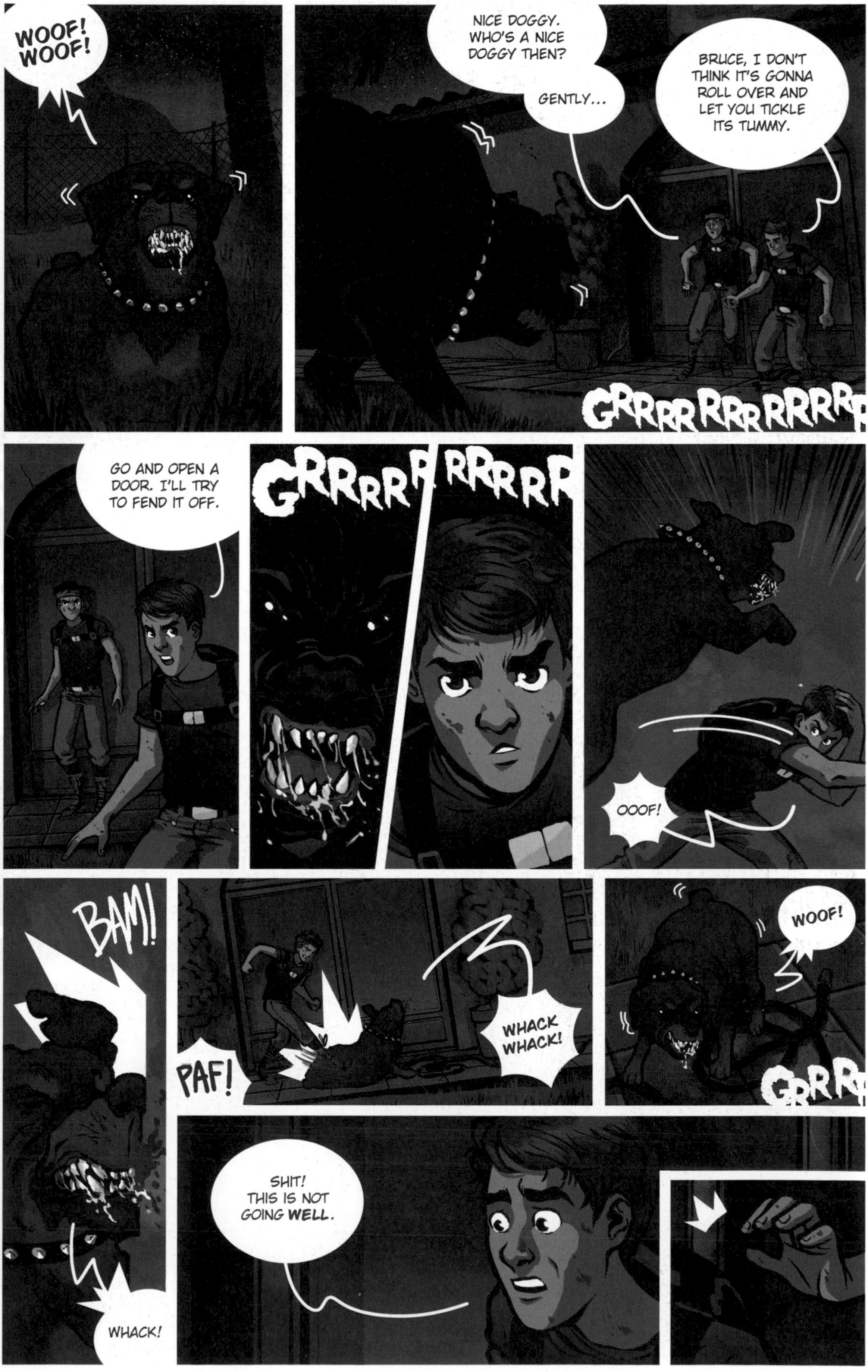
WOOF! WOOF!
NICE DOGGY. WHO'S A NICE DOGGY THEN?
GENTLY...
BRUCE, I DON'T THINK IT'S GONNA ROLL OVER AND LET YOU TICKLE ITS TUMMY.
GRRRRRRRRRRRR
GO AND OPEN A DOOR. I'LL TRY TO FEND IT OFF.
GRRRRR RRRRRR
OOOF!
BAM!
WHACK!
PAF!
WHACK WHACK!
WOOF!
GRRR
SHIT! THIS IS NOT GOING **WELL**.

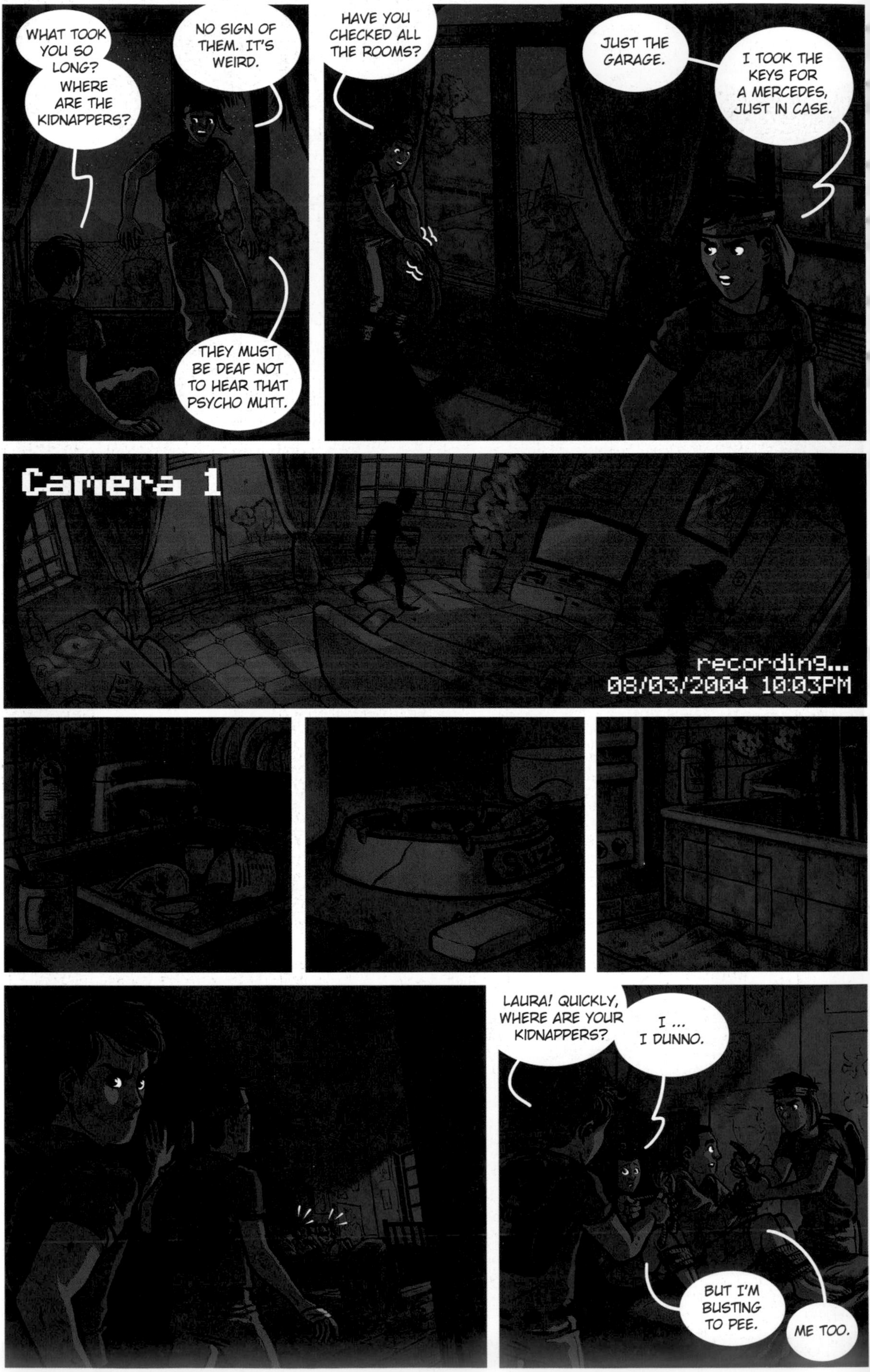
WHAT TOOK YOU SO LONG?
WHERE ARE THE KIDNAPPERS?
NO SIGN OF THEM. IT'S WEIRD.
THEY MUST BE DEAF NOT TO HEAR THAT PSYCHO MUTT.
HAVE YOU CHECKED ALL THE ROOMS?
JUST THE GARAGE.
I TOOK THE KEYS FOR A MERCEDES, JUST IN CASE.
Camera 1
recording...
08/03/2004 10:03PM
LAURA! QUICKLY, WHERE ARE YOUR KIDNAPPERS?
I ... I DUNNO.
BUT I'M BUSTING TO PEE.
ME TOO.

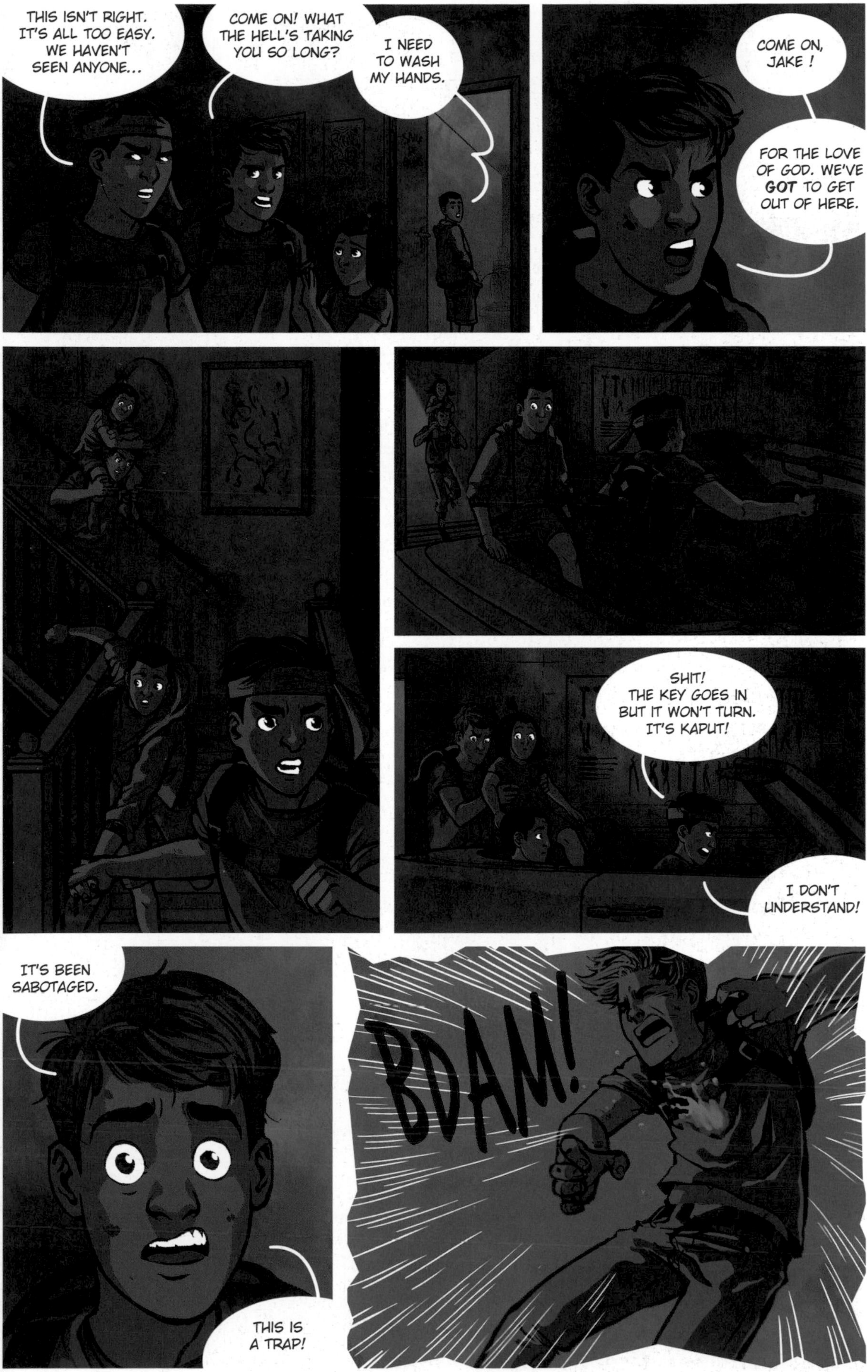
THIS ISN'T RIGHT. IT'S ALL TOO EASY. WE HAVEN'T SEEN ANYONE...
COME ON! WHAT THE HELL'S TAKING YOU SO LONG?
I NEED TO WASH MY HANDS.
COME ON, JAKE !
FOR THE LOVE OF GOD. WE'VE **GOT** TO GET OUT OF HERE.
SHIT! THE KEY GOES IN BUT IT WON'T TURN. IT'S KAPUT!
I DON'T UNDERSTAND!
IT'S BEEN SABOTAGED.
THIS IS A TRAP!
BDAM!

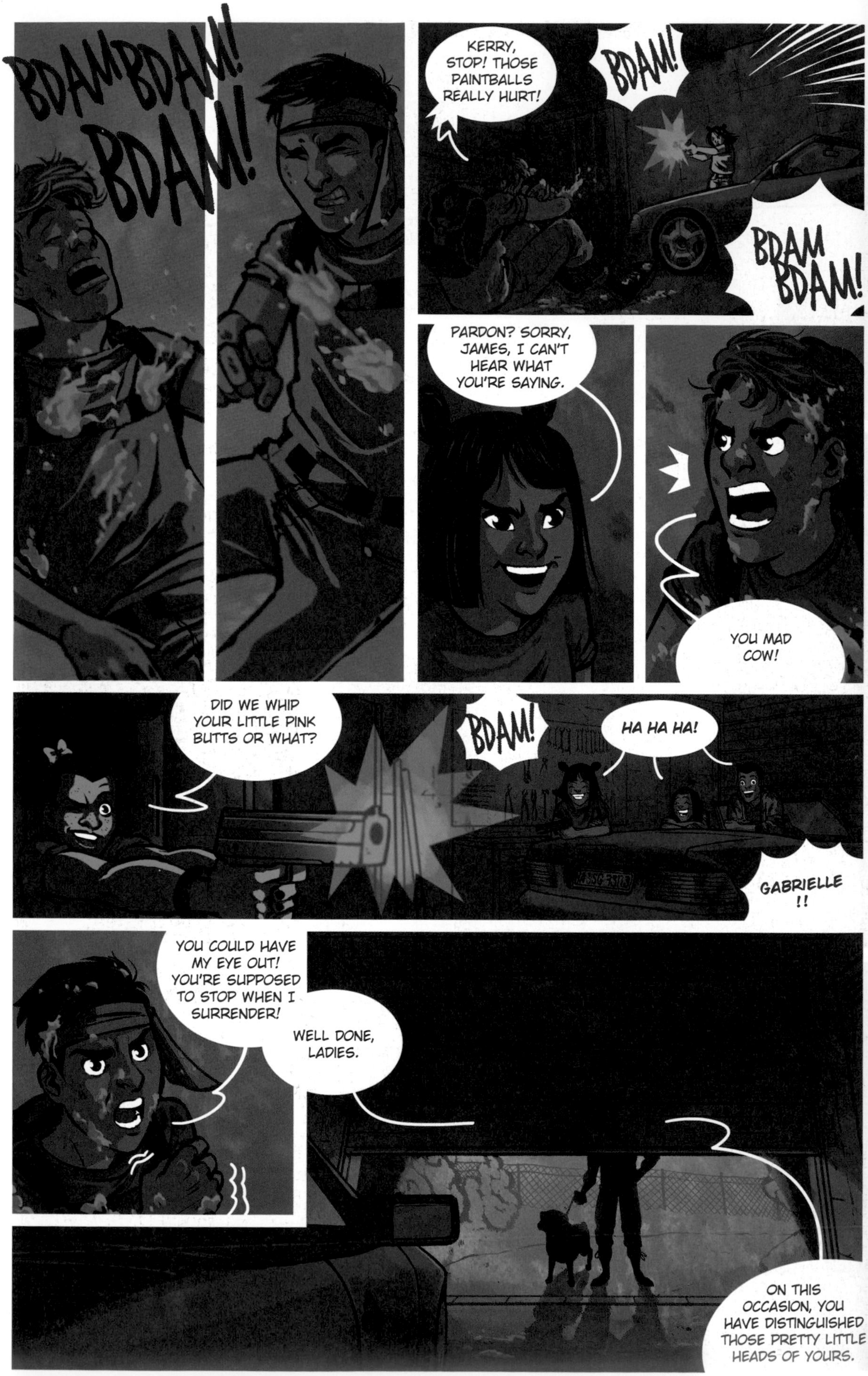
BDAMBDAM!
BDAM!
KERRY, STOP! THOSE PAINTBALLS REALLY HURT!
BDAM!
BDAM BDAM!
PARDON? SORRY, JAMES, I CAN'T HEAR WHAT YOU'RE SAYING.
YOU MAD COW!
DID WE WHIP YOUR LITTLE PINK BUTTS OR WHAT?
BDAM!
HA HA HA!
GABRIELLE !!
YOU COULD HAVE MY EYE OUT! YOU'RE SUPPOSED TO STOP WHEN I SURRENDER!
WELL DONE, LADIES.
ON THIS OCCASION, YOU HAVE DISTINGUISHED THOSE PRETTY LITTLE HEADS OF YOURS.

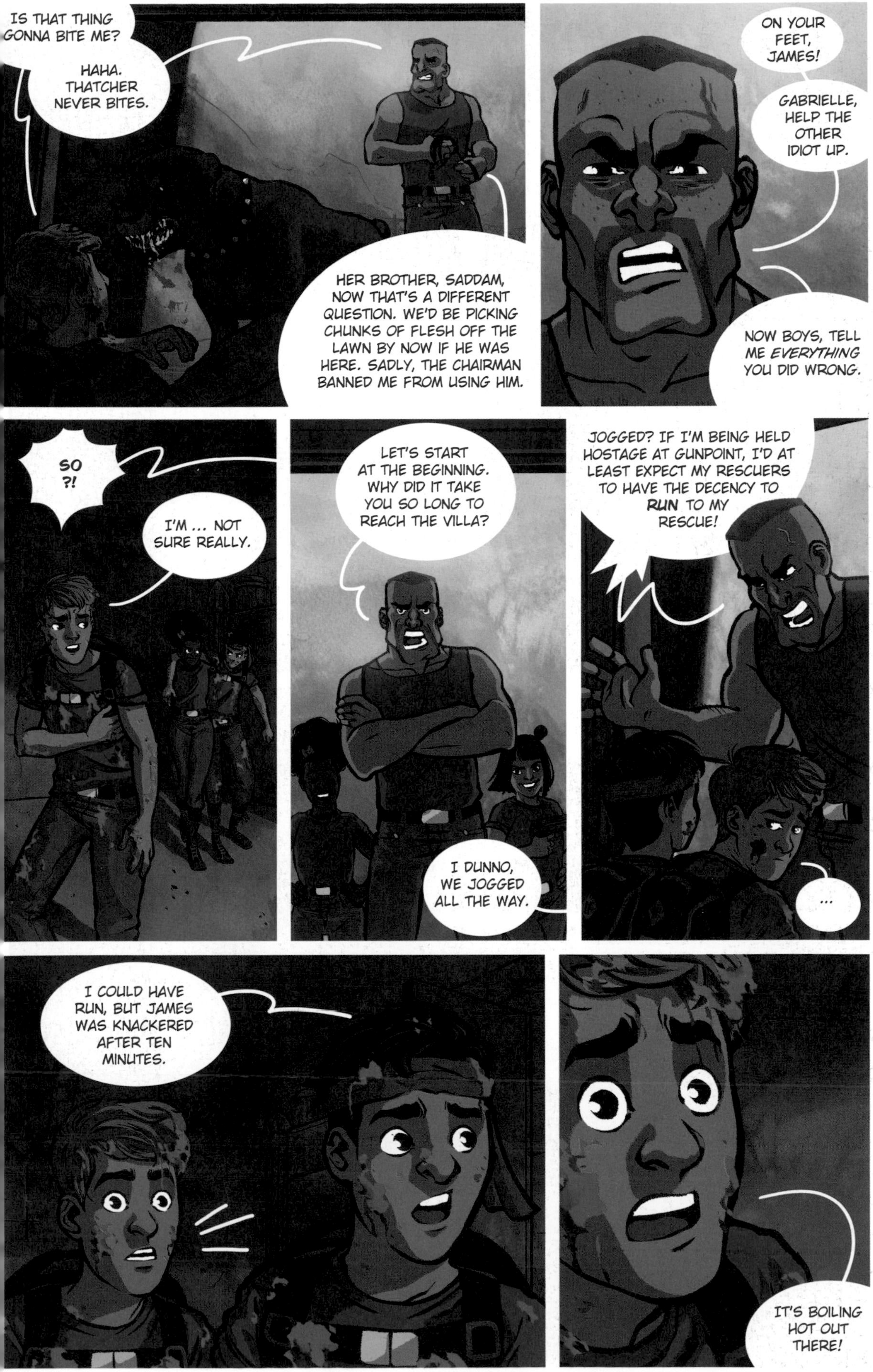
IS THAT THING GONNA BITE ME?
HAHA. THATCHER NEVER BITES.
HER BROTHER, SADDAM, NOW THAT'S A DIFFERENT QUESTION. WE'D BE PICKING CHUNKS OF FLESH OFF THE LAWN BY NOW IF HE WAS HERE. SADLY, THE CHAIRMAN BANNED ME FROM USING HIM.
ON YOUR FEET, JAMES!
GABRIELLE, HELP THE OTHER IDIOT UP.
NOW BOYS, TELL ME *EVERYTHING* YOU DID WRONG.
SO ?!
I'M ... NOT SURE REALLY.
LET'S START AT THE BEGINNING. WHY DID IT TAKE YOU SO LONG TO REACH THE VILLA?
I DUNNO, WE JOGGED ALL THE WAY.
JOGGED? IF I'M BEING HELD HOSTAGE AT GUNPOINT, I'D AT LEAST EXPECT MY RESCUERS TO HAVE THE DECENCY TO **RUN** TO MY RESCUE!
...
I COULD HAVE RUN, BUT JAMES WAS KNACKERED AFTER TEN MINUTES.
IT'S BOILING HOT OUT THERE!

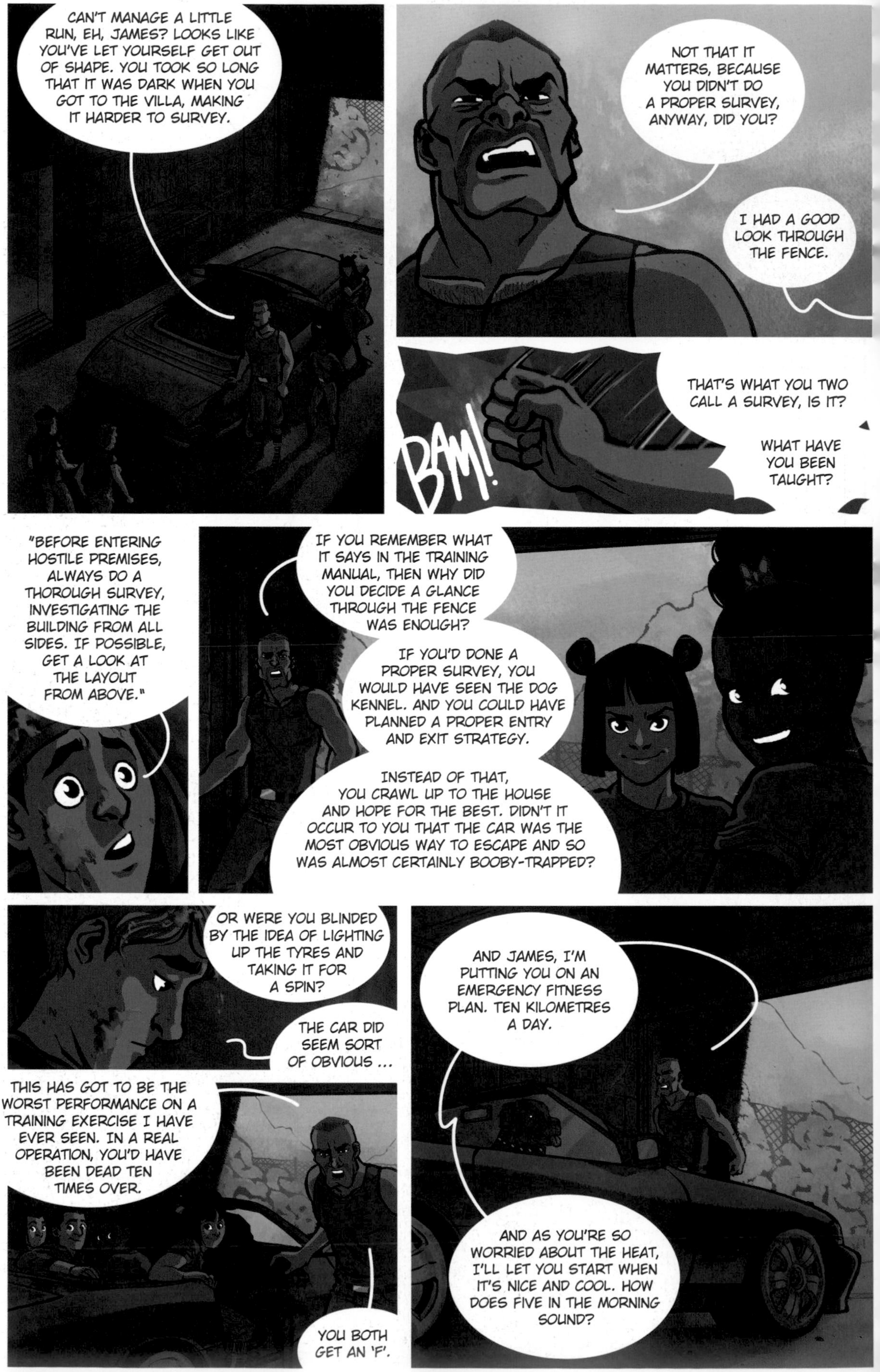
CAN'T MANAGE A LITTLE RUN, EH, JAMES? LOOKS LIKE YOU'VE LET YOURSELF GET OUT OF SHAPE. YOU TOOK SO LONG THAT IT WAS DARK WHEN YOU GOT TO THE VILLA, MAKING IT HARDER TO SURVEY.
NOT THAT IT MATTERS, BECAUSE YOU DIDN'T DO A PROPER SURVEY, ANYWAY, DID YOU?
I HAD A GOOD LOOK THROUGH THE FENCE.
BAM!
THAT'S WHAT YOU TWO CALL A SURVEY, IS IT?
WHAT HAVE YOU BEEN TAUGHT?
"BEFORE ENTERING HOSTILE PREMISES, ALWAYS DO A THOROUGH SURVEY, INVESTIGATING THE BUILDING FROM ALL SIDES. IF POSSIBLE, GET A LOOK AT THE LAYOUT FROM ABOVE."
IF YOU REMEMBER WHAT IT SAYS IN THE TRAINING MANUAL, THEN WHY DID YOU DECIDE A GLANCE THROUGH THE FENCE WAS ENOUGH?
IF YOU'D DONE A PROPER SURVEY, YOU WOULD HAVE SEEN THE DOG KENNEL. AND YOU COULD HAVE PLANNED A PROPER ENTRY AND EXIT STRATEGY.
INSTEAD OF THAT, YOU CRAWL UP TO THE HOUSE AND HOPE FOR THE BEST. DIDN'T IT OCCUR TO YOU THAT THE CAR WAS THE MOST OBVIOUS WAY TO ESCAPE AND SO WAS ALMOST CERTAINLY BOOBY-TRAPPED?
OR WERE YOU BLINDED BY THE IDEA OF LIGHTING UP THE TYRES AND TAKING IT FOR A SPIN?
THE CAR DID SEEM SORT OF OBVIOUS ...
THIS HAS GOT TO BE THE WORST PERFORMANCE ON A TRAINING EXERCISE I HAVE EVER SEEN. IN A REAL OPERATION, YOU'D HAVE BEEN DEAD TEN TIMES OVER.
YOU BOTH GET AN 'F'.
AND JAMES, I'M PUTTING YOU ON AN EMERGENCY FITNESS PLAN. TEN KILOMETRES A DAY.
AND AS YOU'RE SO WORRIED ABOUT THE HEAT, I'LL LET YOU START WHEN IT'S NICE AND COOL. HOW DOES FIVE IN THE MORNING SOUND?

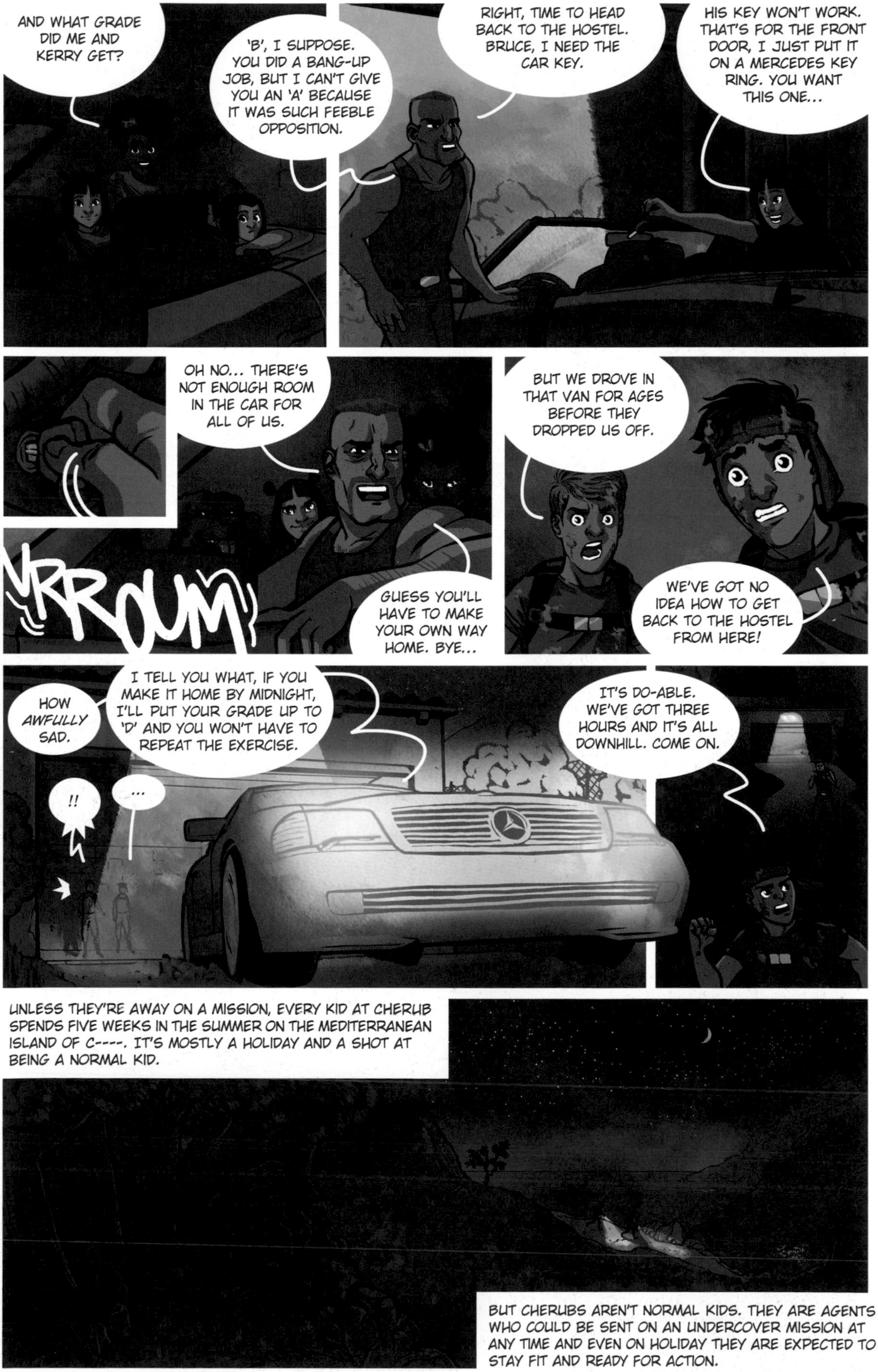
AND WHAT GRADE DID ME AND KERRY GET?
'B', I SUPPOSE. YOU DID A BANG-UP JOB, BUT I CAN'T GIVE YOU AN 'A' BECAUSE IT WAS SUCH FEEBLE OPPOSITION.
RIGHT, TIME TO HEAD BACK TO THE HOSTEL. BRUCE, I NEED THE CAR KEY.
HIS KEY WON'T WORK. THAT'S FOR THE FRONT DOOR, I JUST PUT IT ON A MERCEDES KEY RING. YOU WANT THIS ONE...
OH NO... THERE'S NOT ENOUGH ROOM IN THE CAR FOR ALL OF US.
VRROUM
GUESS YOU'LL HAVE TO MAKE YOUR OWN WAY HOME. BYE...
BUT WE DROVE IN THAT VAN FOR AGES BEFORE THEY DROPPED US OFF.
WE'VE GOT NO IDEA HOW TO GET BACK TO THE HOSTEL FROM HERE!
HOW AWFULLY SAD.
I TELL YOU WHAT, IF YOU MAKE IT HOME BY MIDNIGHT, I'LL PUT YOUR GRADE UP TO 'D' AND YOU WON'T HAVE TO REPEAT THE EXERCISE.
!!
...
IT'S DO-ABLE. WE'VE GOT THREE HOURS AND IT'S ALL DOWNHILL. COME ON.
UNLESS THEY'RE AWAY ON A MISSION, EVERY KID AT CHERUB SPENDS FIVE WEEKS IN THE SUMMER ON THE MEDITERRANEAN ISLAND OF C----. IT'S MOSTLY A HOLIDAY AND A SHOT AT BEING A NORMAL KID.
BUT CHERUBS AREN'T NORMAL KIDS. THEY ARE AGENTS WHO COULD BE SENT ON AN UNDERCOVER MISSION AT ANY TIME AND EVEN ON HOLIDAY THEY ARE EXPECTED TO STAY FIT AND READY FOR ACTION.

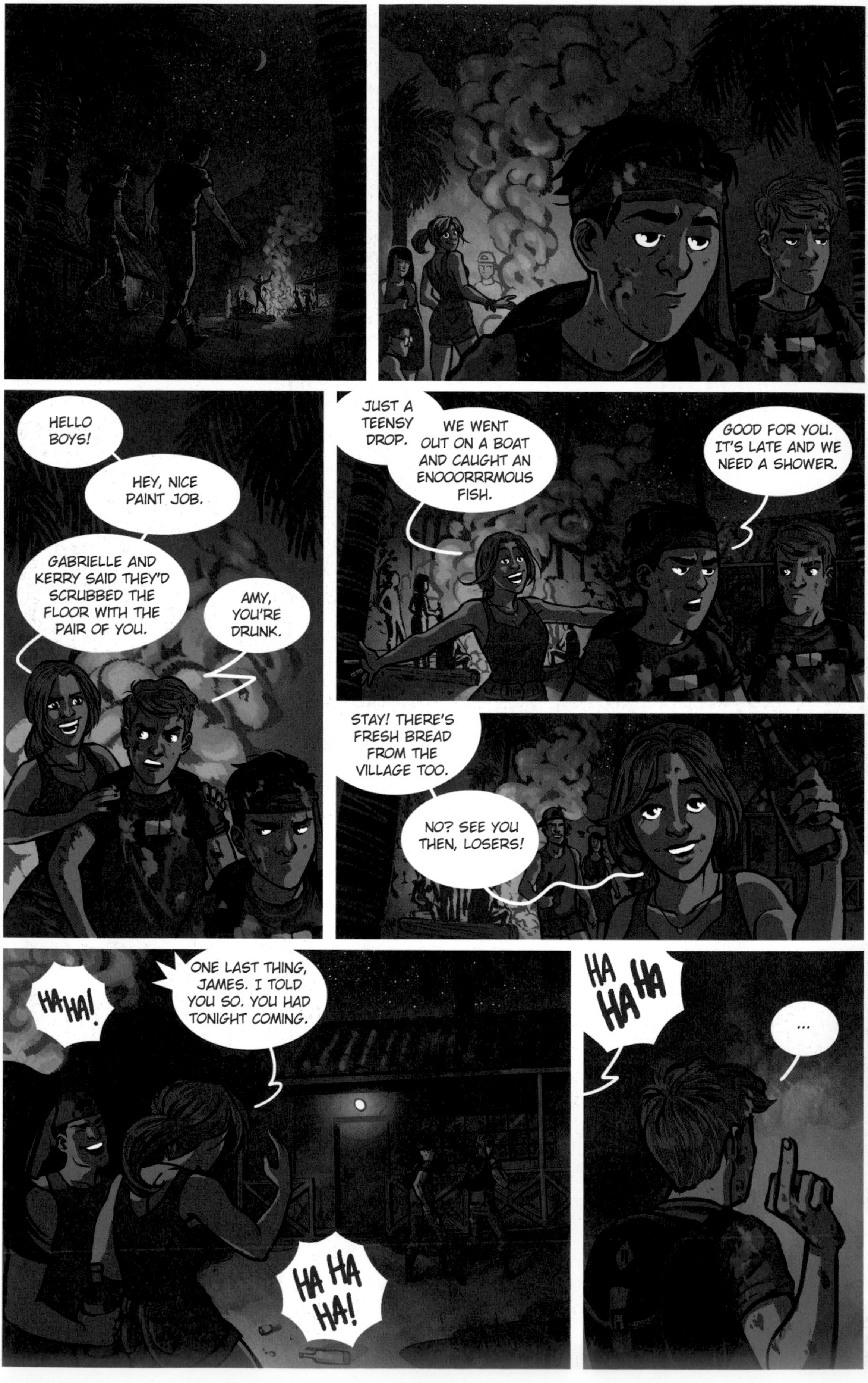
HELLO BOYS!
HEY, NICE PAINT JOB.
GABRIELLE AND KERRY SAID THEY'D SCRUBBED THE FLOOR WITH THE PAIR OF YOU.
AMY, YOU'RE DRUNK.
JUST A TEENSY DROP.
WE WENT OUT ON A BOAT AND CAUGHT AN ENOOORRRMOUS FISH.
GOOD FOR YOU. IT'S LATE AND WE NEED A SHOWER.
STAY! THERE'S FRESH BREAD FROM THE VILLAGE TOO.
NO? SEE YOU THEN, LOSERS!
HA HA!
ONE LAST THING, JAMES. I TOLD YOU SO. YOU HAD TONIGHT COMING.
HA HA HA!
HA HA HA HA
...

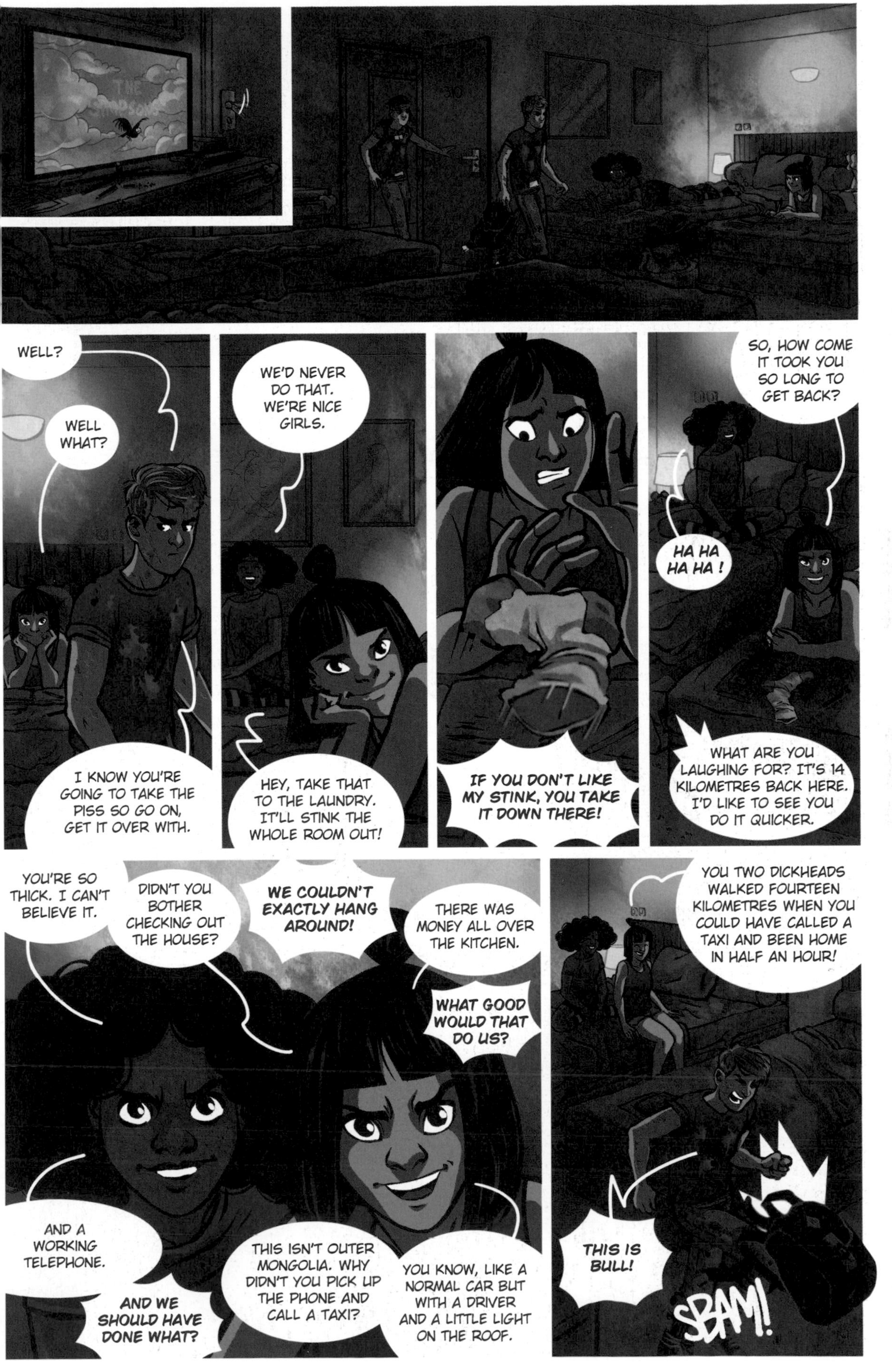
WELL?
WELL WHAT?
I KNOW YOU'RE GOING TO TAKE THE PISS SO GO ON, GET IT OVER WITH.
WE'D NEVER DO THAT. WE'RE NICE GIRLS.
HEY, TAKE THAT TO THE LAUNDRY. IT'LL STINK THE WHOLE ROOM OUT!
IF YOU DON'T LIKE MY STINK, YOU TAKE IT DOWN THERE!
SO, HOW COME IT TOOK YOU SO LONG TO GET BACK?
HA HA HA HA !
WHAT ARE YOU LAUGHING FOR? IT'S 14 KILOMETRES BACK HERE. I'D LIKE TO SEE YOU DO IT QUICKER.
YOU'RE SO THICK. I CAN'T BELIEVE IT.
DIDN'T YOU BOTHER CHECKING OUT THE HOUSE?
WE COULDN'T EXACTLY HANG AROUND!
THERE WAS MONEY ALL OVER THE KITCHEN.
WHAT GOOD WOULD THAT DO US?
AND A WORKING TELEPHONE.
AND WE SHOULD HAVE DONE WHAT?
THIS ISN'T OUTER MONGOLIA. WHY DIDN'T YOU PICK UP THE PHONE AND CALL A TAXI?
YOU KNOW, LIKE A NORMAL CAR BUT WITH A DRIVER AND A LITTLE LIGHT ON THE ROOF.
YOU TWO DICKHEADS WALKED FOURTEEN KILOMETRES WHEN YOU COULD HAVE CALLED A TAXI AND BEEN HOME IN HALF AN HOUR!
THIS IS BULL!
SBAM!

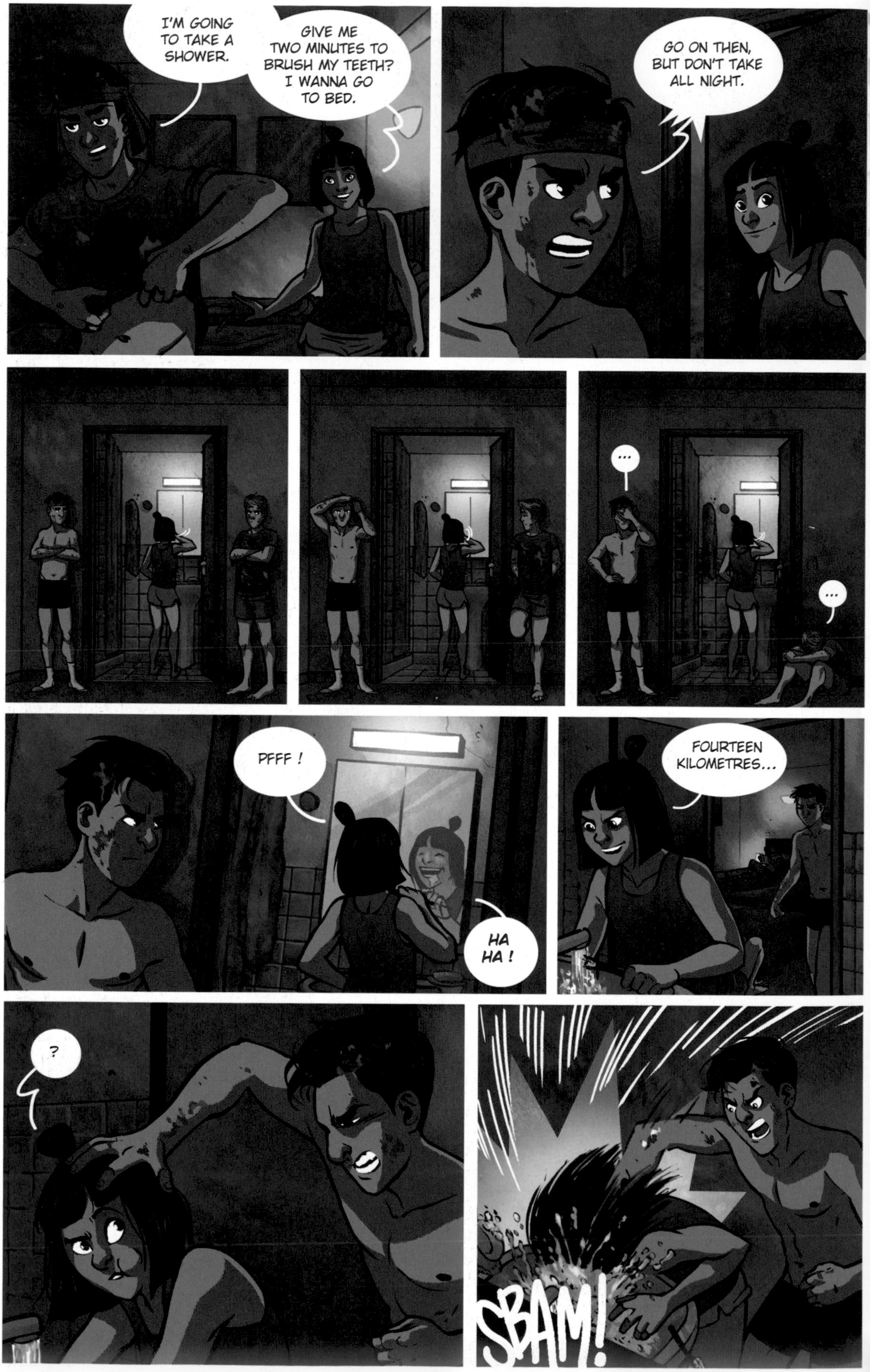
I'M GOING TO TAKE A SHOWER.
GIVE ME TWO MINUTES TO BRUSH MY TEETH? I WANNA GO TO BED.
GO ON THEN, BUT DON'T TAKE ALL NIGHT.
...
...
PFFF !
HA HA !
FOURTEEN KILOMETRES...
?
SBAM!

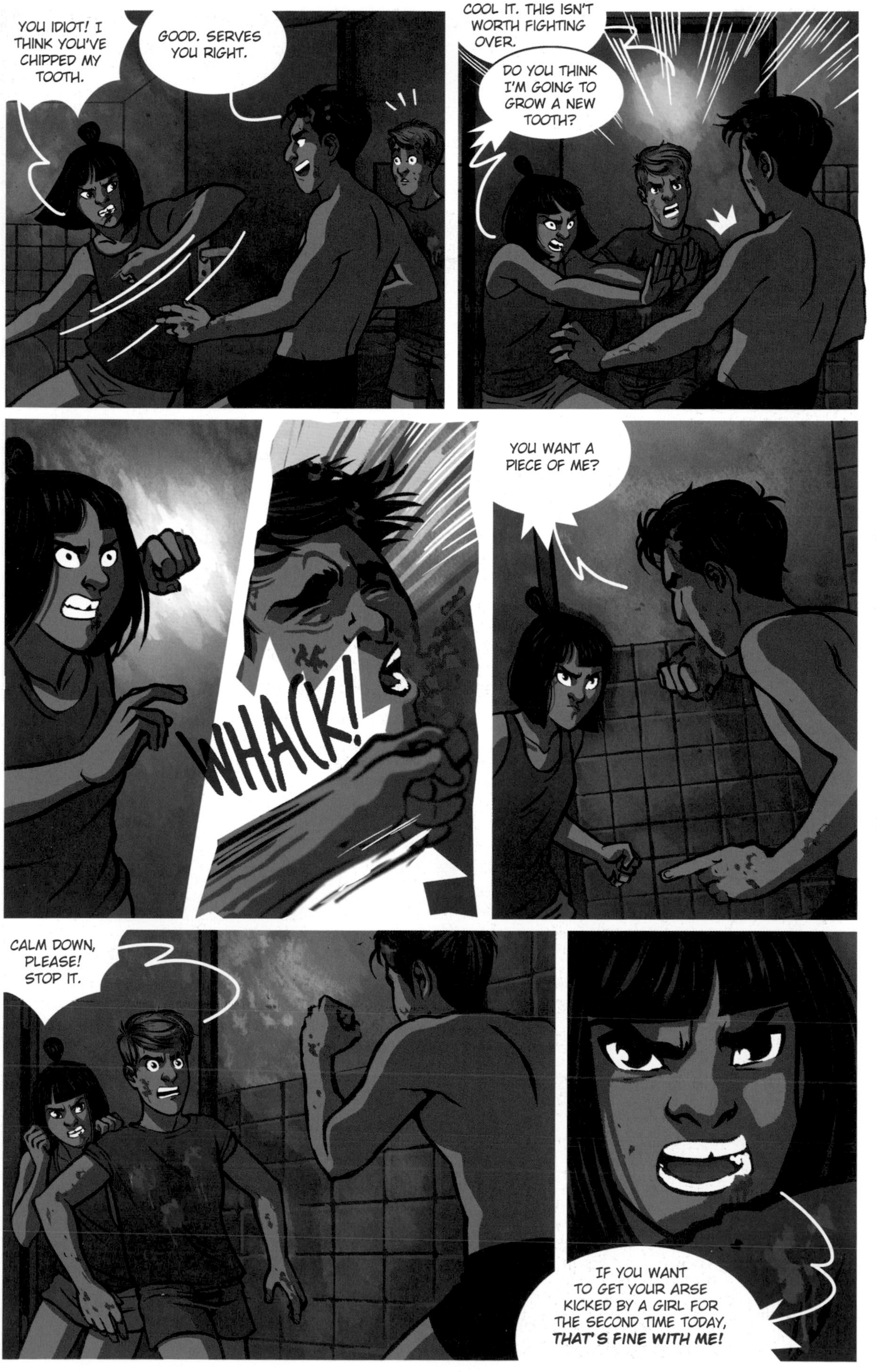
YOU IDIOT! I THINK YOU'VE CHIPPED MY TOOTH.
GOOD. SERVES YOU RIGHT.
COOL IT. THIS ISN'T WORTH FIGHTING OVER.
DO YOU THINK I'M GOING TO GROW A NEW TOOTH?
WHACK!
YOU WANT A PIECE OF ME?
CALM DOWN, PLEASE! STOP IT.
IF YOU WANT TO GET YOUR ARSE KICKED BY A GIRL FOR THE SECOND TIME TODAY, **THAT'S FINE WITH ME!**

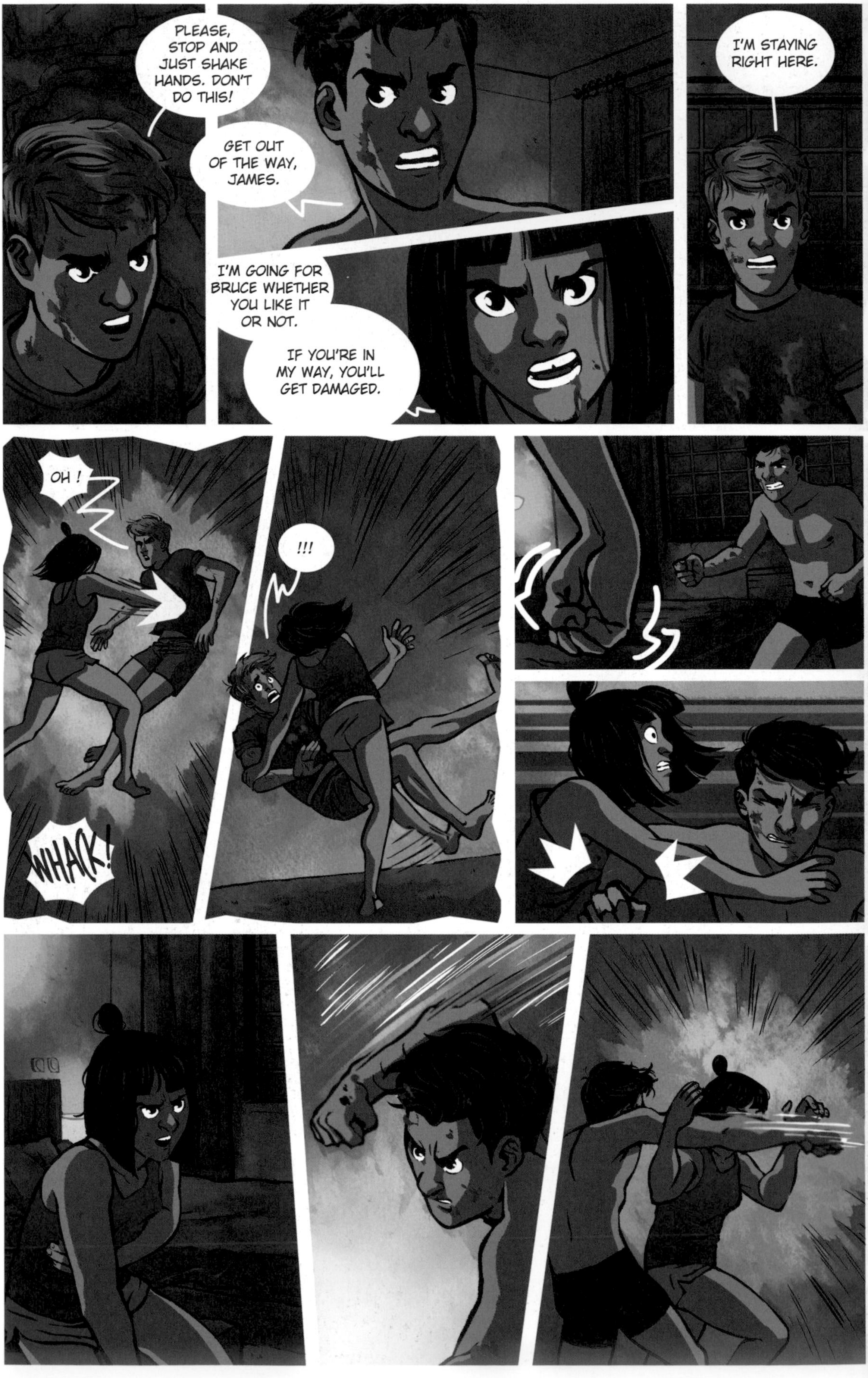
PLEASE, STOP AND JUST SHAKE HANDS. DON'T DO THIS!
GET OUT OF THE WAY, JAMES.
I'M STAYING RIGHT HERE.
I'M GOING FOR BRUCE WHETHER YOU LIKE IT OR NOT.
IF YOU'RE IN MY WAY, YOU'LL GET DAMAGED.
OH !
WHACK!
!!!

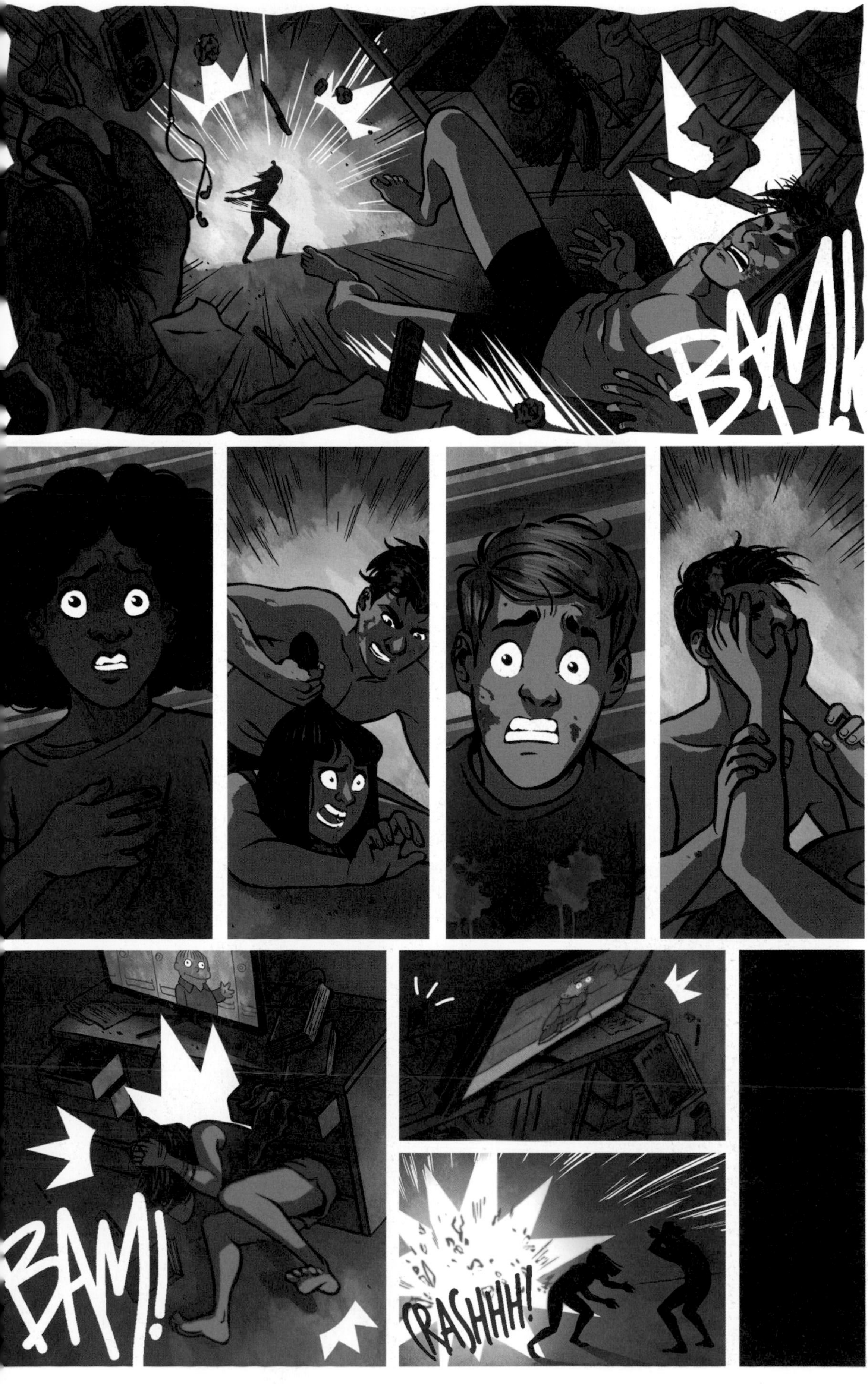
BAM!
BAM!
CRASHHH!

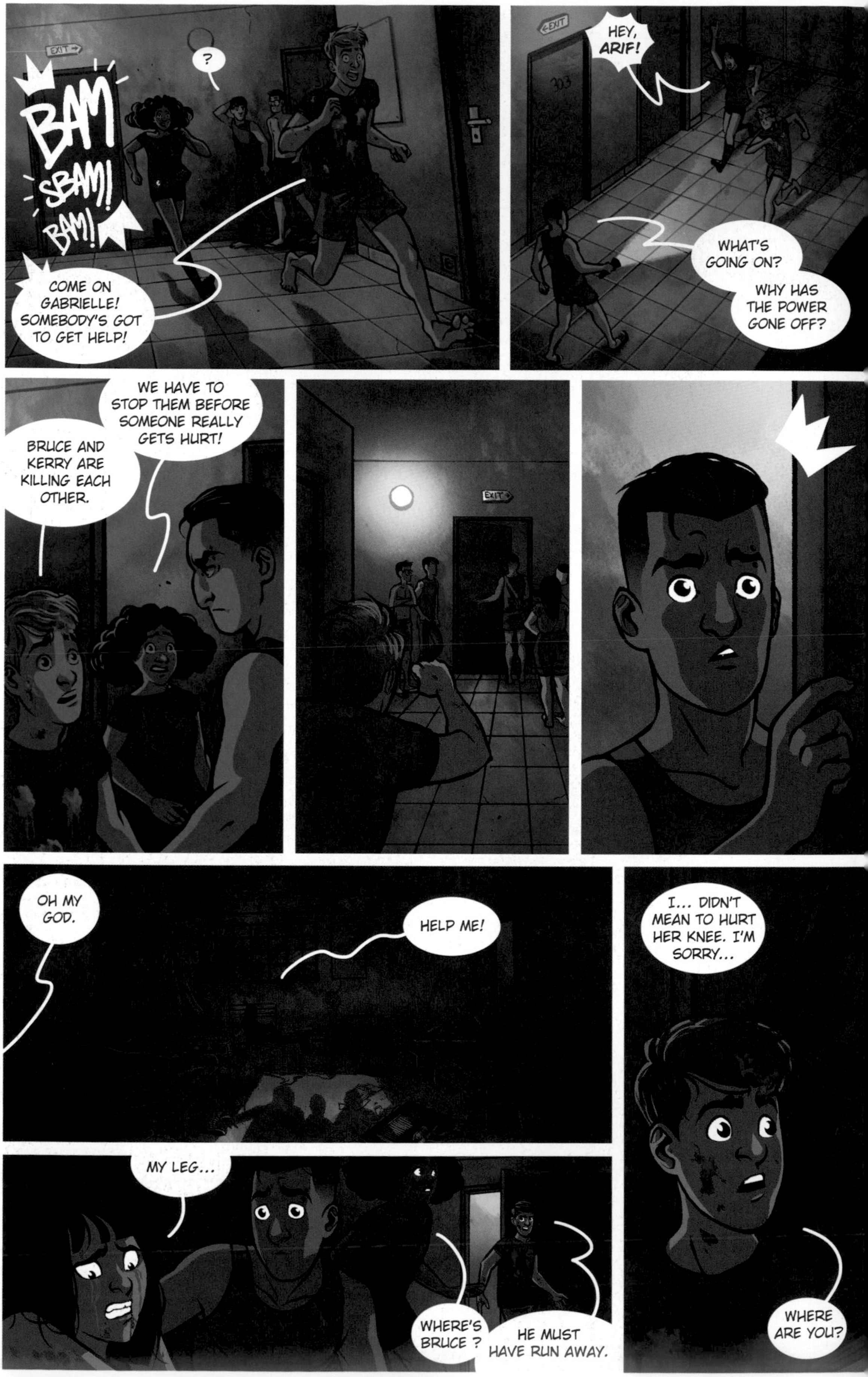
BAM SBAM! BAM!
?
COME ON GABRIELLE! SOMEBODY'S GOT TO GET HELP!
HEY, ARIF!
WHAT'S GOING ON?
WHY HAS THE POWER GONE OFF?
BRUCE AND KERRY ARE KILLING EACH OTHER.
WE HAVE TO STOP THEM BEFORE SOMEONE REALLY GETS HURT!
OH MY GOD.
HELP ME!
I... DIDN'T MEAN TO HURT HER KNEE. I'M SORRY...
MY LEG...
WHERE'S BRUCE ?
HE MUST HAVE RUN AWAY.
WHERE ARE YOU?

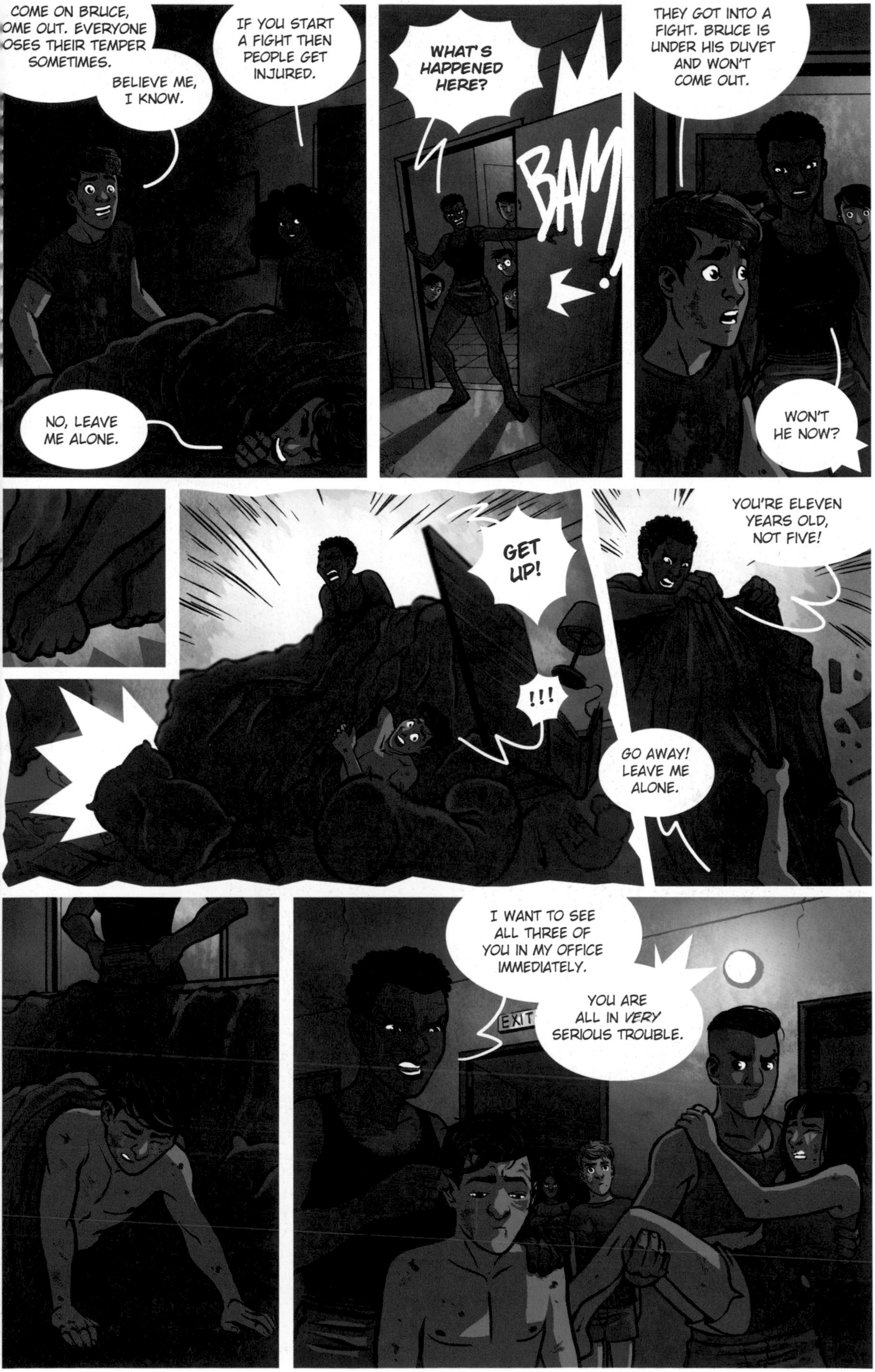
COME ON BRUCE, COME OUT. EVERYONE LOSES THEIR TEMPER SOMETIMES.
BELIEVE ME, I KNOW.
IF YOU START A FIGHT THEN PEOPLE GET INJURED.
NO, LEAVE ME ALONE.
WHAT'S HAPPENED HERE?
BAM
THEY GOT INTO A FIGHT. BRUCE IS UNDER HIS DUVET AND WON'T COME OUT.
WON'T HE NOW?
GET UP!
!!!
YOU'RE ELEVEN YEARS OLD, NOT FIVE!
GO AWAY! LEAVE ME ALONE.
I WANT TO SEE ALL THREE OF YOU IN MY OFFICE IMMEDIATELY.
YOU ARE ALL IN *VERY* SERIOUS TROUBLE.
EXIT

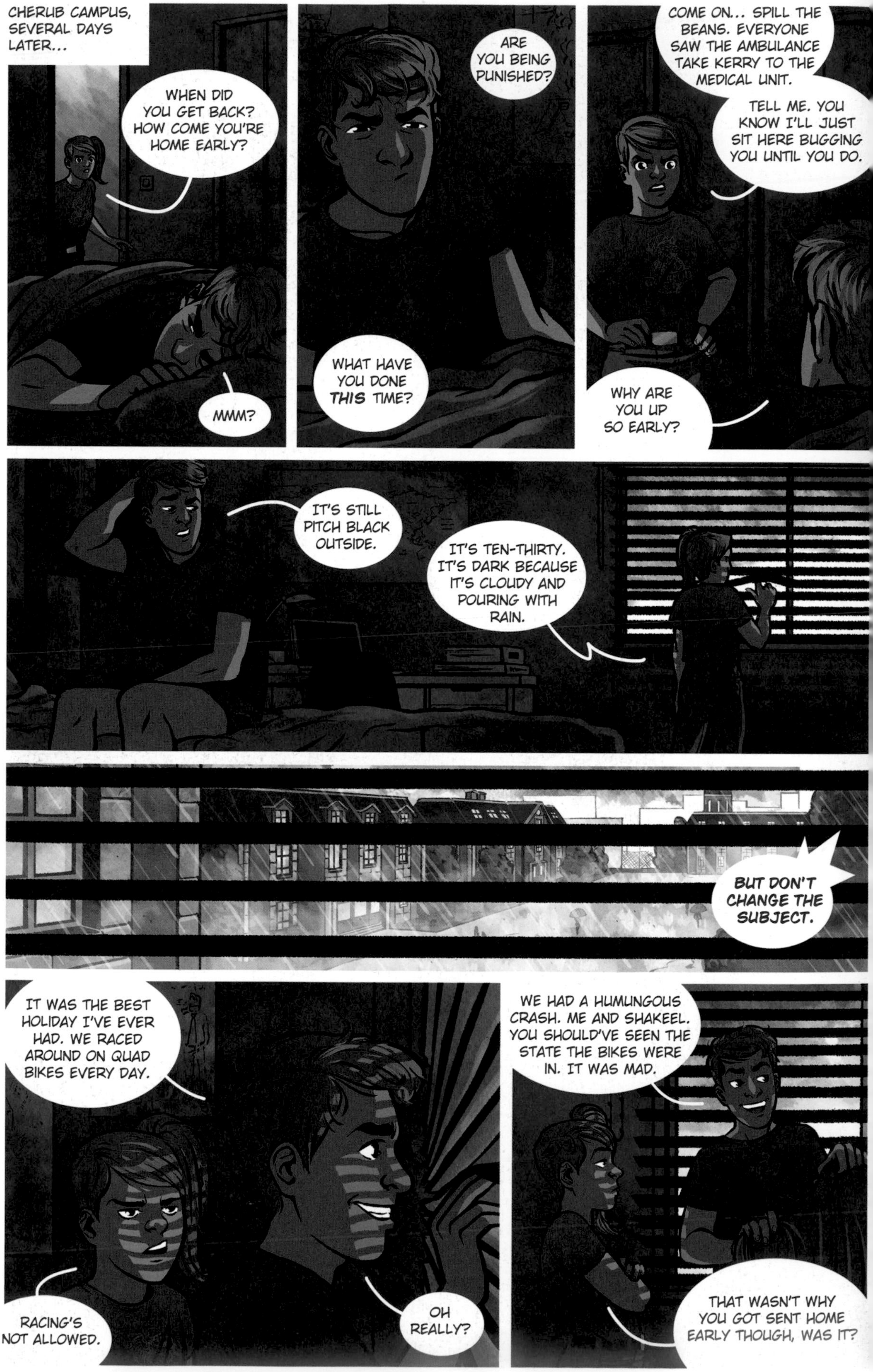
CHERUB CAMPUS, SEVERAL DAYS LATER...
WHEN DID YOU GET BACK? HOW COME YOU'RE HOME EARLY?
MMM?
ARE YOU BEING PUNISHED?
WHAT HAVE YOU DONE **THIS** TIME?
COME ON... SPILL THE BEANS. EVERYONE SAW THE AMBULANCE TAKE KERRY TO THE MEDICAL UNIT.
TELL ME. YOU KNOW I'LL JUST SIT HERE BUGGING YOU UNTIL YOU DO.
WHY ARE YOU UP SO EARLY?
IT'S STILL PITCH BLACK OUTSIDE.
IT'S TEN-THIRTY. IT'S DARK BECAUSE IT'S CLOUDY AND POURING WITH RAIN.
BUT DON'T CHANGE THE SUBJECT.
IT WAS THE BEST HOLIDAY I'VE EVER HAD. WE RACED AROUND ON QUAD BIKES EVERY DAY.
RACING'S NOT ALLOWED.
OH REALLY?
WE HAD A HUMUNGOUS CRASH. ME AND SHAKEEL. YOU SHOULD'VE SEEN THE STATE THE BIKES WERE IN. IT WAS MAD.
THAT WASN'T WHY YOU GOT SENT HOME EARLY THOUGH, WAS IT?

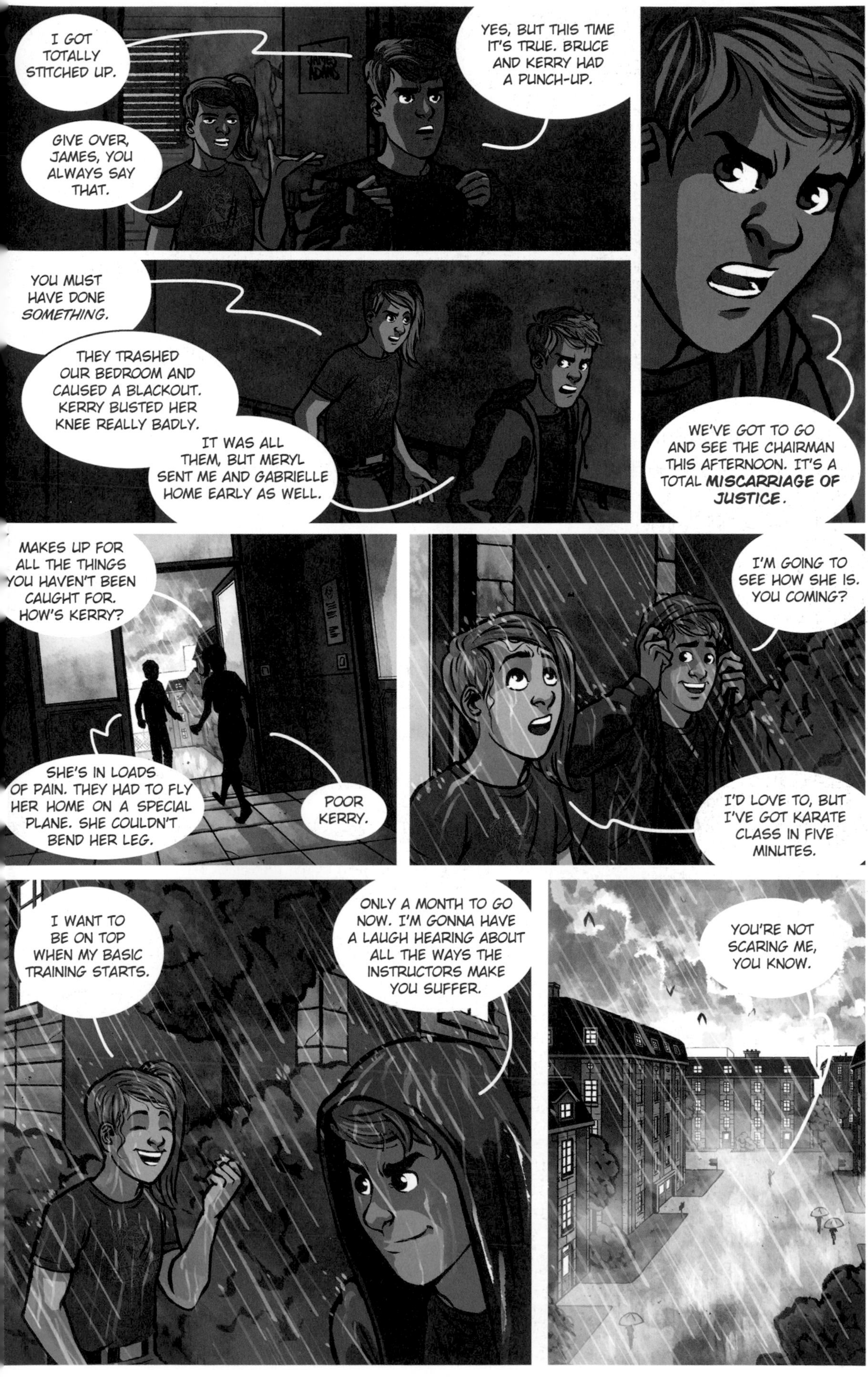
I GOT TOTALLY STITCHED UP.
YES, BUT THIS TIME IT'S TRUE. BRUCE AND KERRY HAD A PUNCH-UP.
GIVE OVER, JAMES, YOU ALWAYS SAY THAT.
YOU MUST HAVE DONE *SOMETHING*.
THEY TRASHED OUR BEDROOM AND CAUSED A BLACKOUT. KERRY BUSTED HER KNEE REALLY BADLY.
IT WAS ALL THEM, BUT MERYL SENT ME AND GABRIELLE HOME EARLY AS WELL.
WE'VE GOT TO GO AND SEE THE CHAIRMAN THIS AFTERNOON. IT'S A TOTAL **MISCARRIAGE OF JUSTICE**.
MAKES UP FOR ALL THE THINGS YOU HAVEN'T BEEN CAUGHT FOR. HOW'S KERRY?
SHE'S IN LOADS OF PAIN. THEY HAD TO FLY HER HOME ON A SPECIAL PLANE. SHE COULDN'T BEND HER LEG.
POOR KERRY.
I'M GOING TO SEE HOW SHE IS. YOU COMING?
I'D LOVE TO, BUT I'VE GOT KARATE CLASS IN FIVE MINUTES.
I WANT TO BE ON TOP WHEN MY BASIC TRAINING STARTS.
ONLY A MONTH TO GO NOW. I'M GONNA HAVE A LAUGH HEARING ABOUT ALL THE WAYS THE INSTRUCTORS MAKE YOU SUFFER.
YOU'RE NOT SCARING ME, YOU KNOW.

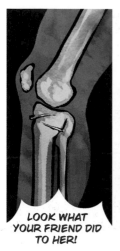

THOSE ARE METAL PINS PUT IN WHEN KERRY BROKE HER KNEECAP TWO YEARS AGO. DURING THE FIGHT, THAT PIN MOVED AND IT'S CUTTING INTO HER TENDONS!

THEY'RE OPERATING THIS AFTERNOON TO CUT OUT THE BENT METAL.

OOOOHHH GOD!

LOOK WHAT YOUR FRIEND DID TO HER!

ARE YOU OK?

IT'S NOTHING. I JUST MOVED MY FOOT. THIS IS ACTUALLY MORE PAINFUL THAN WHEN I BROKE MY KNEE.

HAS BRUCE BEEN TO SEE YOU?

NO! LIKE THAT LITTLE JERK WOULD HAVE ENOUGH CLASS TO COME AND APOLOGISE.

JAMES...

DO ME A FAVOUR. GO AND TELL BRUCE THAT I DON'T BLAME HIM.

WHAT! ARE YOU KIDDING?

REMEMBER I TOLD YOU I BROKE BRUCE'S LEG WHEN WE WERE RED SHIRTS?

EVEN THOUGH IT WAS COMPLETELY MY FAULT, BRUCE WAS COOL ABOUT IT. HE FORGAVE ME STRAIGHT AWAY.

EVERYONE DOES STUPID STUFF SOMETIMES. REMEMBER THIS ONE, JAMES?

THAT SCAR ON MY HAND IS WHERE YOU STOMPED IT DURING TRAINING. YOU CAN'T HOLD GRUDGES.

POINT TAKEN. I'LL SPEAK TO HIM WHEN WE SEE MAC IN A BIT.

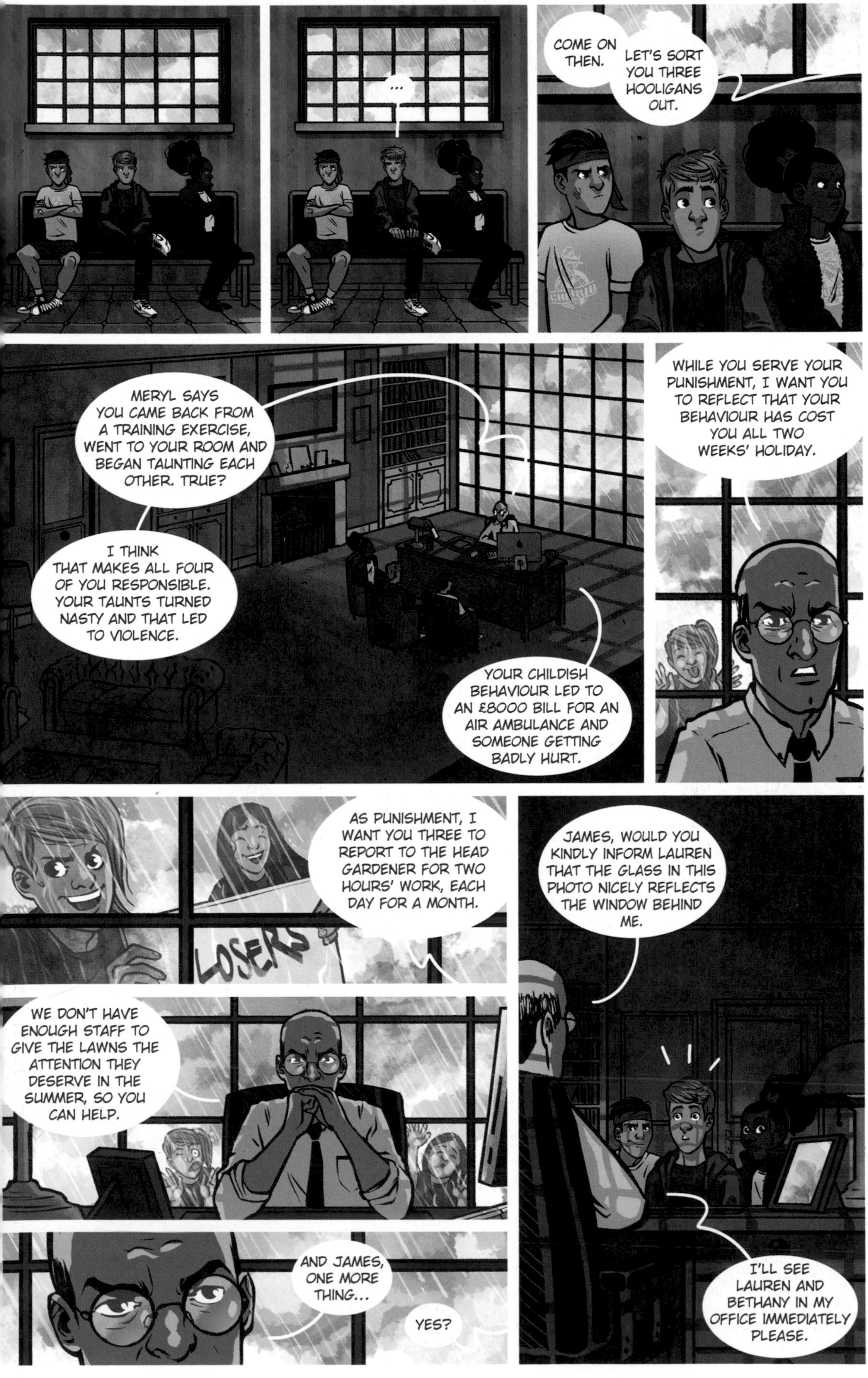
...
COME ON THEN.
LET'S SORT YOU THREE HOOLIGANS OUT.
MERYL SAYS YOU CAME BACK FROM A TRAINING EXERCISE, WENT TO YOUR ROOM AND BEGAN TAUNTING EACH OTHER. TRUE?
I THINK THAT MAKES ALL FOUR OF YOU RESPONSIBLE. YOUR TAUNTS TURNED NASTY AND THAT LED TO VIOLENCE.
YOUR CHILDISH BEHAVIOUR LED TO AN £8000 BILL FOR AN AIR AMBULANCE AND SOMEONE GETTING BADLY HURT.
WHILE YOU SERVE YOUR PUNISHMENT, I WANT YOU TO REFLECT THAT YOUR BEHAVIOUR HAS COST YOU ALL TWO WEEKS' HOLIDAY.
LOSERS
AS PUNISHMENT, I WANT YOU THREE TO REPORT TO THE HEAD GARDENER FOR TWO HOURS' WORK, EACH DAY FOR A MONTH.
WE DON'T HAVE ENOUGH STAFF TO GIVE THE LAWNS THE ATTENTION THEY DESERVE IN THE SUMMER, SO YOU CAN HELP.
AND JAMES, ONE MORE THING...
YES?
JAMES, WOULD YOU KINDLY INFORM LAUREN THAT THE GLASS IN THIS PHOTO NICELY REFLECTS THE WINDOW BEHIND ME.
I'LL SEE LAUREN AND BETHANY IN MY OFFICE IMMEDIATELY PLEASE.

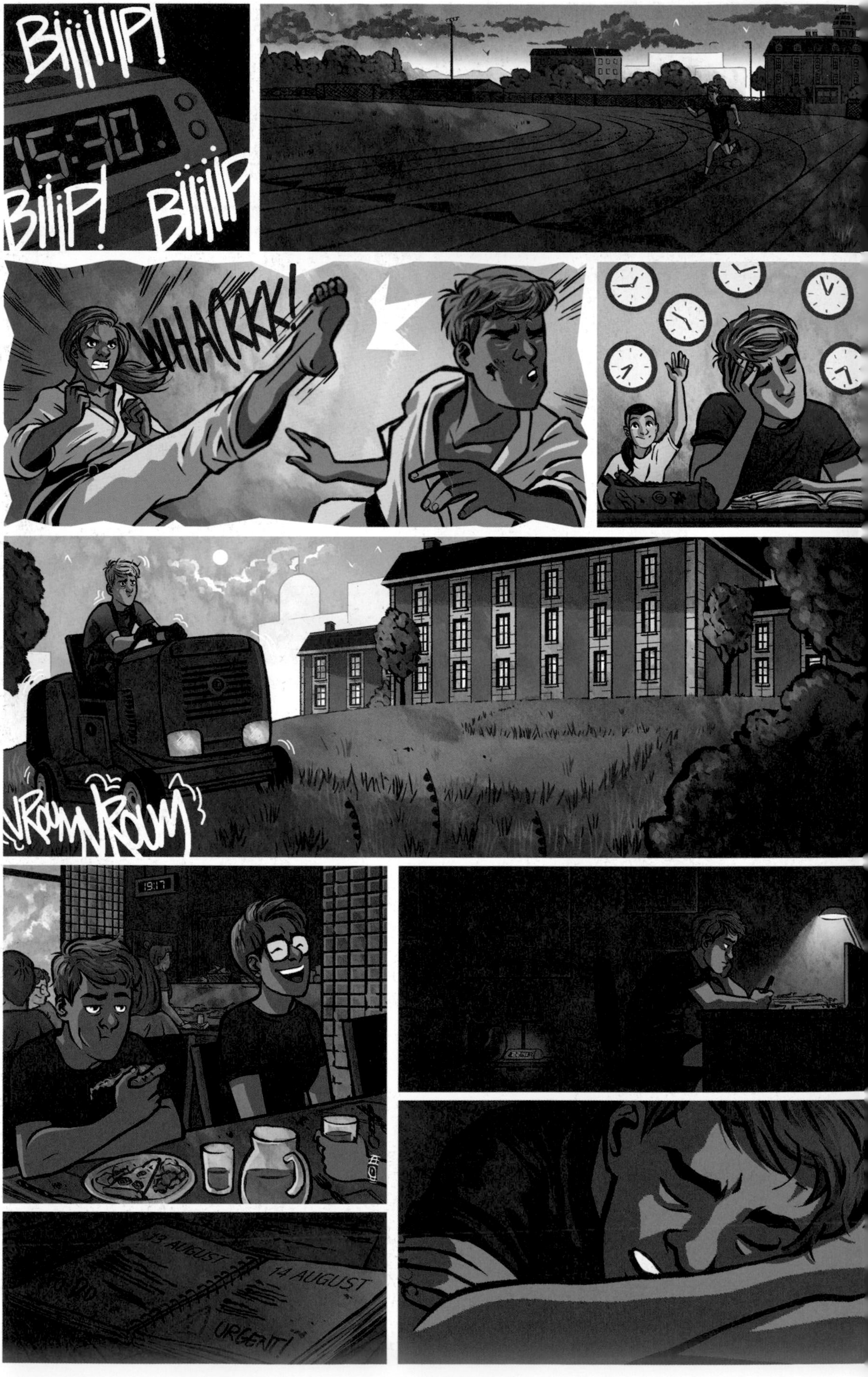
BIIIIIIP!
05:30
BIIIP!
BIIIIIP!
WHACKKK!
VROUM VROUM
19:17
13 AUGUST
14 AUGUST
URGENT!

WAKEY WAKEY!

WHAT? UH!

WAS I SLEEPING?

?

OH CRAP.

IF I DON'T GET THIS HISTORY REPORT DONE BY TOMORROW, I'M DEAD MEAT.

GET A DEFERRAL.

I'VE ALREADY DONE THAT. TWICE.

I SWEAR, THEY WANT TO KILL ME.

THERE AREN'T ENOUGH HOURS IN THE DAY. I SPENT ALL DAY SUNDAY DOING HOMEWORK.

AND THE ONLY THING THAT HAPPENS IS THAT I GET FURTHER AND FURTHER BEHIND.

THEY'RE TRYING TO INSTIL A SENSE OF DISCIPLINE IN YOU.

AFTER A MONTH OF BEING WORKED LIKE A DOG, MAYBE YOU'LL FOLLOW THE RULES.

EVERYBODY WARNED YOU, BUT...

OH, SPARE ME ANOTHER LECTURE!

YEAH, THROWING STUFF AROUND WILL REALLY HELP.

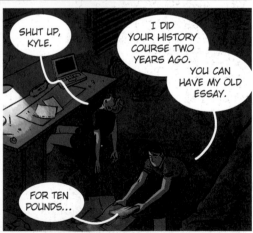

SHUT UP, KYLE.

I DID YOUR HISTORY COURSE TWO YEARS AGO.

YOU CAN HAVE MY OLD ESSAY.

FOR TEN POUNDS...

WHAT! SOME FRIEND YOU ARE, TRYING TO MAKE MONEY OUT OF ME!

THIS ESSAY IS GRADE 'A' MATERIAL. THE GIRL I NICKED IT OFF IS AT HARVARD NOW.

I'LL STILL HAVE TO EDIT IT. TAKE OUT PIECES, CHANGE THE WORDING.

I'LL GIVE YOU A FIVER.

OK, YOU CAN HAVE IT FOR A FIVER IF YOU PAY ME RIGHT NOW.

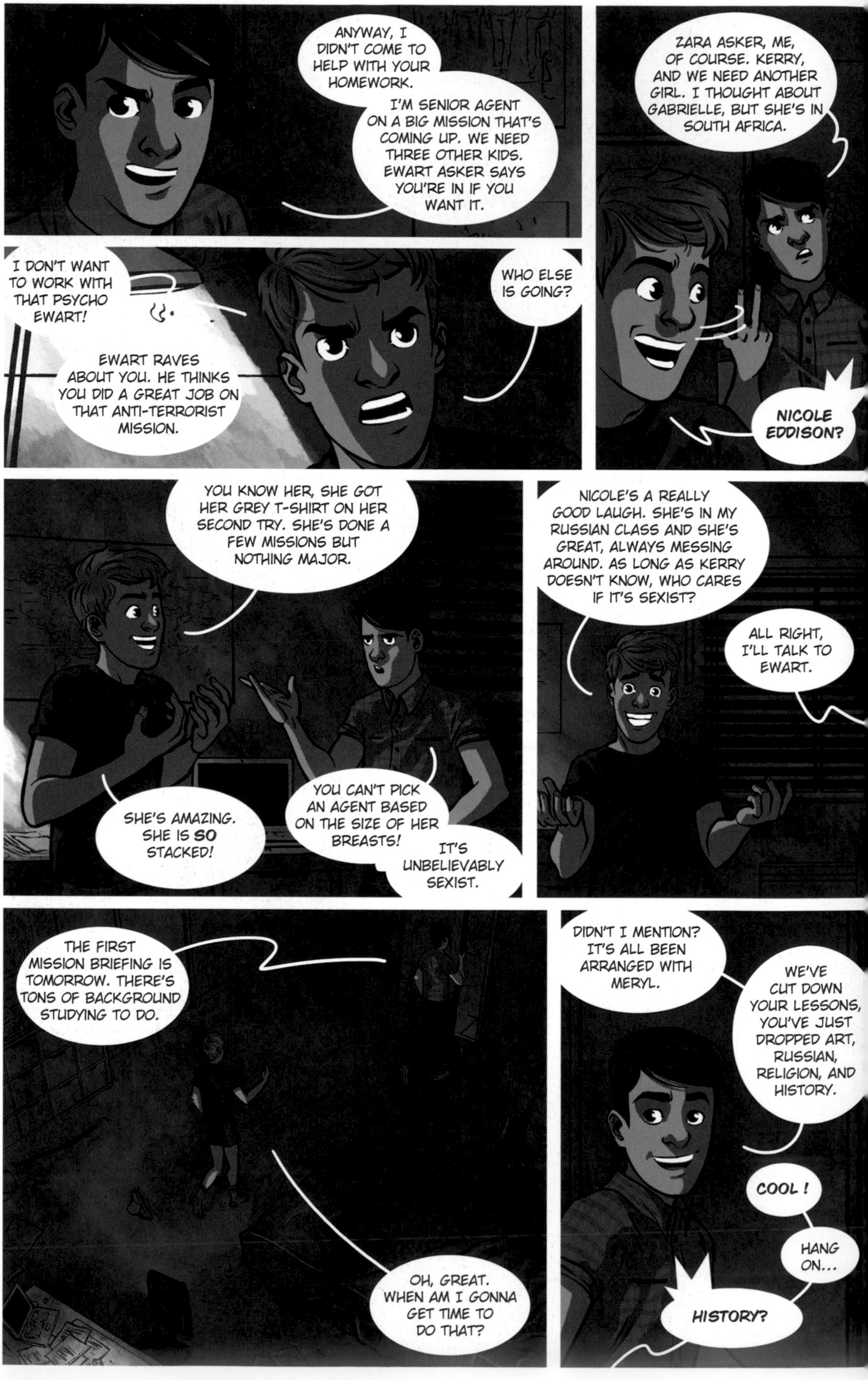
ANYWAY, I DIDN'T COME TO HELP WITH YOUR HOMEWORK.
I'M SENIOR AGENT ON A BIG MISSION THAT'S COMING UP. WE NEED THREE OTHER KIDS. EWART ASKER SAYS YOU'RE IN IF YOU WANT IT.
ZARA ASKER, ME, OF COURSE. KERRY, AND WE NEED ANOTHER GIRL. I THOUGHT ABOUT GABRIELLE, BUT SHE'S IN SOUTH AFRICA.
I DON'T WANT TO WORK WITH THAT PSYCHO EWART!
EWART RAVES ABOUT YOU. HE THINKS YOU DID A GREAT JOB ON THAT ANTI-TERRORIST MISSION.
WHO ELSE IS GOING?
NICOLE EDDISON?
YOU KNOW HER, SHE GOT HER GREY T-SHIRT ON HER SECOND TRY. SHE'S DONE A FEW MISSIONS BUT NOTHING MAJOR.
SHE'S AMAZING. SHE IS SO STACKED!
YOU CAN'T PICK AN AGENT BASED ON THE SIZE OF HER BREASTS!
IT'S UNBELIEVABLY SEXIST.
NICOLE'S A REALLY GOOD LAUGH. SHE'S IN MY RUSSIAN CLASS AND SHE'S GREAT, ALWAYS MESSING AROUND. AS LONG AS KERRY DOESN'T KNOW, WHO CARES IF IT'S SEXIST?
ALL RIGHT, I'LL TALK TO EWART.
THE FIRST MISSION BRIEFING IS TOMORROW. THERE'S TONS OF BACKGROUND STUDYING TO DO.
OH, GREAT. WHEN AM I GONNA GET TIME TO DO THAT?
DIDN'T I MENTION? IT'S ALL BEEN ARRANGED WITH MERYL.
WE'VE CUT DOWN YOUR LESSONS, YOU'VE JUST DROPPED ART, RUSSIAN, RELIGION, AND HISTORY.
COOL!
HANG ON...
HISTORY?

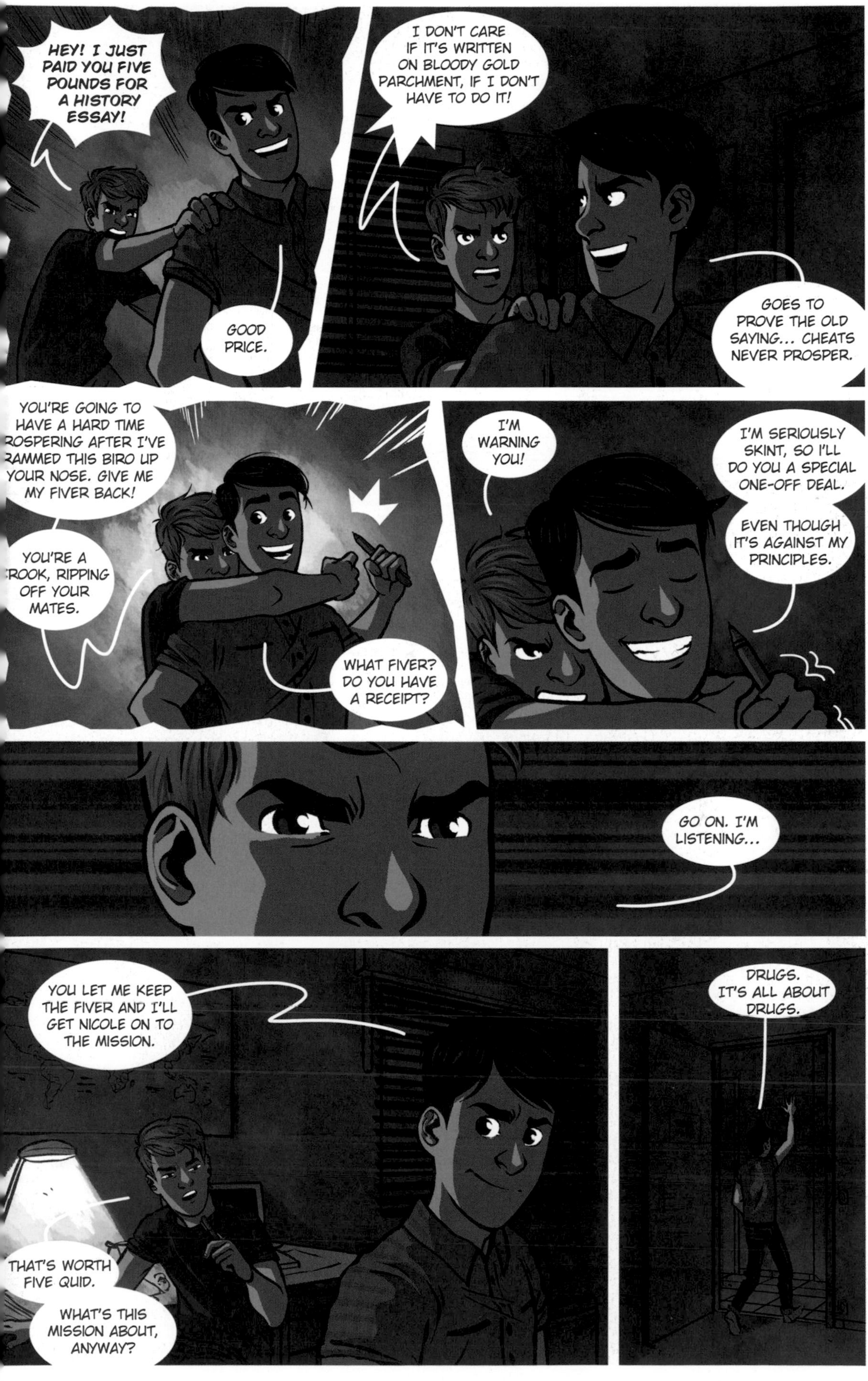
HEY! I JUST PAID YOU FIVE POUNDS FOR A HISTORY ESSAY!
GOOD PRICE.
I DON'T CARE IF IT'S WRITTEN ON BLOODY GOLD PARCHMENT, IF I DON'T HAVE TO DO IT!
GOES TO PROVE THE OLD SAYING... CHEATS NEVER PROSPER.
YOU'RE GOING TO HAVE A HARD TIME ROSPERING AFTER I'VE RAMMED THIS BIRO UP YOUR NOSE. GIVE ME MY FIVER BACK!
YOU'RE A ROOK, RIPPING OFF YOUR MATES.
WHAT FIVER? DO YOU HAVE A RECEIPT?
I'M WARNING YOU!
I'M SERIOUSLY SKINT, SO I'LL DO YOU A SPECIAL ONE-OFF DEAL.
EVEN THOUGH IT'S AGAINST MY PRINCIPLES.
GO ON. I'M LISTENING...
YOU LET ME KEEP THE FIVER AND I'LL GET NICOLE ON TO THE MISSION.
THAT'S WORTH FIVE QUID.
WHAT'S THIS MISSION ABOUT, ANYWAY?
DRUGS. IT'S ALL ABOUT DRUGS.

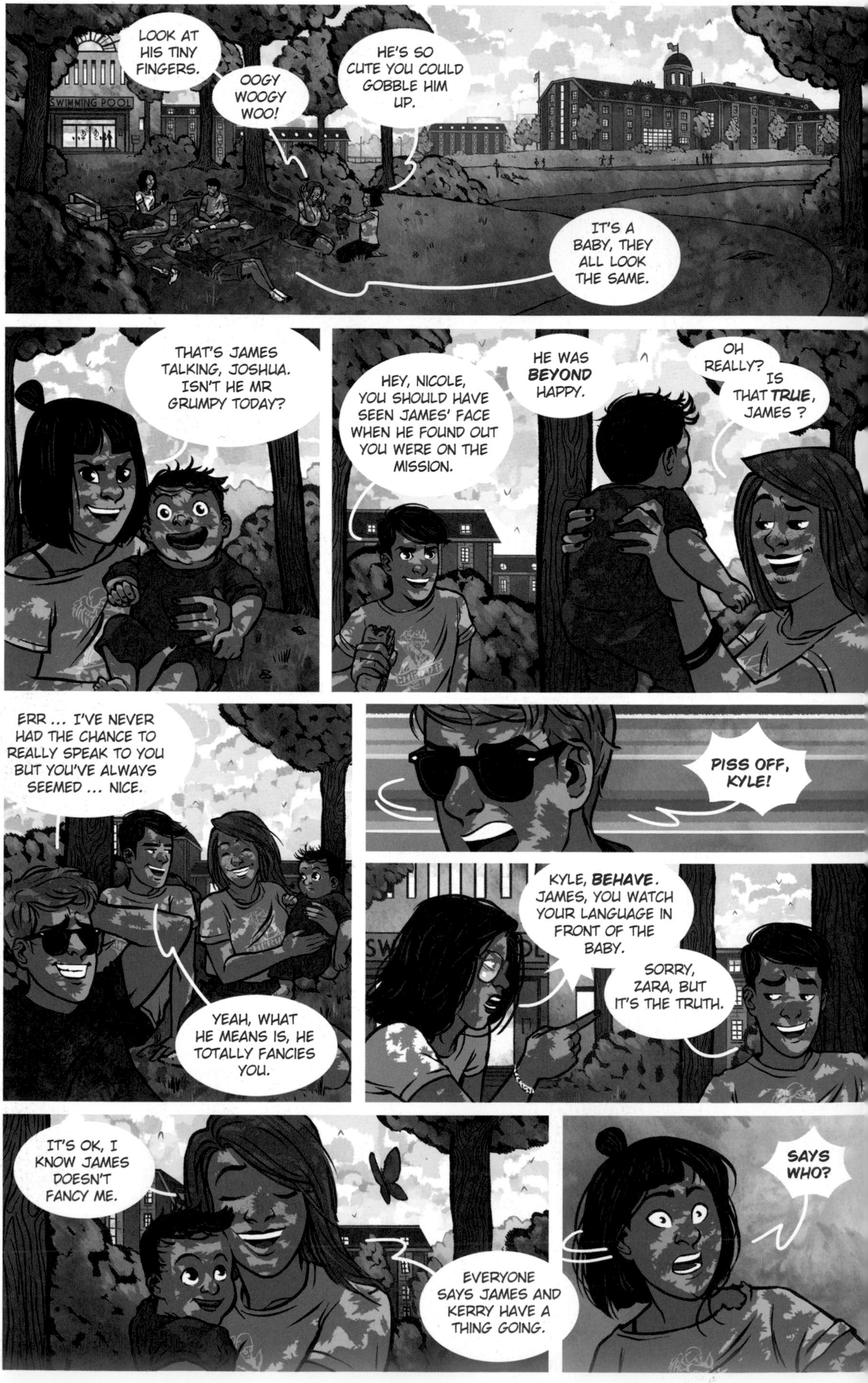

SWIMMING POOL
LOOK AT HIS TINY FINGERS.
OOGY WOOGY WOO!
HE'S SO CUTE YOU COULD GOBBLE HIM UP.
IT'S A BABY, THEY ALL LOOK THE SAME.
THAT'S JAMES TALKING, JOSHUA. ISN'T HE MR GRUMPY TODAY?
HEY, NICOLE, YOU SHOULD HAVE SEEN JAMES' FACE WHEN HE FOUND OUT YOU WERE ON THE MISSION.
HE WAS **BEYOND** HAPPY.
OH REALLY?
IS THAT **TRUE**, JAMES ?
ERR ... I'VE NEVER HAD THE CHANCE TO REALLY SPEAK TO YOU BUT YOU'VE ALWAYS SEEMED ... NICE.
YEAH, WHAT HE MEANS IS, HE TOTALLY FANCIES YOU.
PISS OFF, KYLE!
KYLE, **BEHAVE**. JAMES, YOU WATCH YOUR LANGUAGE IN FRONT OF THE BABY.
SORRY, ZARA, BUT IT'S THE TRUTH.
IT'S OK, I KNOW JAMES DOESN'T FANCY ME.
EVERYONE SAYS JAMES AND KERRY HAVE A THING GOING.
SAYS WHO?

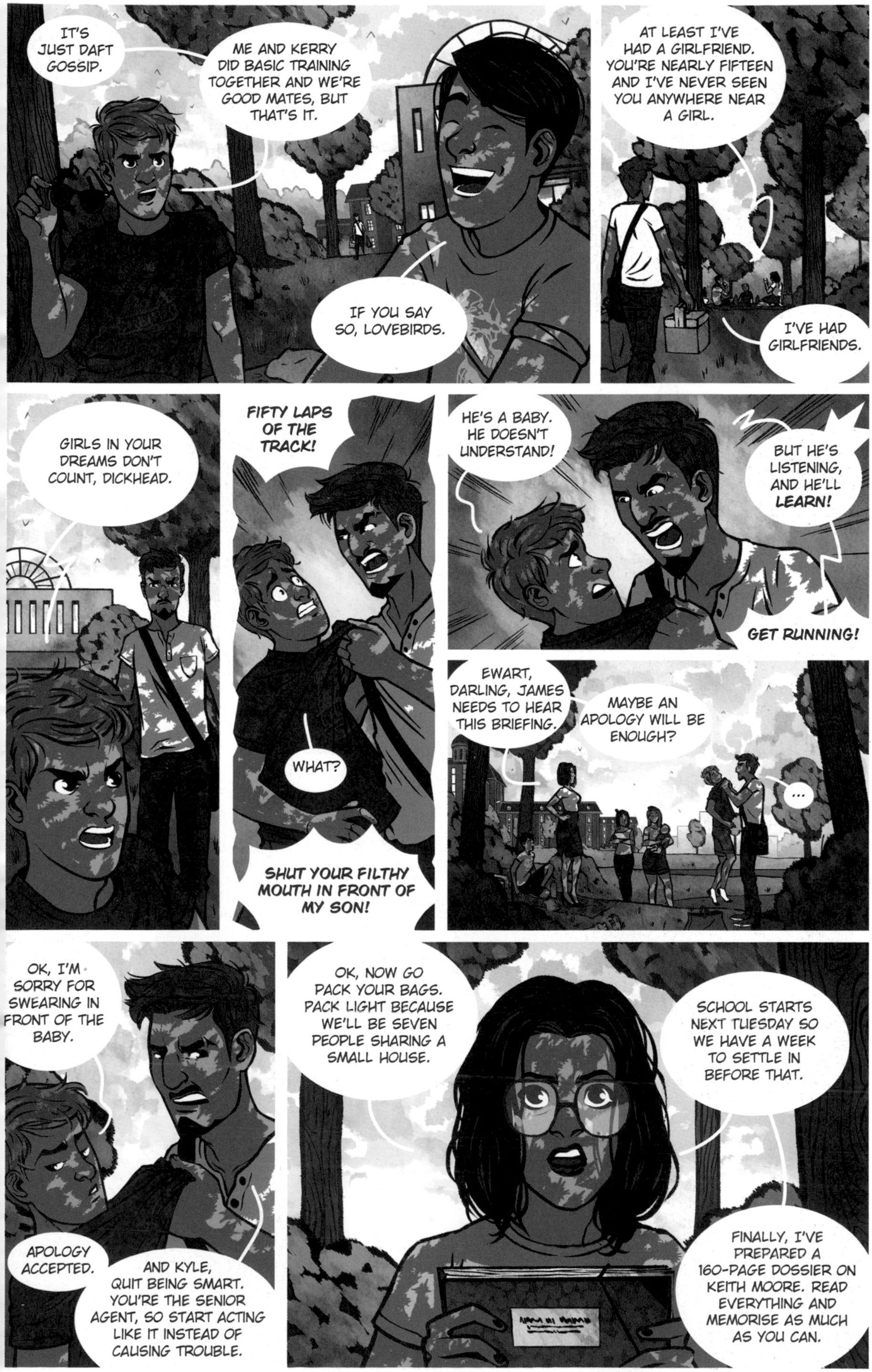
IT'S JUST DAFT GOSSIP.
ME AND KERRY DID BASIC TRAINING TOGETHER AND WE'RE GOOD MATES, BUT THAT'S IT.
IF YOU SAY SO, LOVEBIRDS.
AT LEAST I'VE HAD A GIRLFRIEND. YOU'RE NEARLY FIFTEEN AND I'VE NEVER SEEN YOU ANYWHERE NEAR A GIRL.
I'VE HAD GIRLFRIENDS.
GIRLS IN YOUR DREAMS DON'T COUNT, DICKHEAD.
FIFTY LAPS OF THE TRACK!
WHAT?
SHUT YOUR FILTHY MOUTH IN FRONT OF MY SON!
HE'S A BABY. HE DOESN'T UNDERSTAND!
BUT HE'S LISTENING, AND HE'LL LEARN!
GET RUNNING!
EWART, DARLING, JAMES NEEDS TO HEAR THIS BRIEFING.
MAYBE AN APOLOGY WILL BE ENOUGH?
...
OK, I'M SORRY FOR SWEARING IN FRONT OF THE BABY.
APOLOGY ACCEPTED.
AND KYLE, QUIT BEING SMART. YOU'RE THE SENIOR AGENT, SO START ACTING LIKE IT INSTEAD OF CAUSING TROUBLE.
OK, NOW GO PACK YOUR BAGS. PACK LIGHT BECAUSE WE'LL BE SEVEN PEOPLE SHARING A SMALL HOUSE.
SCHOOL STARTS NEXT TUESDAY SO WE HAVE A WEEK TO SETTLE IN BEFORE THAT.
FINALLY, I'VE PREPARED A 160-PAGE DOSSIER ON KEITH MOORE. READ EVERYTHING AND MEMORISE AS MUCH AS YOU CAN.

MISSION BRIEFING

ADAMS James,
CHA

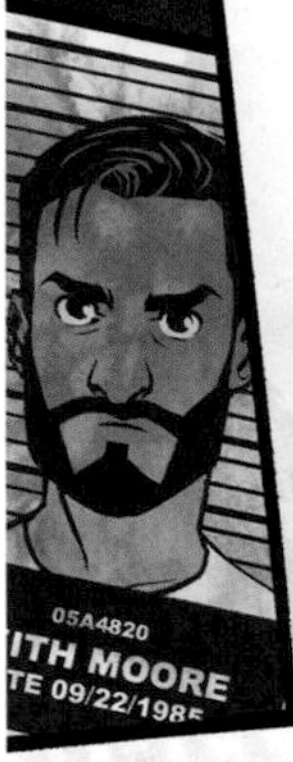
05A4820
ITH MOORE
TE 09/22/198

- **CHILDREN IN THE DRUGS BUSINESS**

Children are employed by drug dealers across the world for three reasons:

1. Kids selling drugs are usually viewed as victims rather than criminals. Unlike adults they incur only a light punishment if caught.
2. Children have easy access to schools and young people where they can distribute free samples.
3. Children have few sources of income and plenty of spare time. They will often work for little or no money.

- **COCAINE IN BRITAIN**

Cocaine is an illegal drug extracted from the leaves of the coc plant. It was once the champagne of the drugs world: a luxury only the ric could afford. However its price has dropped to less than £50 a gram. Th majority of the cocaine flooding the UK market arrives via the Caribbean.

It is impossible to catch every smuggler entering Britain. The poli must aim higher and capture the people in control of the drugs gangs. Clo to one third of the cocaine entering Britain passes through an organisati commonly referred to as KMG. The initials stand for Keith Moore's Gang.

YO

- **BIOGRAPHY OF KEITH MOORE AND KMG**

1964 : Keith Moore was born on the newly built Thornton estate on the outskirts of Luton, Bedfordshire.

1978 : Keith began training as a boxer at the JT Martin Youth Centre. JT Martin was a retired boxer and armed robber who controlled the local underworld. He used his boxing club to recruit young criminals.

1980 : Keith was spotted in police photographs of JT Martin. He was a weedy sixteen-year-old who looked out of place amongst the tougher boxers.

1981 : Keith became JT Martin's chauffeur. Moving around with JT gave the seventeen-year-old an insight into all aspects of the drug business.

1985 : Police captured JT Martin and a number of associates selling drugs. JT goes to prison.

1986 : Keith kept out of the violent power struggle for control of Martin's empire, which included cannabis, heroin, pubs, nightclubs and casinos. Instead, Keith focused on the cocaine business.

1987 : The price of cocaine kept falling and supply was growing. Keith Moore was one of the first people in Britain to realise that the cocaine business was about to explode. Keith clinches a deal with a Peruvian drug cartel and develops a phone ordering service so his customers simply have to dial a number to have cocaine delivered within the hour.

1988 : The cocaine business was earning Keith over £10,000 per week allowing him to take over Martin's criminal empire at 23 years of age.

1989 : Keith and wife, Julie, have their first son, Ringo (now aged 15).

1990 : Keith's business grew tenfold in three years. Began selling wholesale quantities to mainland Europe.

1992 : Keith and wife, Julie, have twins April and Keith Jr (now aged 12).

1993 : Keith and Julie's youngest child, Erin, was born (now agec 11).

1998 : Police tried to get undercover officers into Keith's inne circle but are unable to get hard evidence against him. Fiercely loya deputies kept Keith out of jail.

2001 : Julie Moore left Keith after eighteen years of marriage.

2003 : Police launched Operation Snort, the largest taskforce drugs officers ever assembled in Britain. Its main target was Keith Moor

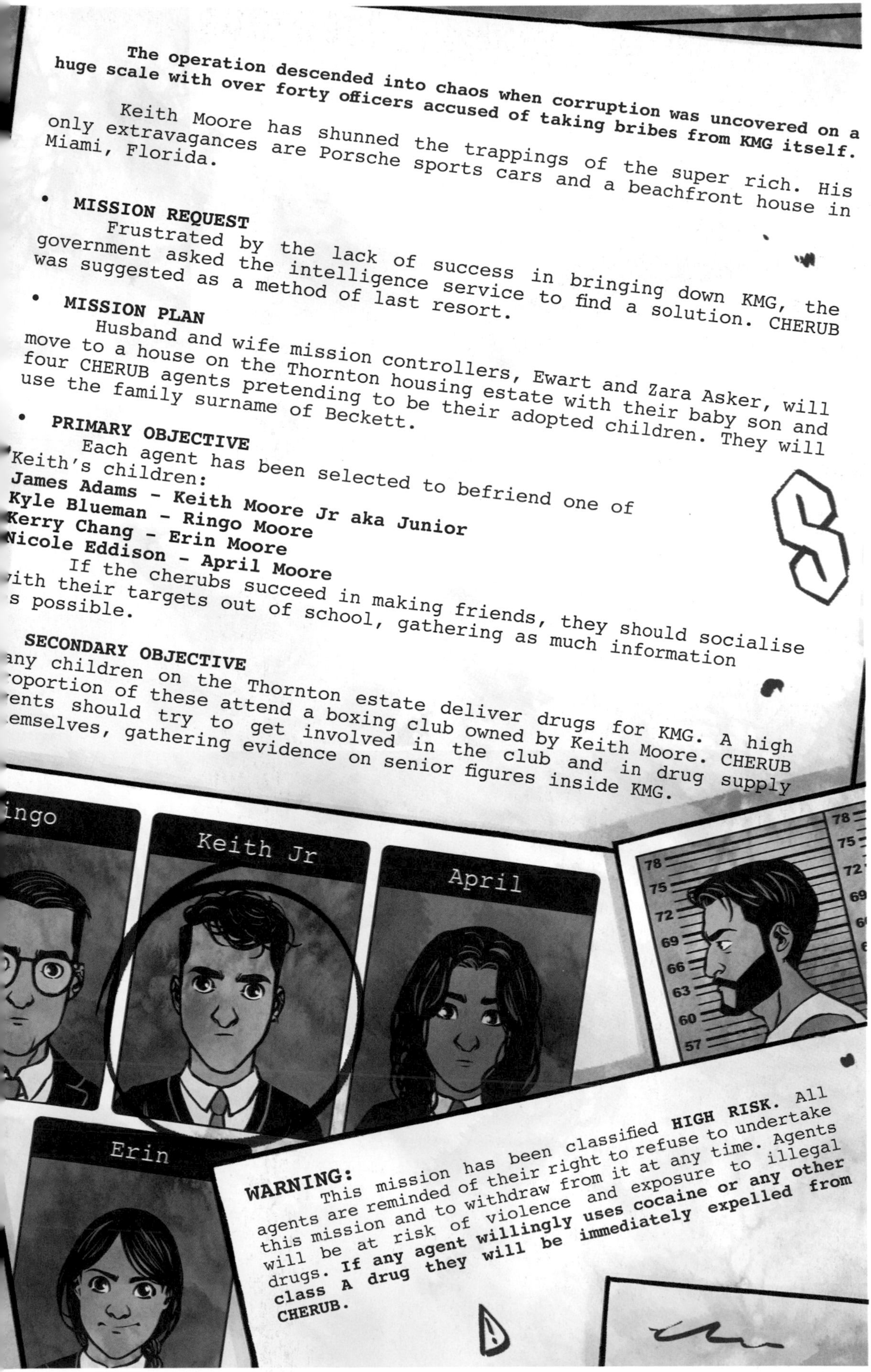
The operation descended into chaos when corruption was uncovered on a huge scale with over forty officers accused of taking bribes from KMG itself.
Keith Moore has shunned the trappings of the super rich. His only extravagances are Porsche sports cars and a beachfront house in Miami, Florida.
• **MISSION REQUEST**
Frustrated by the lack of success in bringing down KMG, the government asked the intelligence service to find a solution. CHERUB was suggested as a method of last resort.
• **MISSION PLAN**
Husband and wife mission controllers, Ewart and Zara Asker, will move to a house on the Thornton housing estate with their baby son and four CHERUB agents pretending to be their adopted children. They will use the family surname of Beckett.
• **PRIMARY OBJECTIVE**
Each agent has been selected to befriend one of Keith's children:
James Adams - Keith Moore Jr aka Junior
Kyle Blueman - Ringo Moore
Kerry Chang - Erin Moore
Nicole Eddison - April Moore
If the cherubs succeed in making friends, they should socialise ith their targets out of school, gathering as much information s possible.
SECONDARY OBJECTIVE
any children on the Thornton estate deliver drugs for KMG. A high roportion of these attend a boxing club owned by Keith Moore. CHERUB ents should try to get involved in the club and in drug supply emselves, gathering evidence on senior figures inside KMG.
ingo
Keith Jr
April
78
75
72
69
66
63
60
57
Erin
WARNING: This mission has been classified **HIGH RISK.** All agents are reminded of their right to refuse to undertake this mission and to withdraw from it at any time. Agents will be at risk of violence and exposure to illegal drugs. **If any agent willingly uses cocaine or any other class A drug they will be immediately expelled from CHERUB.**

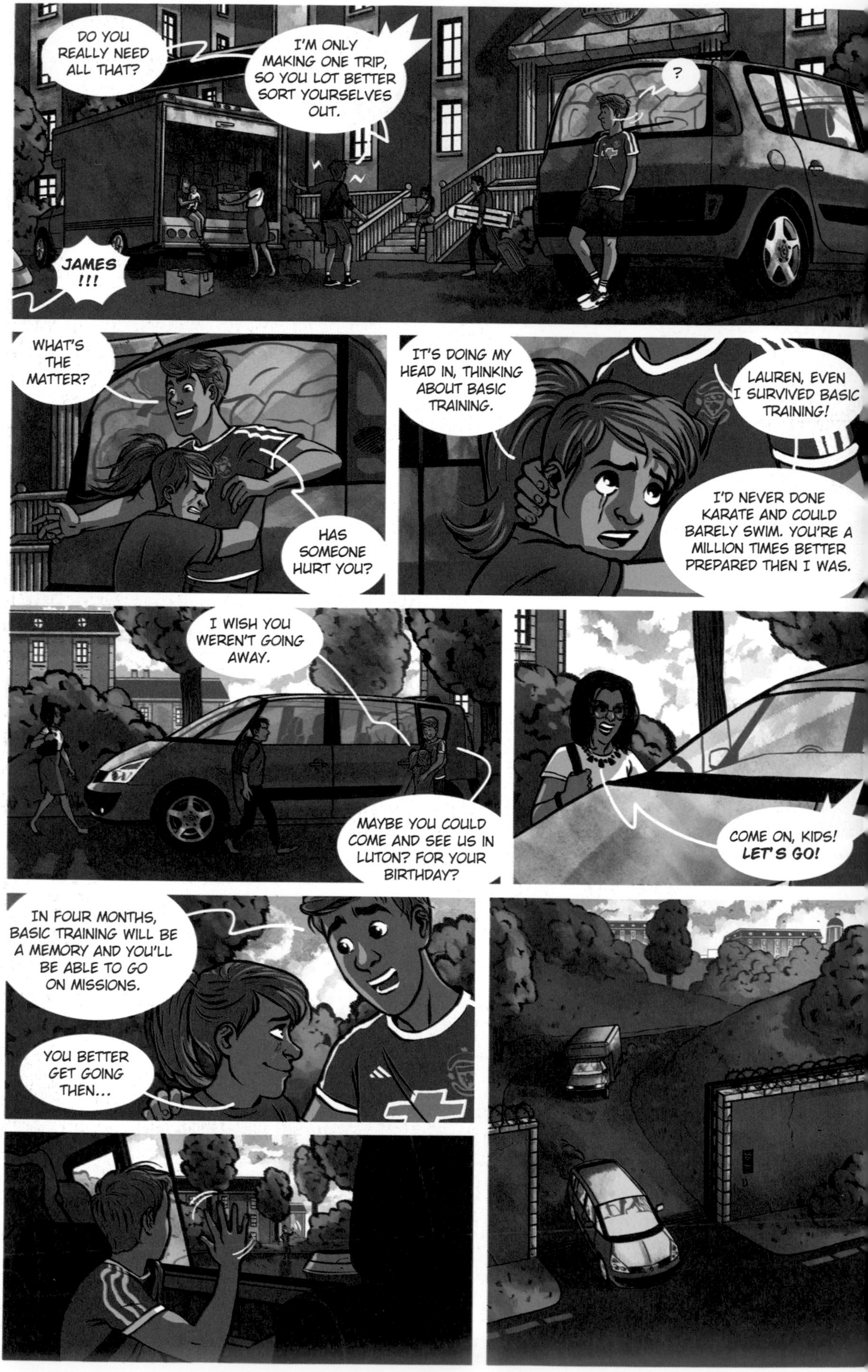
DO YOU REALLY NEED ALL THAT?
I'M ONLY MAKING ONE TRIP, SO YOU LOT BETTER SORT YOURSELVES OUT.
?
JAMES !!!
WHAT'S THE MATTER?
HAS SOMEONE HURT YOU?
IT'S DOING MY HEAD IN, THINKING ABOUT BASIC TRAINING.
LAUREN, EVEN I SURVIVED BASIC TRAINING!
I'D NEVER DONE KARATE AND COULD BARELY SWIM. YOU'RE A MILLION TIMES BETTER PREPARED THEN I WAS.
I WISH YOU WEREN'T GOING AWAY.
MAYBE YOU COULD COME AND SEE US IN LUTON? FOR YOUR BIRTHDAY?
COME ON, KIDS! LET'S GO!
IN FOUR MONTHS, BASIC TRAINING WILL BE A MEMORY AND YOU'LL BE ABLE TO GO ON MISSIONS.
YOU BETTER GET GOING THEN...

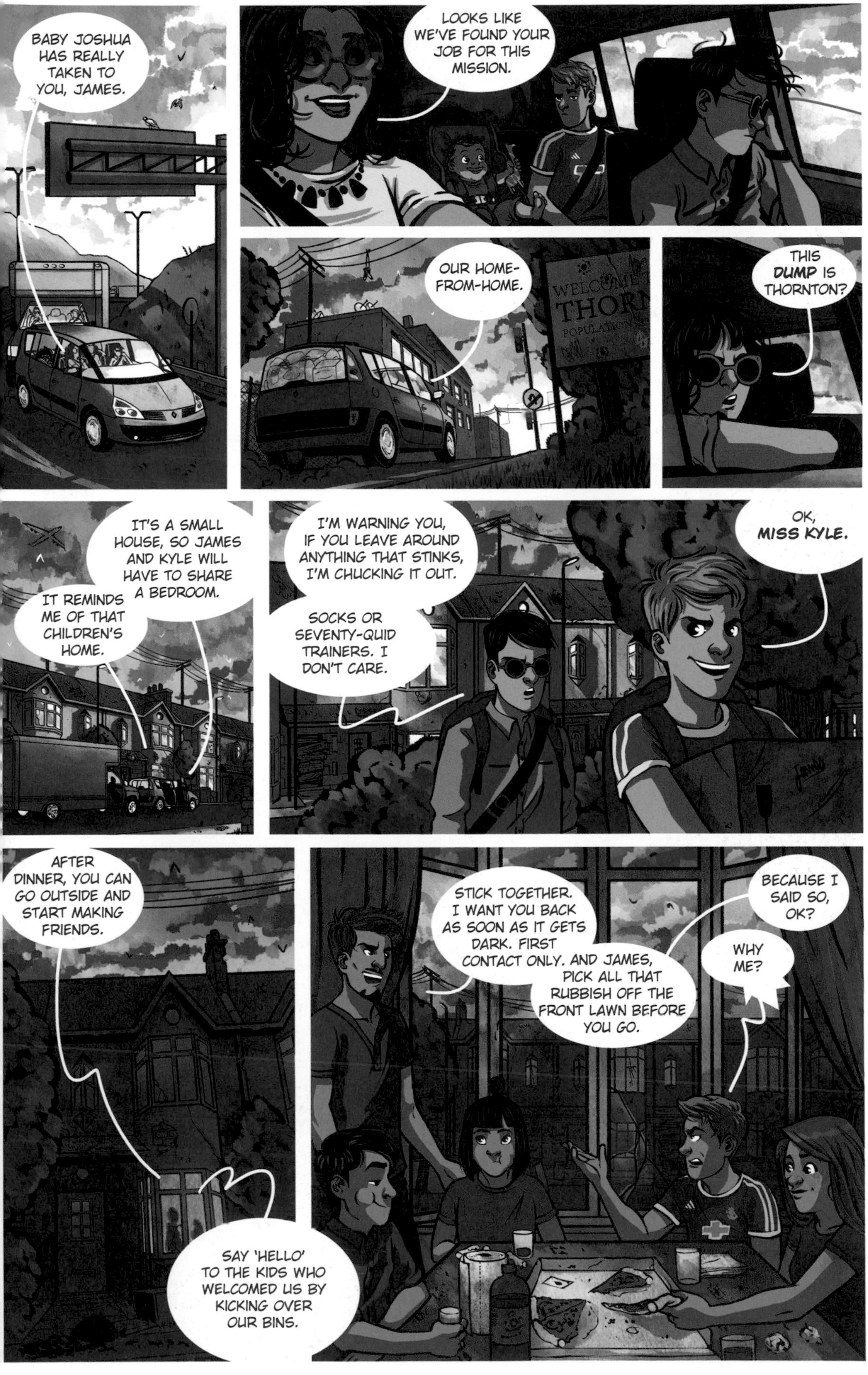
BABY JOSHUA HAS REALLY TAKEN TO YOU, JAMES.
LOOKS LIKE WE'VE FOUND YOUR JOB FOR THIS MISSION.
OUR HOME-FROM-HOME.
WELCOME TO THORN... POPULATION
THIS DUMP IS THORNTON?
IT'S A SMALL HOUSE, SO JAMES AND KYLE WILL HAVE TO SHARE A BEDROOM.
IT REMINDS ME OF THAT CHILDREN'S HOME.
I'M WARNING YOU, IF YOU LEAVE AROUND ANYTHING THAT STINKS, I'M CHUCKING IT OUT.
SOCKS OR SEVENTY-QUID TRAINERS. I DON'T CARE.
OK, MISS KYLE.
AFTER DINNER, YOU CAN GO OUTSIDE AND START MAKING FRIENDS.
SAY 'HELLO' TO THE KIDS WHO WELCOMED US BY KICKING OVER OUR BINS.
STICK TOGETHER. I WANT YOU BACK AS SOON AS IT GETS DARK. FIRST CONTACT ONLY. AND JAMES, PICK ALL THAT RUBBISH OFF THE FRONT LAWN BEFORE YOU GO.
WHY ME?
BECAUSE I SAID SO, OK?

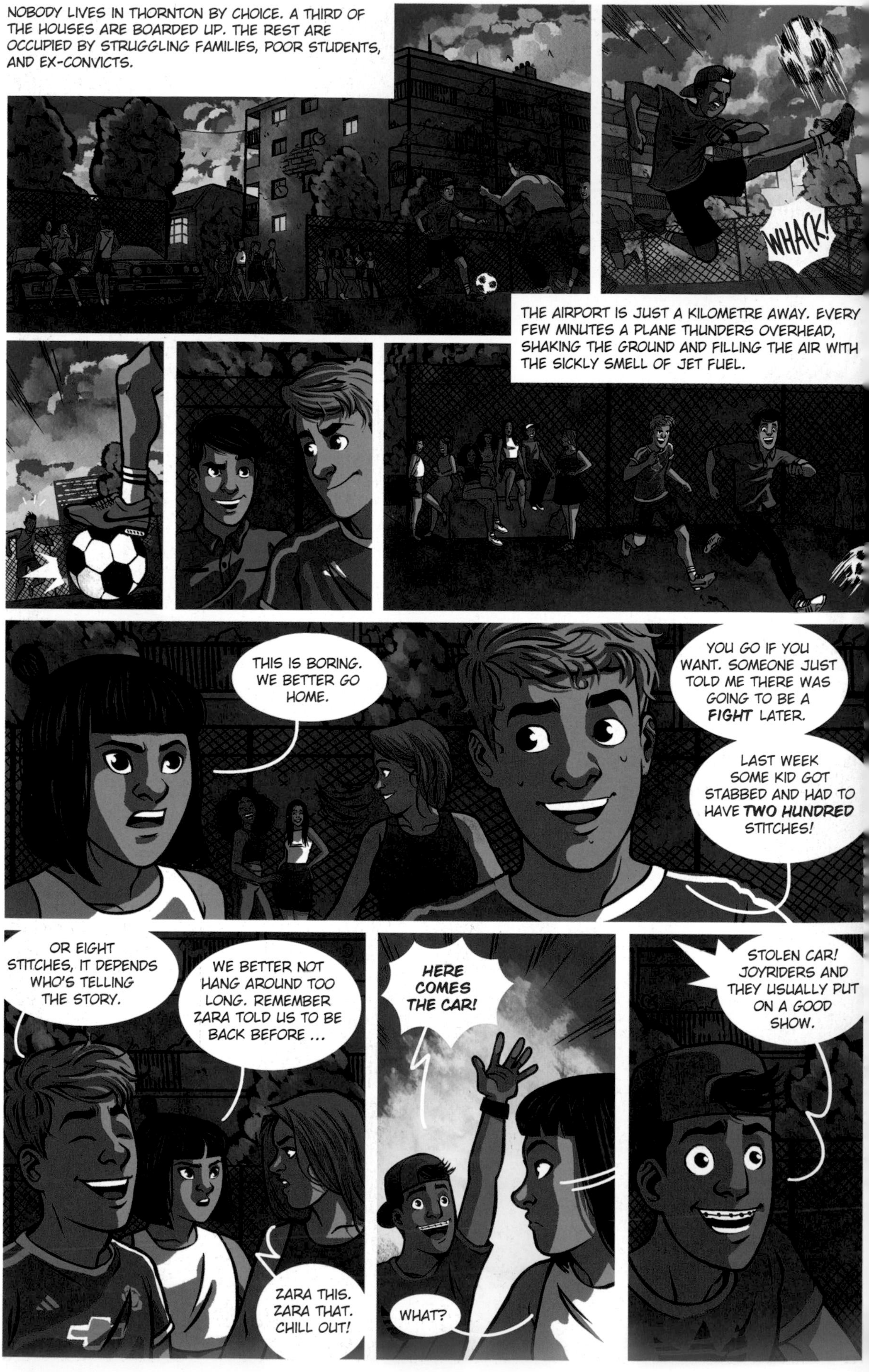
NOBODY LIVES IN THORNTON BY CHOICE. A THIRD OF THE HOUSES ARE BOARDED UP. THE REST ARE OCCUPIED BY STRUGGLING FAMILIES, POOR STUDENTS, AND EX-CONVICTS.
WHACK!
THE AIRPORT IS JUST A KILOMETRE AWAY. EVERY FEW MINUTES A PLANE THUNDERS OVERHEAD, SHAKING THE GROUND AND FILLING THE AIR WITH THE SICKLY SMELL OF JET FUEL.
THIS IS BORING. WE BETTER GO HOME.
YOU GO IF YOU WANT. SOMEONE JUST TOLD ME THERE WAS GOING TO BE A **FIGHT** LATER.
LAST WEEK SOME KID GOT STABBED AND HAD TO HAVE **TWO HUNDRED** STITCHES!
OR EIGHT STITCHES, IT DEPENDS WHO'S TELLING THE STORY.
WE BETTER NOT HANG AROUND TOO LONG. REMEMBER ZARA TOLD US TO BE BACK BEFORE ...
ZARA THIS. ZARA THAT. CHILL OUT!
HERE COMES THE CAR!
WHAT?
STOLEN CAR! JOYRIDERS AND THEY USUALLY PUT ON A GOOD SHOW.

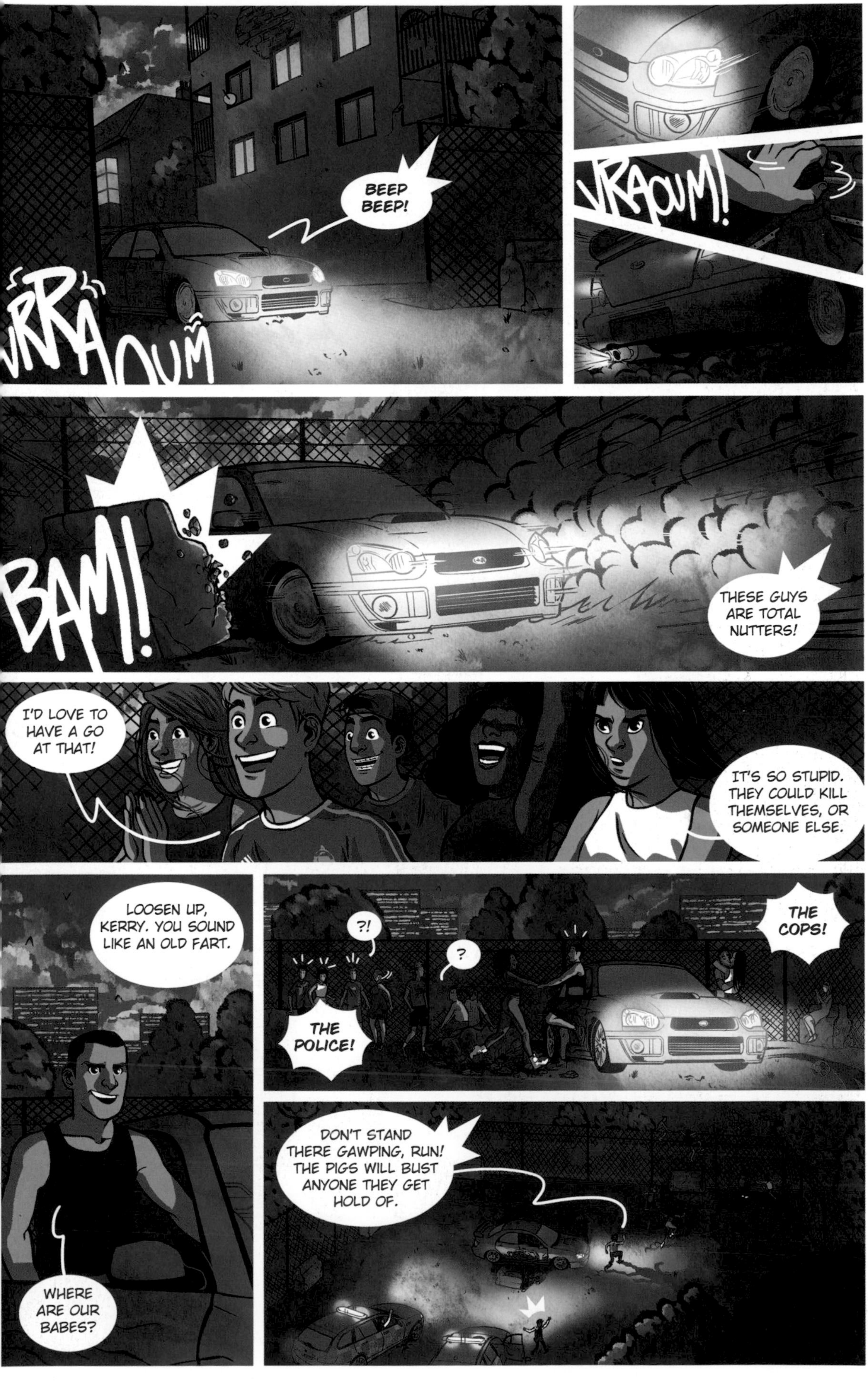
BEEP BEEP!
VRRRAOUM
VRAOUM!
BAM!
THESE GUYS ARE TOTAL NUTTERS!
I'D LOVE TO HAVE A GO AT THAT!
IT'S SO STUPID. THEY COULD KILL THEMSELVES, OR SOMEONE ELSE.
LOOSEN UP, KERRY. YOU SOUND LIKE AN OLD FART.
WHERE ARE OUR BABES?
?!
?
THE POLICE!
THE COPS!
DON'T STAND THERE GAWPING, RUN! THE PIGS WILL BUST ANYONE THEY GET HOLD OF.

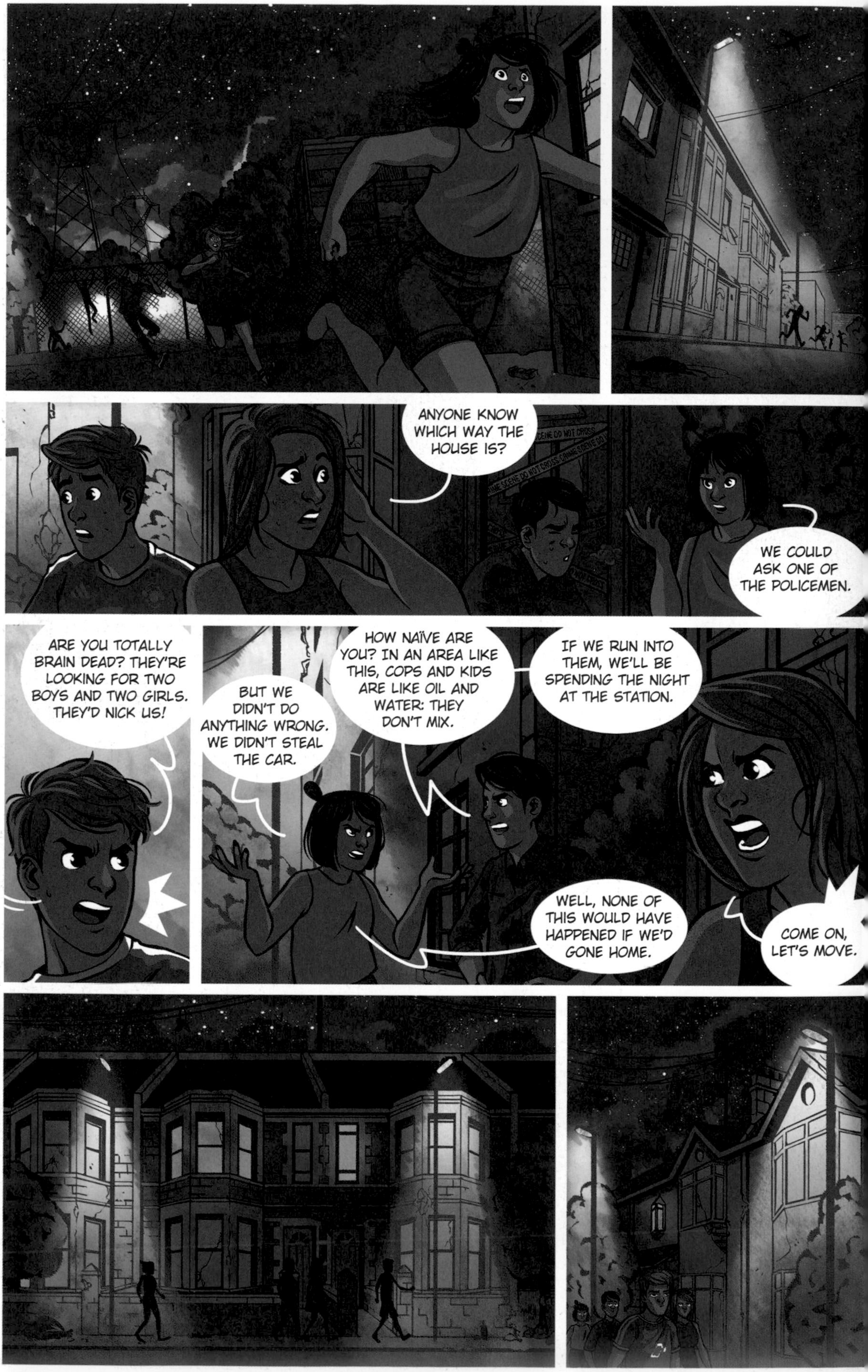
ANYONE KNOW WHICH WAY THE HOUSE IS?
WE COULD ASK ONE OF THE POLICEMEN.
ARE YOU TOTALLY BRAIN DEAD? THEY'RE LOOKING FOR TWO BOYS AND TWO GIRLS. THEY'D NICK US!
BUT WE DIDN'T DO ANYTHING WRONG. WE DIDN'T STEAL THE CAR.
HOW NAÏVE ARE YOU? IN AN AREA LIKE THIS, COPS AND KIDS ARE LIKE OIL AND WATER: THEY DON'T MIX.
IF WE RUN INTO THEM, WE'LL BE SPENDING THE NIGHT AT THE STATION.
WELL, NONE OF THIS WOULD HAVE HAPPENED IF WE'D GONE HOME.
COME ON, LET'S MOVE.

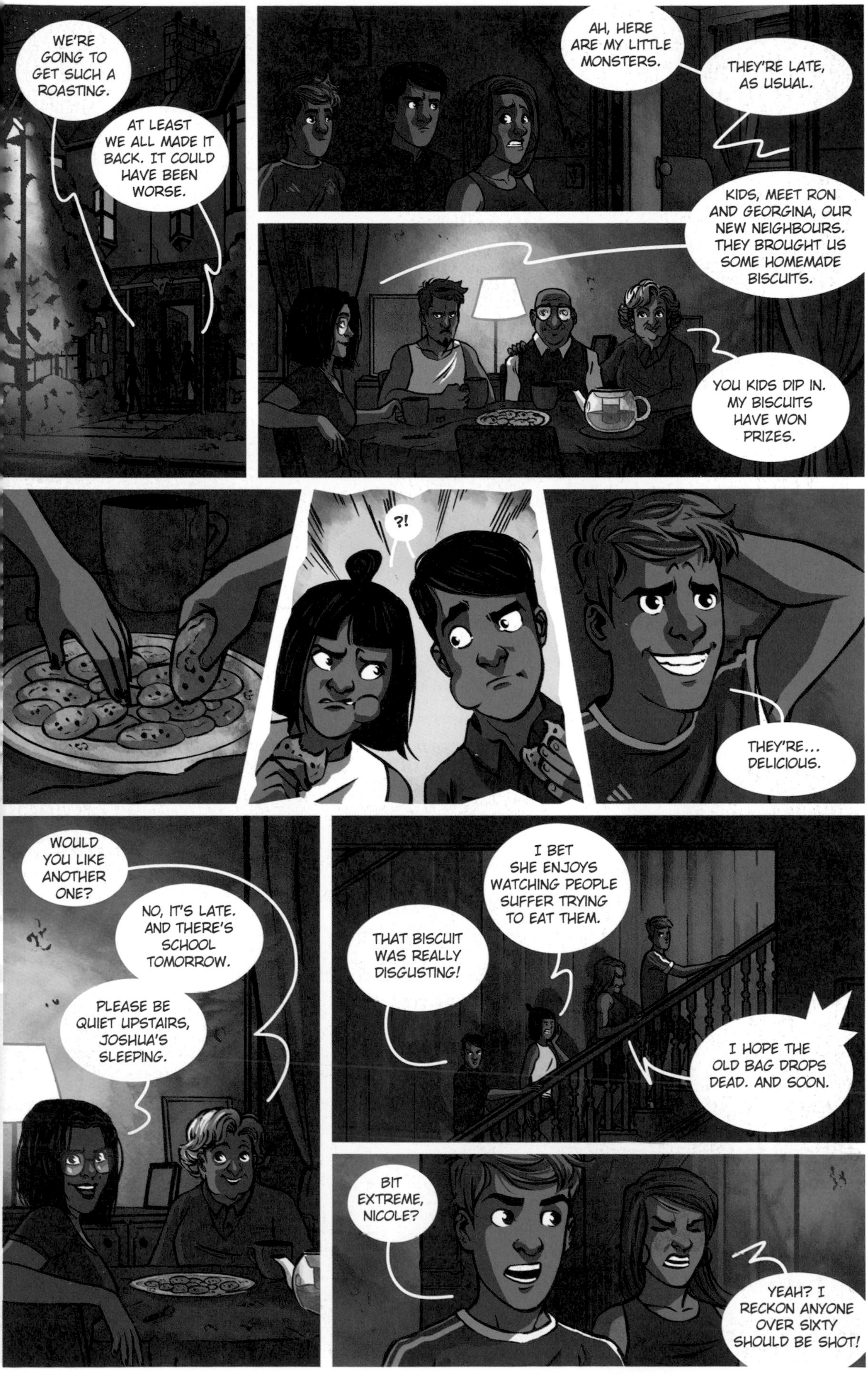
WE'RE GOING TO GET SUCH A ROASTING.
AT LEAST WE ALL MADE IT BACK. IT COULD HAVE BEEN WORSE.
AH, HERE ARE MY LITTLE MONSTERS.
THEY'RE LATE, AS USUAL.
KIDS, MEET RON AND GEORGINA, OUR NEW NEIGHBOURS. THEY BROUGHT US SOME HOMEMADE BISCUITS.
YOU KIDS DIP IN. MY BISCUITS HAVE WON PRIZES.
?!
THEY'RE... DELICIOUS.
WOULD YOU LIKE ANOTHER ONE?
NO, IT'S LATE. AND THERE'S SCHOOL TOMORROW.
PLEASE BE QUIET UPSTAIRS, JOSHUA'S SLEEPING.
THAT BISCUIT WAS REALLY DISGUSTING!
I BET SHE ENJOYS WATCHING PEOPLE SUFFER TRYING TO EAT THEM.
I HOPE THE OLD BAG DROPS DEAD. AND SOON.
BIT EXTREME, NICOLE?
YEAH? I RECKON ANYONE OVER SIXTY SHOULD BE SHOT!

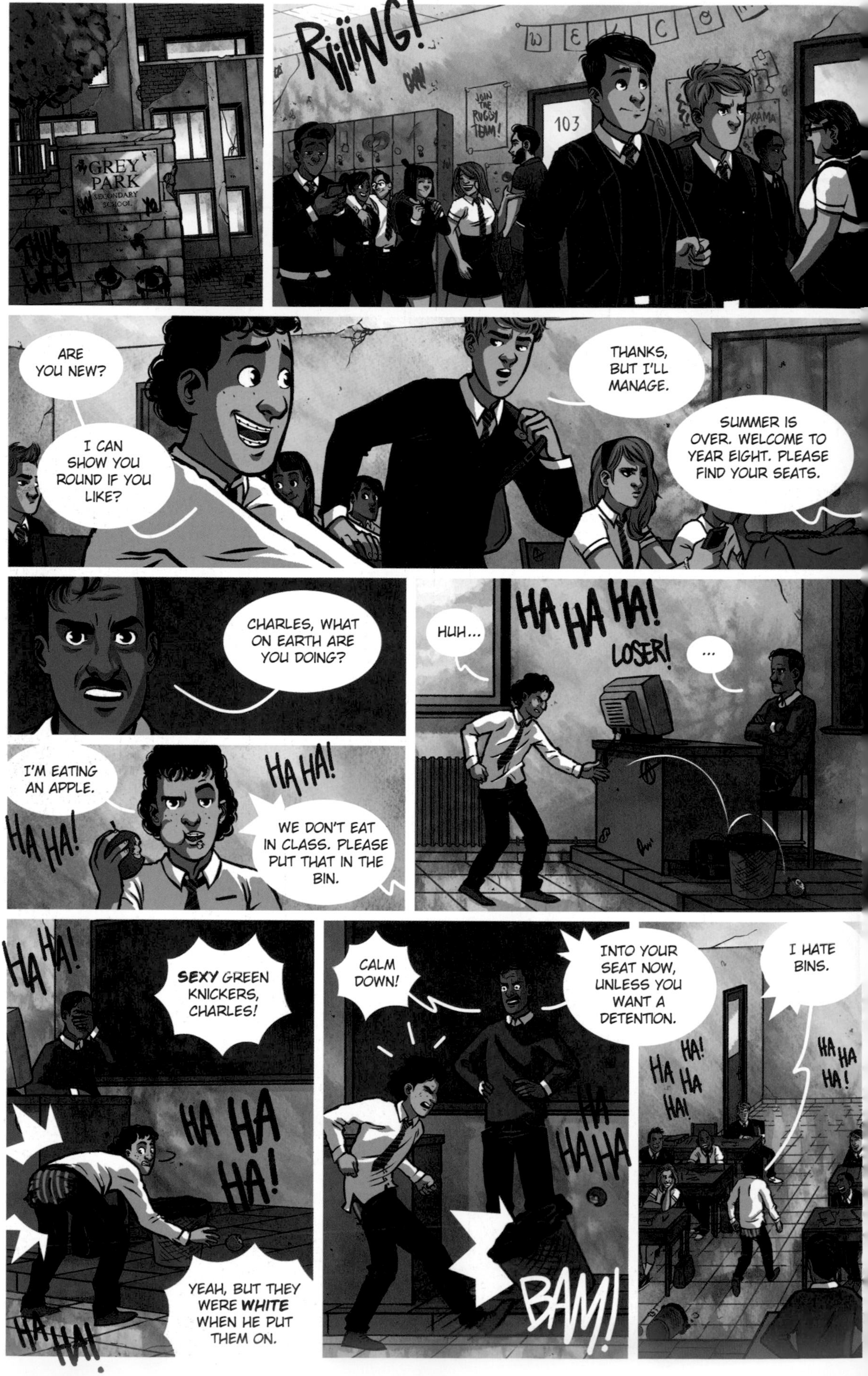
GREY PARK SECONDARY SCHOOL
THUG LIFE!
RIIIING!
JOIN THE RUGBY TEAM!
103
ARE YOU NEW?
I CAN SHOW YOU ROUND IF YOU LIKE?
THANKS, BUT I'LL MANAGE.
SUMMER IS OVER. WELCOME TO YEAR EIGHT. PLEASE FIND YOUR SEATS.
CHARLES, WHAT ON EARTH ARE YOU DOING?
I'M EATING AN APPLE.
HA HA!
HA HA!
WE DON'T EAT IN CLASS. PLEASE PUT THAT IN THE BIN.
HUH...
HA HA HA!
LOSER!
...
HA HA!
SEXY GREEN KNICKERS, CHARLES!
HA HA HA!
YEAH, BUT THEY WERE WHITE WHEN HE PUT THEM ON.
HA HA!
CALM DOWN!
INTO YOUR SEAT NOW, UNLESS YOU WANT A DETENTION.
HA HA HA
BAM!
I HATE BINS.
HA! HA HA HA!
HA HA HA!

RIIING!

U.N. CLUB
INFO

WHACK!

MISS US IN THE HOLIDAYS, CHARLES?

DID YOU BRING US ANY SOUVENIRS?

NO...

SELFISH. YOU DESERVE TO BE SLAPPED.

WHACK!

AND WHO'S YOUR NEW LITTLE FRIEND HERE?

U.N CLUB
INFO

I WOULDN'T RECOMMEND YOU TRY THAT AGAIN.

LOOKS LIKE THE NEW BOY THINKS HE'S A BIT OF A HARD MAN.

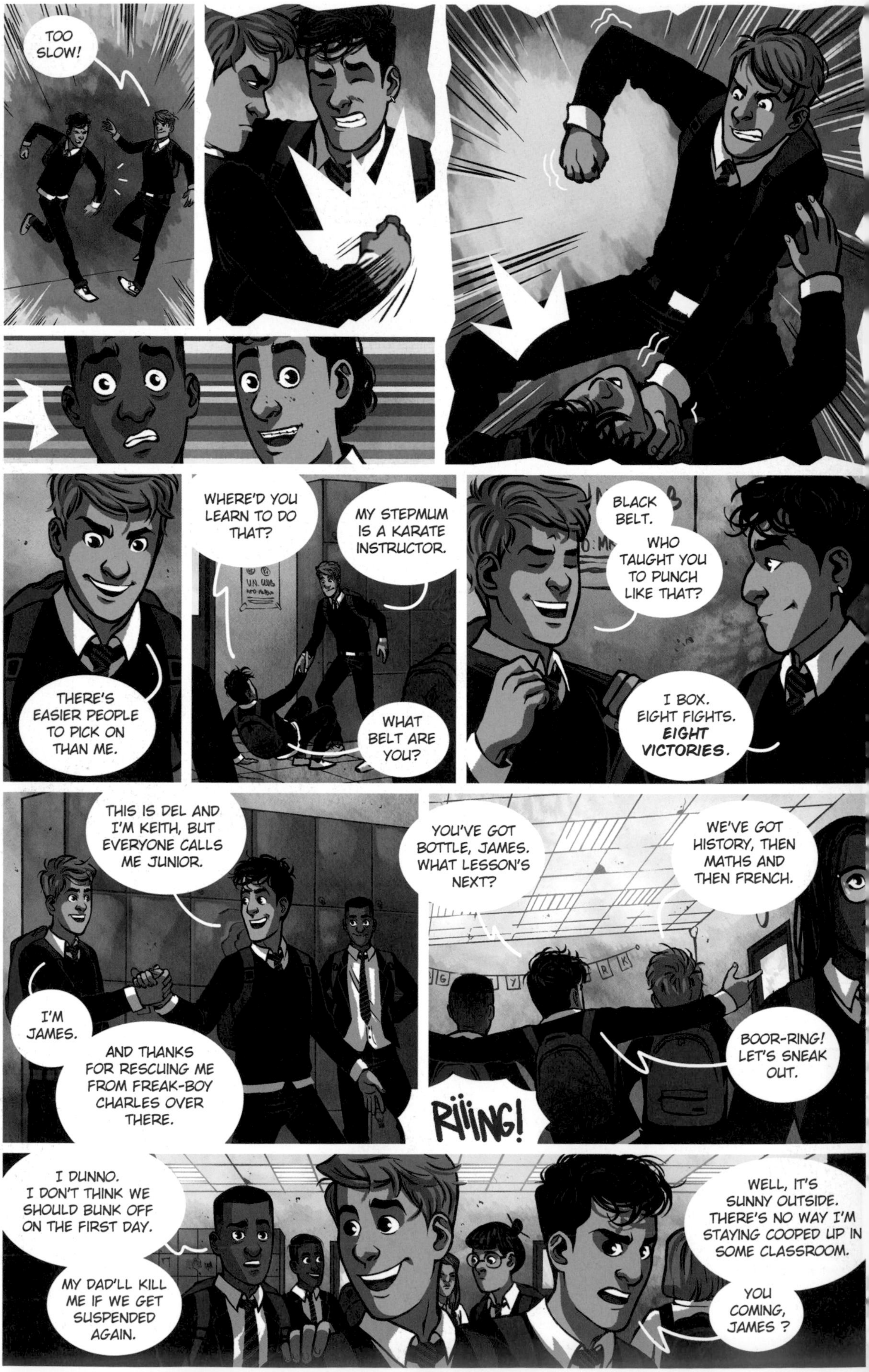
TOO SLOW!
THERE'S EASIER PEOPLE TO PICK ON THAN ME.
WHERE'D YOU LEARN TO DO THAT?
MY STEPMUM IS A KARATE INSTRUCTOR.
WHAT BELT ARE YOU?
BLACK BELT.
WHO TAUGHT YOU TO PUNCH LIKE THAT?
I BOX. EIGHT FIGHTS. **EIGHT VICTORIES**.
THIS IS DEL AND I'M KEITH, BUT EVERYONE CALLS ME JUNIOR.
I'M JAMES.
AND THANKS FOR RESCUING ME FROM FREAK-BOY CHARLES OVER THERE.
YOU'VE GOT BOTTLE, JAMES. WHAT LESSON'S NEXT?
WE'VE GOT HISTORY, THEN MATHS AND THEN FRENCH.
BOOR-RING! LET'S SNEAK OUT.
RIIING!
I DUNNO. I DON'T THINK WE SHOULD BUNK OFF ON THE FIRST DAY.
MY DAD'LL KILL ME IF WE GET SUSPENDED AGAIN.
WELL, IT'S SUNNY OUTSIDE. THERE'S NO WAY I'M STAYING COOPED UP IN SOME CLASSROOM.
YOU COMING, JAMES ?

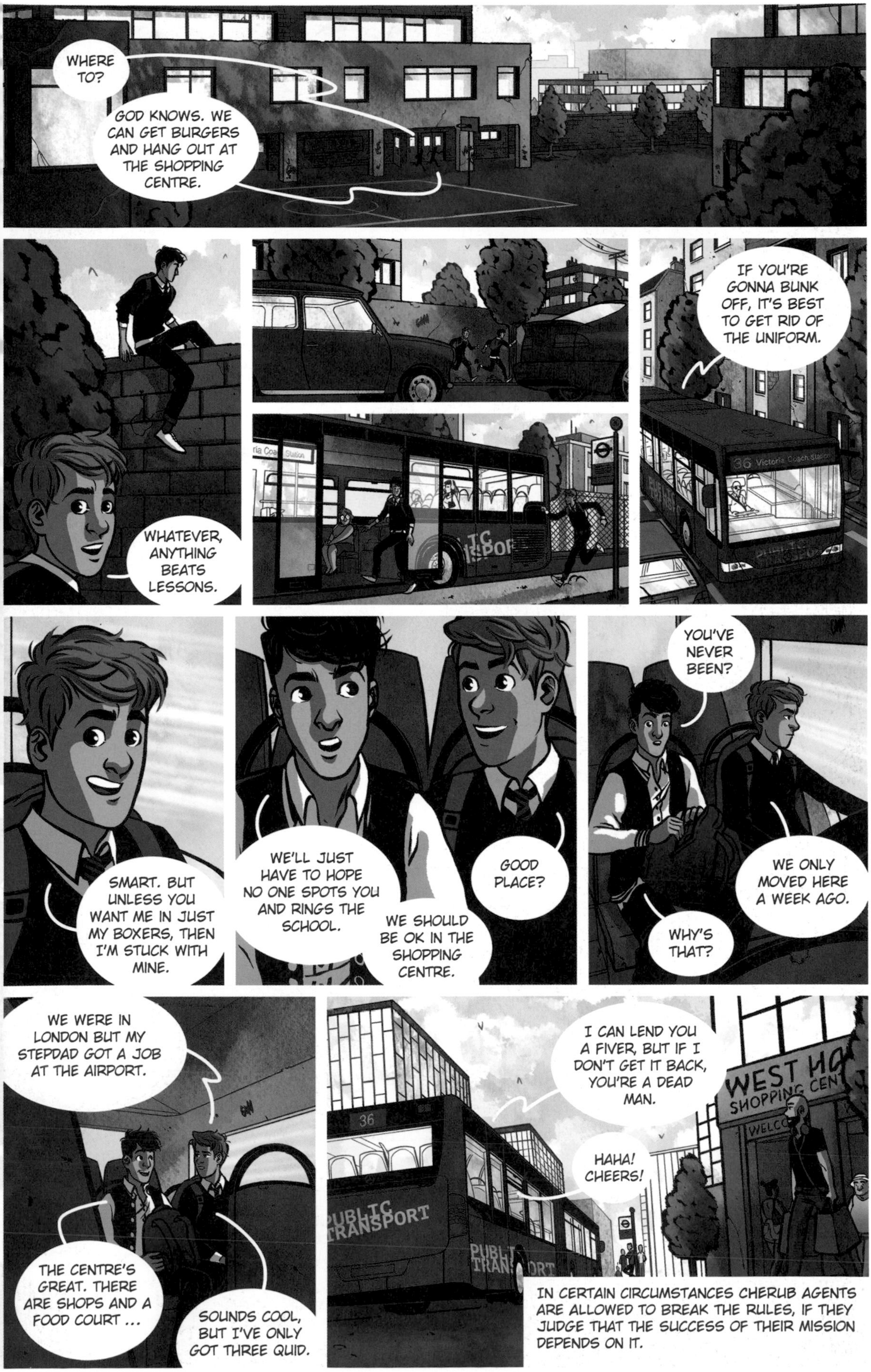
WHERE TO?
GOD KNOWS. WE CAN GET BURGERS AND HANG OUT AT THE SHOPPING CENTRE.
WHATEVER, ANYTHING BEATS LESSONS.
IF YOU'RE GONNA BUNK OFF, IT'S BEST TO GET RID OF THE UNIFORM.
SMART. BUT UNLESS YOU WANT ME IN JUST MY BOXERS, THEN I'M STUCK WITH MINE.
WE'LL JUST HAVE TO HOPE NO ONE SPOTS YOU AND RINGS THE SCHOOL.
WE SHOULD BE OK IN THE SHOPPING CENTRE.
GOOD PLACE?
YOU'VE NEVER BEEN?
WHY'S THAT?
WE ONLY MOVED HERE A WEEK AGO.
WE WERE IN LONDON BUT MY STEPDAD GOT A JOB AT THE AIRPORT.
THE CENTRE'S GREAT. THERE ARE SHOPS AND A FOOD COURT ...
SOUNDS COOL, BUT I'VE ONLY GOT THREE QUID.
I CAN LEND YOU A FIVER, BUT IF I DON'T GET IT BACK, YOU'RE A DEAD MAN.
HAHA! CHEERS!
IN CERTAIN CIRCUMSTANCES CHERUB AGENTS ARE ALLOWED TO BREAK THE RULES, IF THEY JUDGE THAT THE SUCCESS OF THEIR MISSION DEPENDS ON IT.

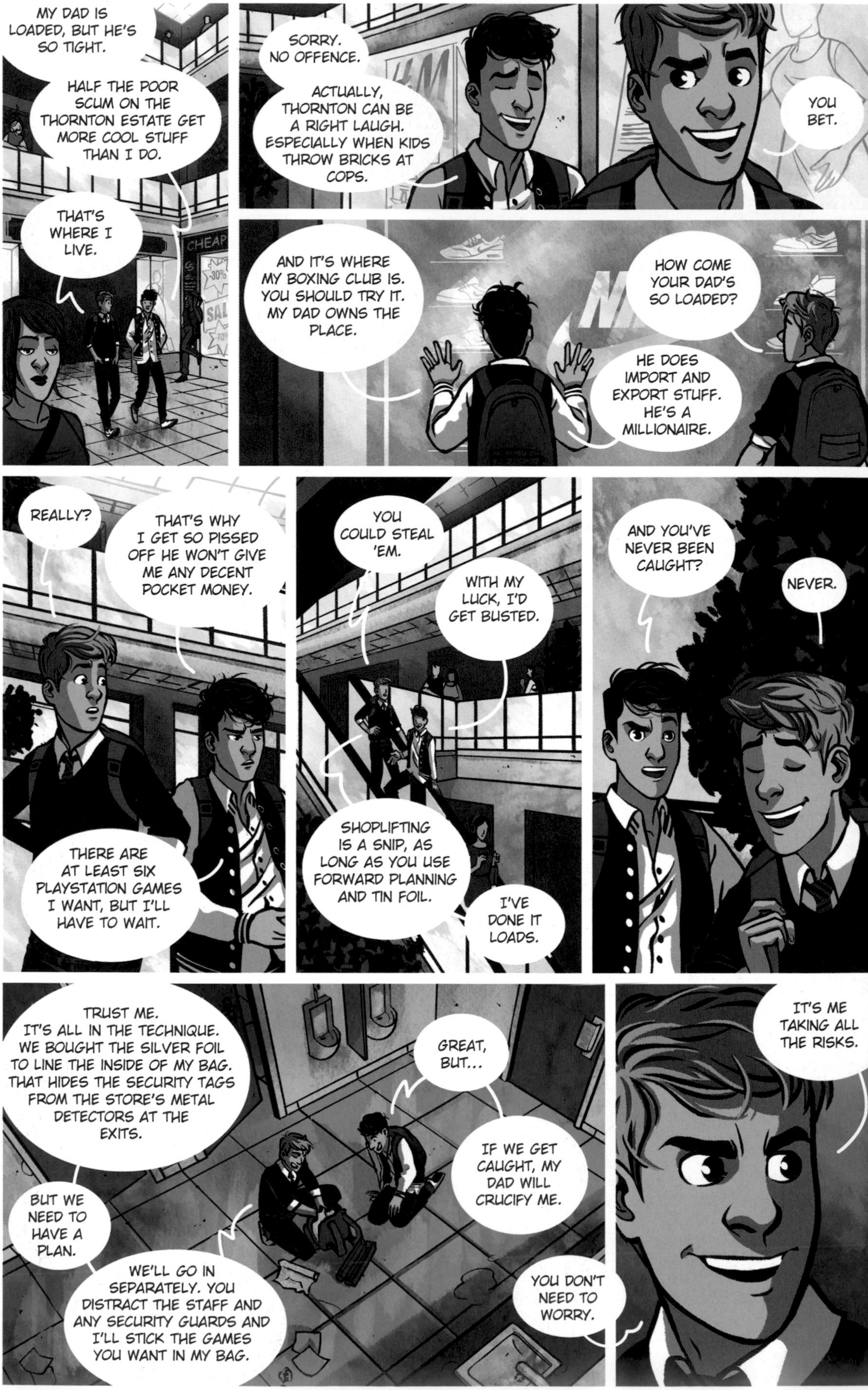
MY DAD IS LOADED, BUT HE'S SO TIGHT.
HALF THE POOR SCUM ON THE THORNTON ESTATE GET MORE COOL STUFF THAN I DO.
THAT'S WHERE I LIVE.
CHEAP
SALE
SORRY. NO OFFENCE.
ACTUALLY, THORNTON CAN BE A RIGHT LAUGH. ESPECIALLY WHEN KIDS THROW BRICKS AT COPS.
YOU BET.
AND IT'S WHERE MY BOXING CLUB IS. YOU SHOULD TRY IT. MY DAD OWNS THE PLACE.
HOW COME YOUR DAD'S SO LOADED?
HE DOES IMPORT AND EXPORT STUFF. HE'S A MILLIONAIRE.
REALLY?
THAT'S WHY I GET SO PISSED OFF HE WON'T GIVE ME ANY DECENT POCKET MONEY.
THERE ARE AT LEAST SIX PLAYSTATION GAMES I WANT, BUT I'LL HAVE TO WAIT.
YOU COULD STEAL 'EM.
WITH MY LUCK, I'D GET BUSTED.
SHOPLIFTING IS A SNIP, AS LONG AS YOU USE FORWARD PLANNING AND TIN FOIL.
I'VE DONE IT LOADS.
AND YOU'VE NEVER BEEN CAUGHT?
NEVER.
TRUST ME. IT'S ALL IN THE TECHNIQUE. WE BOUGHT THE SILVER FOIL TO LINE THE INSIDE OF MY BAG. THAT HIDES THE SECURITY TAGS FROM THE STORE'S METAL DETECTORS AT THE EXITS.
BUT WE NEED TO HAVE A PLAN.
WE'LL GO IN SEPARATELY. YOU DISTRACT THE STAFF AND ANY SECURITY GUARDS AND I'LL STICK THE GAMES YOU WANT IN MY BAG.
GREAT, BUT...
IF WE GET CAUGHT, MY DAD WILL CRUCIFY ME.
YOU DON'T NEED TO WORRY.
IT'S ME TAKING ALL THE RISKS.

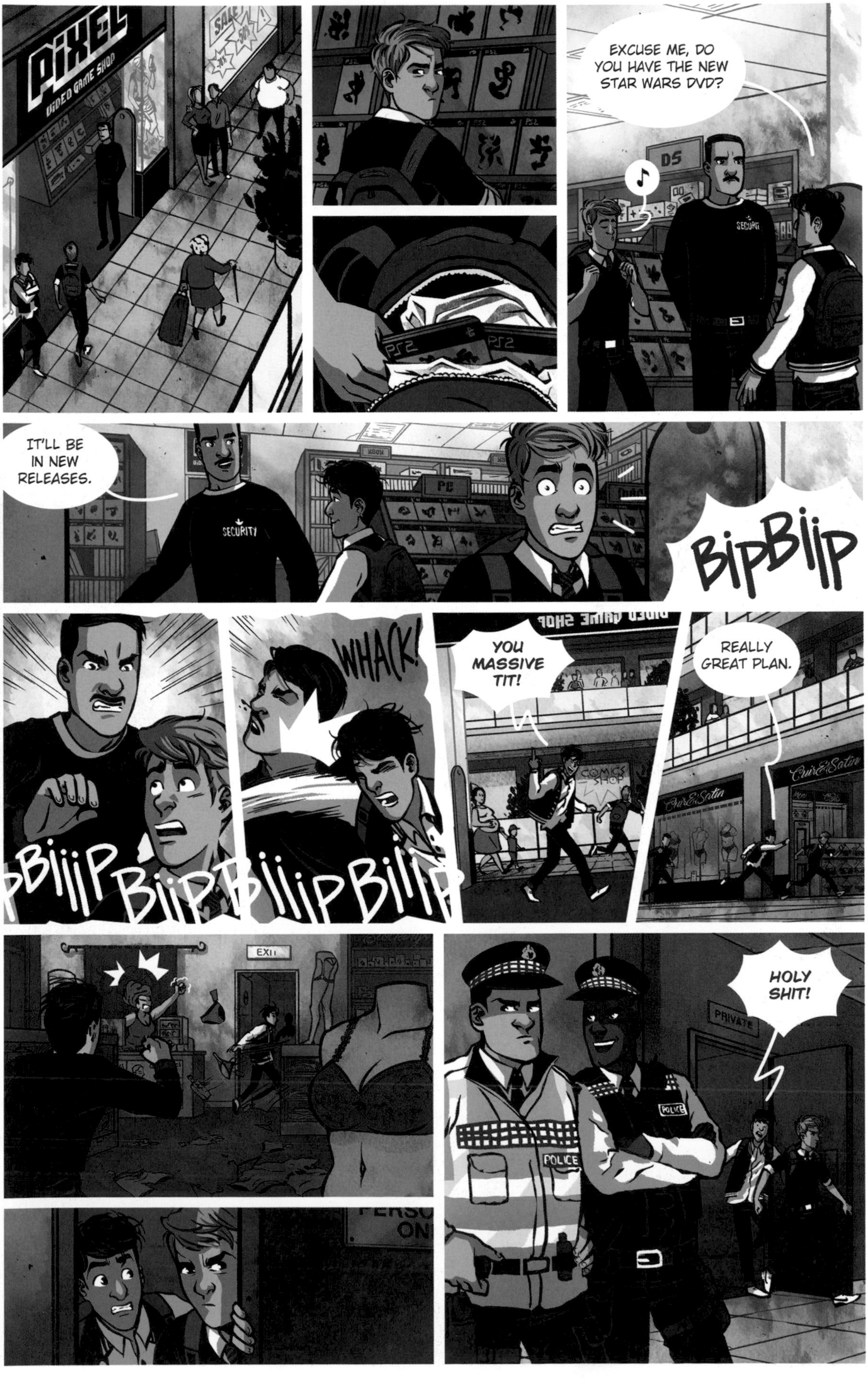
PIXEL
VIDEO GAME SHOP
EXCUSE ME, DO YOU HAVE THE NEW STAR WARS DVD?
DS
SECURITY
IT'LL BE IN NEW RELEASES.
SECURITY
PC
BIPBIIP
BIIIP BIIP BIIIP BIIIP
WHACK!
YOU MASSIVE TIT!
COMICS SHOP
REALLY GREAT PLAN.
Cuir&Satin
EXIT
HOLY SHIT!
PRIVATE
POLICE
POLICE

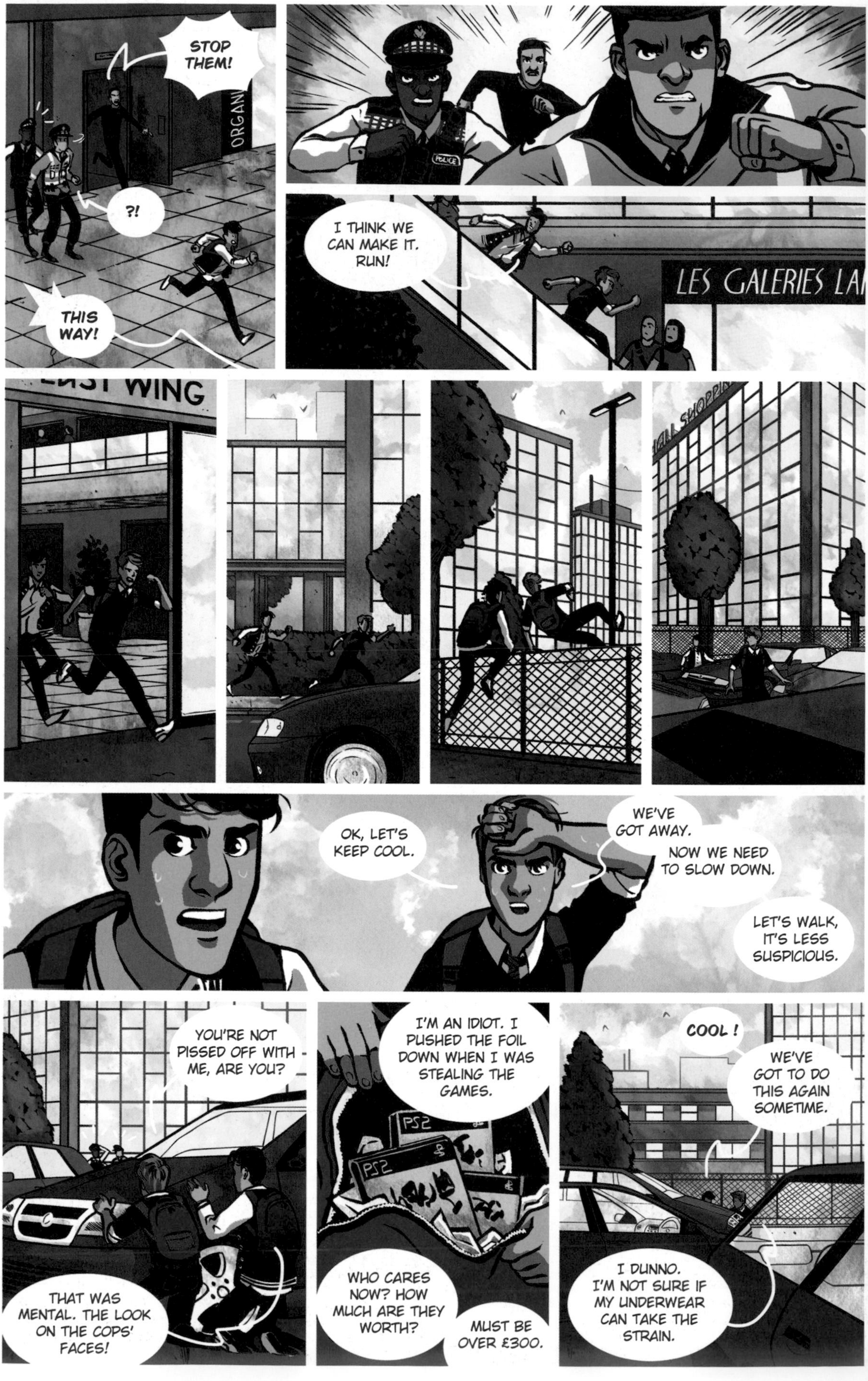
STOP THEM!
ORGAN
?!
THIS WAY!
I THINK WE CAN MAKE IT. RUN!
LES GALERIES LA
WING
OK, LET'S KEEP COOL.
WE'VE GOT AWAY.
NOW WE NEED TO SLOW DOWN.
LET'S WALK, IT'S LESS SUSPICIOUS.
YOU'RE NOT PISSED OFF WITH ME, ARE YOU?
THAT WAS MENTAL. THE LOOK ON THE COPS' FACES!
I'M AN IDIOT. I PUSHED THE FOIL DOWN WHEN I WAS STEALING THE GAMES.
PS2
PS2
WHO CARES NOW? HOW MUCH ARE THEY WORTH?
MUST BE OVER £300.
COOL!
WE'VE GOT TO DO THIS AGAIN SOMETIME.
I DUNNO. I'M NOT SURE IF MY UNDERWEAR CAN TAKE THE STRAIN.

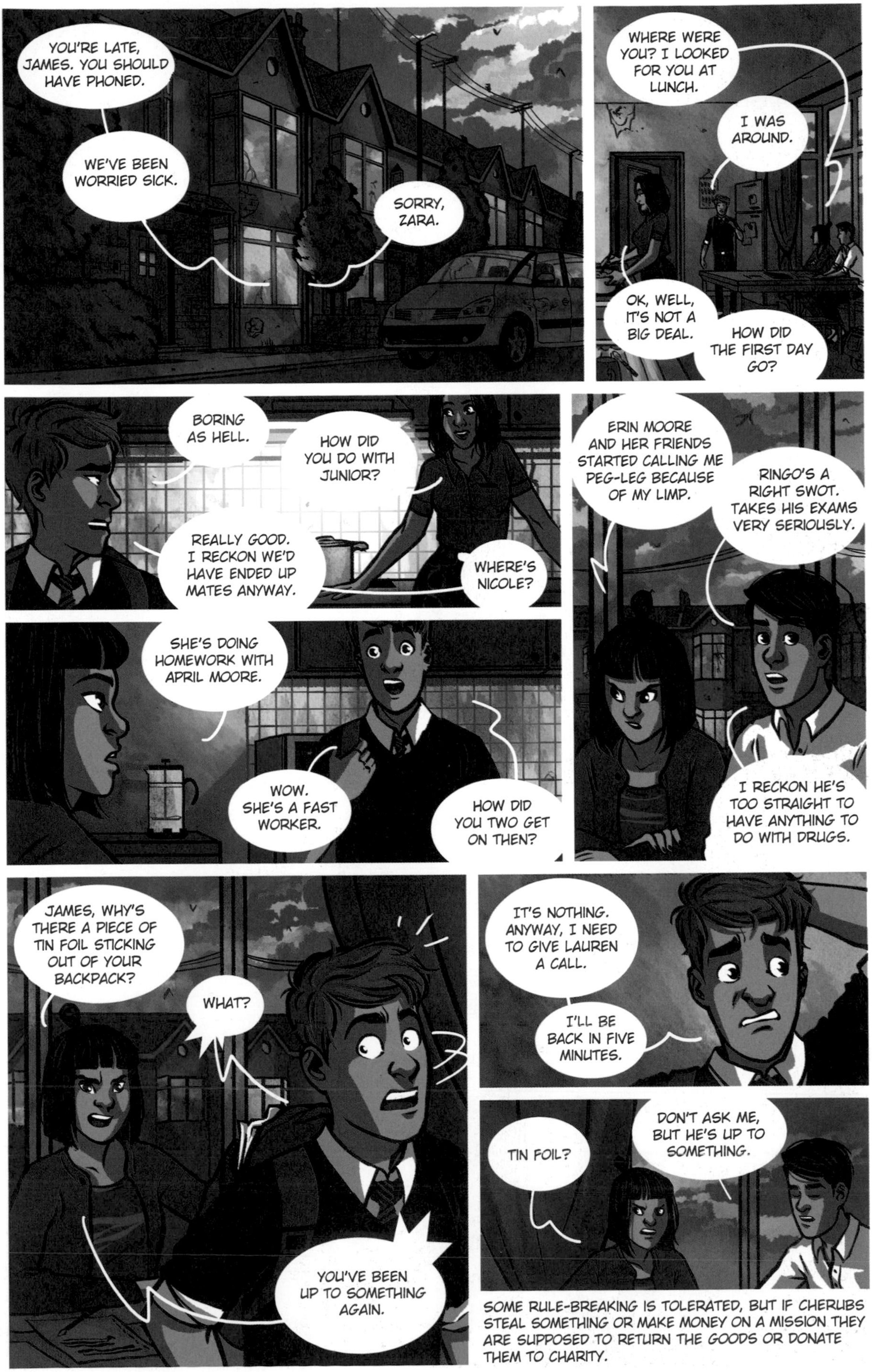
YOU'RE LATE, JAMES. YOU SHOULD HAVE PHONED.
WE'VE BEEN WORRIED SICK.
SORRY, ZARA.
WHERE WERE YOU? I LOOKED FOR YOU AT LUNCH.
I WAS AROUND.
OK, WELL, IT'S NOT A BIG DEAL.
HOW DID THE FIRST DAY GO?
BORING AS HELL.
HOW DID YOU DO WITH JUNIOR?
REALLY GOOD. I RECKON WE'D HAVE ENDED UP MATES ANYWAY.
WHERE'S NICOLE?
SHE'S DOING HOMEWORK WITH APRIL MOORE.
WOW. SHE'S A FAST WORKER.
HOW DID YOU TWO GET ON THEN?
ERIN MOORE AND HER FRIENDS STARTED CALLING ME PEG-LEG BECAUSE OF MY LIMP.
RINGO'S A RIGHT SWOT. TAKES HIS EXAMS VERY SERIOUSLY.
I RECKON HE'S TOO STRAIGHT TO HAVE ANYTHING TO DO WITH DRUGS.
JAMES, WHY'S THERE A PIECE OF TIN FOIL STICKING OUT OF YOUR BACKPACK?
WHAT?
YOU'VE BEEN UP TO SOMETHING AGAIN.
IT'S NOTHING. ANYWAY, I NEED TO GIVE LAUREN A CALL.
I'LL BE BACK IN FIVE MINUTES.
TIN FOIL?
DON'T ASK ME, BUT HE'S UP TO SOMETHING.
SOME RULE-BREAKING IS TOLERATED, BUT IF CHERUBS STEAL SOMETHING OR MAKE MONEY ON A MISSION THEY ARE SUPPOSED TO RETURN THE GOODS OR DONATE THEM TO CHARITY.

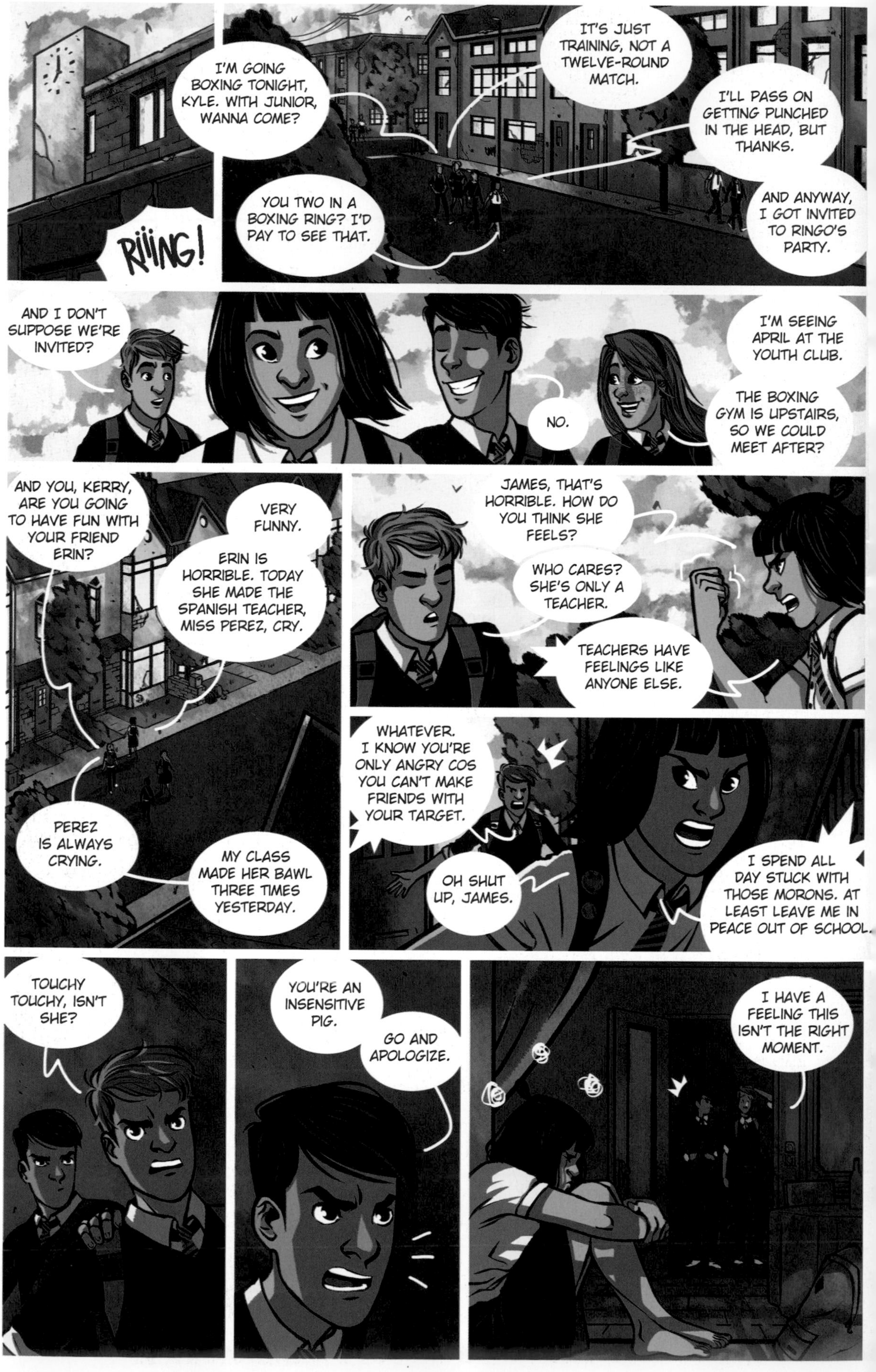
RIIING!
I'M GOING BOXING TONIGHT, KYLE. WITH JUNIOR, WANNA COME?
IT'S JUST TRAINING, NOT A TWELVE-ROUND MATCH.
I'LL PASS ON GETTING PUNCHED IN THE HEAD, BUT THANKS.
YOU TWO IN A BOXING RING? I'D PAY TO SEE THAT.
AND ANYWAY, I GOT INVITED TO RINGO'S PARTY.
AND I DON'T SUPPOSE WE'RE INVITED?
NO.
I'M SEEING APRIL AT THE YOUTH CLUB.
THE BOXING GYM IS UPSTAIRS, SO WE COULD MEET AFTER?
AND YOU, KERRY, ARE YOU GOING TO HAVE FUN WITH YOUR FRIEND ERIN?
VERY FUNNY.
ERIN IS HORRIBLE. TODAY SHE MADE THE SPANISH TEACHER, MISS PEREZ, CRY.
PEREZ IS ALWAYS CRYING.
MY CLASS MADE HER BAWL THREE TIMES YESTERDAY.
JAMES, THAT'S HORRIBLE. HOW DO YOU THINK SHE FEELS?
WHO CARES? SHE'S ONLY A TEACHER.
TEACHERS HAVE FEELINGS LIKE ANYONE ELSE.
WHATEVER. I KNOW YOU'RE ONLY ANGRY COS YOU CAN'T MAKE FRIENDS WITH YOUR TARGET.
OH SHUT UP, JAMES.
I SPEND ALL DAY STUCK WITH THOSE MORONS. AT LEAST LEAVE ME IN PEACE OUT OF SCHOOL.
TOUCHY TOUCHY, ISN'T SHE?
YOU'RE AN INSENSITIVE PIG.
GO AND APOLOGIZE.
I HAVE A FEELING THIS ISN'T THE RIGHT MOMENT.

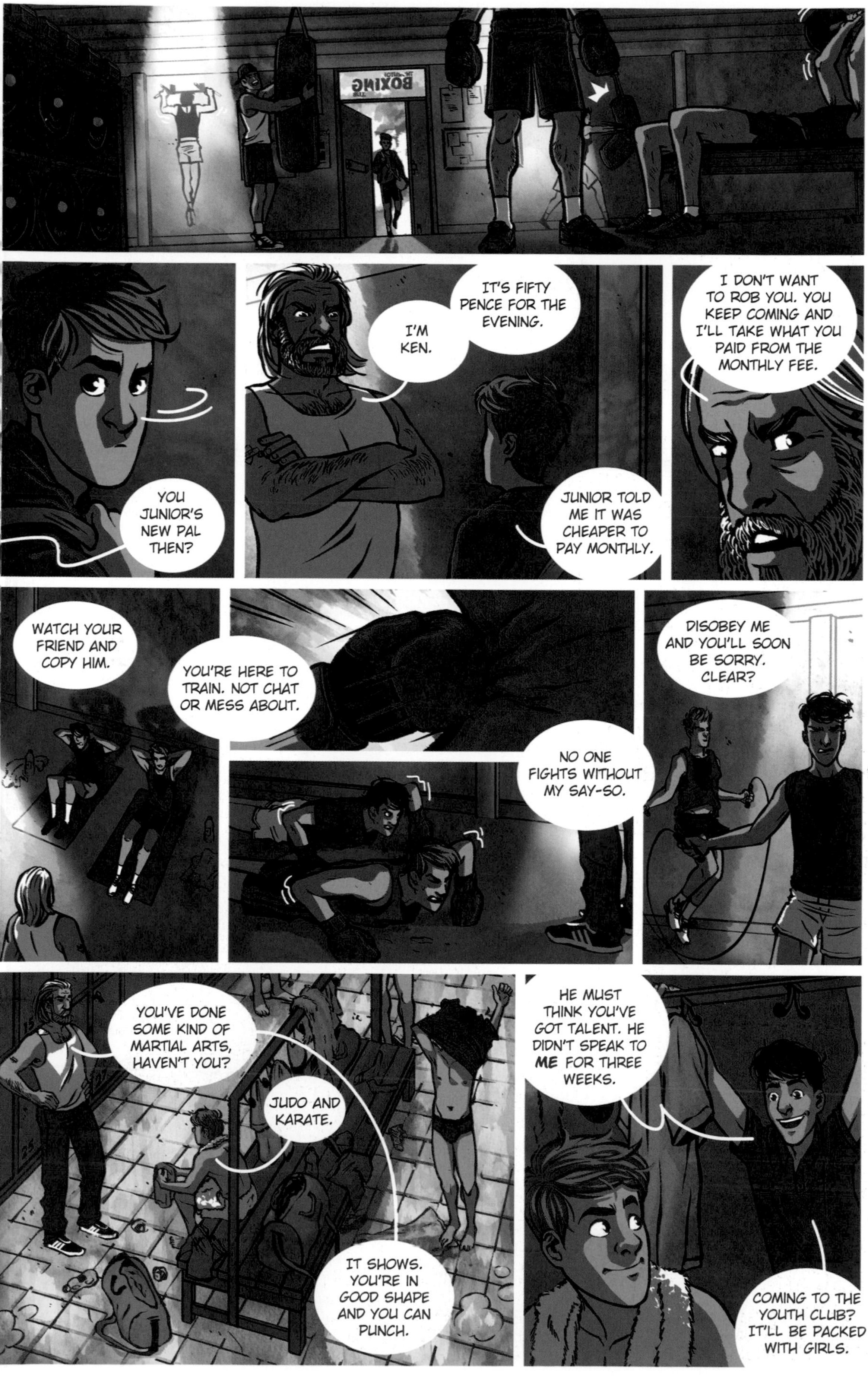
YOU JUNIOR'S NEW PAL THEN?
I'M KEN.
IT'S FIFTY PENCE FOR THE EVENING.
JUNIOR TOLD ME IT WAS CHEAPER TO PAY MONTHLY.
I DON'T WANT TO ROB YOU. YOU KEEP COMING AND I'LL TAKE WHAT YOU PAID FROM THE MONTHLY FEE.
WATCH YOUR FRIEND AND COPY HIM.
YOU'RE HERE TO TRAIN. NOT CHAT OR MESS ABOUT.
NO ONE FIGHTS WITHOUT MY SAY-SO.
DISOBEY ME AND YOU'LL SOON BE SORRY. CLEAR?
YOU'VE DONE SOME KIND OF MARTIAL ARTS, HAVEN'T YOU?
JUDO AND KARATE.
IT SHOWS. YOU'RE IN GOOD SHAPE AND YOU CAN PUNCH.
HE MUST THINK YOU'VE GOT TALENT. HE DIDN'T SPEAK TO **ME** FOR THREE WEEKS.
COMING TO THE YOUTH CLUB? IT'LL BE PACKED WITH GIRLS.

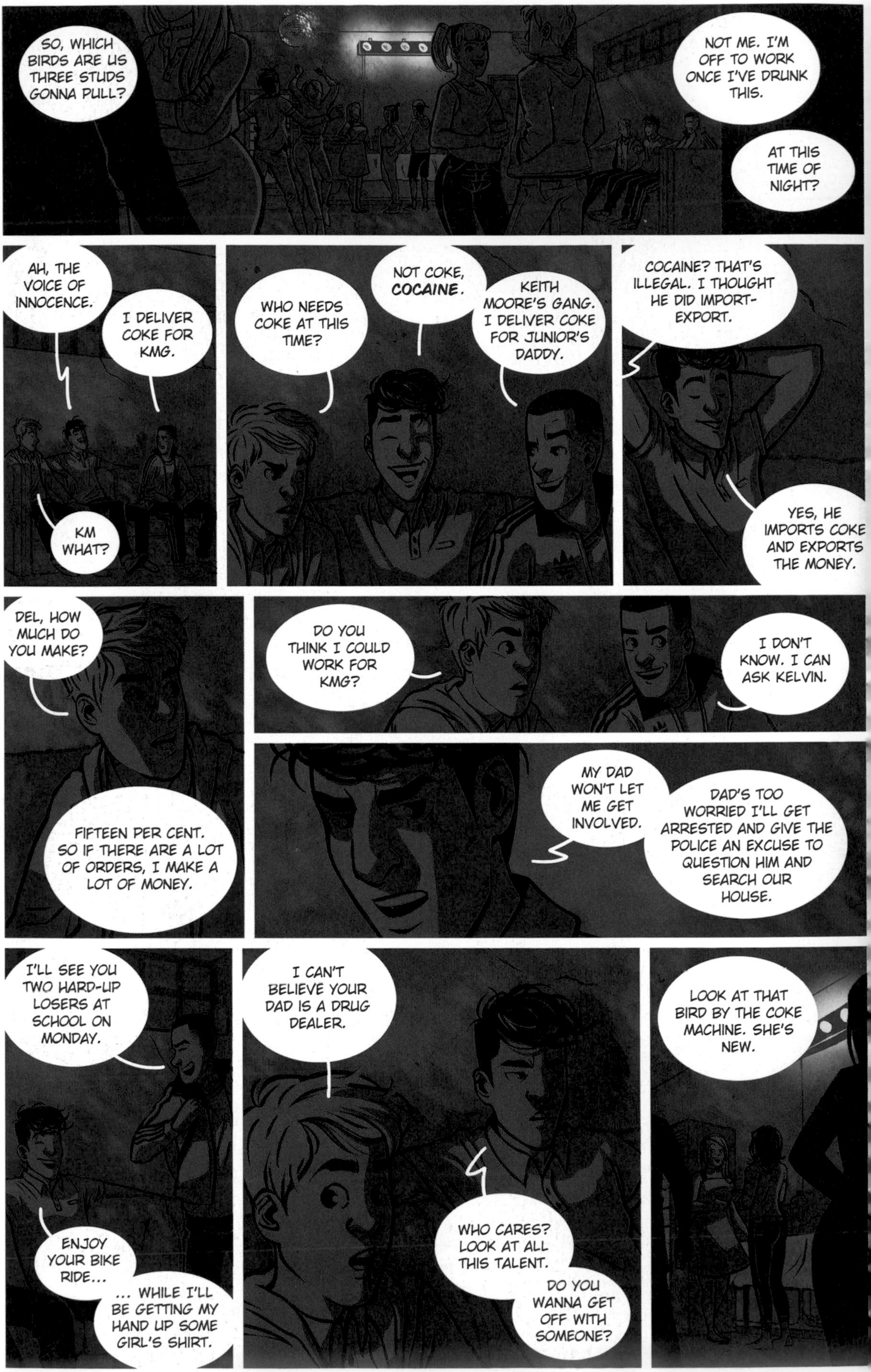
SO, WHICH BIRDS ARE US THREE STUDS GONNA PULL?
NOT ME. I'M OFF TO WORK ONCE I'VE DRUNK THIS.
AT THIS TIME OF NIGHT?
AH, THE VOICE OF INNOCENCE.
I DELIVER COKE FOR KMG.
KM WHAT?
WHO NEEDS COKE AT THIS TIME?
NOT COKE, **COCAINE**.
KEITH MOORE'S GANG. I DELIVER COKE FOR JUNIOR'S DADDY.
COCAINE? THAT'S ILLEGAL. I THOUGHT HE DID IMPORT-EXPORT.
YES, HE IMPORTS COKE AND EXPORTS THE MONEY.
DEL, HOW MUCH DO YOU MAKE?
FIFTEEN PER CENT. SO IF THERE ARE A LOT OF ORDERS, I MAKE A LOT OF MONEY.
DO YOU THINK I COULD WORK FOR KMG?
I DON'T KNOW. I CAN ASK KELVIN.
MY DAD WON'T LET ME GET INVOLVED.
DAD'S TOO WORRIED I'LL GET ARRESTED AND GIVE THE POLICE AN EXCUSE TO QUESTION HIM AND SEARCH OUR HOUSE.
I'LL SEE YOU TWO HARD-UP LOSERS AT SCHOOL ON MONDAY.
ENJOY YOUR BIKE RIDE...
... WHILE I'LL BE GETTING MY HAND UP SOME GIRL'S SHIRT.
I CAN'T BELIEVE YOUR DAD IS A DRUG DEALER.
WHO CARES? LOOK AT ALL THIS TALENT.
DO YOU WANNA GET OFF WITH SOMEONE?
LOOK AT THAT BIRD BY THE COKE MACHINE. SHE'S NEW.

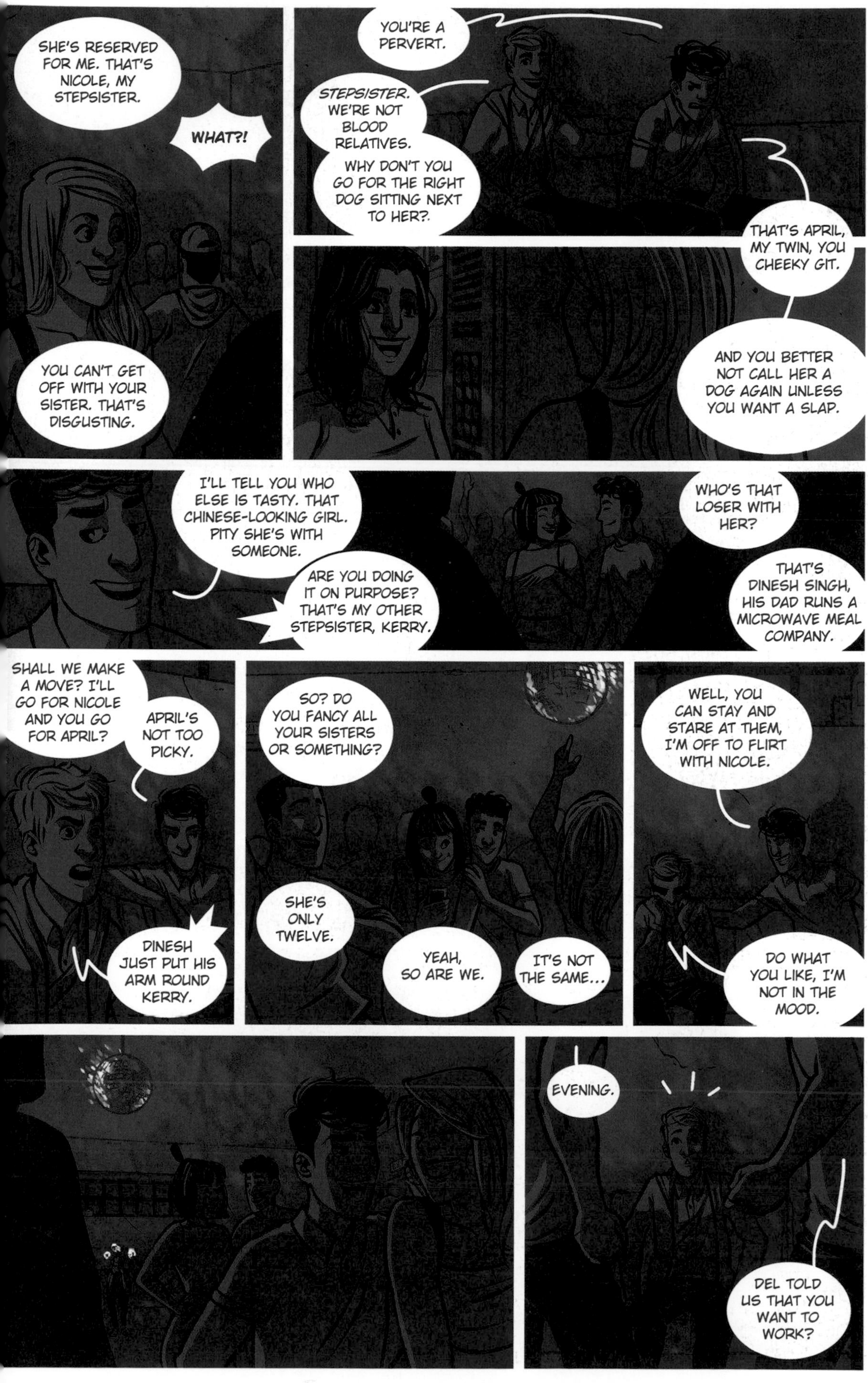
SHE'S RESERVED FOR ME. THAT'S NICOLE, MY STEPSISTER.
WHAT?!
YOU CAN'T GET OFF WITH YOUR SISTER. THAT'S DISGUSTING.
YOU'RE A PERVERT.
STEPSISTER. WE'RE NOT BLOOD RELATIVES.
WHY DON'T YOU GO FOR THE RIGHT DOG SITTING NEXT TO HER?.
THAT'S APRIL, MY TWIN, YOU CHEEKY GIT.
AND YOU BETTER NOT CALL HER A DOG AGAIN UNLESS YOU WANT A SLAP.
I'LL TELL YOU WHO ELSE IS TASTY. THAT CHINESE-LOOKING GIRL. PITY SHE'S WITH SOMEONE.
ARE YOU DOING IT ON PURPOSE? THAT'S MY OTHER STEPSISTER, KERRY.
WHO'S THAT LOSER WITH HER?
THAT'S DINESH SINGH, HIS DAD RUNS A MICROWAVE MEAL COMPANY.
SHALL WE MAKE A MOVE? I'LL GO FOR NICOLE AND YOU GO FOR APRIL?
APRIL'S NOT TOO PICKY.
DINESH JUST PUT HIS ARM ROUND KERRY.
SO? DO YOU FANCY ALL YOUR SISTERS OR SOMETHING?
SHE'S ONLY TWELVE.
YEAH, SO ARE WE.
IT'S NOT THE SAME...
WELL, YOU CAN STAY AND STARE AT THEM, I'M OFF TO FLIRT WITH NICOLE.
DO WHAT YOU LIKE, I'M NOT IN THE MOOD.
EVENING.
DEL TOLD US THAT YOU WANT TO WORK?

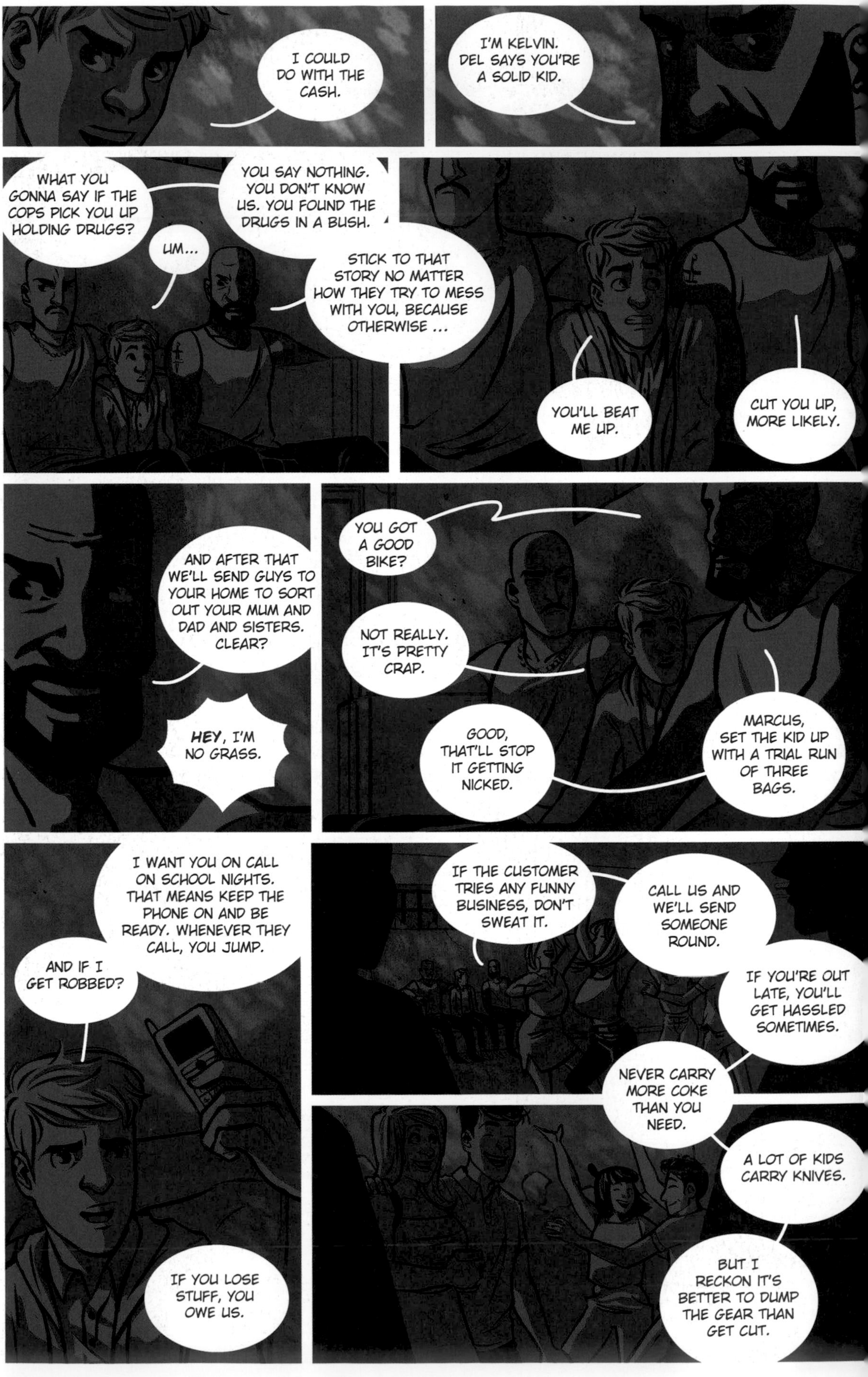
I COULD DO WITH THE CASH.
I'M KELVIN. DEL SAYS YOU'RE A SOLID KID.
WHAT YOU GONNA SAY IF THE COPS PICK YOU UP HOLDING DRUGS?
UM...
YOU SAY NOTHING. YOU DON'T KNOW US. YOU FOUND THE DRUGS IN A BUSH.
STICK TO THAT STORY NO MATTER HOW THEY TRY TO MESS WITH YOU, BECAUSE OTHERWISE ...
YOU'LL BEAT ME UP.
CUT YOU UP, MORE LIKELY.
AND AFTER THAT WE'LL SEND GUYS TO YOUR HOME TO SORT OUT YOUR MUM AND DAD AND SISTERS. CLEAR?
HEY, I'M NO GRASS.
YOU GOT A GOOD BIKE?
NOT REALLY. IT'S PRETTY CRAP.
GOOD, THAT'LL STOP IT GETTING NICKED.
MARCUS, SET THE KID UP WITH A TRIAL RUN OF THREE BAGS.
I WANT YOU ON CALL ON SCHOOL NIGHTS. THAT MEANS KEEP THE PHONE ON AND BE READY. WHENEVER THEY CALL, YOU JUMP.
AND IF I GET ROBBED?
IF YOU LOSE STUFF, YOU OWE US.
IF THE CUSTOMER TRIES ANY FUNNY BUSINESS, DON'T SWEAT IT.
CALL US AND WE'LL SEND SOMEONE ROUND.
IF YOU'RE OUT LATE, YOU'LL GET HASSLED SOMETIMES.
NEVER CARRY MORE COKE THAN YOU NEED.
A LOT OF KIDS CARRY KNIVES.
BUT I RECKON IT'S BETTER TO DUMP THE GEAR THAN GET CUT.

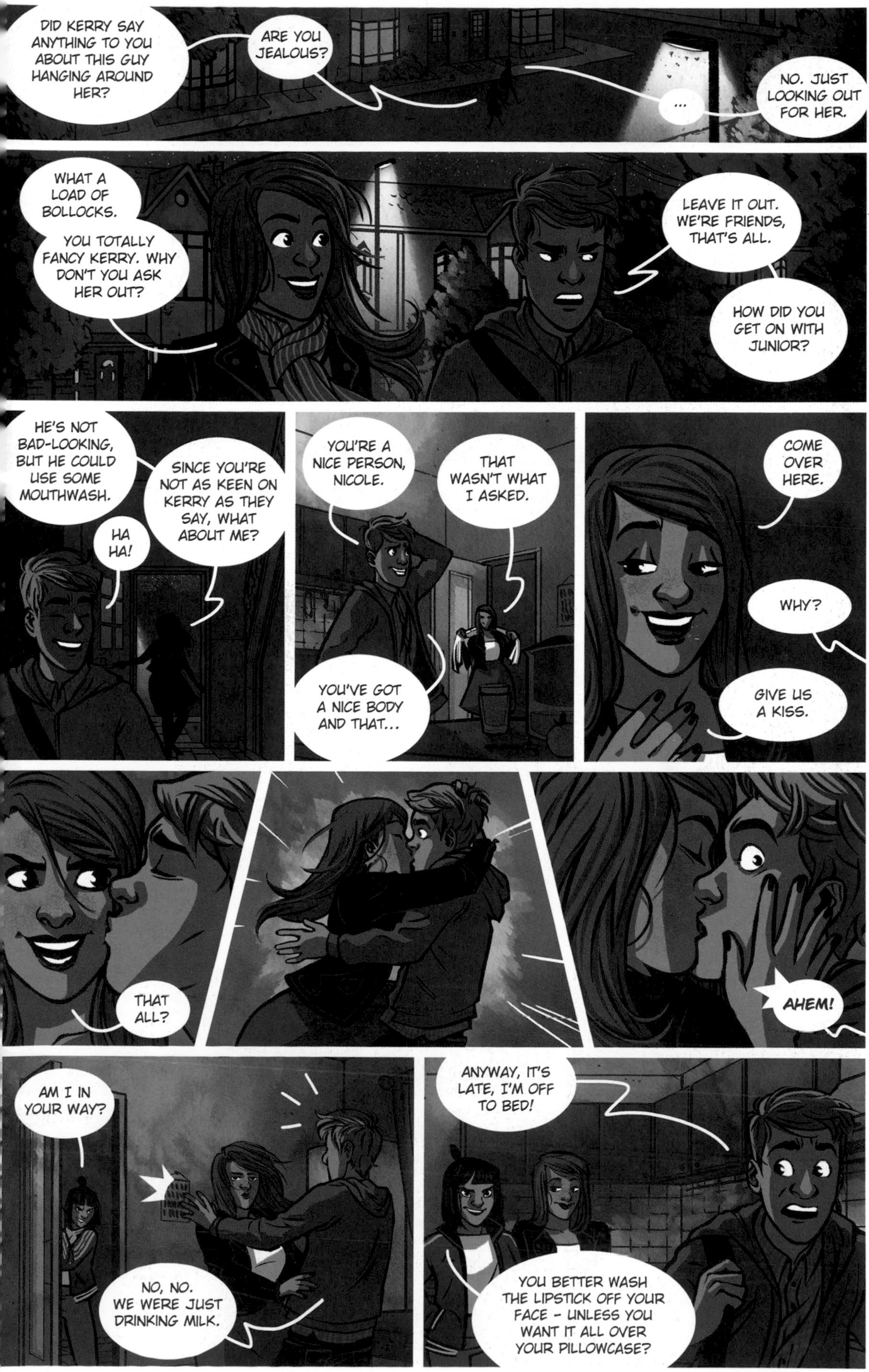
DID KERRY SAY ANYTHING TO YOU ABOUT THIS GUY HANGING AROUND HER?
ARE YOU JEALOUS?
...
NO. JUST LOOKING OUT FOR HER.
WHAT A LOAD OF BOLLOCKS.
YOU TOTALLY FANCY KERRY. WHY DON'T YOU ASK HER OUT?
LEAVE IT OUT. WE'RE FRIENDS, THAT'S ALL.
HOW DID YOU GET ON WITH JUNIOR?
HE'S NOT BAD-LOOKING, BUT HE COULD USE SOME MOUTHWASH.
HA HA!
SINCE YOU'RE NOT AS KEEN ON KERRY AS THEY SAY, WHAT ABOUT ME?
YOU'RE A NICE PERSON, NICOLE.
THAT WASN'T WHAT I ASKED.
YOU'VE GOT A NICE BODY AND THAT...
COME OVER HERE.
WHY?
GIVE US A KISS.
THAT ALL?
AHEM!
AM I IN YOUR WAY?
NO, NO. WE WERE JUST DRINKING MILK.
ANYWAY, IT'S LATE, I'M OFF TO BED!
YOU BETTER WASH THE LIPSTICK OFF YOUR FACE - UNLESS YOU WANT IT ALL OVER YOUR PILLOWCASE?

YOU OK, JAMES?

NICOLE KISSED ME.

SO WHY AREN'T YOU HAPPY?

KERRY SAW US.

KERRY'S NOT A LOOKER LIKE NICOLE, BUT THERE'S SOMETHING...

I CAN'T GET HER OUT MY HEAD.

JAMES, YOU HAVE TO ASK HER OUT.

YOU JUST GOT OFF WITH NICOLE, BUT ALL YOU CAN TALK ABOUT IS KERRY, KERRY, KERRY.

WHAT IF I MESS UP OUR FRIENDSHIP?

YOU'VE GOT TO RISK IT.

MAYBE YOU'RE RIGHT. I'LL TALK TO HER.

BUT WHAT SHOULD I SAY?

TELL HER THE TRUTH.

EXPLAIN THE WAY YOU FEEL, AND THEN IT'S UP TO HER.

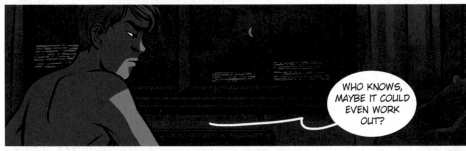

WHO KNOWS, MAYBE IT COULD EVEN WORK OUT?

CLICK!

KYLE, THERE'S ONE THING THAT I DON'T GET.

HOW COME I'M TAKING ALL THIS ADVICE OFF YOU, BUT I'VE NEVER EVEN SEEN YOU WITH A GIRL?

I'VE NEVER *HAD* A GIRLFRIEND.

REALLY?

YES, REALLY.

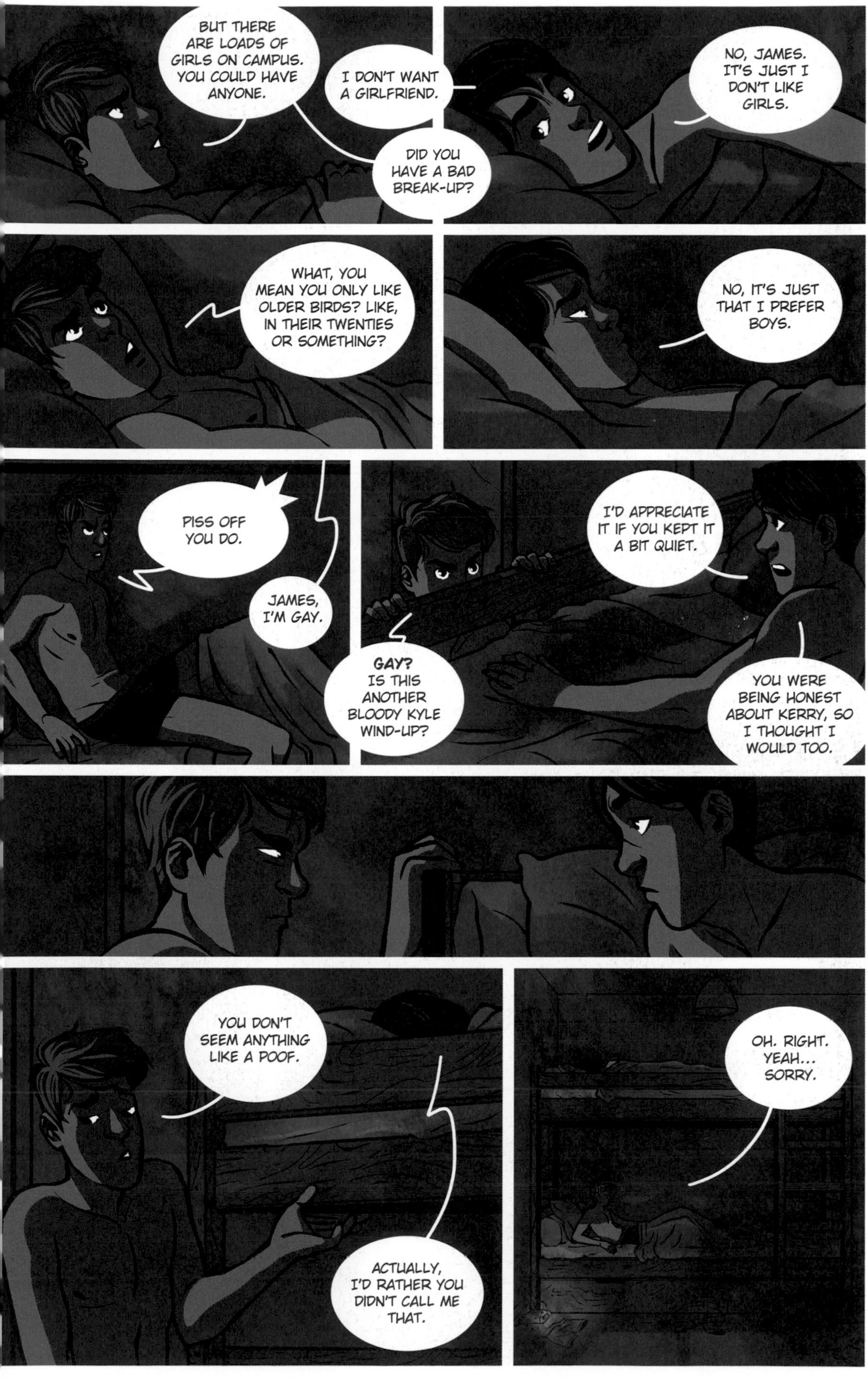
BUT THERE ARE LOADS OF GIRLS ON CAMPUS. YOU COULD HAVE ANYONE.
I DON'T WANT A GIRLFRIEND.
DID YOU HAVE A BAD BREAK-UP?
NO, JAMES. IT'S JUST I DON'T LIKE GIRLS.
WHAT, YOU MEAN YOU ONLY LIKE OLDER BIRDS? LIKE, IN THEIR TWENTIES OR SOMETHING?
NO, IT'S JUST THAT I PREFER BOYS.
PISS OFF YOU DO.
JAMES, I'M GAY.
GAY? IS THIS ANOTHER BLOODY KYLE WIND-UP?
I'D APPRECIATE IT IF YOU KEPT IT A BIT QUIET.
YOU WERE BEING HONEST ABOUT KERRY, SO I THOUGHT I WOULD TOO.
YOU DON'T SEEM ANYTHING LIKE A POOF.
ACTUALLY, I'D RATHER YOU DIDN'T CALL ME THAT.
OH. RIGHT. YEAH... SORRY.

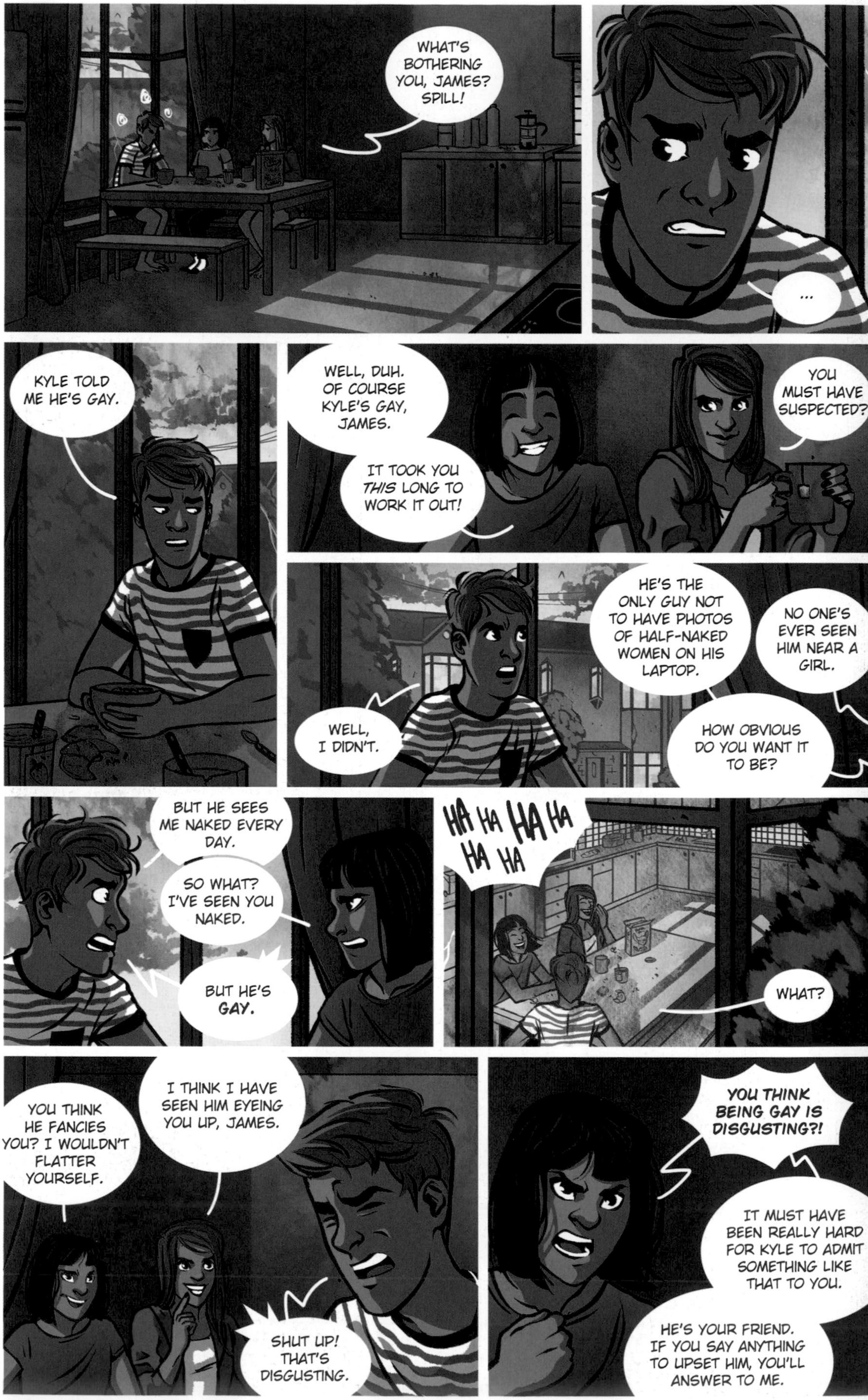
WHAT'S BOTHERING YOU, JAMES? SPILL!
...
KYLE TOLD ME HE'S GAY.
WELL, DUH. OF COURSE KYLE'S GAY, JAMES.
IT TOOK YOU *THIS* LONG TO WORK IT OUT!
YOU MUST HAVE SUSPECTED?
WELL, I DIDN'T.
HE'S THE ONLY GUY NOT TO HAVE PHOTOS OF HALF-NAKED WOMEN ON HIS LAPTOP.
NO ONE'S EVER SEEN HIM NEAR A GIRL.
HOW OBVIOUS DO YOU WANT IT TO BE?
BUT HE SEES ME NAKED EVERY DAY.
SO WHAT? I'VE SEEN YOU NAKED.
BUT HE'S **GAY.**
HA HA HA HA HA HA
WHAT?
YOU THINK HE FANCIES YOU? I WOULDN'T FLATTER YOURSELF.
I THINK I HAVE SEEN HIM EYEING YOU UP, JAMES.
SHUT UP! THAT'S DISGUSTING.
YOU THINK BEING GAY IS DISGUSTING?!
IT MUST HAVE BEEN REALLY HARD FOR KYLE TO ADMIT SOMETHING LIKE THAT TO YOU.
HE'S YOUR FRIEND. IF YOU SAY ANYTHING TO UPSET HIM, YOU'LL ANSWER TO ME.

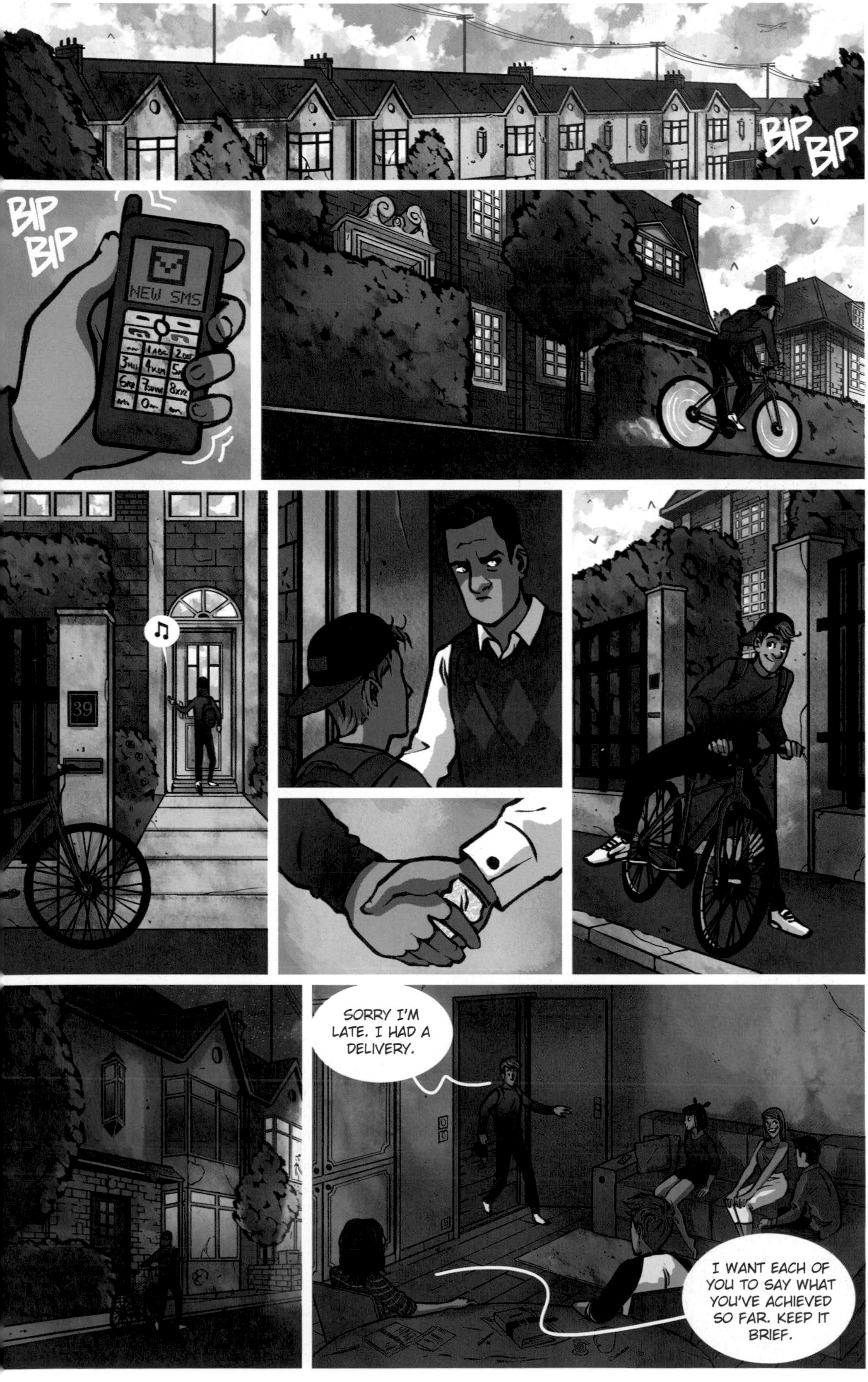
BIP BIP
BIP BIP
NEW SMS
39
SORRY I'M LATE. I HAD A DELIVERY.
I WANT EACH OF YOU TO SAY WHAT YOU'VE ACHIEVED SO FAR. KEEP IT BRIEF.

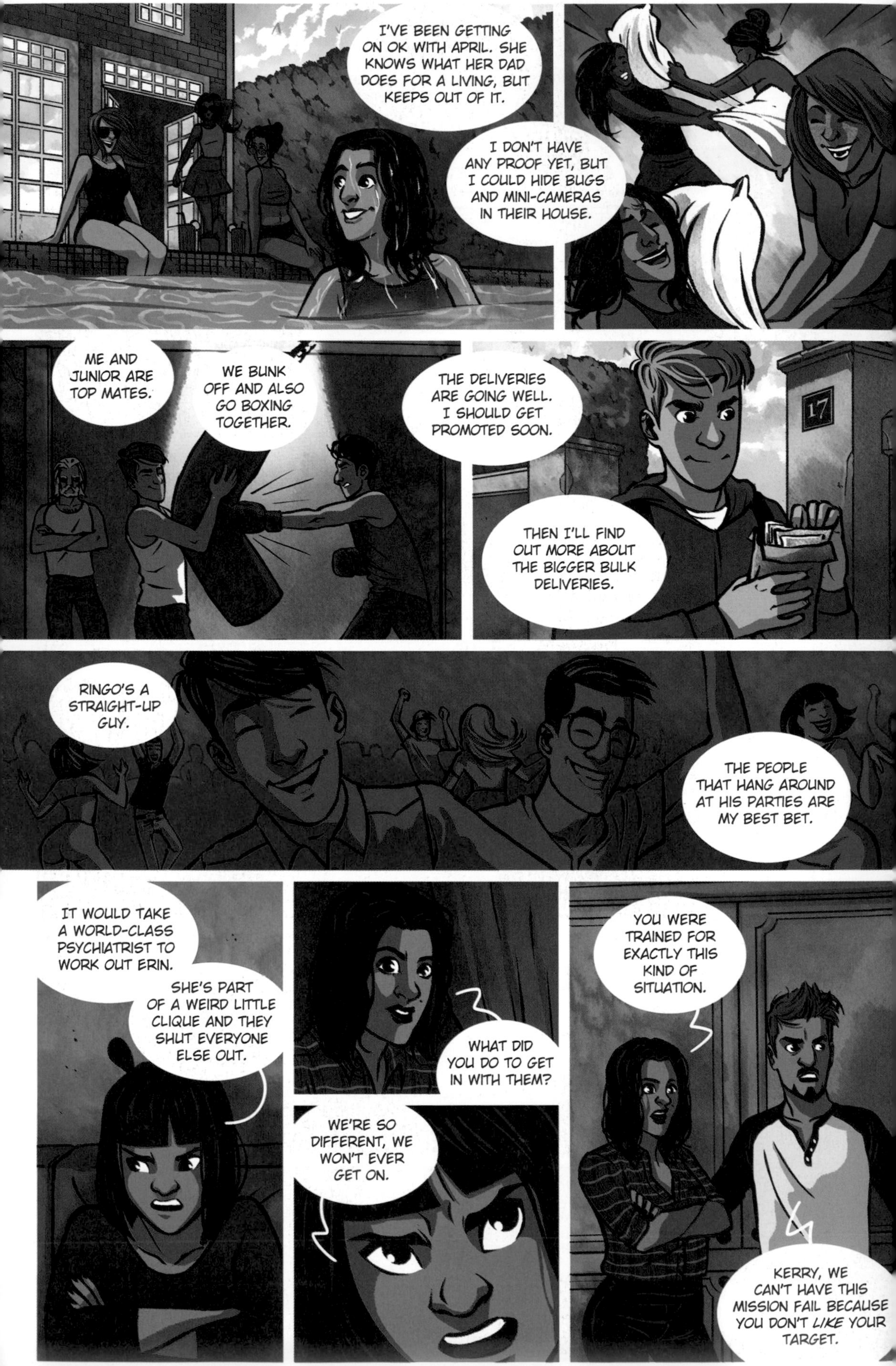
I'VE BEEN GETTING ON OK WITH APRIL. SHE KNOWS WHAT HER DAD DOES FOR A LIVING, BUT KEEPS OUT OF IT.
I DON'T HAVE ANY PROOF YET, BUT I COULD HIDE BUGS AND MINI-CAMERAS IN THEIR HOUSE.
ME AND JUNIOR ARE TOP MATES.
WE BUNK OFF AND ALSO GO BOXING TOGETHER.
THE DELIVERIES ARE GOING WELL. I SHOULD GET PROMOTED SOON.
17
THEN I'LL FIND OUT MORE ABOUT THE BIGGER BULK DELIVERIES.
RINGO'S A STRAIGHT-UP GUY.
THE PEOPLE THAT HANG AROUND AT HIS PARTIES ARE MY BEST BET.
IT WOULD TAKE A WORLD-CLASS PSYCHIATRIST TO WORK OUT ERIN.
SHE'S PART OF A WEIRD LITTLE CLIQUE AND THEY SHUT EVERYONE ELSE OUT.
WHAT DID YOU DO TO GET IN WITH THEM?
WE'RE SO DIFFERENT, WE WON'T EVER GET ON.
YOU WERE TRAINED FOR EXACTLY THIS KIND OF SITUATION.
KERRY, WE CAN'T HAVE THIS MISSION FAIL BECAUSE YOU DON'T *LIKE* YOUR TARGET.

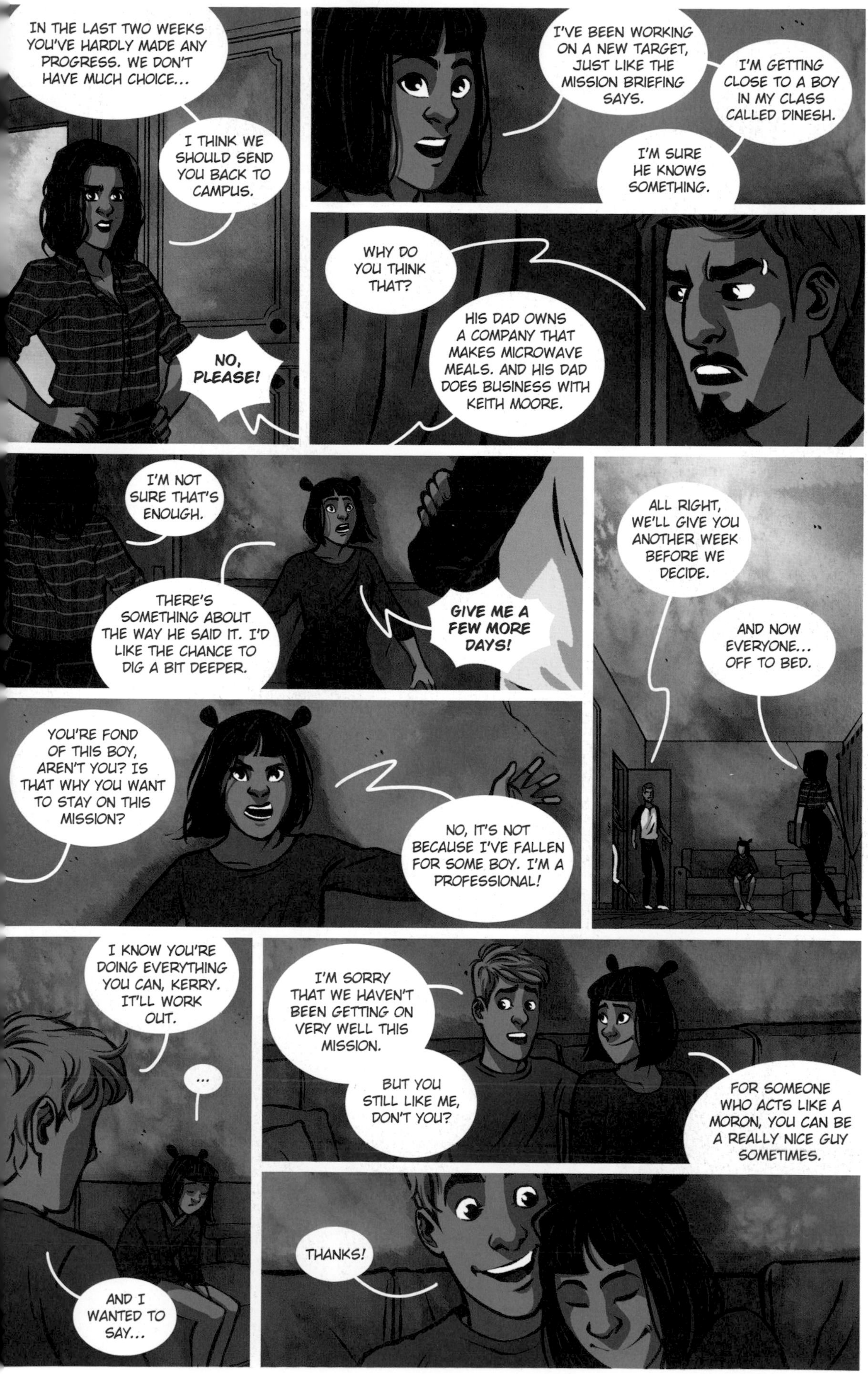
IN THE LAST TWO WEEKS YOU'VE HARDLY MADE ANY PROGRESS. WE DON'T HAVE MUCH CHOICE...
I THINK WE SHOULD SEND YOU BACK TO CAMPUS.
NO, PLEASE!
I'VE BEEN WORKING ON A NEW TARGET, JUST LIKE THE MISSION BRIEFING SAYS.
I'M GETTING CLOSE TO A BOY IN MY CLASS CALLED DINESH.
I'M SURE HE KNOWS SOMETHING.
WHY DO YOU THINK THAT?
HIS DAD OWNS A COMPANY THAT MAKES MICROWAVE MEALS. AND HIS DAD DOES BUSINESS WITH KEITH MOORE.
I'M NOT SURE THAT'S ENOUGH.
THERE'S SOMETHING ABOUT THE WAY HE SAID IT. I'D LIKE THE CHANCE TO DIG A BIT DEEPER.
GIVE ME A FEW MORE DAYS!
YOU'RE FOND OF THIS BOY, AREN'T YOU? IS THAT WHY YOU WANT TO STAY ON THIS MISSION?
NO, IT'S NOT BECAUSE I'VE FALLEN FOR SOME BOY. I'M A PROFESSIONAL!
ALL RIGHT, WE'LL GIVE YOU ANOTHER WEEK BEFORE WE DECIDE.
AND NOW EVERYONE... OFF TO BED.
I KNOW YOU'RE DOING EVERYTHING YOU CAN, KERRY. IT'LL WORK OUT.
...
AND I WANTED TO SAY...
I'M SORRY THAT WE HAVEN'T BEEN GETTING ON VERY WELL THIS MISSION.
BUT YOU STILL LIKE ME, DON'T YOU?
FOR SOMEONE WHO ACTS LIKE A MORON, YOU CAN BE A REALLY NICE GUY SOMETIMES.
THANKS!

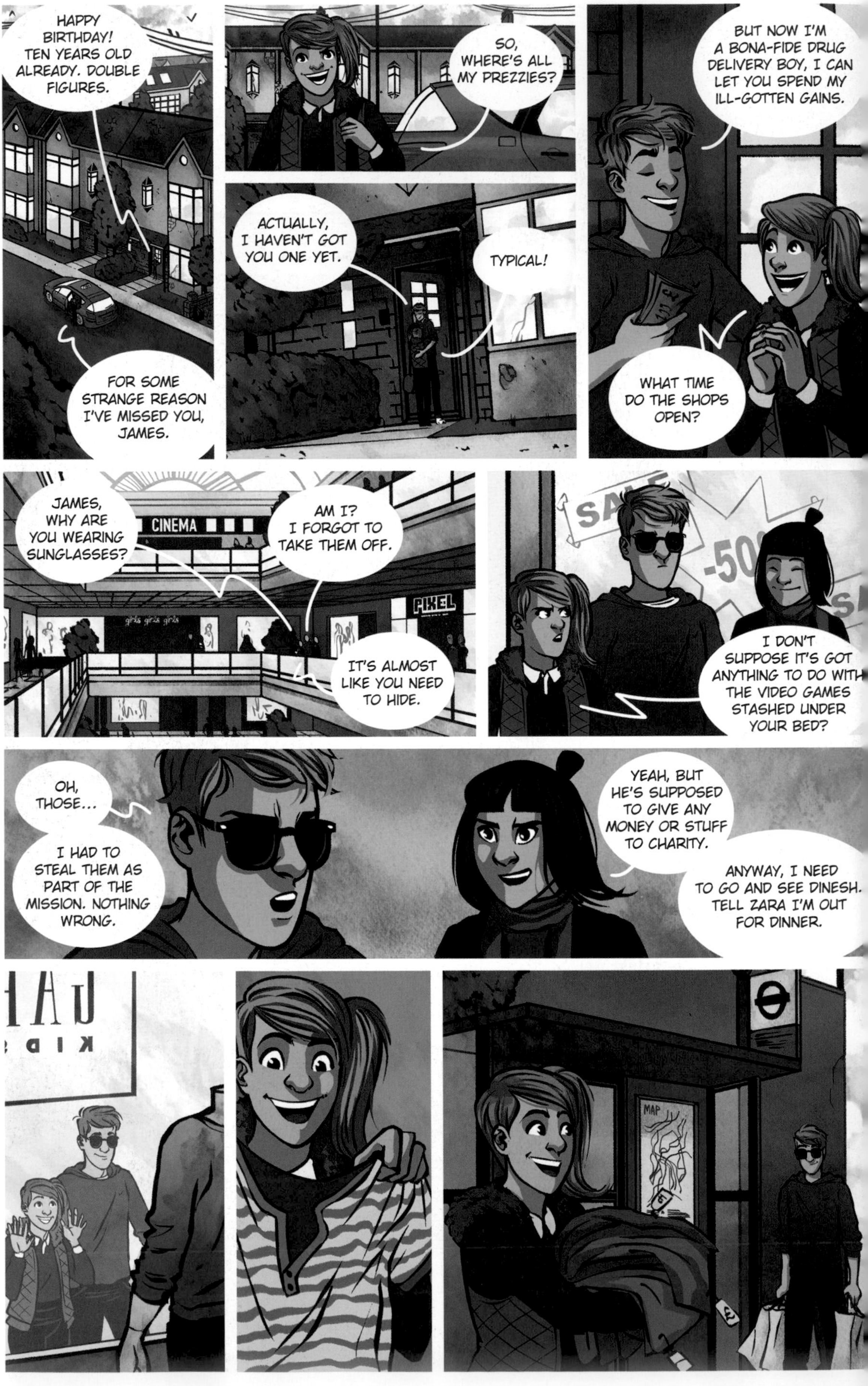
HAPPY BIRTHDAY! TEN YEARS OLD ALREADY. DOUBLE FIGURES.
FOR SOME STRANGE REASON I'VE MISSED YOU, JAMES.
SO, WHERE'S ALL MY PREZZIES?
ACTUALLY, I HAVEN'T GOT YOU ONE YET.
TYPICAL!
BUT NOW I'M A BONA-FIDE DRUG DELIVERY BOY, I CAN LET YOU SPEND MY ILL-GOTTEN GAINS.
WHAT TIME DO THE SHOPS OPEN?
CINEMA
JAMES, WHY ARE YOU WEARING SUNGLASSES?
AM I? I FORGOT TO TAKE THEM OFF.
PIXEL
IT'S ALMOST LIKE YOU NEED TO HIDE.
I DON'T SUPPOSE IT'S GOT ANYTHING TO DO WITH THE VIDEO GAMES STASHED UNDER YOUR BED?
OH, THOSE...
I HAD TO STEAL THEM AS PART OF THE MISSION. NOTHING WRONG.
YEAH, BUT HE'S SUPPOSED TO GIVE ANY MONEY OR STUFF TO CHARITY.
ANYWAY, I NEED TO GO AND SEE DINESH. TELL ZARA I'M OUT FOR DINNER.
MAP

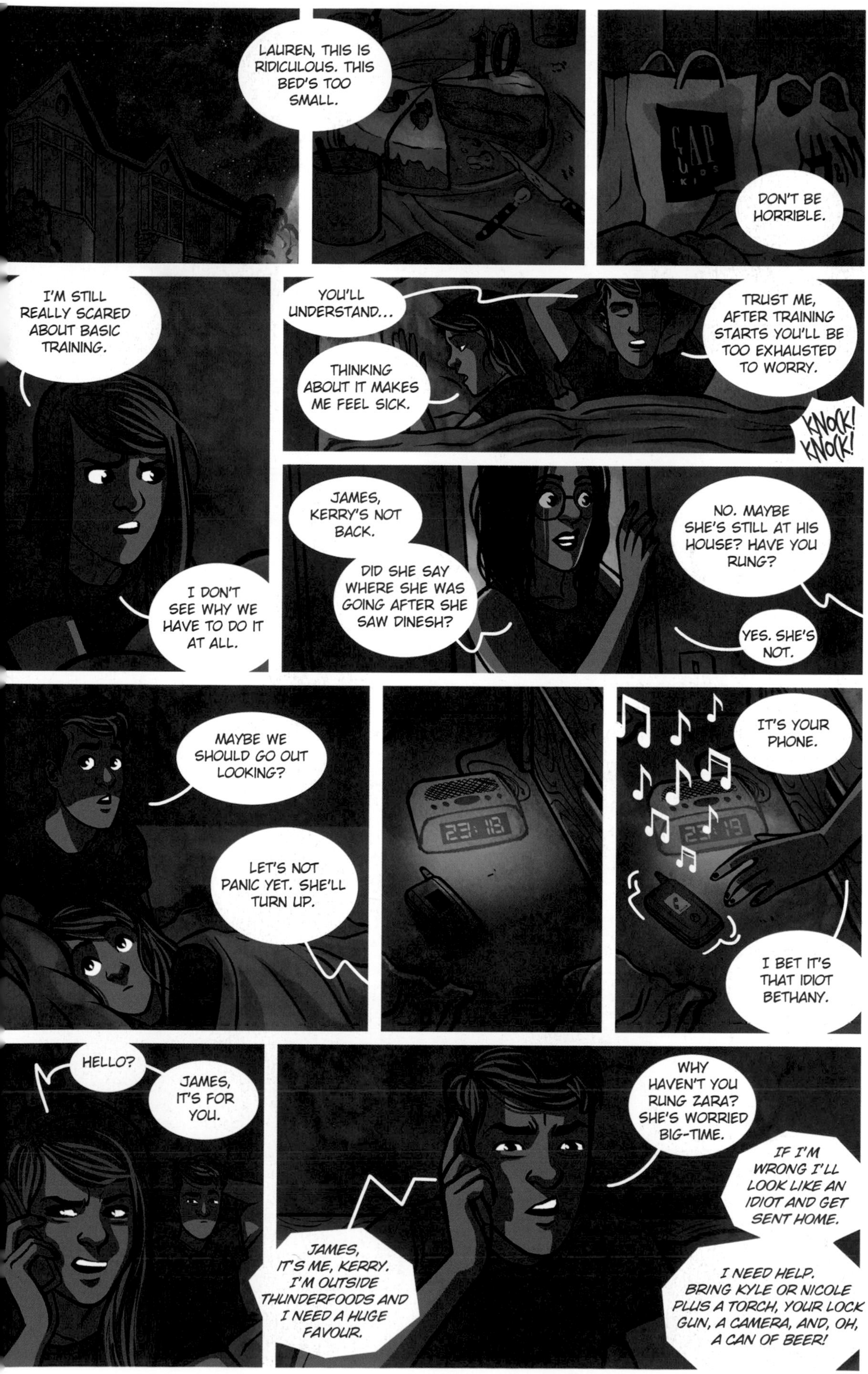
LAUREN, THIS IS RIDICULOUS. THIS BED'S TOO SMALL.
DON'T BE HORRIBLE.
I'M STILL REALLY SCARED ABOUT BASIC TRAINING.
I DON'T SEE WHY WE HAVE TO DO IT AT ALL.
YOU'LL UNDERSTAND...
THINKING ABOUT IT MAKES ME FEEL SICK.
TRUST ME, AFTER TRAINING STARTS YOU'LL BE TOO EXHAUSTED TO WORRY.
KNOCK! KNOCK!
JAMES, KERRY'S NOT BACK.
DID SHE SAY WHERE SHE WAS GOING AFTER SHE SAW DINESH?
NO. MAYBE SHE'S STILL AT HIS HOUSE? HAVE YOU RUNG?
YES. SHE'S NOT.
MAYBE WE SHOULD GO OUT LOOKING?
LET'S NOT PANIC YET. SHE'LL TURN UP.
IT'S YOUR PHONE.
I BET IT'S THAT IDIOT BETHANY.
HELLO?
JAMES, IT'S FOR YOU.
WHY HAVEN'T YOU RUNG ZARA? SHE'S WORRIED BIG-TIME.
JAMES, IT'S ME, KERRY. I'M OUTSIDE THUNDERFOODS AND I NEED A HUGE FAVOUR.
IF I'M WRONG I'LL LOOK LIKE AN IDIOT AND GET SENT HOME.
I NEED HELP. BRING KYLE OR NICOLE PLUS A TORCH, YOUR LOCK GUN, A CAMERA, AND, OH, A CAN OF BEER!

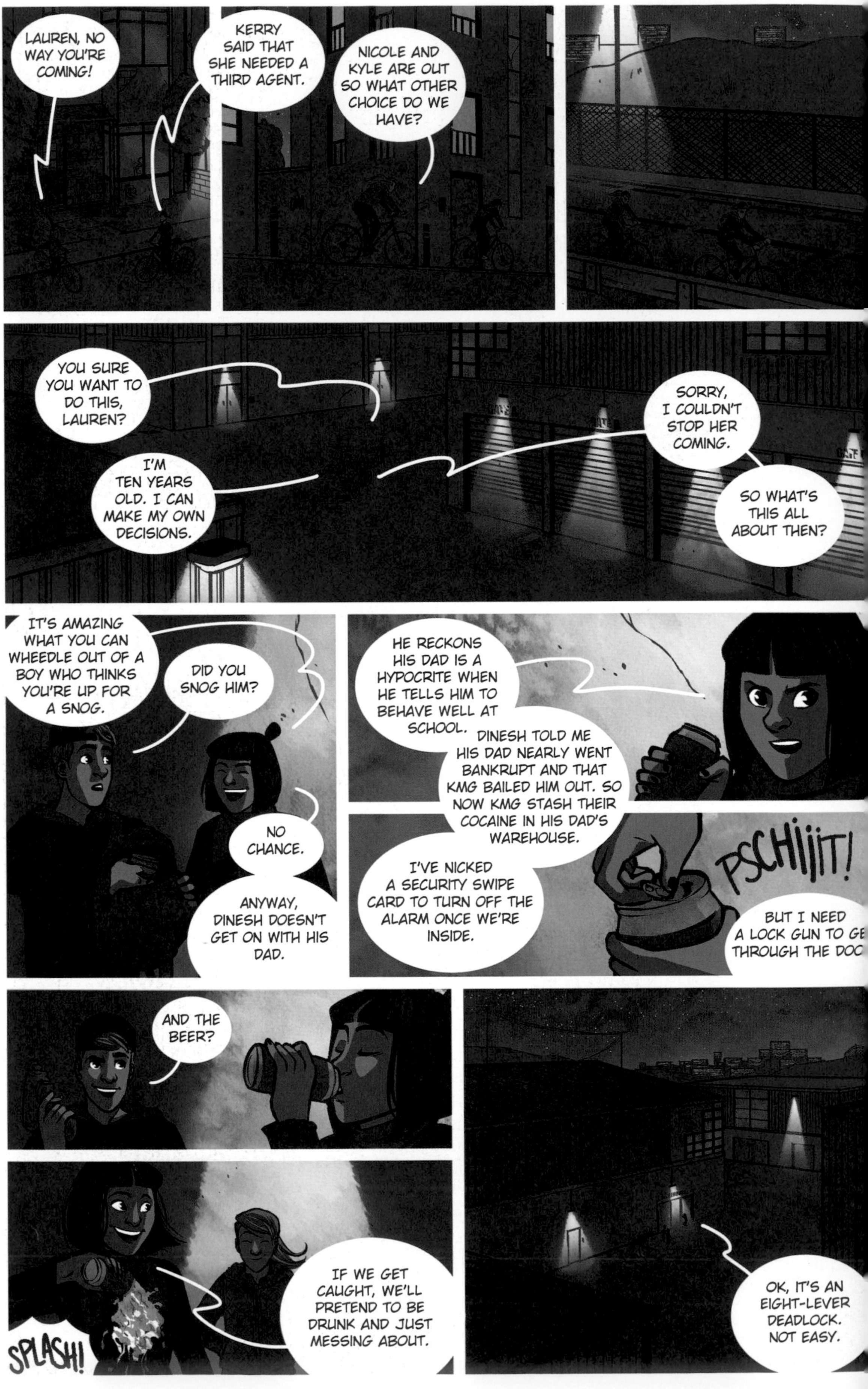
LAUREN, NO WAY YOU'RE COMING!
KERRY SAID THAT SHE NEEDED A THIRD AGENT.
NICOLE AND KYLE ARE OUT SO WHAT OTHER CHOICE DO WE HAVE?
YOU SURE YOU WANT TO DO THIS, LAUREN?
I'M TEN YEARS OLD. I CAN MAKE MY OWN DECISIONS.
SORRY, I COULDN'T STOP HER COMING.
SO WHAT'S THIS ALL ABOUT THEN?
IT'S AMAZING WHAT YOU CAN WHEEDLE OUT OF A BOY WHO THINKS YOU'RE UP FOR A SNOG.
DID YOU SNOG HIM?
NO CHANCE.
ANYWAY, DINESH DOESN'T GET ON WITH HIS DAD.
HE RECKONS HIS DAD IS A HYPOCRITE WHEN HE TELLS HIM TO BEHAVE WELL AT SCHOOL.
DINESH TOLD ME HIS DAD NEARLY WENT BANKRUPT AND THAT KMG BAILED HIM OUT. SO NOW KMG STASH THEIR COCAINE IN HIS DAD'S WAREHOUSE.
I'VE NICKED A SECURITY SWIPE CARD TO TURN OFF THE ALARM ONCE WE'RE INSIDE.
PSCHIIIIT!
BUT I NEED A LOCK GUN TO GE THROUGH THE DOC
AND THE BEER?
SPLASH!
IF WE GET CAUGHT, WE'LL PRETEND TO BE DRUNK AND JUST MESSING ABOUT.
OK, IT'S AN EIGHT-LEVER DEADLOCK. NOT EASY.

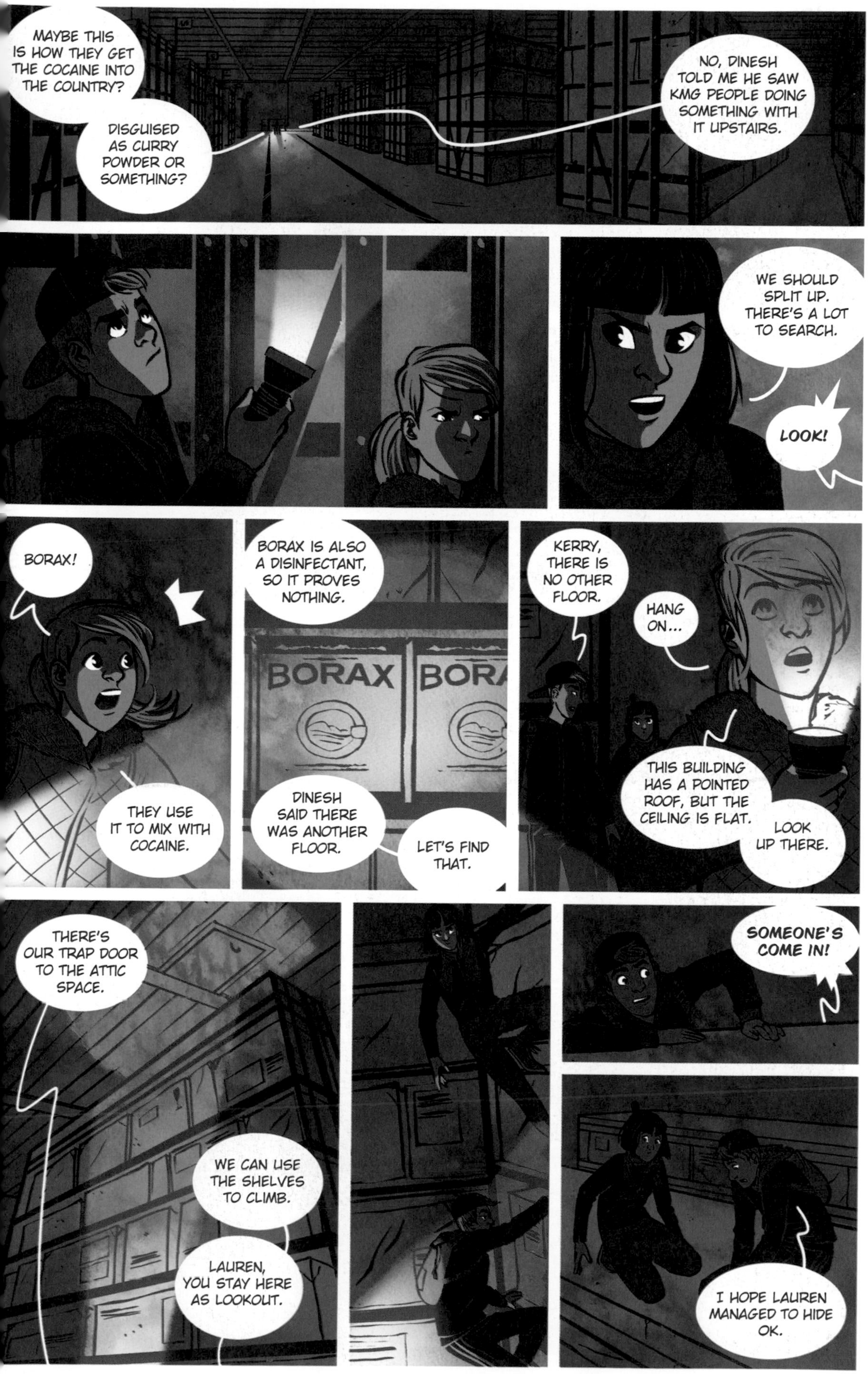
MAYBE THIS IS HOW THEY GET THE COCAINE INTO THE COUNTRY?
DISGUISED AS CURRY POWDER OR SOMETHING?
NO, DINESH TOLD ME HE SAW KMG PEOPLE DOING SOMETHING WITH IT UPSTAIRS.
WE SHOULD SPLIT UP. THERE'S A LOT TO SEARCH.
LOOK!
BORAX!
THEY USE IT TO MIX WITH COCAINE.
BORAX IS ALSO A DISINFECTANT, SO IT PROVES NOTHING.
BORAX
BORA
DINESH SAID THERE WAS ANOTHER FLOOR.
LET'S FIND THAT.
KERRY, THERE IS NO OTHER FLOOR.
HANG ON...
THIS BUILDING HAS A POINTED ROOF, BUT THE CEILING IS FLAT.
LOOK UP THERE.
THERE'S OUR TRAP DOOR TO THE ATTIC SPACE.
WE CAN USE THE SHELVES TO CLIMB.
LAUREN, YOU STAY HERE AS LOOKOUT.
SOMEONE'S COME IN!
I HOPE LAUREN MANAGED TO HIDE OK.

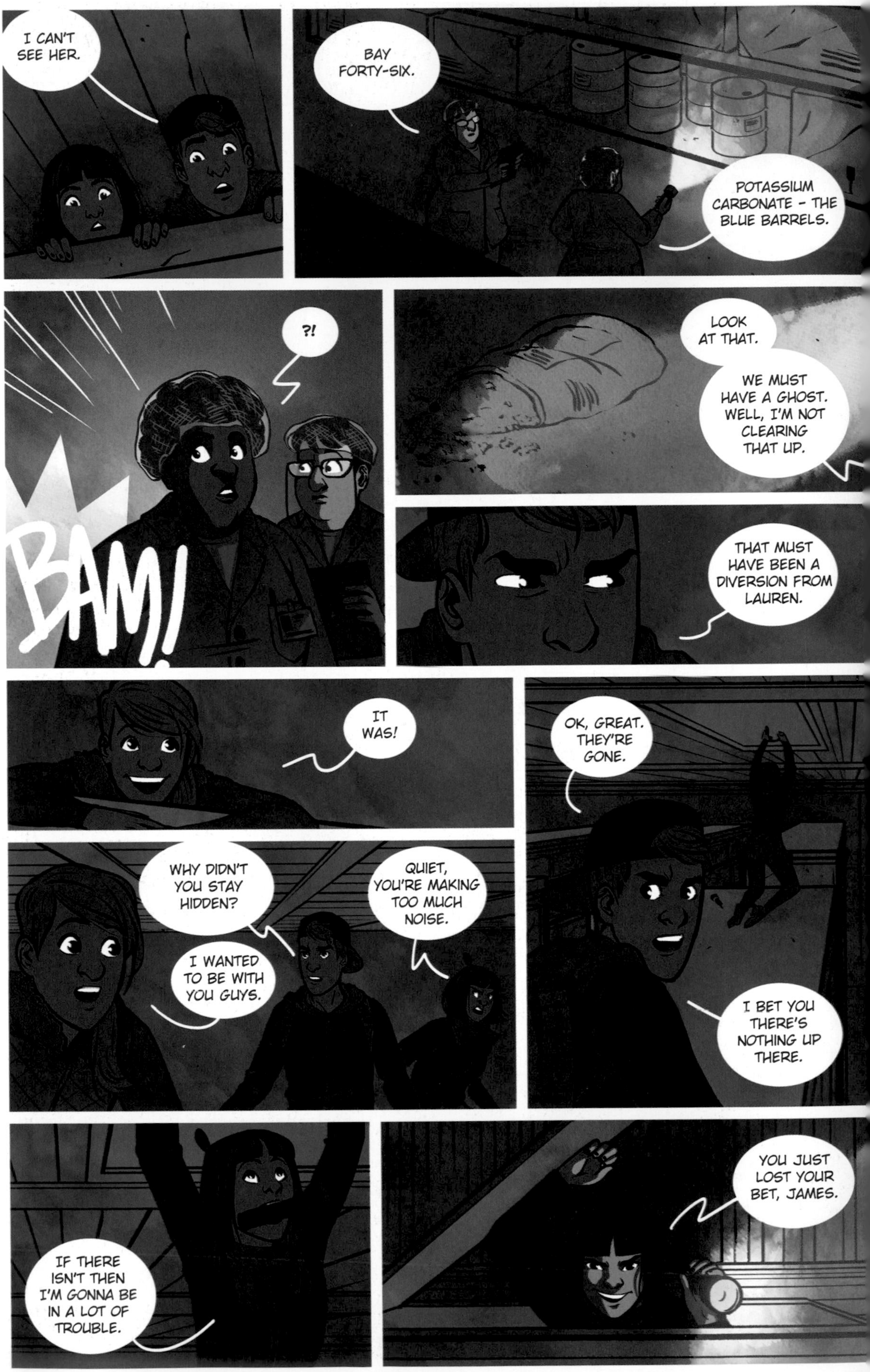
I CAN'T SEE HER.
BAY FORTY-SIX.
POTASSIUM CARBONATE - THE BLUE BARRELS.
?!
BAM!!
LOOK AT THAT.
WE MUST HAVE A GHOST. WELL, I'M NOT CLEARING THAT UP.
THAT MUST HAVE BEEN A DIVERSION FROM LAUREN.
IT WAS!
WHY DIDN'T YOU STAY HIDDEN?
QUIET, YOU'RE MAKING TOO MUCH NOISE.
I WANTED TO BE WITH YOU GUYS.
OK, GREAT. THEY'RE GONE.
I BET YOU THERE'S NOTHING UP THERE.
IF THERE ISN'T THEN I'M GONNA BE IN A LOT OF TROUBLE.
YOU JUST LOST YOUR BET, JAMES.

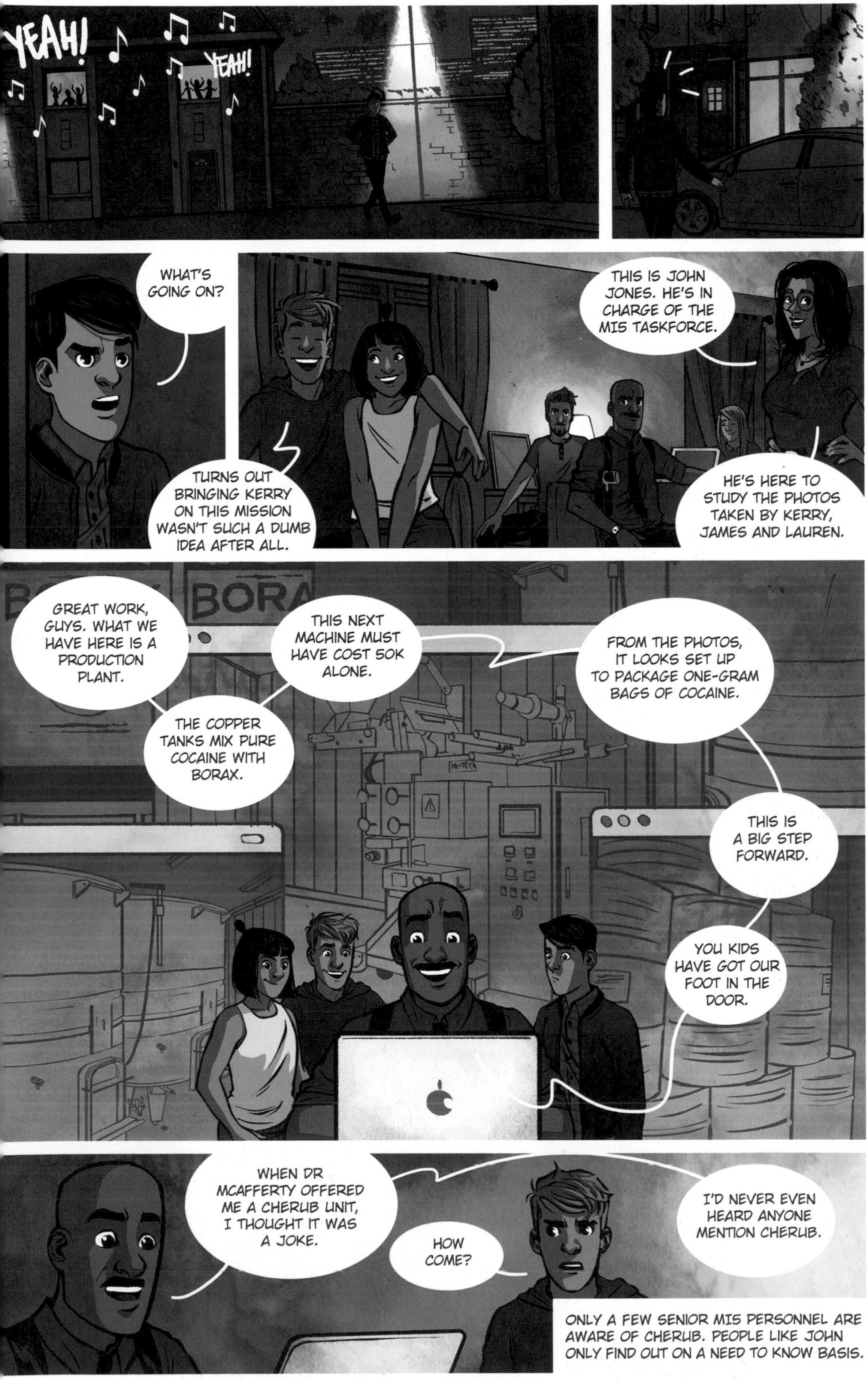
YEAH!
YEAH!
WHAT'S GOING ON?
TURNS OUT BRINGING KERRY ON THIS MISSION WASN'T SUCH A DUMB IDEA AFTER ALL.
THIS IS JOHN JONES. HE'S IN CHARGE OF THE MI5 TASKFORCE.
HE'S HERE TO STUDY THE PHOTOS TAKEN BY KERRY, JAMES AND LAUREN.
GREAT WORK, GUYS. WHAT WE HAVE HERE IS A PRODUCTION PLANT.
THE COPPER TANKS MIX PURE COCAINE WITH BORAX.
THIS NEXT MACHINE MUST HAVE COST 50K ALONE.
FROM THE PHOTOS, IT LOOKS SET UP TO PACKAGE ONE-GRAM BAGS OF COCAINE.
THIS IS A BIG STEP FORWARD.
YOU KIDS HAVE GOT OUR FOOT IN THE DOOR.
WHEN DR MCAFFERTY OFFERED ME A CHERUB UNIT, I THOUGHT IT WAS A JOKE.
HOW COME?
I'D NEVER EVEN HEARD ANYONE MENTION CHERUB.
ONLY A FEW SENIOR MI5 PERSONNEL ARE AWARE OF CHERUB. PEOPLE LIKE JOHN ONLY FIND OUT ON A NEED TO KNOW BASIS.

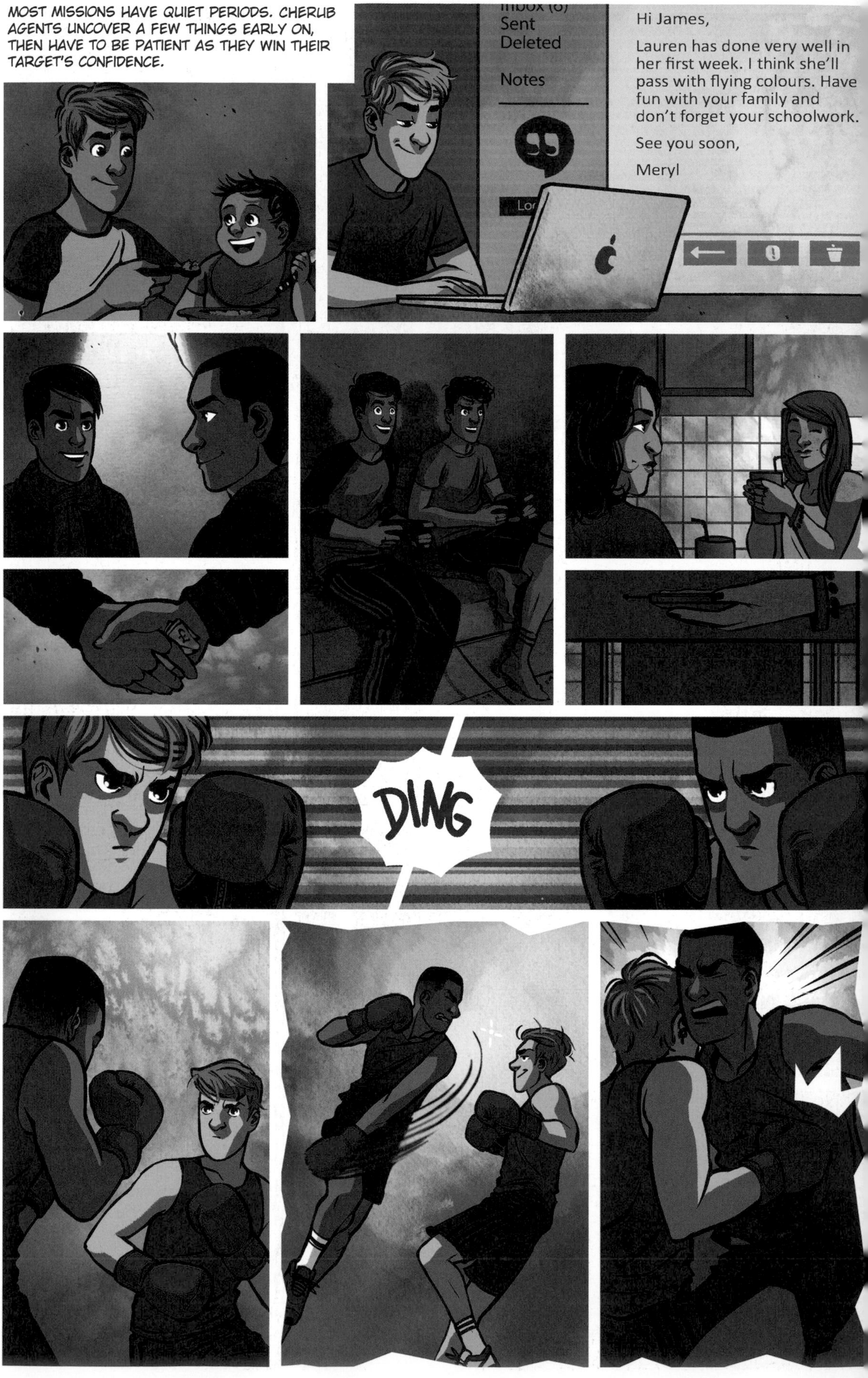
MOST MISSIONS HAVE QUIET PERIODS. CHERUB AGENTS UNCOVER A FEW THINGS EARLY ON, THEN HAVE TO BE PATIENT AS THEY WIN THEIR TARGET'S CONFIDENCE.
Sent
Deleted
Notes
Hi James,
Lauren has done very well in her first week. I think she'll pass with flying colours. Have fun with your family and don't forget your schoolwork.
See you soon,
Meryl
DING

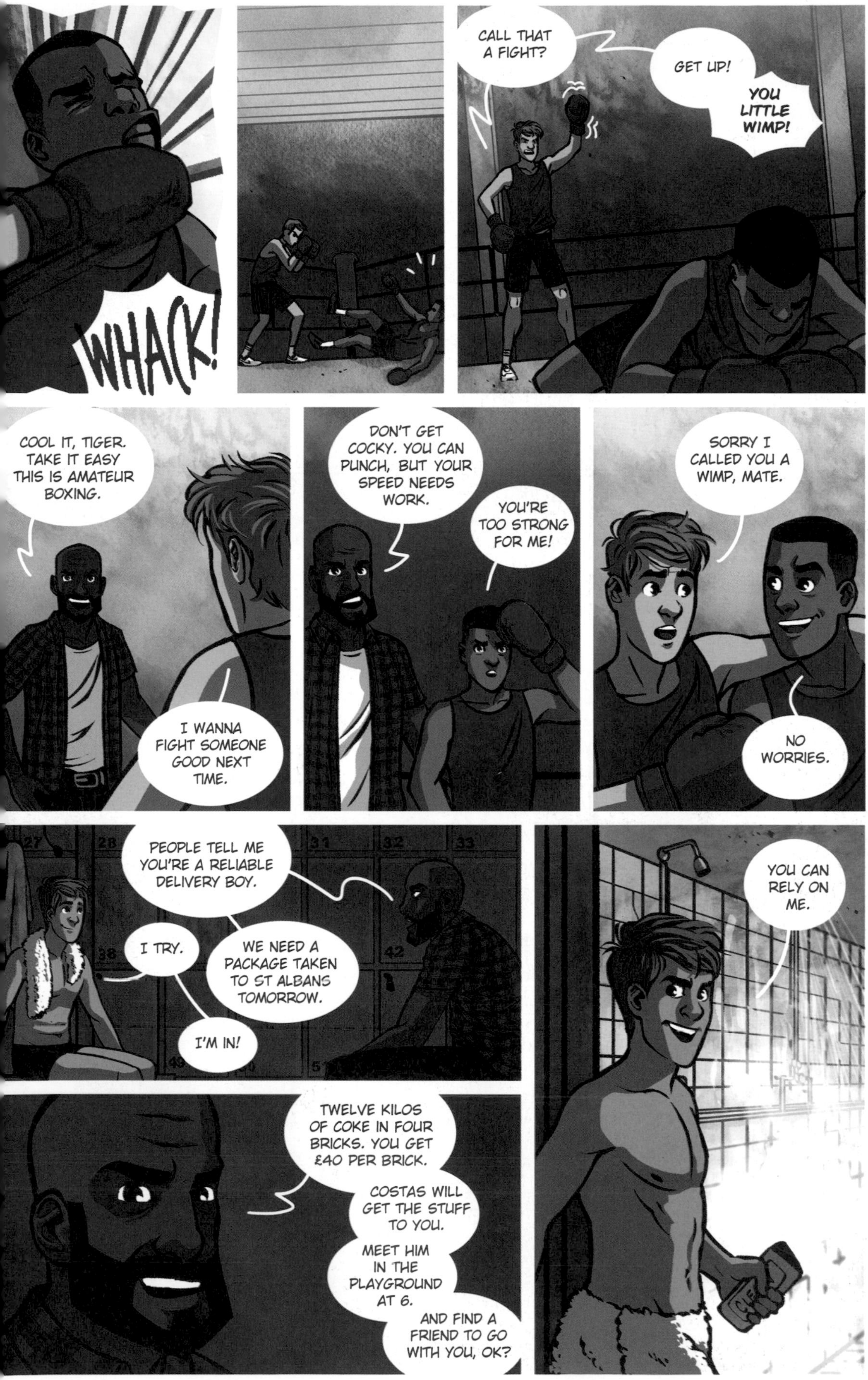
WHACK!
CALL THAT A FIGHT?
GET UP!
YOU LITTLE WIMP!
COOL IT, TIGER. TAKE IT EASY THIS IS AMATEUR BOXING.
I WANNA FIGHT SOMEONE GOOD NEXT TIME.
DON'T GET COCKY. YOU CAN PUNCH, BUT YOUR SPEED NEEDS WORK.
YOU'RE TOO STRONG FOR ME!
SORRY I CALLED YOU A WIMP, MATE.
NO WORRIES.
PEOPLE TELL ME YOU'RE A RELIABLE DELIVERY BOY.
I TRY.
WE NEED A PACKAGE TAKEN TO ST ALBANS TOMORROW.
I'M IN!
TWELVE KILOS OF COKE IN FOUR BRICKS. YOU GET £40 PER BRICK.
COSTAS WILL GET THE STUFF TO YOU.
MEET HIM IN THE PLAYGROUND AT 6.
AND FIND A FRIEND TO GO WITH YOU, OK?
YOU CAN RELY ON ME.

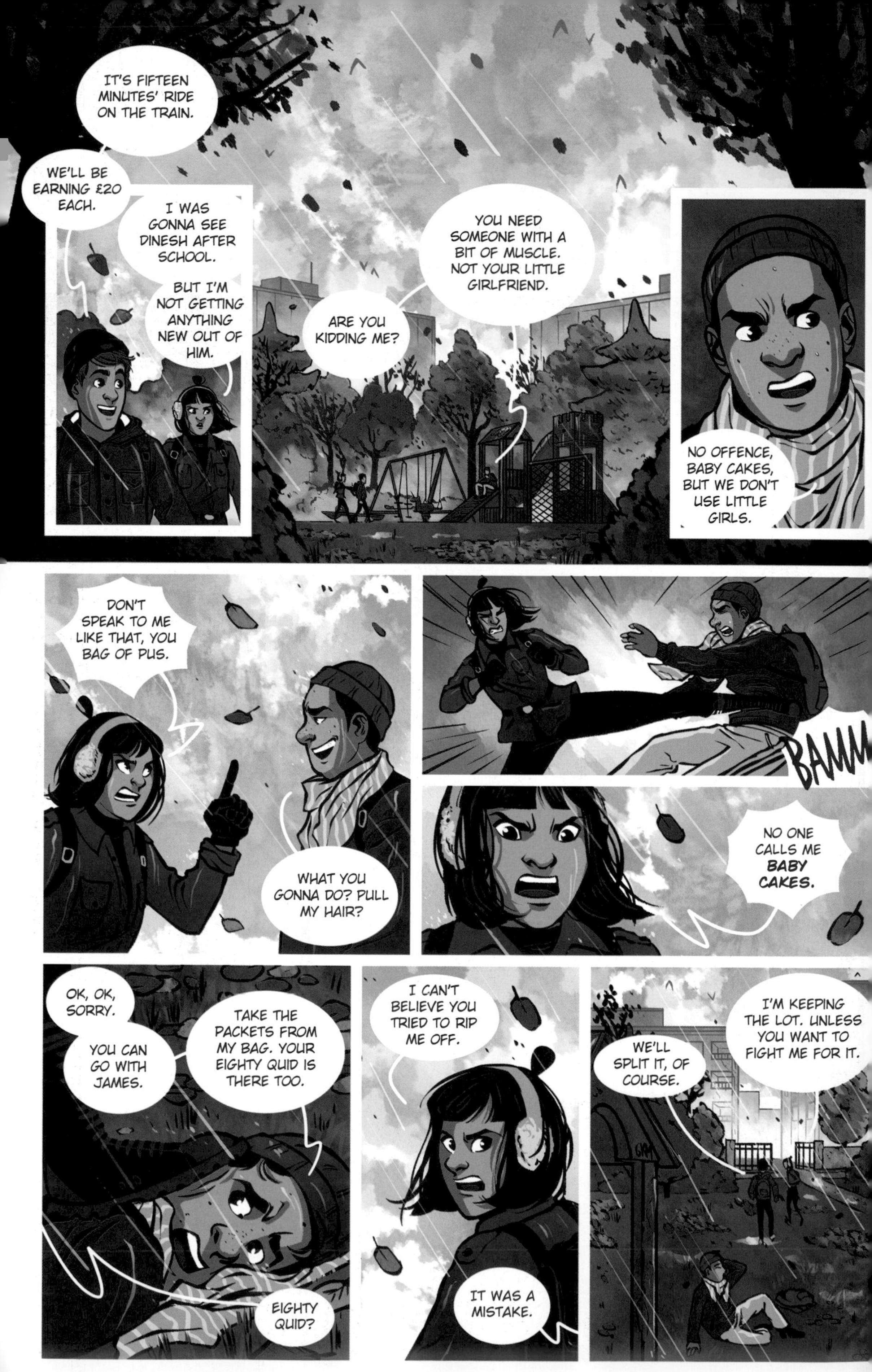
IT'S FIFTEEN MINUTES' RIDE ON THE TRAIN.
WE'LL BE EARNING £20 EACH.
I WAS GONNA SEE DINESH AFTER SCHOOL.
BUT I'M NOT GETTING ANYTHING NEW OUT OF HIM.
ARE YOU KIDDING ME?
YOU NEED SOMEONE WITH A BIT OF MUSCLE. NOT YOUR LITTLE GIRLFRIEND.
NO OFFENCE, BABY CAKES, BUT WE DON'T USE LITTLE GIRLS.
DON'T SPEAK TO ME LIKE THAT, YOU BAG OF PUS.
WHAT YOU GONNA DO? PULL MY HAIR?
BAMM
NO ONE CALLS ME **BABY CAKES.**
OK, OK, SORRY.
YOU CAN GO WITH JAMES.
TAKE THE PACKETS FROM MY BAG. YOUR EIGHTY QUID IS THERE TOO.
EIGHTY QUID?
I CAN'T BELIEVE YOU TRIED TO RIP ME OFF.
IT WAS A MISTAKE.
WE'LL SPLIT IT, OF COURSE.
I'M KEEPING THE LOT. UNLESS YOU WANT TO FIGHT ME FOR IT.

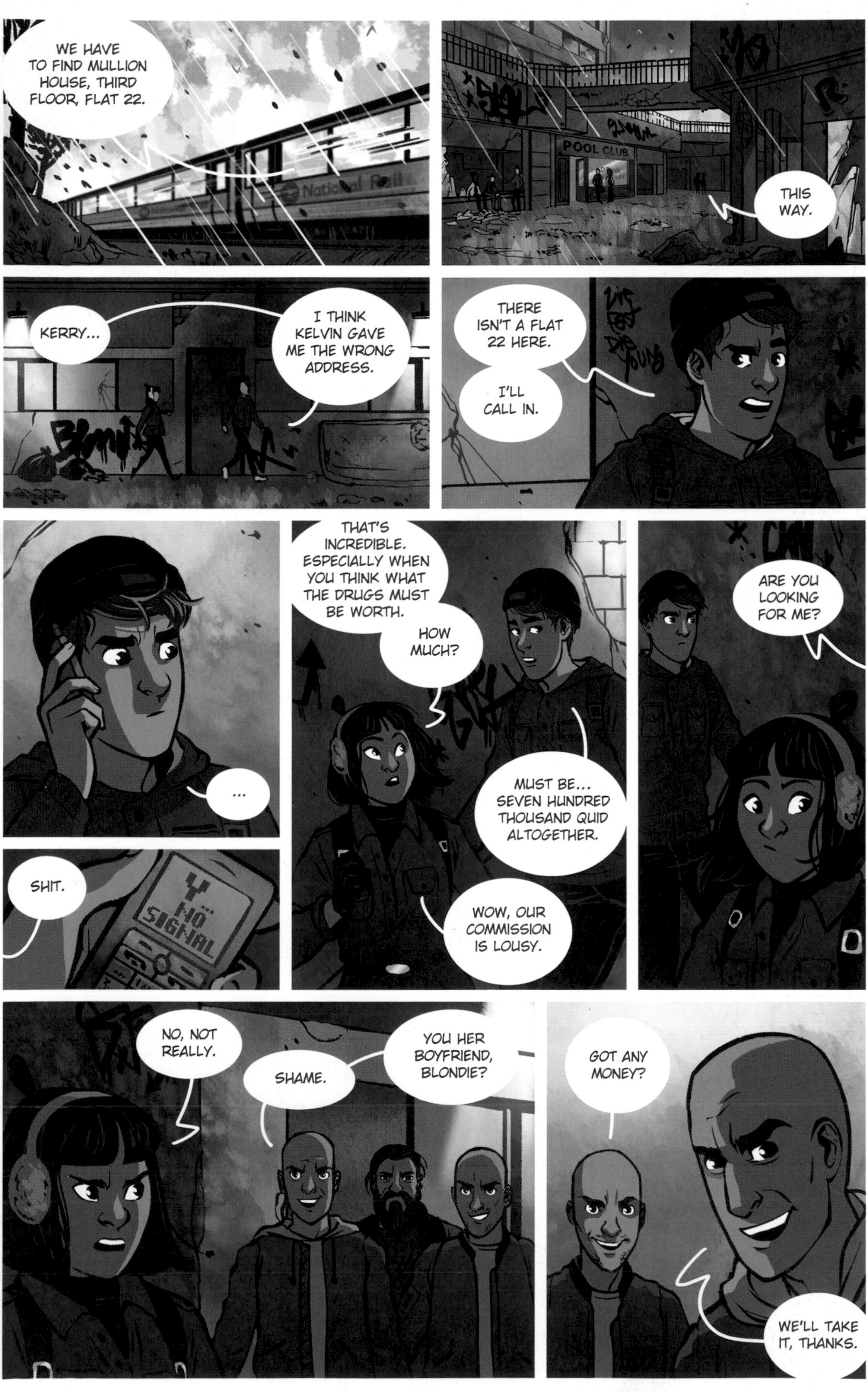
WE HAVE TO FIND MULLION HOUSE, THIRD FLOOR, FLAT 22.
POOL CLUB
THIS WAY.
KERRY...
I THINK KELVIN GAVE ME THE WRONG ADDRESS.
THERE ISN'T A FLAT 22 HERE.
I'LL CALL IN.
...
SHIT.
NO SIGNAL
THAT'S INCREDIBLE. ESPECIALLY WHEN YOU THINK WHAT THE DRUGS MUST BE WORTH.
HOW MUCH?
MUST BE... SEVEN HUNDRED THOUSAND QUID ALTOGETHER.
WOW, OUR COMMISSION IS LOUSY.
ARE YOU LOOKING FOR ME?
YOU HER BOYFRIEND, BLONDIE?
NO, NOT REALLY.
SHAME.
GOT ANY MONEY?
WE'LL TAKE IT, THANKS.

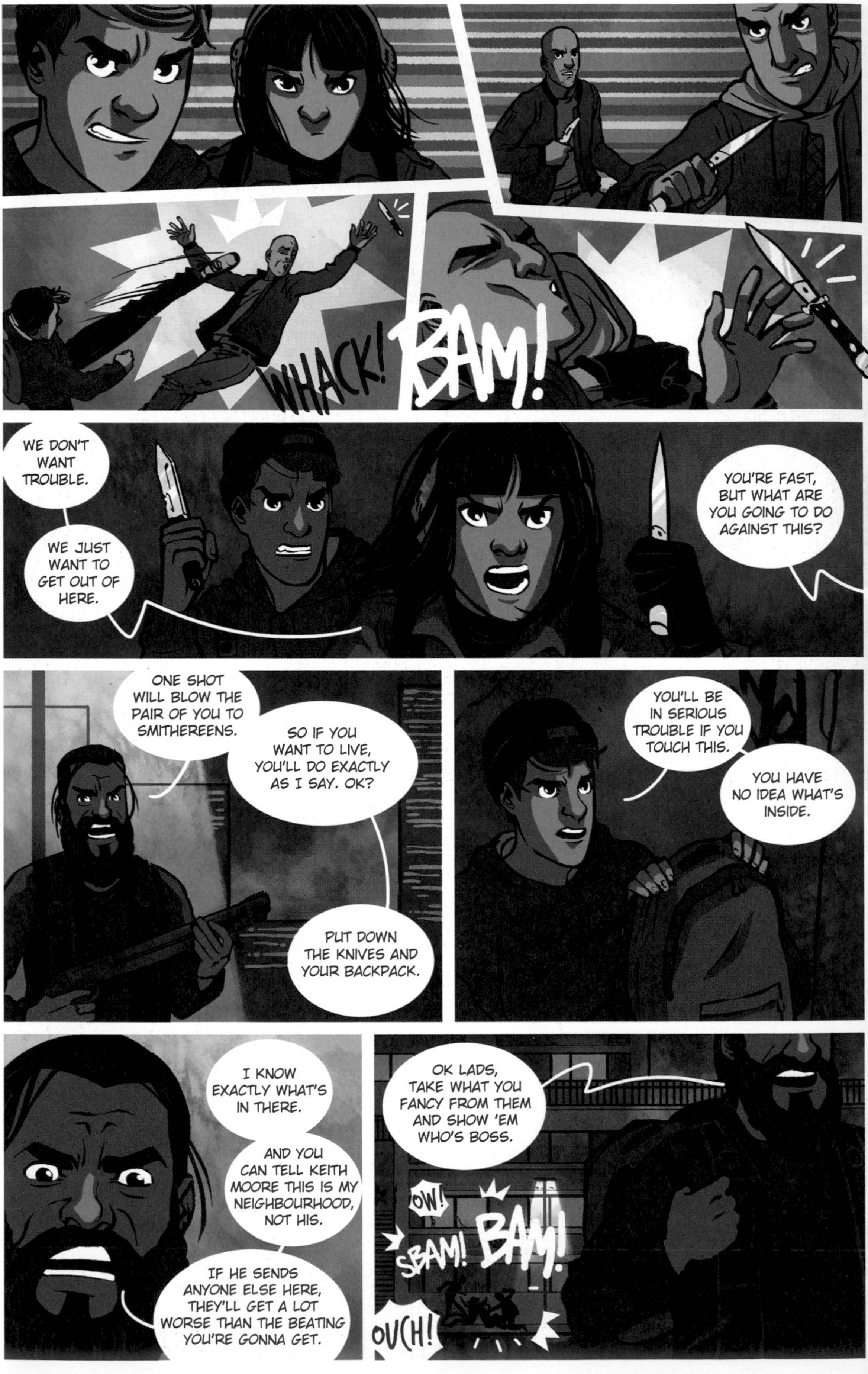
WHACK!
BAM!
WE DON'T WANT TROUBLE.
WE JUST WANT TO GET OUT OF HERE.
YOU'RE FAST, BUT WHAT ARE YOU GOING TO DO AGAINST THIS?
ONE SHOT WILL BLOW THE PAIR OF YOU TO SMITHEREENS.
SO IF YOU WANT TO LIVE, YOU'LL DO EXACTLY AS I SAY. OK?
PUT DOWN THE KNIVES AND YOUR BACKPACK.
YOU'LL BE IN SERIOUS TROUBLE IF YOU TOUCH THIS.
YOU HAVE NO IDEA WHAT'S INSIDE.
I KNOW EXACTLY WHAT'S IN THERE.
AND YOU CAN TELL KEITH MOORE THIS IS MY NEIGHBOURHOOD, NOT HIS.
IF HE SENDS ANYONE ELSE HERE, THEY'LL GET A LOT WORSE THAN THE BEATING YOU'RE GONNA GET.
OK LADS, TAKE WHAT YOU FANCY FROM THEM AND SHOW 'EM WHO'S BOSS.
OW!
SBAM!
BAM!
OUCH!

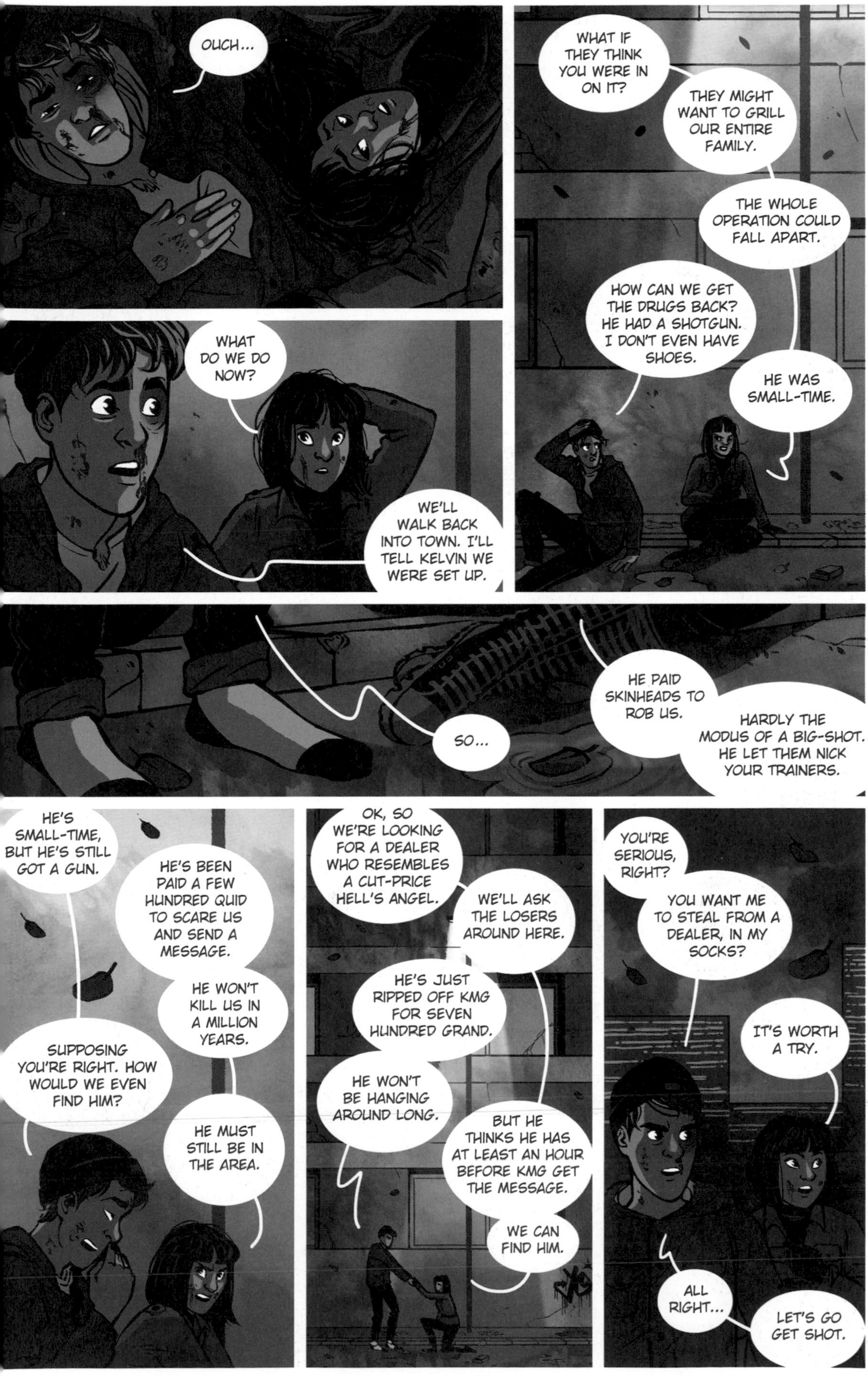
OUCH...
WHAT IF THEY THINK YOU WERE IN ON IT?
THEY MIGHT WANT TO GRILL OUR ENTIRE FAMILY.
THE WHOLE OPERATION COULD FALL APART.
WHAT DO WE DO NOW?
WE'LL WALK BACK INTO TOWN. I'LL TELL KELVIN WE WERE SET UP.
HOW CAN WE GET THE DRUGS BACK? HE HAD A SHOTGUN. I DON'T EVEN HAVE SHOES.
HE WAS SMALL-TIME.
SO...
HE PAID SKINHEADS TO ROB US.
HARDLY THE MODUS OF A BIG-SHOT. HE LET THEM NICK YOUR TRAINERS.
HE'S SMALL-TIME, BUT HE'S STILL GOT A GUN.
HE'S BEEN PAID A FEW HUNDRED QUID TO SCARE US AND SEND A MESSAGE.
HE WON'T KILL US IN A MILLION YEARS.
SUPPOSING YOU'RE RIGHT. HOW WOULD WE EVEN FIND HIM?
HE MUST STILL BE IN THE AREA.
OK, SO WE'RE LOOKING FOR A DEALER WHO RESEMBLES A CUT-PRICE HELL'S ANGEL.
WE'LL ASK THE LOSERS AROUND HERE.
HE'S JUST RIPPED OFF KMG FOR SEVEN HUNDRED GRAND.
HE WON'T BE HANGING AROUND LONG.
BUT HE THINKS HE HAS AT LEAST AN HOUR BEFORE KMG GET THE MESSAGE.
WE CAN FIND HIM.
YOU'RE SERIOUS, RIGHT?
YOU WANT ME TO STEAL FROM A DEALER, IN MY SOCKS?
IT'S WORTH A TRY.
ALL RIGHT...
LET'S GO GET SHOT.

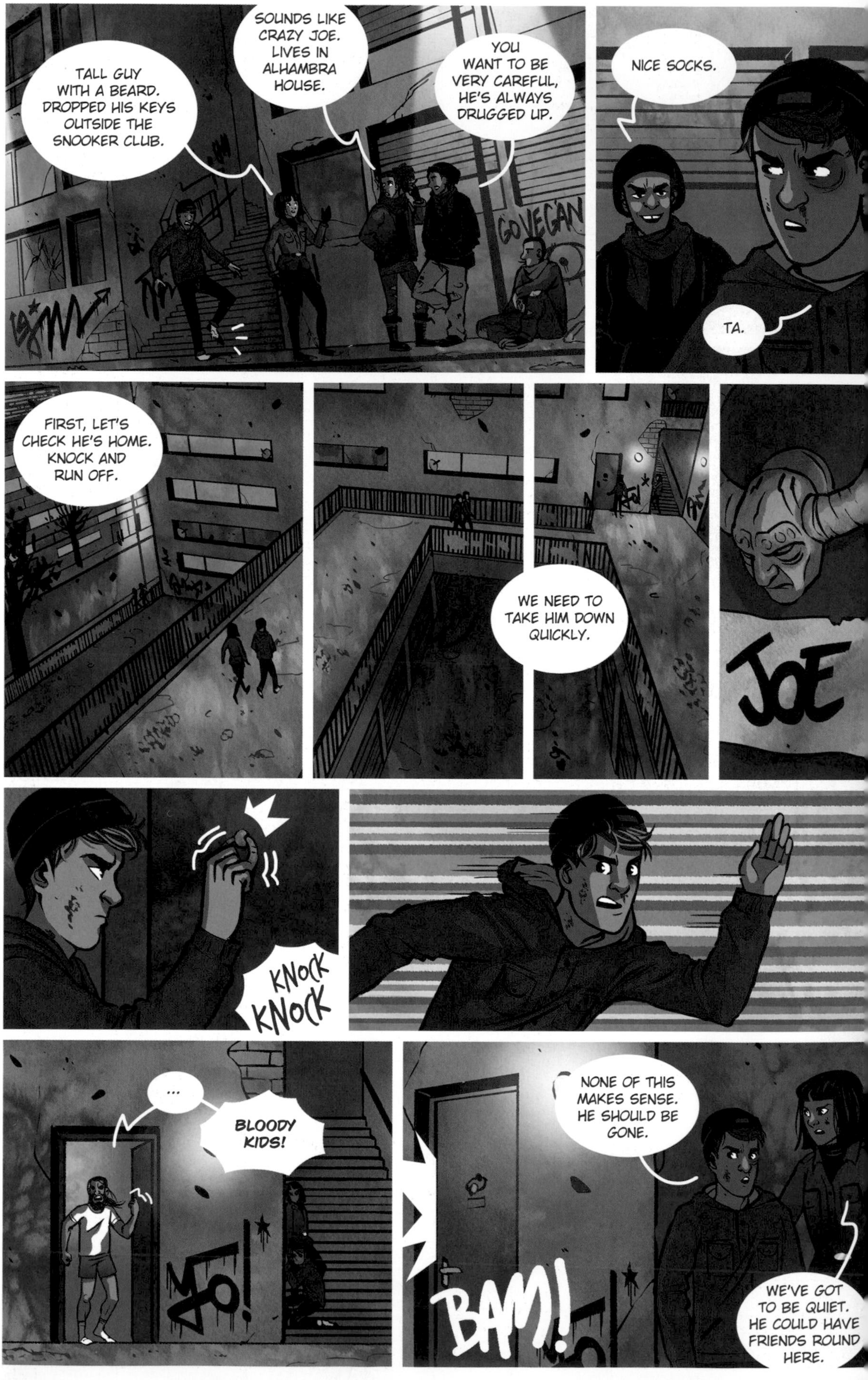
TALL GUY WITH A BEARD. DROPPED HIS KEYS OUTSIDE THE SNOOKER CLUB.
SOUNDS LIKE CRAZY JOE. LIVES IN ALHAMBRA HOUSE.
YOU WANT TO BE VERY CAREFUL, HE'S ALWAYS DRUGGED UP.
GO VEGAN
NICE SOCKS.
TA.
FIRST, LET'S CHECK HE'S HOME. KNOCK AND RUN OFF.
WE NEED TO TAKE HIM DOWN QUICKLY.
JOE
KNOCK KNOCK
...
BLOODY KIDS!
BAM!
NONE OF THIS MAKES SENSE. HE SHOULD BE GONE.
WE'VE GOT TO BE QUIET. HE COULD HAVE FRIENDS ROUND HERE.

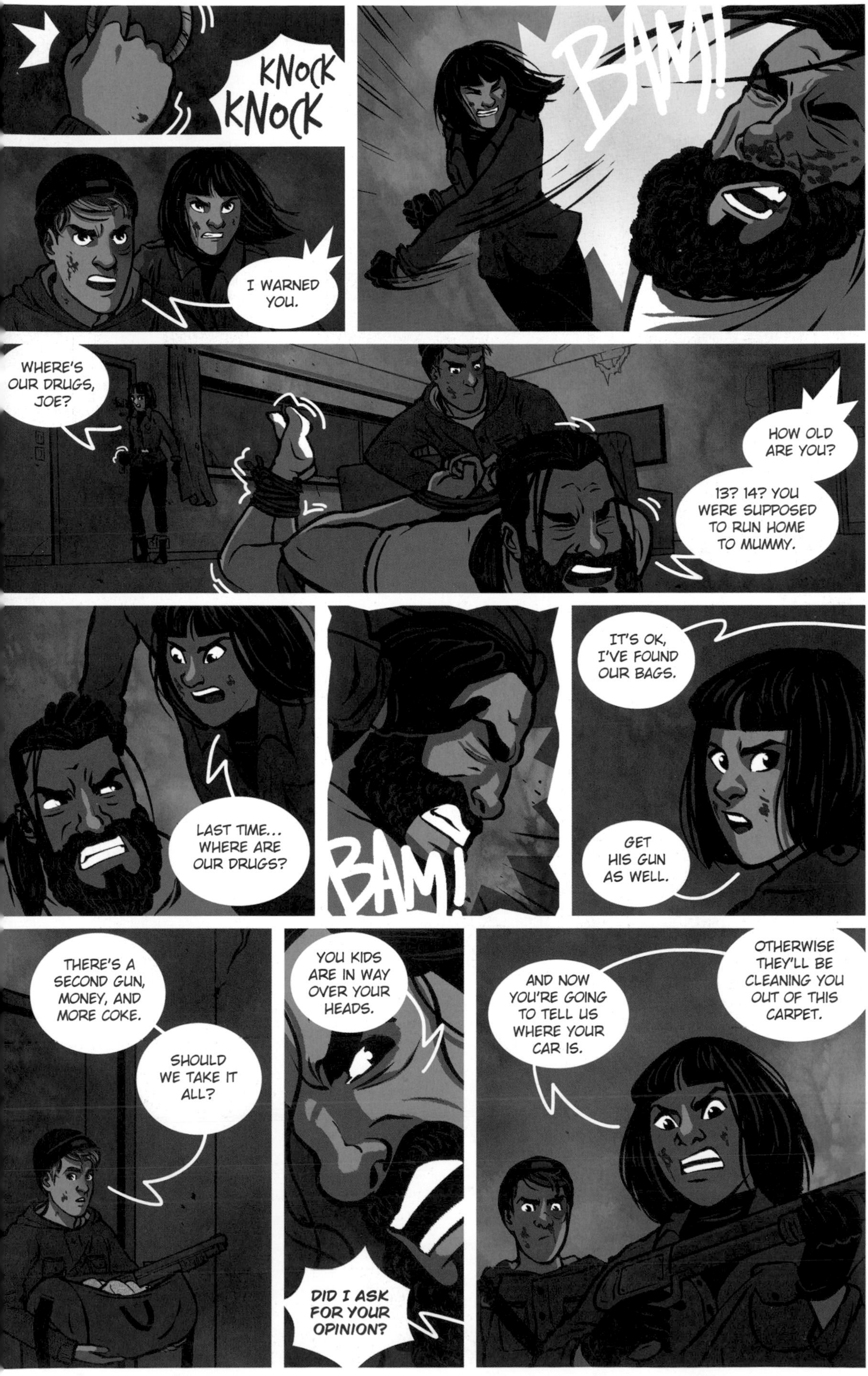
KNOCK KNOCK
I WARNED YOU.
BAM!
WHERE'S OUR DRUGS, JOE?
HOW OLD ARE YOU?
13? 14? YOU WERE SUPPOSED TO RUN HOME TO MUMMY.
LAST TIME... WHERE ARE OUR DRUGS?
BAM!
IT'S OK, I'VE FOUND OUR BAGS.
GET HIS GUN AS WELL.
THERE'S A SECOND GUN, MONEY, AND MORE COKE.
SHOULD WE TAKE IT ALL?
YOU KIDS ARE IN WAY OVER YOUR HEADS.
DID I ASK FOR YOUR OPINION?
AND NOW YOU'RE GOING TO TELL US WHERE YOUR CAR IS.
OTHERWISE THEY'LL BE CLEANING YOU OUT OF THIS CARPET.

IT'S HERE.

BAM

HOLY MOTHER.

BAGS I DRIVE.

GO AHEAD.

WE'LL NEED TO GET RID OF THIS ONCE WE GET HOME.

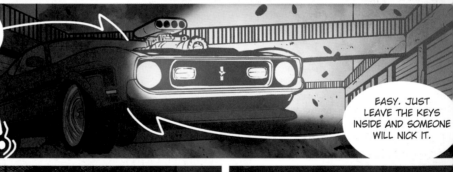

VROOM!

EASY. JUST LEAVE THE KEYS INSIDE AND SOMEONE WILL NICK IT.

ACTUALLY, OUR FINGERPRINTS ARE ON IT.

WE'LL HAVE TO DO WHAT THE JOYRIDERS USUALLY DO AND BURN IT.

AH, SEEMS A SHAME TO KILL IT.

HOW FAR IS OUR HOUSE FROM HERE?

MAYBE A KILOMETRE?

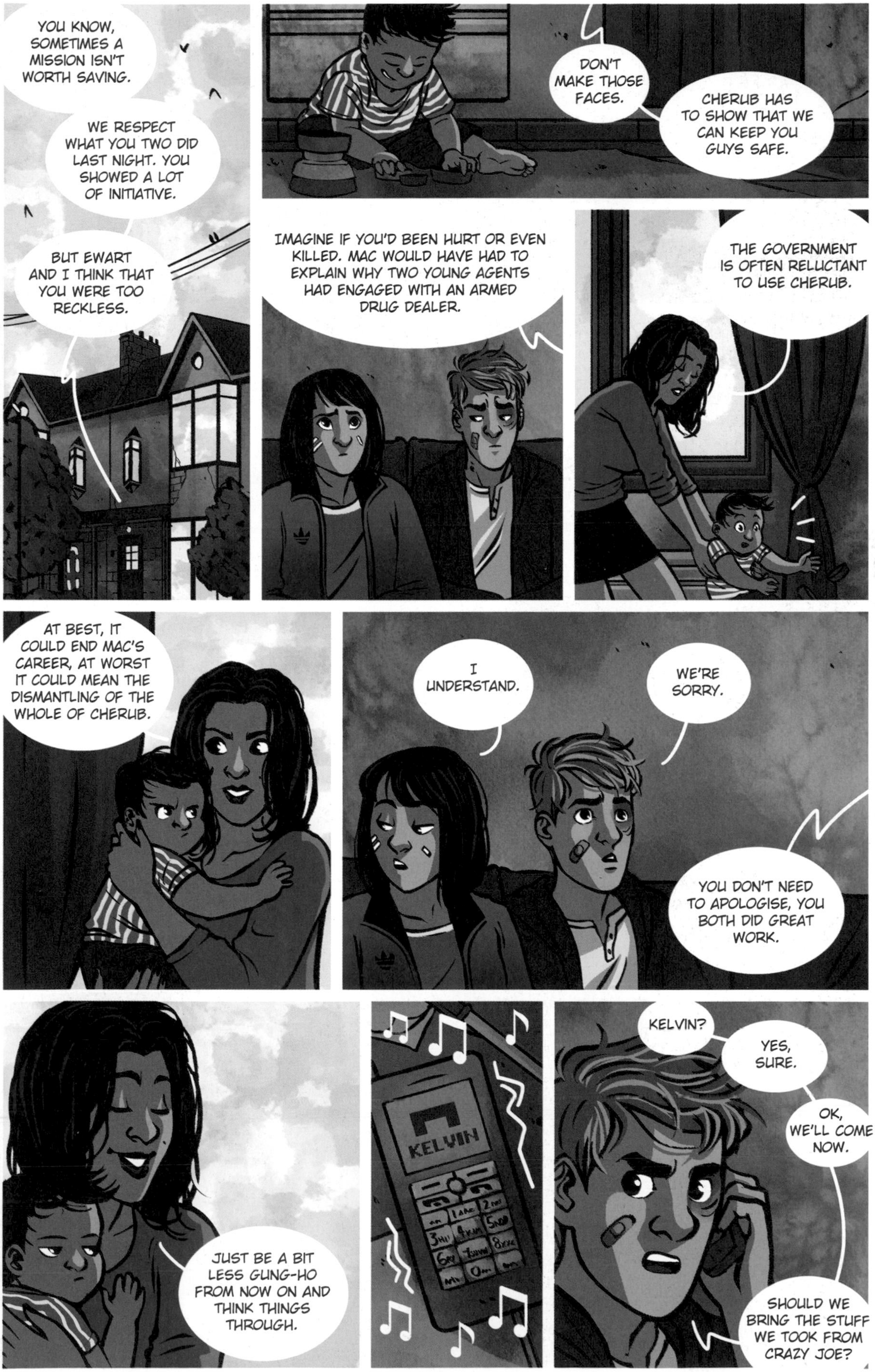
YOU KNOW, SOMETIMES A MISSION ISN'T WORTH SAVING.
WE RESPECT WHAT YOU TWO DID LAST NIGHT. YOU SHOWED A LOT OF INITIATIVE.
BUT EWART AND I THINK THAT YOU WERE TOO RECKLESS.
DON'T MAKE THOSE FACES.
CHERUB HAS TO SHOW THAT WE CAN KEEP YOU GUYS SAFE.
IMAGINE IF YOU'D BEEN HURT OR EVEN KILLED. MAC WOULD HAVE HAD TO EXPLAIN WHY TWO YOUNG AGENTS HAD ENGAGED WITH AN ARMED DRUG DEALER.
THE GOVERNMENT IS OFTEN RELUCTANT TO USE CHERUB.
AT BEST, IT COULD END MAC'S CAREER, AT WORST IT COULD MEAN THE DISMANTLING OF THE WHOLE OF CHERUB.
I UNDERSTAND.
WE'RE SORRY.
YOU DON'T NEED TO APOLOGISE, YOU BOTH DID GREAT WORK.
JUST BE A BIT LESS GUNG-HO FROM NOW ON AND THINK THINGS THROUGH.
KELVIN
KELVIN?
YES, SURE.
OK, WE'LL COME NOW.
SHOULD WE BRING THE STUFF WE TOOK FROM CRAZY JOE?

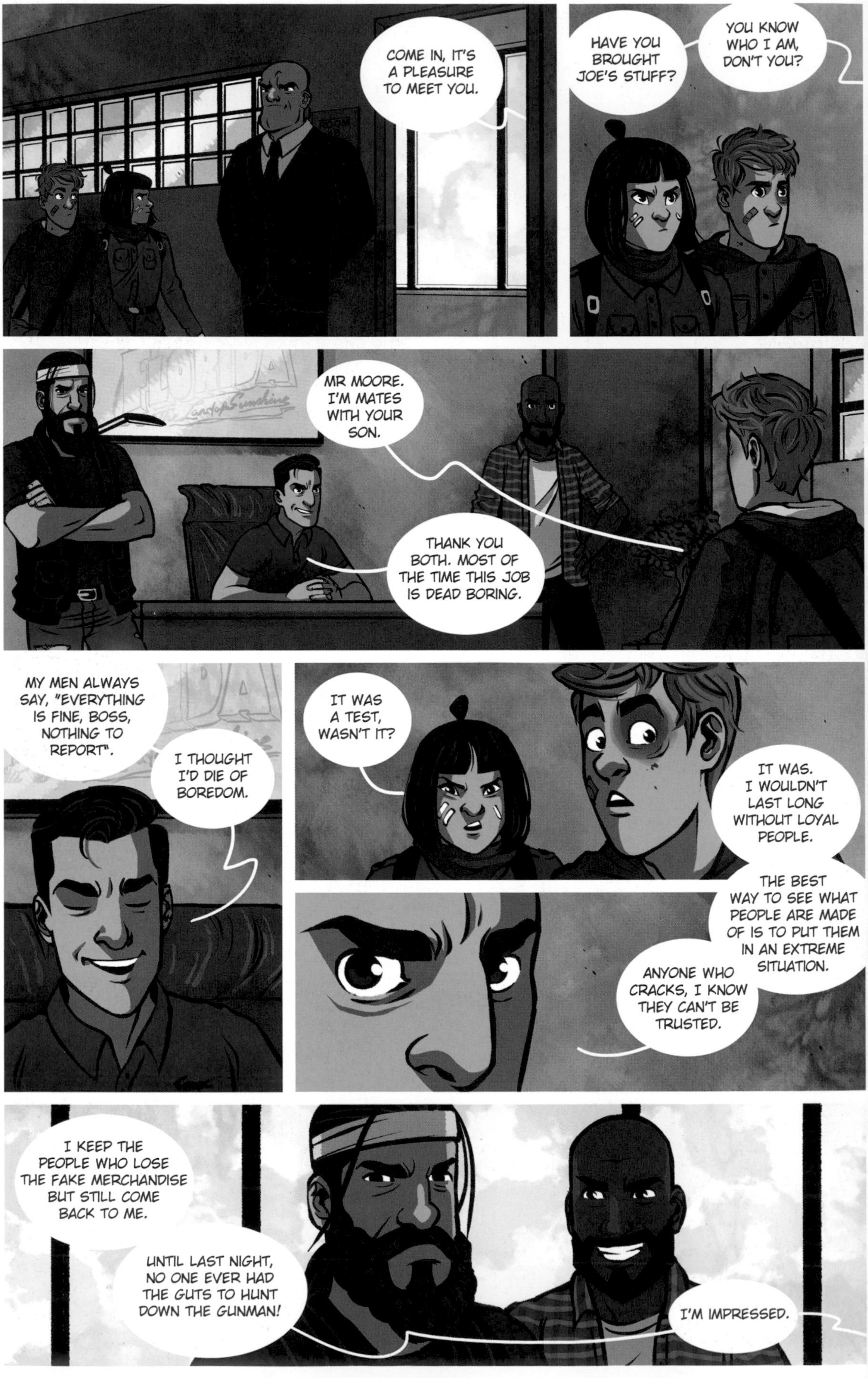
COME IN, IT'S A PLEASURE TO MEET YOU.
HAVE YOU BROUGHT JOE'S STUFF?
YOU KNOW WHO I AM, DON'T YOU?
MR MOORE. I'M MATES WITH YOUR SON.
THANK YOU BOTH. MOST OF THE TIME THIS JOB IS DEAD BORING.
MY MEN ALWAYS SAY, "EVERYTHING IS FINE, BOSS, NOTHING TO REPORT".
I THOUGHT I'D DIE OF BOREDOM.
IT WAS A TEST, WASN'T IT?
IT WAS. I WOULDN'T LAST LONG WITHOUT LOYAL PEOPLE.
THE BEST WAY TO SEE WHAT PEOPLE ARE MADE OF IS TO PUT THEM IN AN EXTREME SITUATION.
ANYONE WHO CRACKS, I KNOW THEY CAN'T BE TRUSTED.
I KEEP THE PEOPLE WHO LOSE THE FAKE MERCHANDISE BUT STILL COME BACK TO ME.
UNTIL LAST NIGHT, NO ONE EVER HAD THE GUTS TO HUNT DOWN THE GUNMAN!
I'M IMPRESSED.

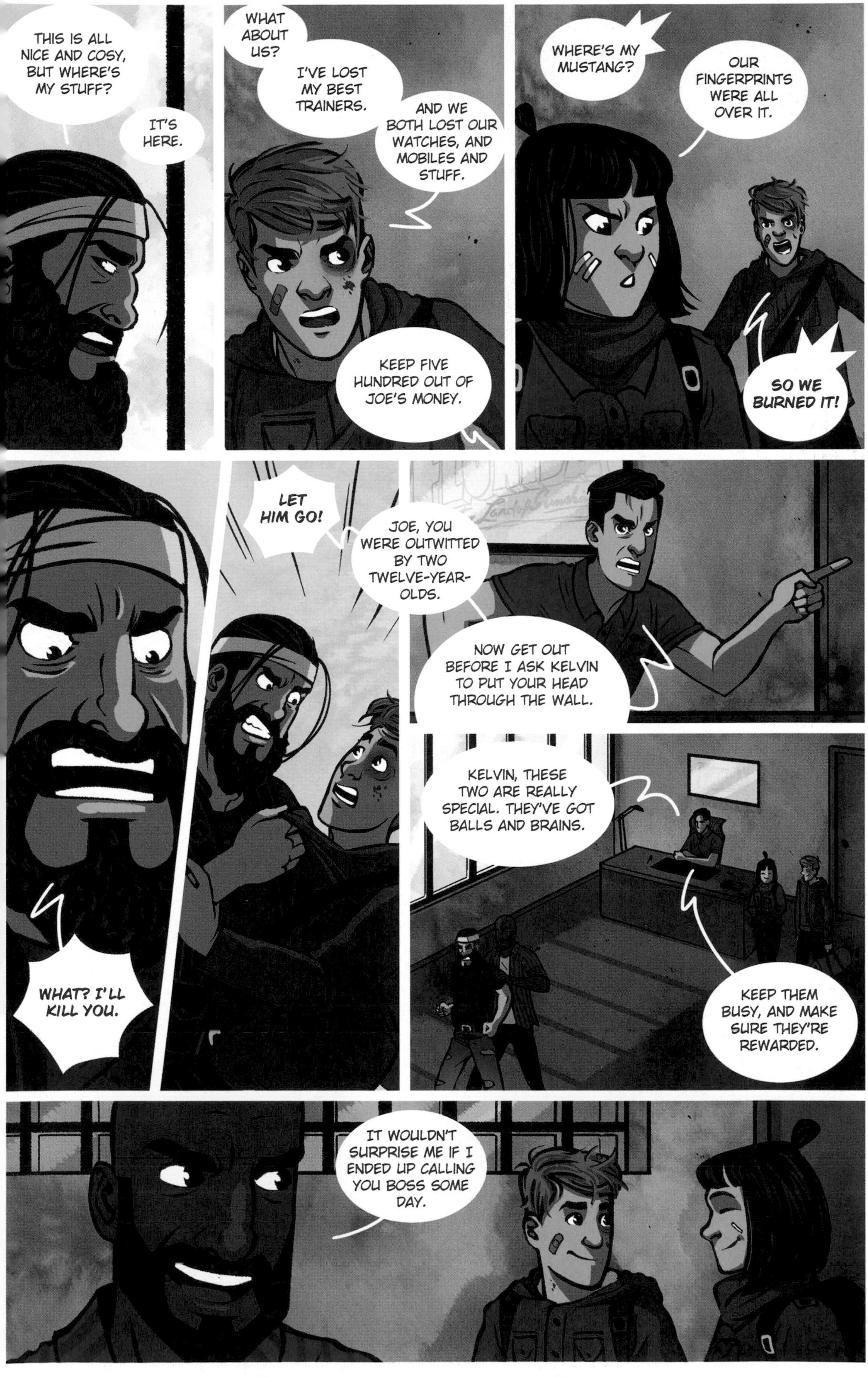
THIS IS ALL NICE AND COSY, BUT WHERE'S MY STUFF?
IT'S HERE.
WHAT ABOUT US?
I'VE LOST MY BEST TRAINERS.
AND WE BOTH LOST OUR WATCHES, AND MOBILES AND STUFF.
KEEP FIVE HUNDRED OUT OF JOE'S MONEY.
WHERE'S MY MUSTANG?
OUR FINGERPRINTS WERE ALL OVER IT.
SO WE BURNED IT!
WHAT? I'LL KILL YOU.
LET HIM GO!
JOE, YOU WERE OUTWITTED BY TWO TWELVE-YEAR-OLDS.
NOW GET OUT BEFORE I ASK KELVIN TO PUT YOUR HEAD THROUGH THE WALL.
KELVIN, THESE TWO ARE REALLY SPECIAL. THEY'VE GOT BALLS AND BRAINS.
KEEP THEM BUSY, AND MAKE SURE THEY'RE REWARDED.
IT WOULDN'T SURPRISE ME IF I ENDED UP CALLING YOU BOSS SOME DAY.

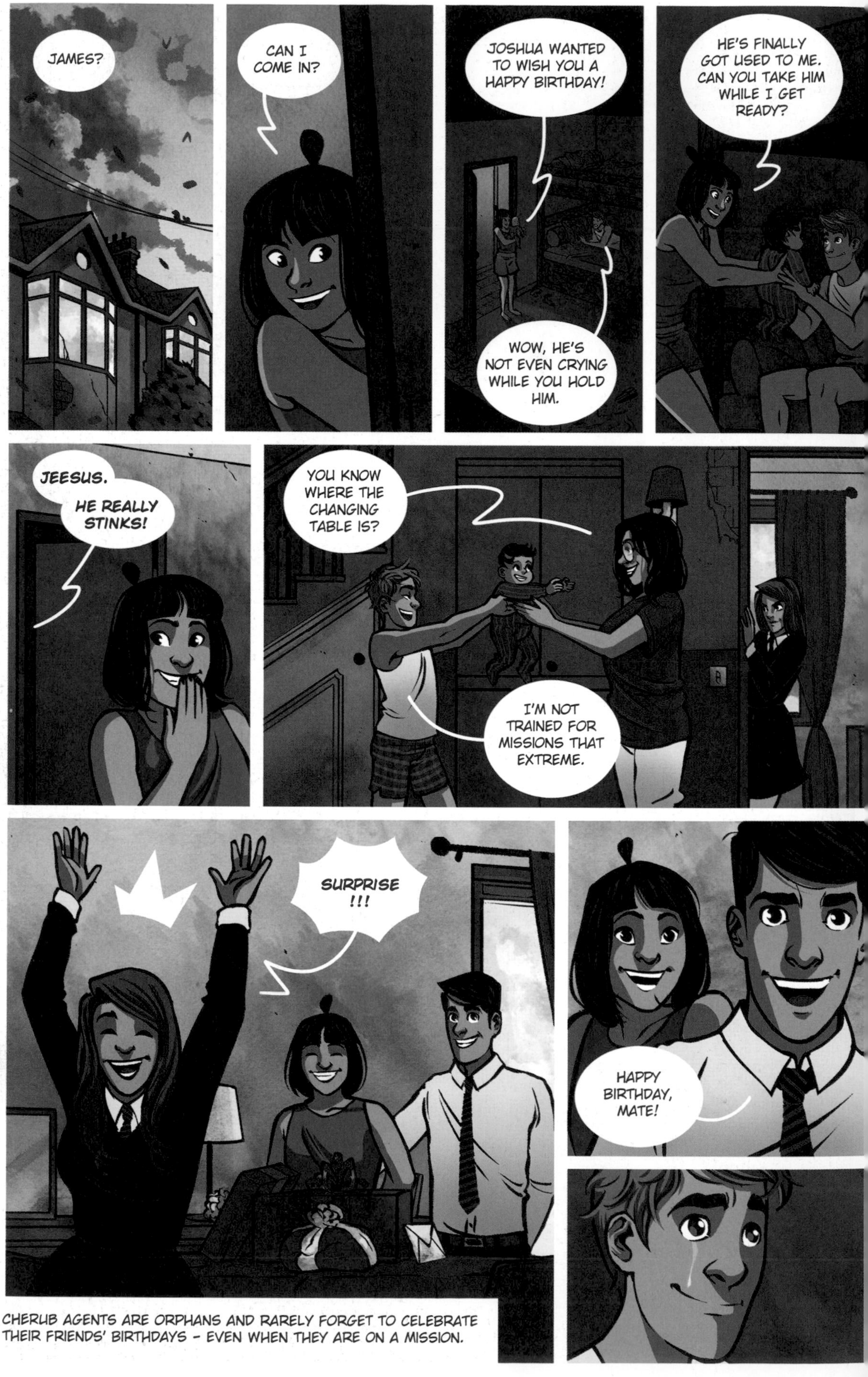
JAMES?
CAN I COME IN?
JOSHUA WANTED TO WISH YOU A HAPPY BIRTHDAY!
WOW, HE'S NOT EVEN CRYING WHILE YOU HOLD HIM.
HE'S FINALLY GOT USED TO ME. CAN YOU TAKE HIM WHILE I GET READY?
JEESUS.
HE REALLY STINKS!
YOU KNOW WHERE THE CHANGING TABLE IS?
I'M NOT TRAINED FOR MISSIONS THAT EXTREME.
SURPRISE !!!
HAPPY BIRTHDAY, MATE!
CHERUB AGENTS ARE ORPHANS AND RARELY FORGET TO CELEBRATE THEIR FRIENDS' BIRTHDAYS – EVEN WHEN THEY ARE ON A MISSION.

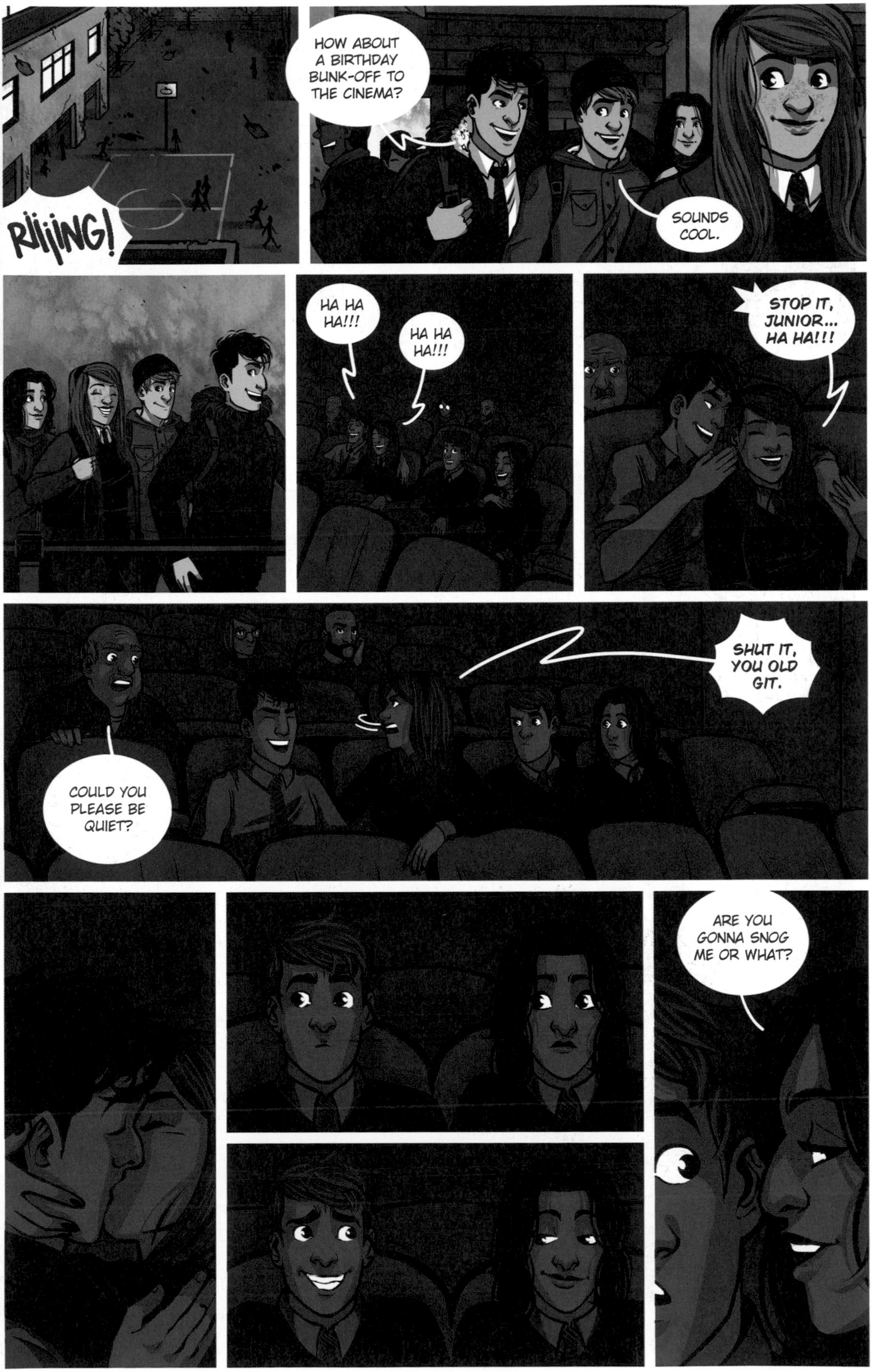
RIIIING!
HOW ABOUT A BIRTHDAY BUNK-OFF TO THE CINEMA?
SOUNDS COOL.
HA HA HA!!!
HA HA HA!!!
STOP IT, JUNIOR... HA HA!!!
COULD YOU PLEASE BE QUIET?
SHUT IT, YOU OLD GIT.
ARE YOU GONNA SNOG ME OR WHAT?

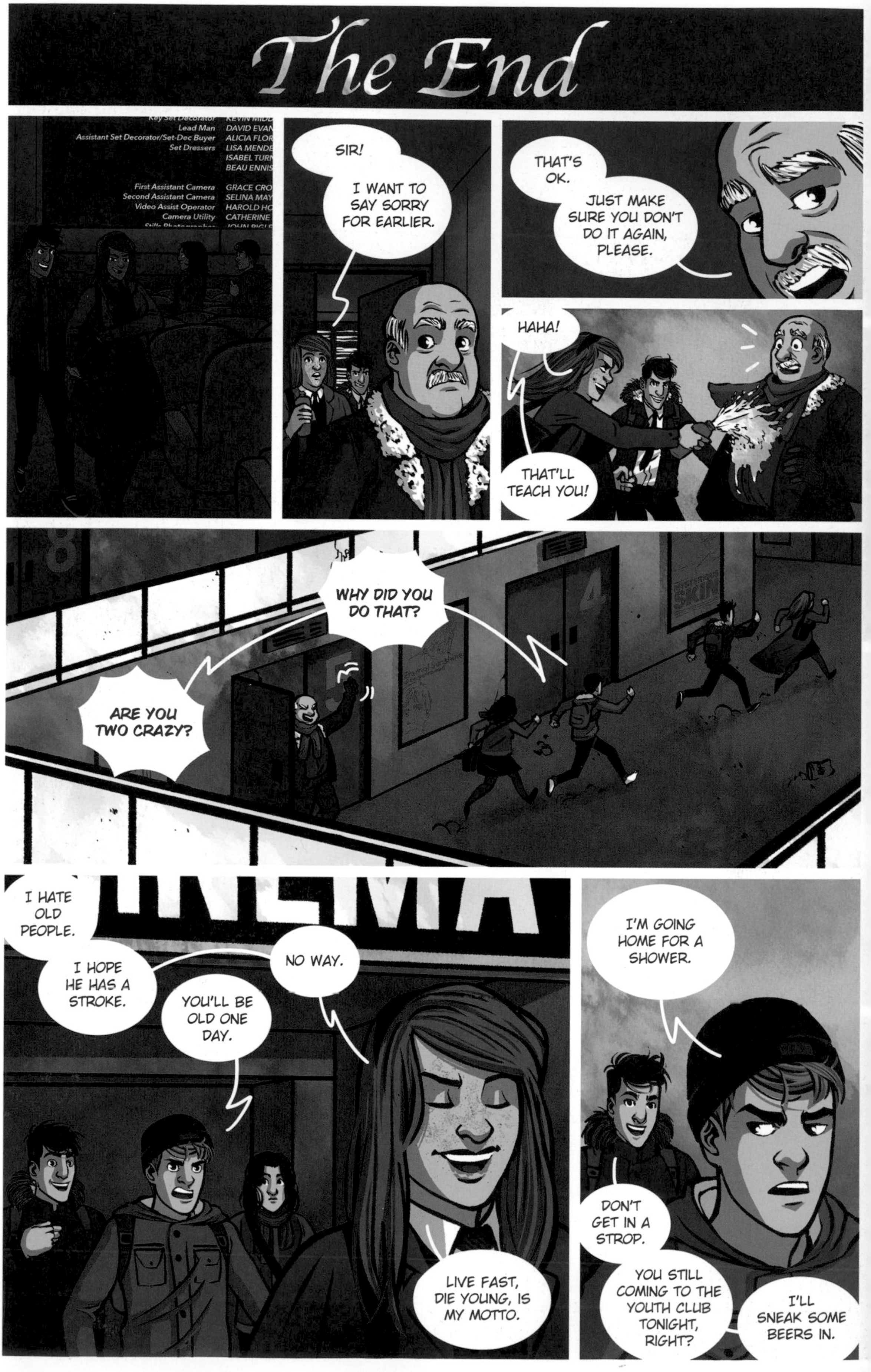
The End
Lead Man DAVID EVAN
Assistant Set Decorator/Set-Dec Buyer ALICIA FLOR
Set Dressers LISA MENDE
ISABEL TURN
BEAU ENNIS
First Assistant Camera GRACE CRO
Second Assistant Camera SELINA MAY
Video Assist Operator HAROLD HO
Camera Utility CATHERINE
SIR!
I WANT TO SAY SORRY FOR EARLIER.
THAT'S OK.
JUST MAKE SURE YOU DON'T DO IT AGAIN, PLEASE.
HAHA!
THAT'LL TEACH YOU!
WHY DID YOU DO THAT?
ARE YOU TWO CRAZY?
I HATE OLD PEOPLE.
I HOPE HE HAS A STROKE.
NO WAY.
YOU'LL BE OLD ONE DAY.
LIVE FAST, DIE YOUNG, IS MY MOTTO.
I'M GOING HOME FOR A SHOWER.
DON'T GET IN A STROP.
YOU STILL COMING TO THE YOUTH CLUB TONIGHT, RIGHT?
I'LL SNEAK SOME BEERS IN.

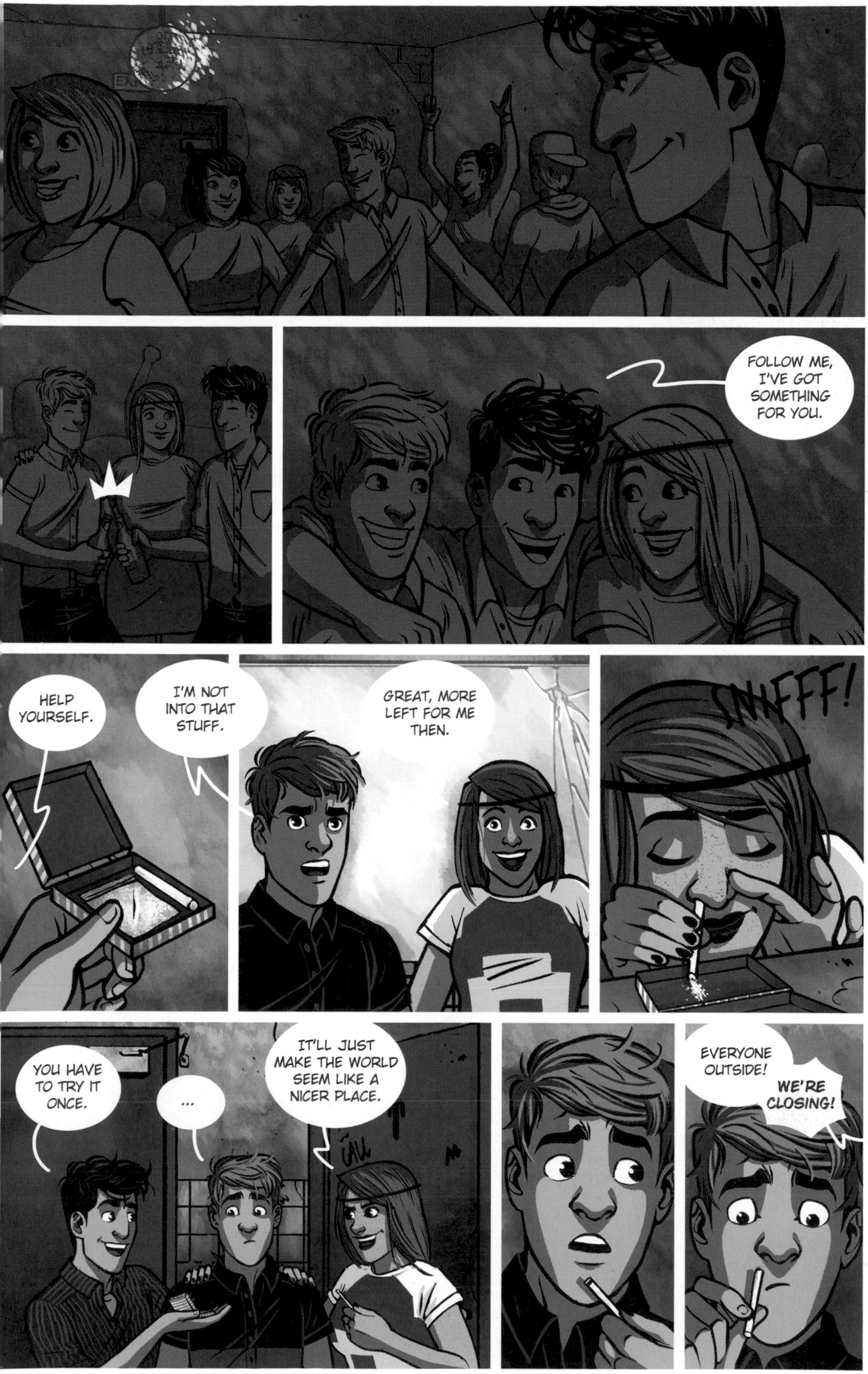
FOLLOW ME, I'VE GOT SOMETHING FOR YOU.
HELP YOURSELF.
I'M NOT INTO THAT STUFF.
GREAT, MORE LEFT FOR ME THEN.
SNIFFF!
YOU HAVE TO TRY IT ONCE.
...
IT'LL JUST MAKE THE WORLD SEEM LIKE A NICER PLACE.
EVERYONE OUTSIDE!
WE'RE CLOSING!

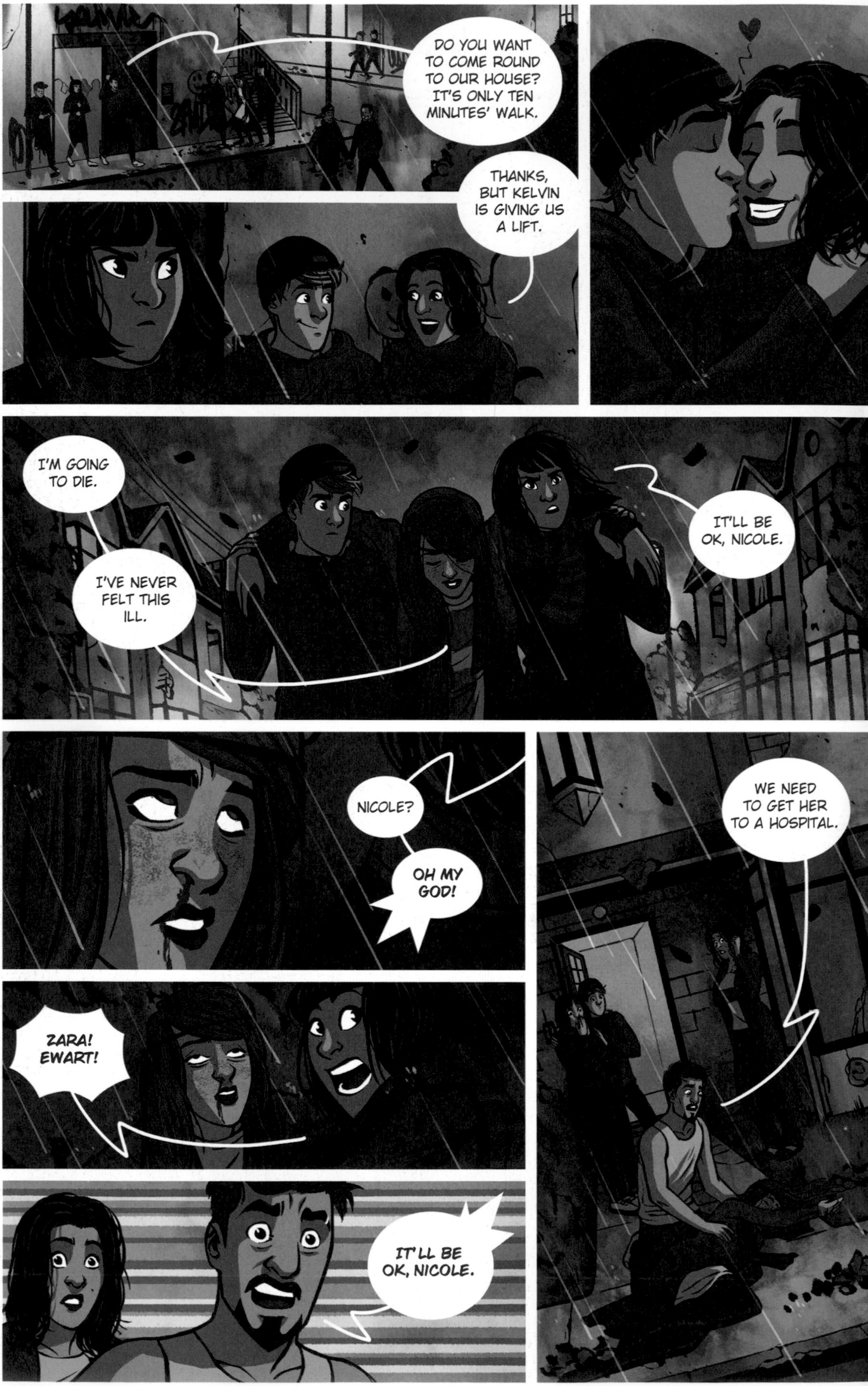
DO YOU WANT TO COME ROUND TO OUR HOUSE? IT'S ONLY TEN MINUTES' WALK.
THANKS, BUT KELVIN IS GIVING US A LIFT.
I'M GOING TO DIE.
I'VE NEVER FELT THIS ILL.
IT'LL BE OK, NICOLE.
NICOLE?
OH MY GOD!
ZARA! EWART!
IT'LL BE OK, NICOLE.
WE NEED TO GET HER TO A HOSPITAL.

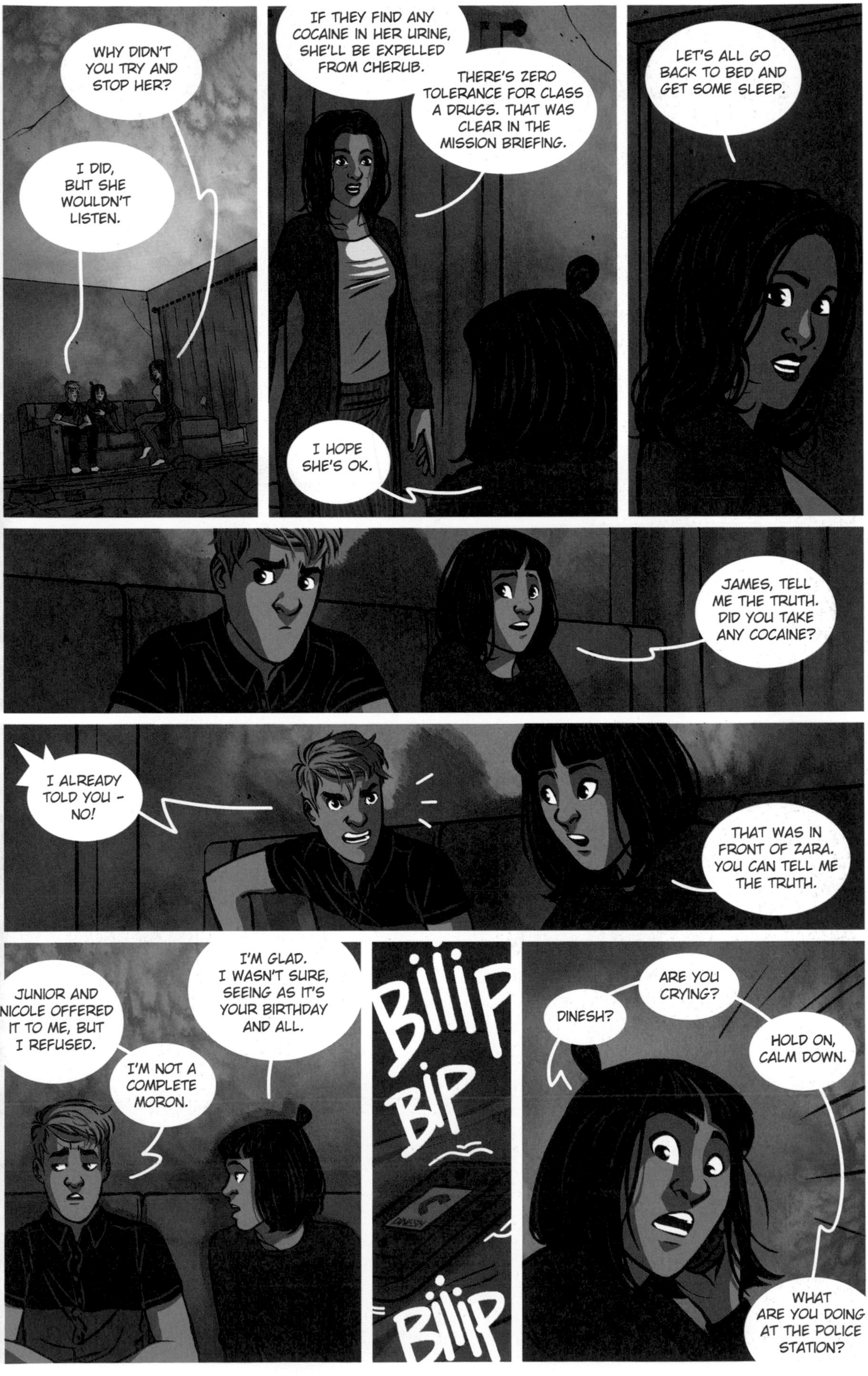
WHY DIDN'T YOU TRY AND STOP HER?
I DID, BUT SHE WOULDN'T LISTEN.
IF THEY FIND ANY COCAINE IN HER URINE, SHE'LL BE EXPELLED FROM CHERUB.
THERE'S ZERO TOLERANCE FOR CLASS A DRUGS. THAT WAS CLEAR IN THE MISSION BRIEFING.
I HOPE SHE'S OK.
LET'S ALL GO BACK TO BED AND GET SOME SLEEP.
JAMES, TELL ME THE TRUTH. DID YOU TAKE ANY COCAINE?
I ALREADY TOLD YOU - NO!
THAT WAS IN FRONT OF ZARA. YOU CAN TELL ME THE TRUTH.
JUNIOR AND NICOLE OFFERED IT TO ME, BUT I REFUSED.
I'M NOT A COMPLETE MORON.
I'M GLAD. I WASN'T SURE, SEEING AS IT'S YOUR BIRTHDAY AND ALL.
BIIIP
BIP
BIIIP
DINESH?
ARE YOU CRYING?
HOLD ON, CALM DOWN.
WHAT ARE YOU DOING AT THE POLICE STATION?

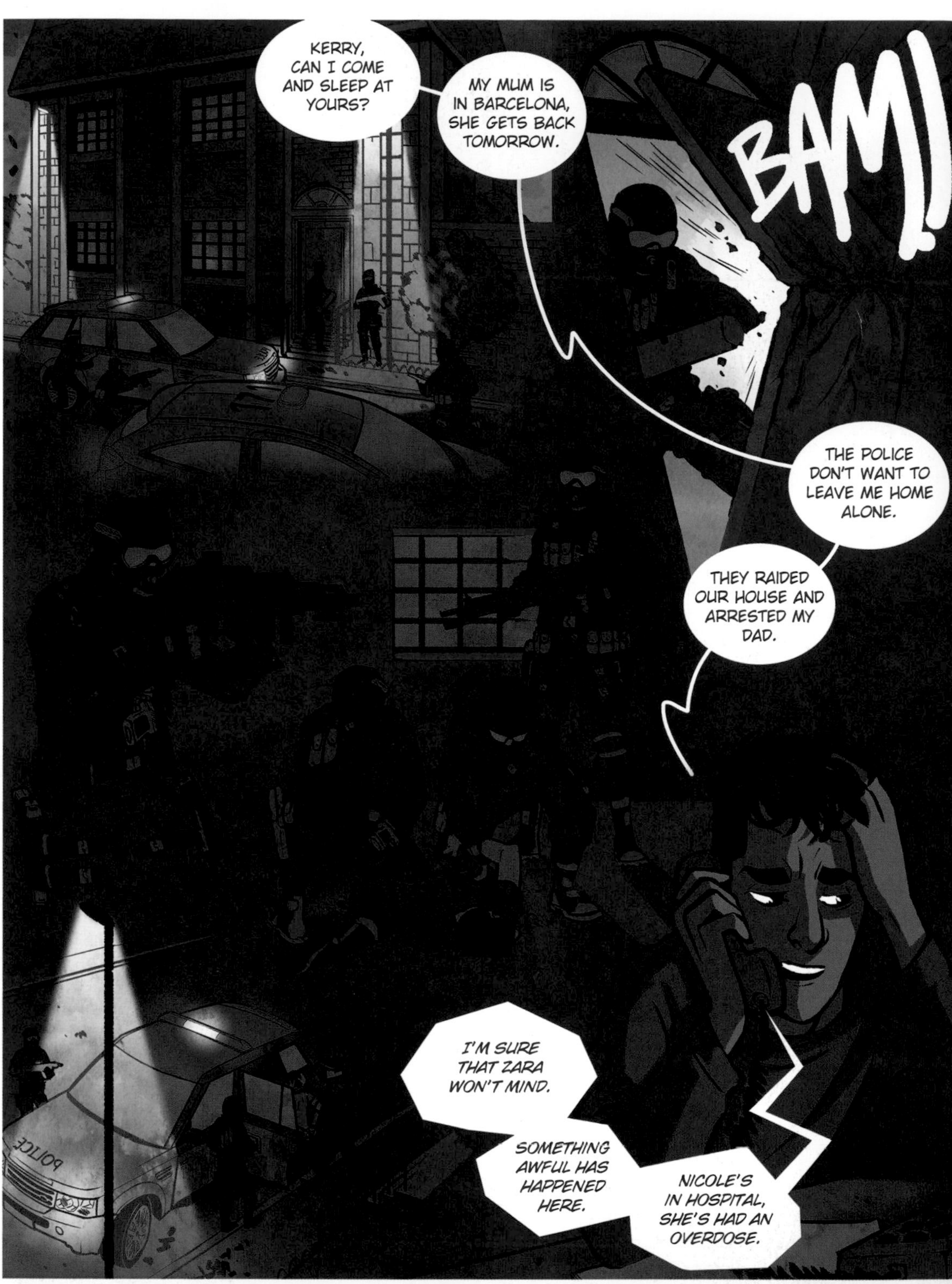
KERRY, CAN I COME AND SLEEP AT YOURS?
MY MUM IS IN BARCELONA, SHE GETS BACK TOMORROW.
BAM!!
THE POLICE DON'T WANT TO LEAVE ME HOME ALONE.
THEY RAIDED OUR HOUSE AND ARRESTED MY DAD.
I'M SURE THAT ZARA WON'T MIND.
SOMETHING AWFUL HAS HAPPENED HERE.
NICOLE'S IN HOSPITAL, SHE'S HAD AN OVERDOSE.
POLICE

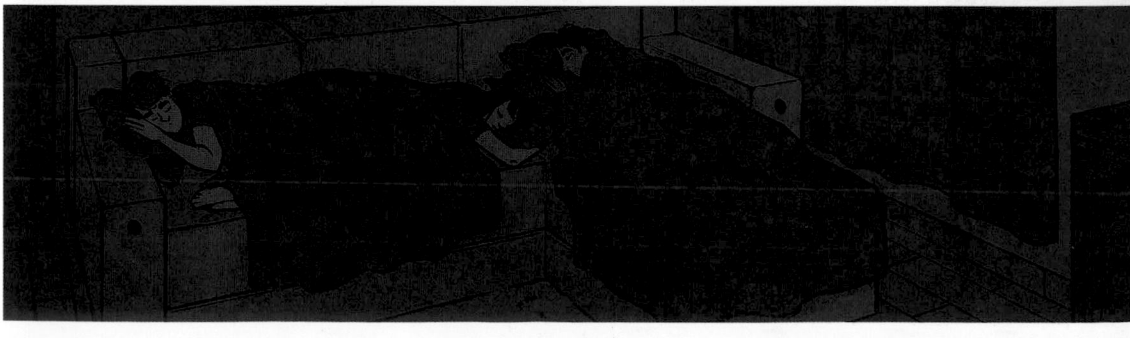

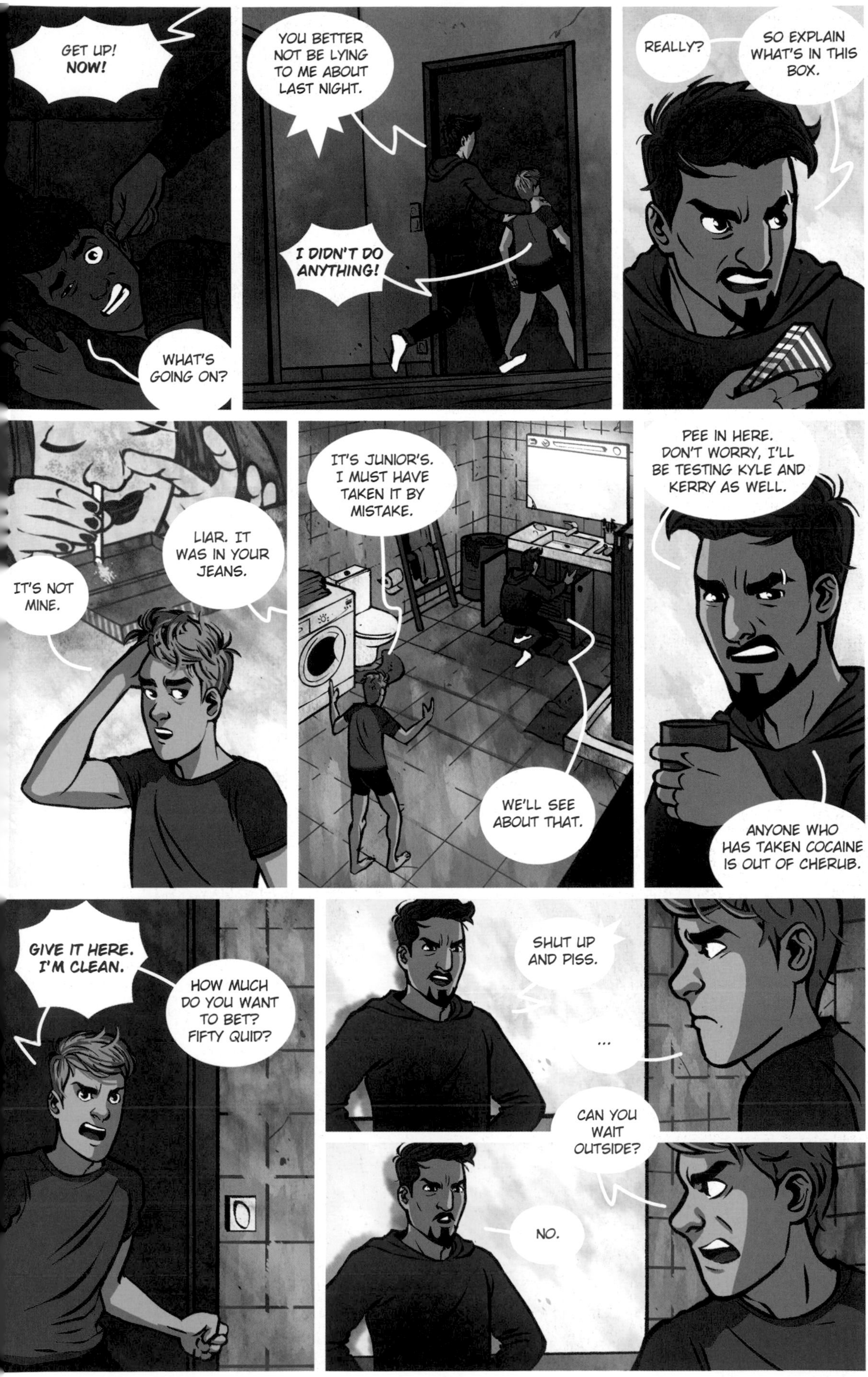
GET UP! **NOW!**
WHAT'S GOING ON?
YOU BETTER NOT BE LYING TO ME ABOUT LAST NIGHT.
I DIDN'T DO ANYTHING!
REALLY?
SO EXPLAIN WHAT'S IN THIS BOX.
IT'S NOT MINE.
LIAR. IT WAS IN YOUR JEANS.
IT'S JUNIOR'S. I MUST HAVE TAKEN IT BY MISTAKE.
WE'LL SEE ABOUT THAT.
PEE IN HERE. DON'T WORRY, I'LL BE TESTING KYLE AND KERRY AS WELL.
ANYONE WHO HAS TAKEN COCAINE IS OUT OF CHERUB.
GIVE IT HERE. I'M CLEAN.
HOW MUCH DO YOU WANT TO BET? FIFTY QUID?
SHUT UP AND PISS.
...
CAN YOU WAIT OUTSIDE?
NO.

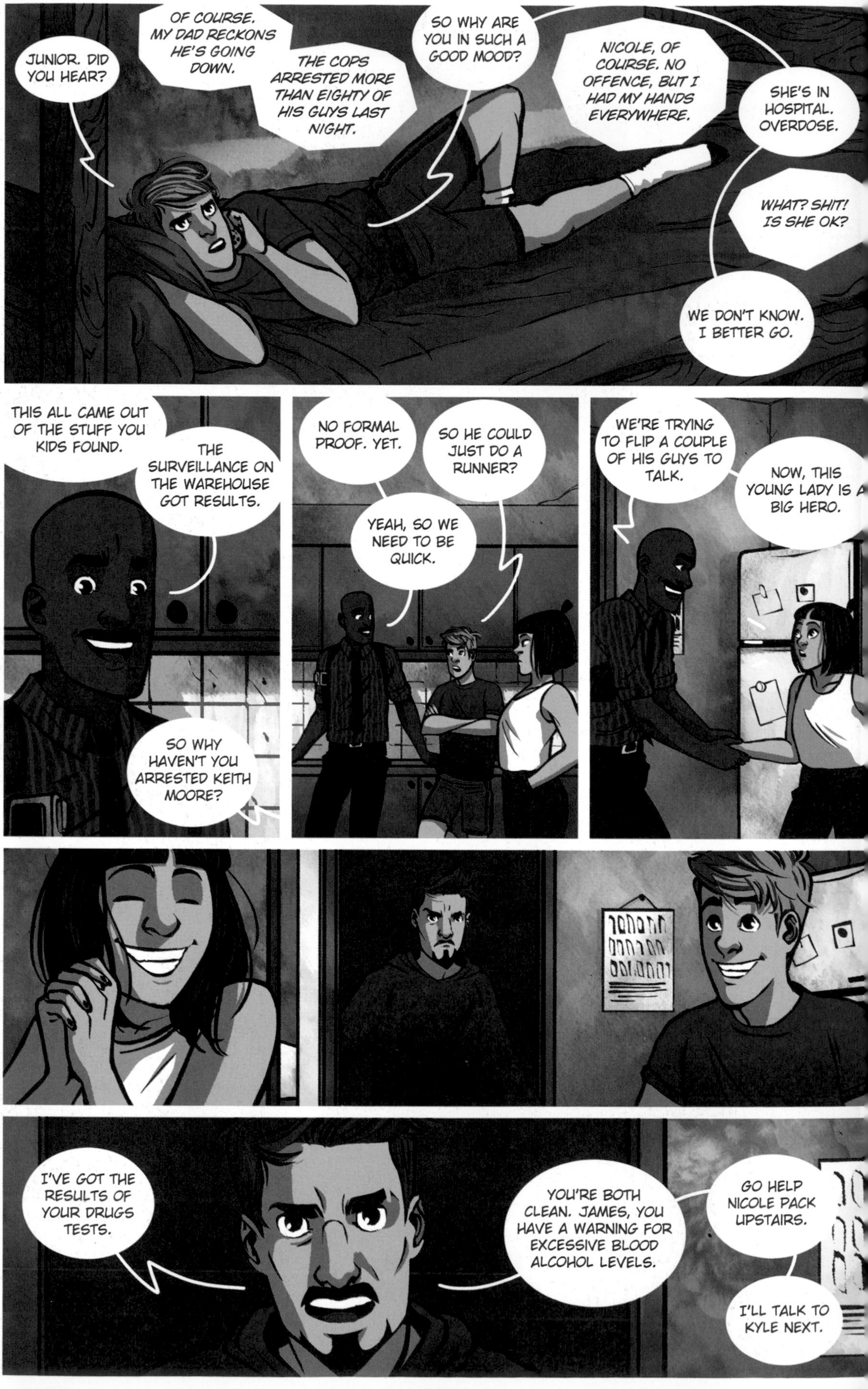
JUNIOR. DID YOU HEAR?
OF COURSE. MY DAD RECKONS HE'S GOING DOWN.
THE COPS ARRESTED MORE THAN EIGHTY OF HIS GUYS LAST NIGHT.
SO WHY ARE YOU IN SUCH A GOOD MOOD?
NICOLE, OF COURSE. NO OFFENCE, BUT I HAD MY HANDS EVERYWHERE.
SHE'S IN HOSPITAL. OVERDOSE.
WHAT? SHIT! IS SHE OK?
WE DON'T KNOW. I BETTER GO.
THIS ALL CAME OUT OF THE STUFF YOU KIDS FOUND.
THE SURVEILLANCE ON THE WAREHOUSE GOT RESULTS.
SO WHY HAVEN'T YOU ARRESTED KEITH MOORE?
NO FORMAL PROOF. YET.
SO HE COULD JUST DO A RUNNER?
YEAH, SO WE NEED TO BE QUICK.
WE'RE TRYING TO FLIP A COUPLE OF HIS GUYS TO TALK.
NOW, THIS YOUNG LADY IS A BIG HERO.
I'VE GOT THE RESULTS OF YOUR DRUGS TESTS.
YOU'RE BOTH CLEAN. JAMES, YOU HAVE A WARNING FOR EXCESSIVE BLOOD ALCOHOL LEVELS.
GO HELP NICOLE PACK UPSTAIRS.
I'LL TALK TO KYLE NEXT.

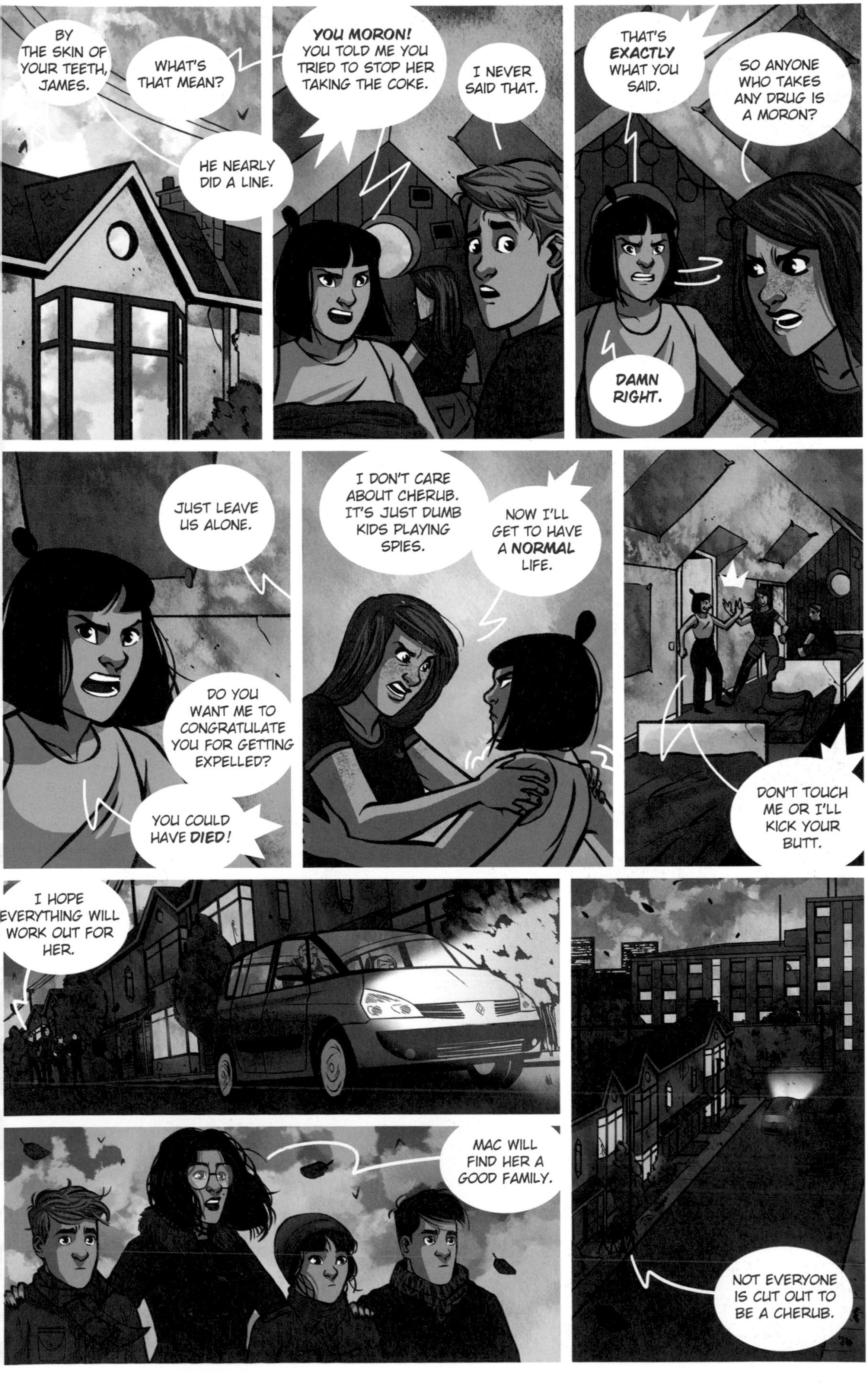
BY THE SKIN OF YOUR TEETH, JAMES.
WHAT'S THAT MEAN?
HE NEARLY DID A LINE.
YOU MORON! YOU TOLD ME YOU TRIED TO STOP HER TAKING THE COKE.
I NEVER SAID THAT.
THAT'S EXACTLY WHAT YOU SAID.
SO ANYONE WHO TAKES ANY DRUG IS A MORON?
DAMN RIGHT.
JUST LEAVE US ALONE.
DO YOU WANT ME TO CONGRATULATE YOU FOR GETTING EXPELLED?
YOU COULD HAVE DIED!
I DON'T CARE ABOUT CHERUB. IT'S JUST DUMB KIDS PLAYING SPIES.
NOW I'LL GET TO HAVE A NORMAL LIFE.
DON'T TOUCH ME OR I'LL KICK YOUR BUTT.
I HOPE EVERYTHING WILL WORK OUT FOR HER.
MAC WILL FIND HER A GOOD FAMILY.
NOT EVERYONE IS CUT OUT TO BE A CHERUB.

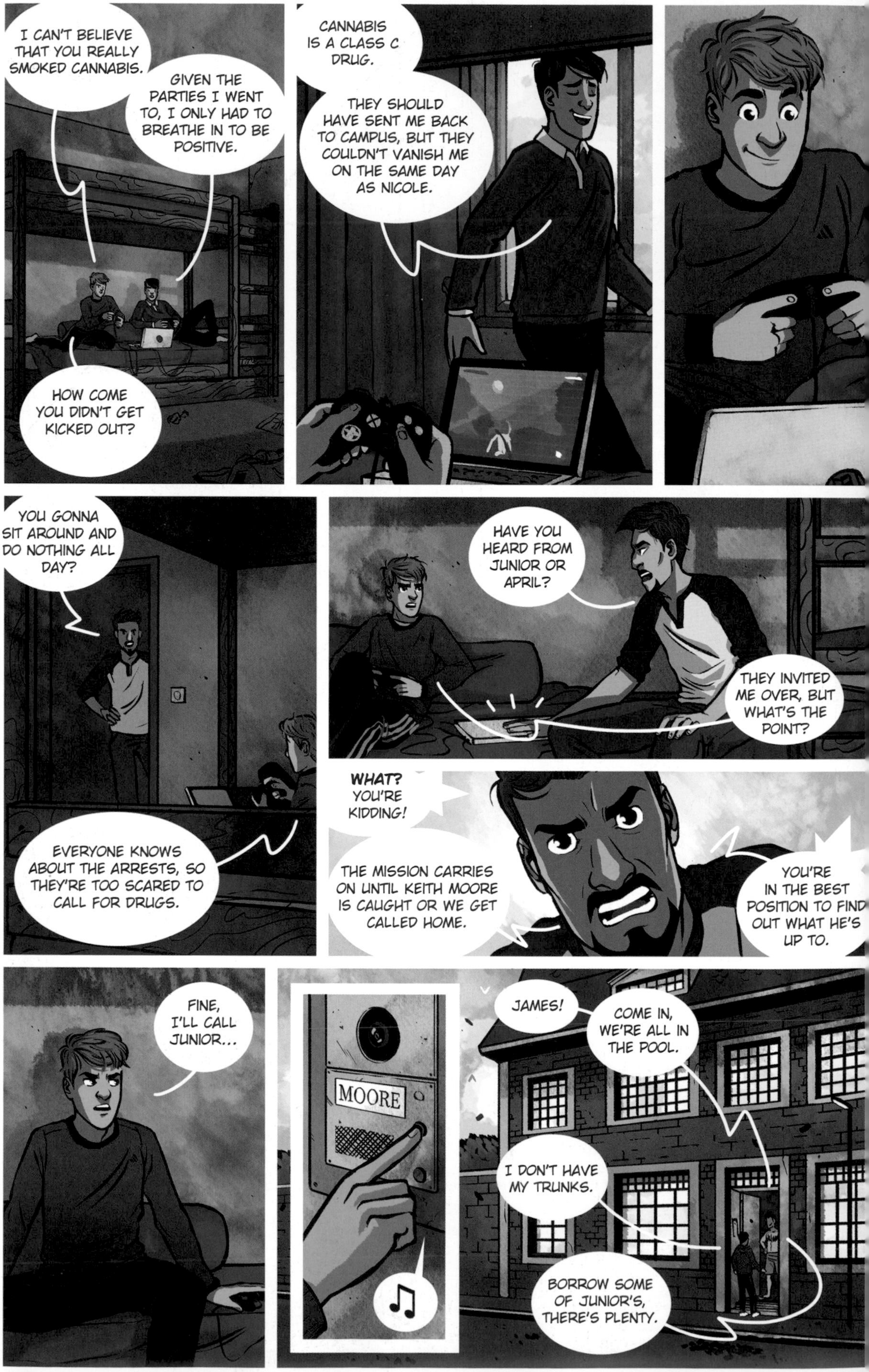

I CAN'T BELIEVE THAT YOU REALLY SMOKED CANNABIS.
GIVEN THE PARTIES I WENT TO, I ONLY HAD TO BREATHE IN TO BE POSITIVE.
HOW COME YOU DIDN'T GET KICKED OUT?
CANNABIS IS A CLASS C DRUG.
THEY SHOULD HAVE SENT ME BACK TO CAMPUS, BUT THEY COULDN'T VANISH ME ON THE SAME DAY AS NICOLE.
YOU GONNA SIT AROUND AND DO NOTHING ALL DAY?
EVERYONE KNOWS ABOUT THE ARRESTS, SO THEY'RE TOO SCARED TO CALL FOR DRUGS.
HAVE YOU HEARD FROM JUNIOR OR APRIL?
THEY INVITED ME OVER, BUT WHAT'S THE POINT?
WHAT? YOU'RE KIDDING!
THE MISSION CARRIES ON UNTIL KEITH MOORE IS CAUGHT OR WE GET CALLED HOME.
YOU'RE IN THE BEST POSITION TO FIND OUT WHAT HE'S UP TO.
FINE, I'LL CALL JUNIOR...
MOORE
JAMES!
COME IN, WE'RE ALL IN THE POOL.
I DON'T HAVE MY TRUNKS.
BORROW SOME OF JUNIOR'S, THERE'S PLENTY.

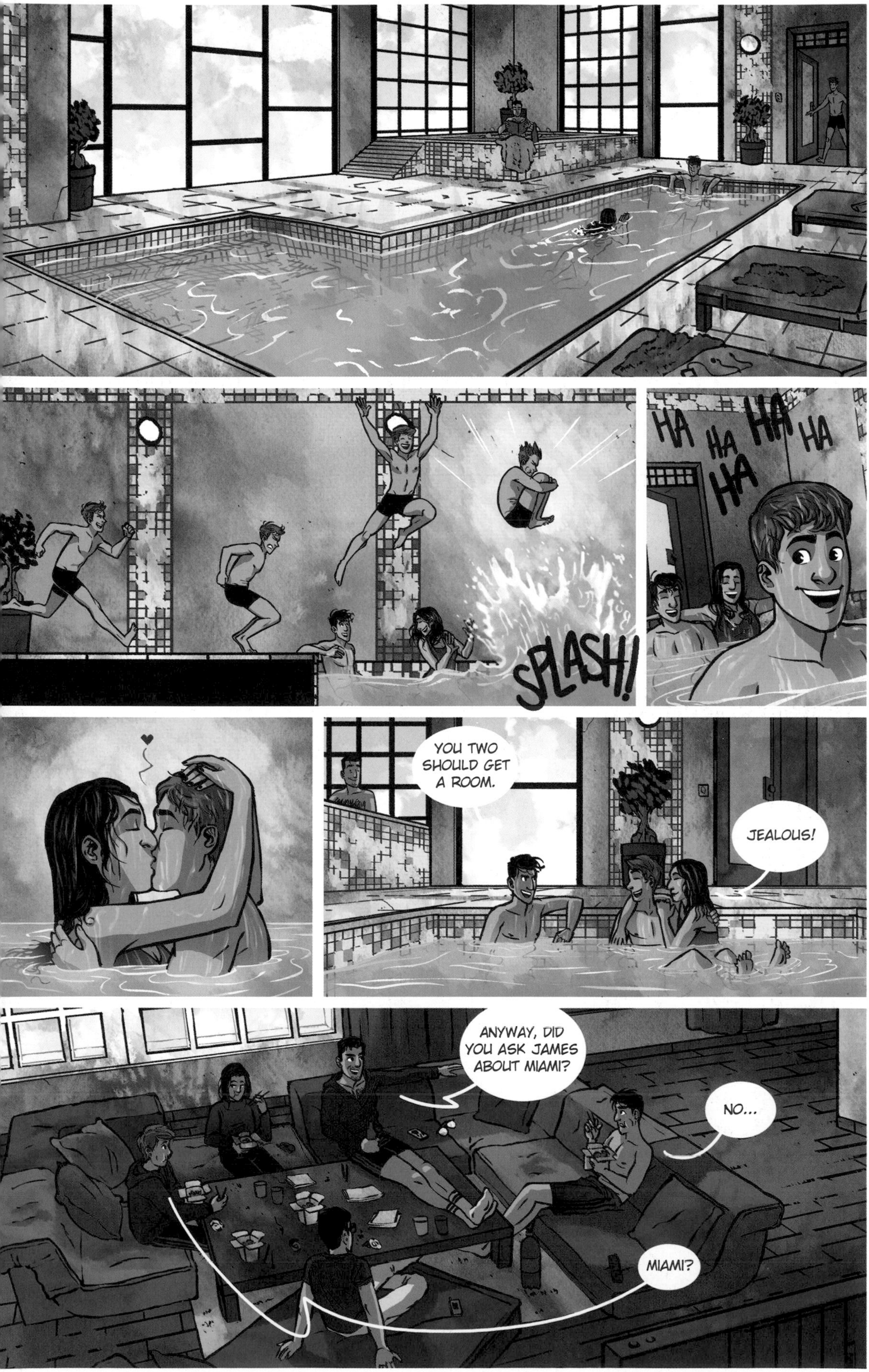
SPLASH!
HA HA HA HA HA HA
YOU TWO SHOULD GET A ROOM.
JEALOUS!
ANYWAY, DID YOU ASK JAMES ABOUT MIAMI?
NO...
MIAMI?

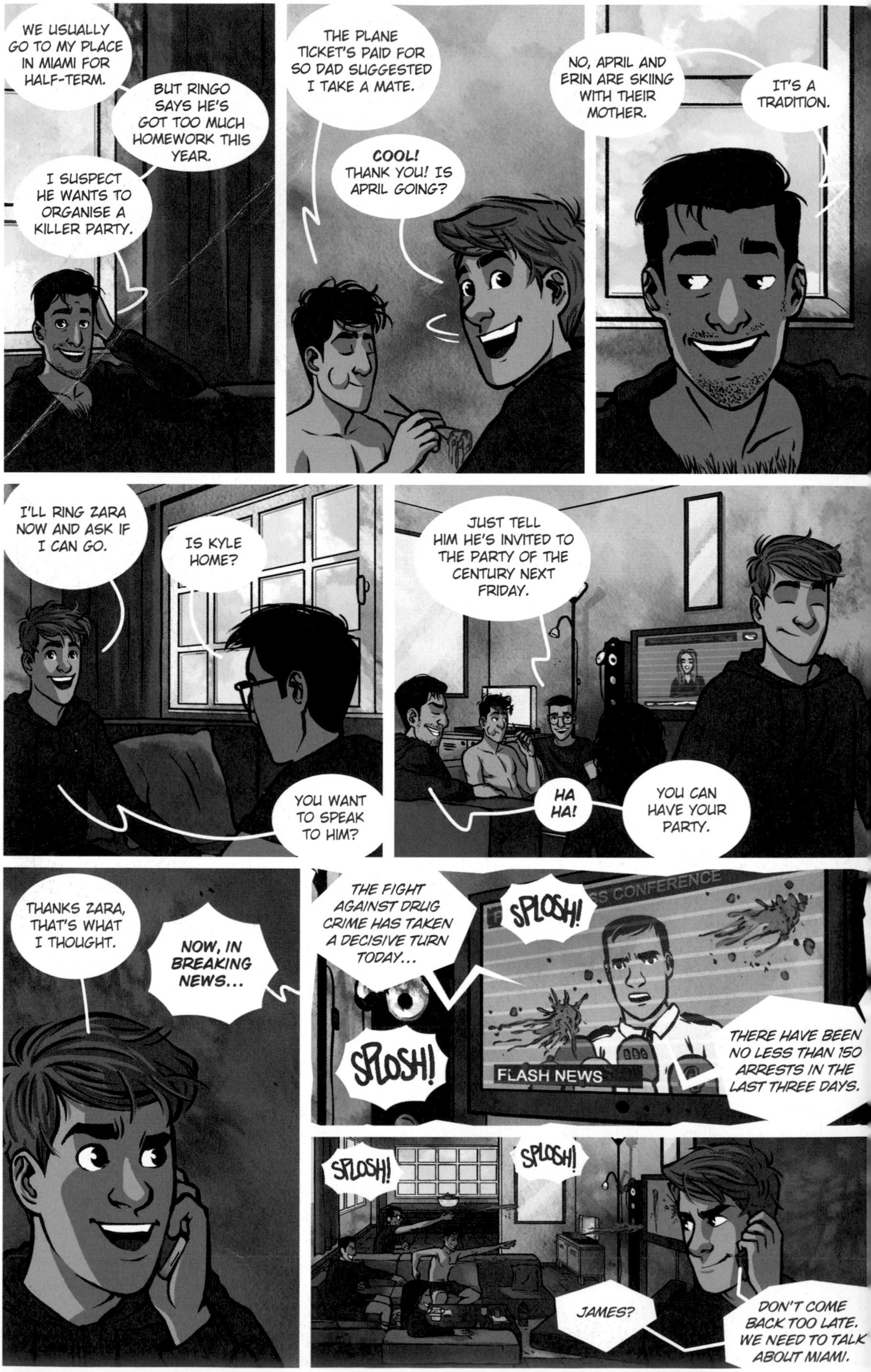
WE USUALLY GO TO MY PLACE IN MIAMI FOR HALF-TERM.
BUT RINGO SAYS HE'S GOT TOO MUCH HOMEWORK THIS YEAR.
I SUSPECT HE WANTS TO ORGANISE A KILLER PARTY.
THE PLANE TICKET'S PAID FOR SO DAD SUGGESTED I TAKE A MATE.
COOL! THANK YOU! IS APRIL GOING?
NO, APRIL AND ERIN ARE SKIING WITH THEIR MOTHER.
IT'S A TRADITION.
I'LL RING ZARA NOW AND ASK IF I CAN GO.
IS KYLE HOME?
YOU WANT TO SPEAK TO HIM?
JUST TELL HIM HE'S INVITED TO THE PARTY OF THE CENTURY NEXT FRIDAY.
HA HA!
YOU CAN HAVE YOUR PARTY.
THANKS ZARA, THAT'S WHAT I THOUGHT.
NOW, IN BREAKING NEWS...
THE FIGHT AGAINST DRUG CRIME HAS TAKEN A DECISIVE TURN TODAY...
SPLOSH!
SPLOSH!
FLASH NEWS
THERE HAVE BEEN NO LESS THAN 150 ARRESTS IN THE LAST THREE DAYS.
SPLOSH!
SPLOSH!
JAMES?
DON'T COME BACK TOO LATE. WE NEED TO TALK ABOUT MIAMI.

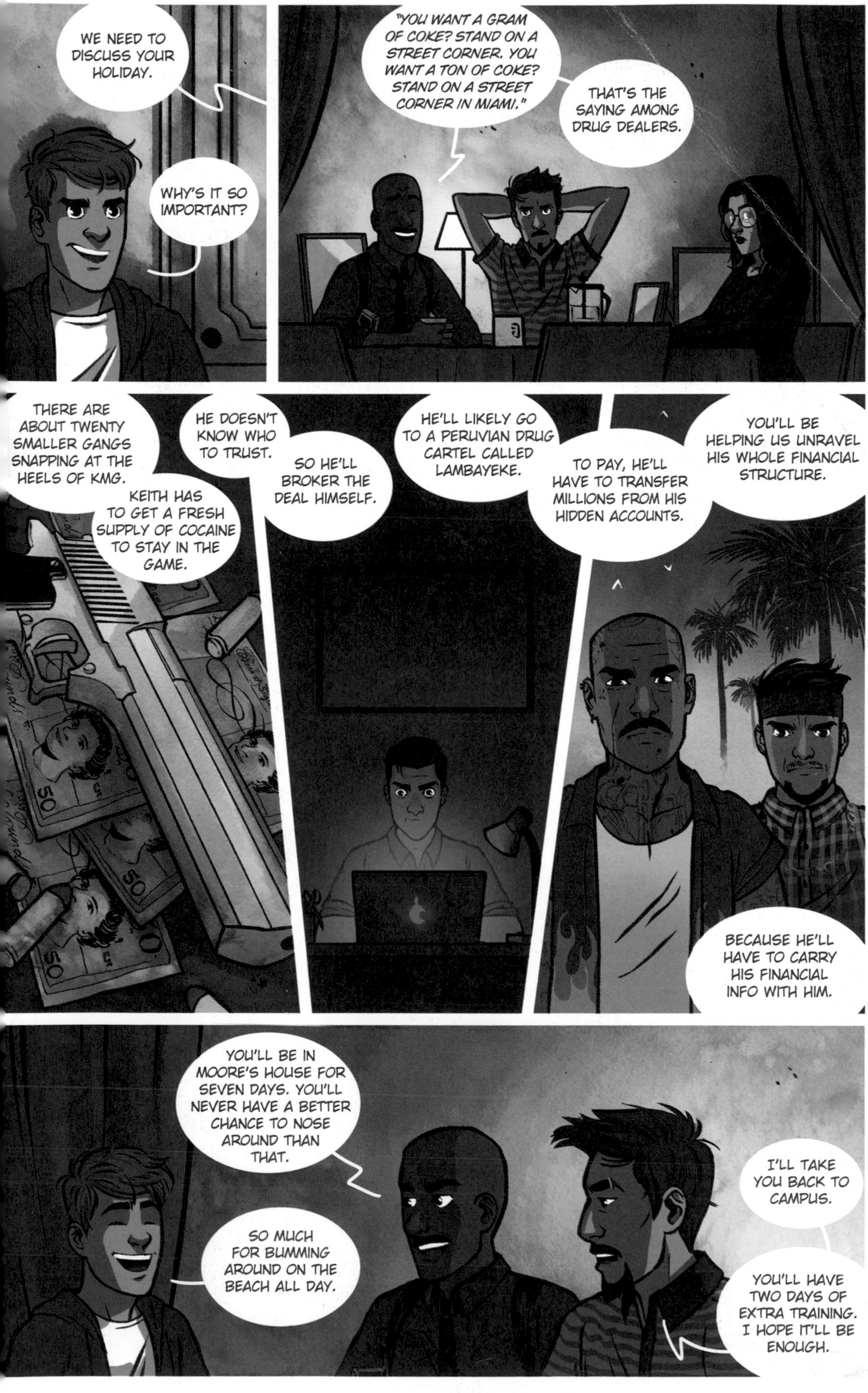

WE NEED TO DISCUSS YOUR HOLIDAY.
WHY'S IT SO IMPORTANT?
"YOU WANT A GRAM OF COKE? STAND ON A STREET CORNER. YOU WANT A TON OF COKE? STAND ON A STREET CORNER IN MIAMI."
THAT'S THE SAYING AMONG DRUG DEALERS.
THERE ARE ABOUT TWENTY SMALLER GANGS SNAPPING AT THE HEELS OF KMG.
KEITH HAS TO GET A FRESH SUPPLY OF COCAINE TO STAY IN THE GAME.
HE DOESN'T KNOW WHO TO TRUST.
SO HE'LL BROKER THE DEAL HIMSELF.
HE'LL LIKELY GO TO A PERUVIAN DRUG CARTEL CALLED LAMBAYEKE.
TO PAY, HE'LL HAVE TO TRANSFER MILLIONS FROM HIS HIDDEN ACCOUNTS.
YOU'LL BE HELPING US UNRAVEL HIS WHOLE FINANCIAL STRUCTURE.
BECAUSE HE'LL HAVE TO CARRY HIS FINANCIAL INFO WITH HIM.
YOU'LL BE IN MOORE'S HOUSE FOR SEVEN DAYS. YOU'LL NEVER HAVE A BETTER CHANCE TO NOSE AROUND THAN THAT.
SO MUCH FOR BUMMING AROUND ON THE BEACH ALL DAY.
I'LL TAKE YOU BACK TO CAMPUS.
YOU'LL HAVE TWO DAYS OF EXTRA TRAINING. I HOPE IT'LL BE ENOUGH.

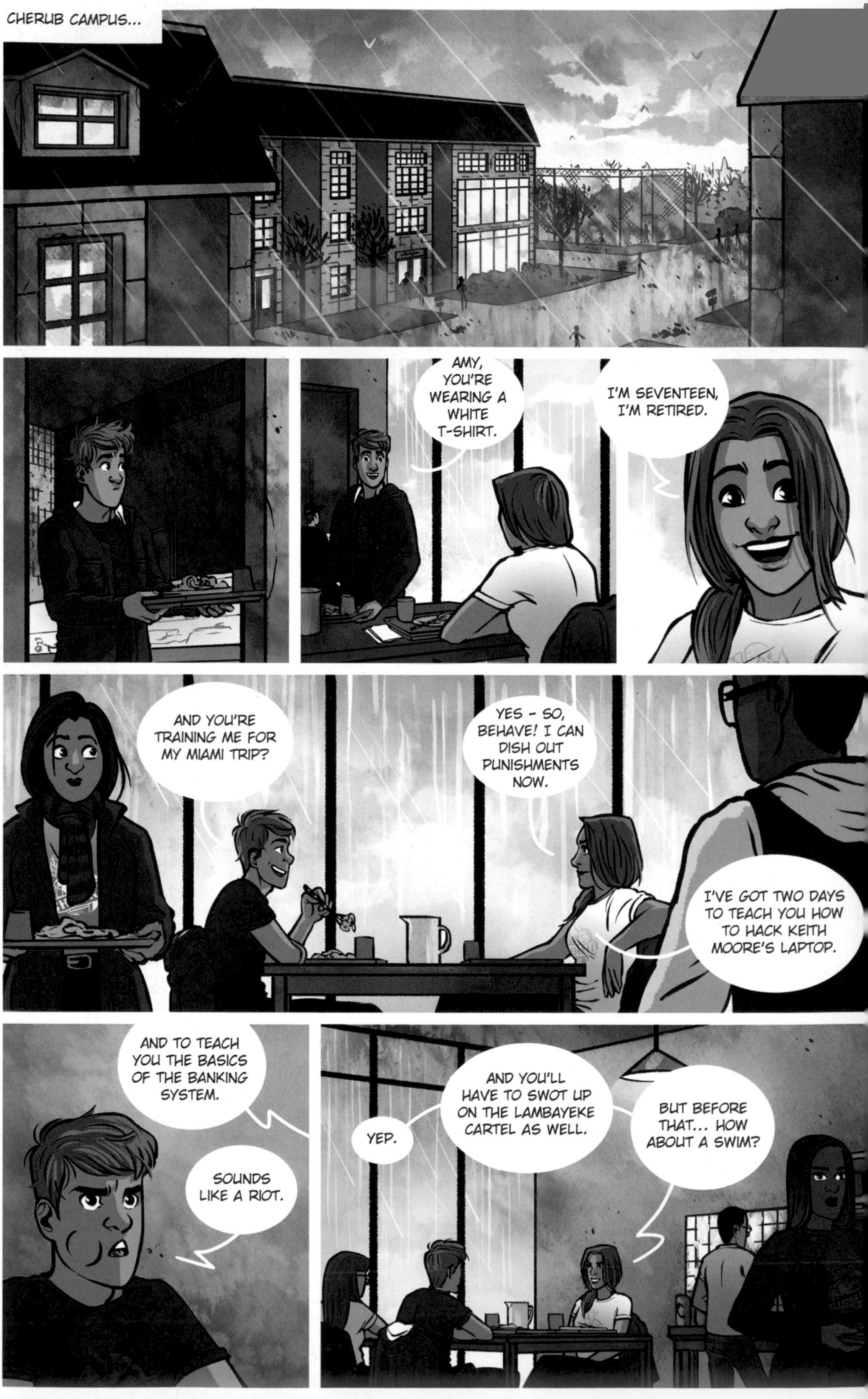
CHERUB CAMPUS...
AMY, YOU'RE WEARING A WHITE T-SHIRT.
I'M SEVENTEEN, I'M RETIRED.
AND YOU'RE TRAINING ME FOR MY MIAMI TRIP?
YES - SO, BEHAVE! I CAN DISH OUT PUNISHMENTS NOW.
I'VE GOT TWO DAYS TO TEACH YOU HOW TO HACK KEITH MOORE'S LAPTOP.
AND TO TEACH YOU THE BASICS OF THE BANKING SYSTEM.
SOUNDS LIKE A RIOT.
YEP.
AND YOU'LL HAVE TO SWOT UP ON THE LAMBAYEKE CARTEL AS WELL.
BUT BEFORE THAT... HOW ABOUT A SWIM?

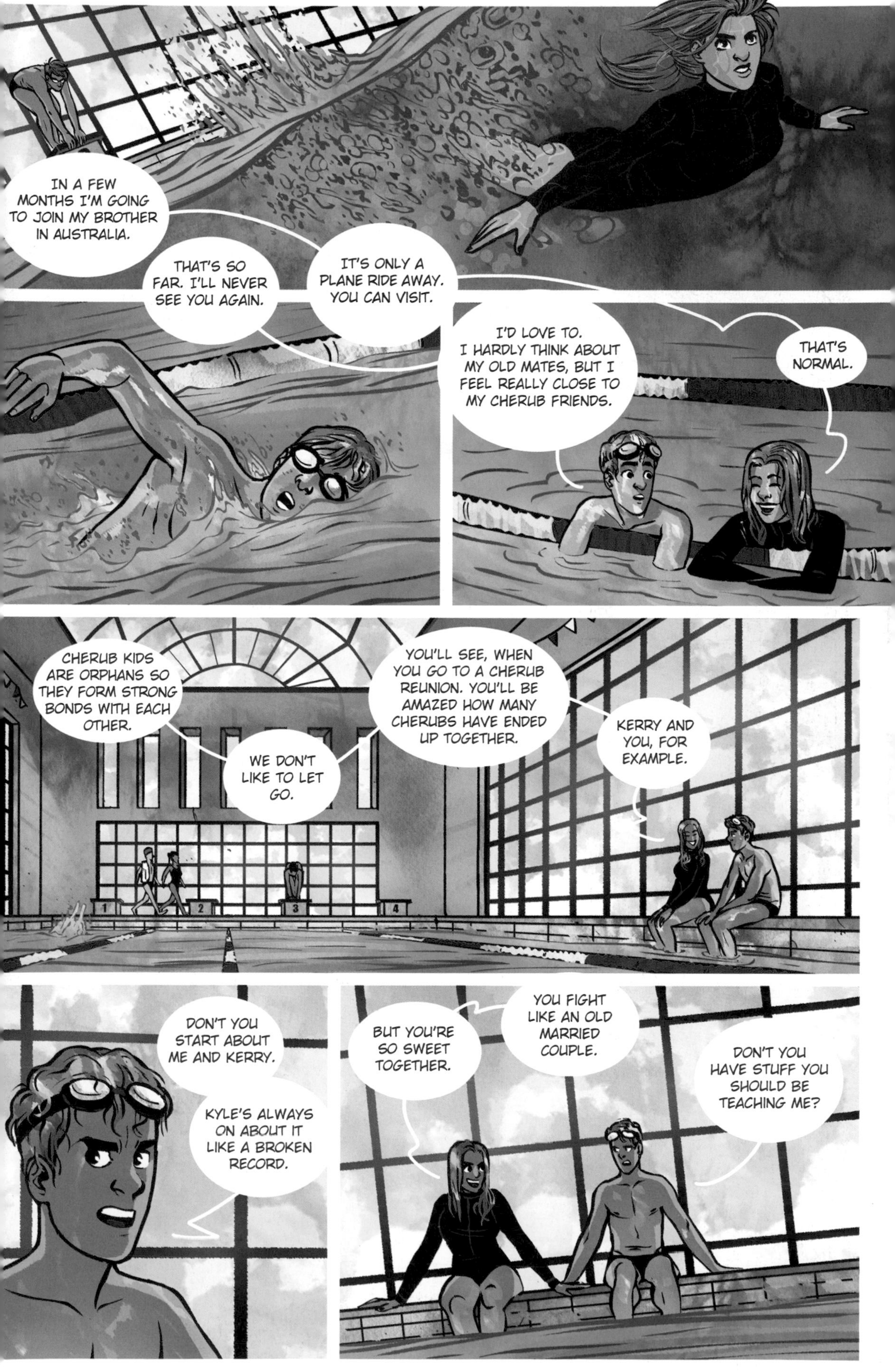
IN A FEW MONTHS I'M GOING TO JOIN MY BROTHER IN AUSTRALIA.
THAT'S SO FAR. I'LL NEVER SEE YOU AGAIN.
IT'S ONLY A PLANE RIDE AWAY. YOU CAN VISIT.
I'D LOVE TO. I HARDLY THINK ABOUT MY OLD MATES, BUT I FEEL REALLY CLOSE TO MY CHERUB FRIENDS.
THAT'S NORMAL.
CHERUB KIDS ARE ORPHANS SO THEY FORM STRONG BONDS WITH EACH OTHER.
WE DON'T LIKE TO LET GO.
YOU'LL SEE, WHEN YOU GO TO A CHERUB REUNION. YOU'LL BE AMAZED HOW MANY CHERUBS HAVE ENDED UP TOGETHER.
KERRY AND YOU, FOR EXAMPLE.
1
2
3
4
DON'T YOU START ABOUT ME AND KERRY.
KYLE'S ALWAYS ON ABOUT IT LIKE A BROKEN RECORD.
BUT YOU'RE SO SWEET TOGETHER.
YOU FIGHT LIKE AN OLD MARRIED COUPLE.
DON'T YOU HAVE STUFF YOU SHOULD BE TEACHING ME?

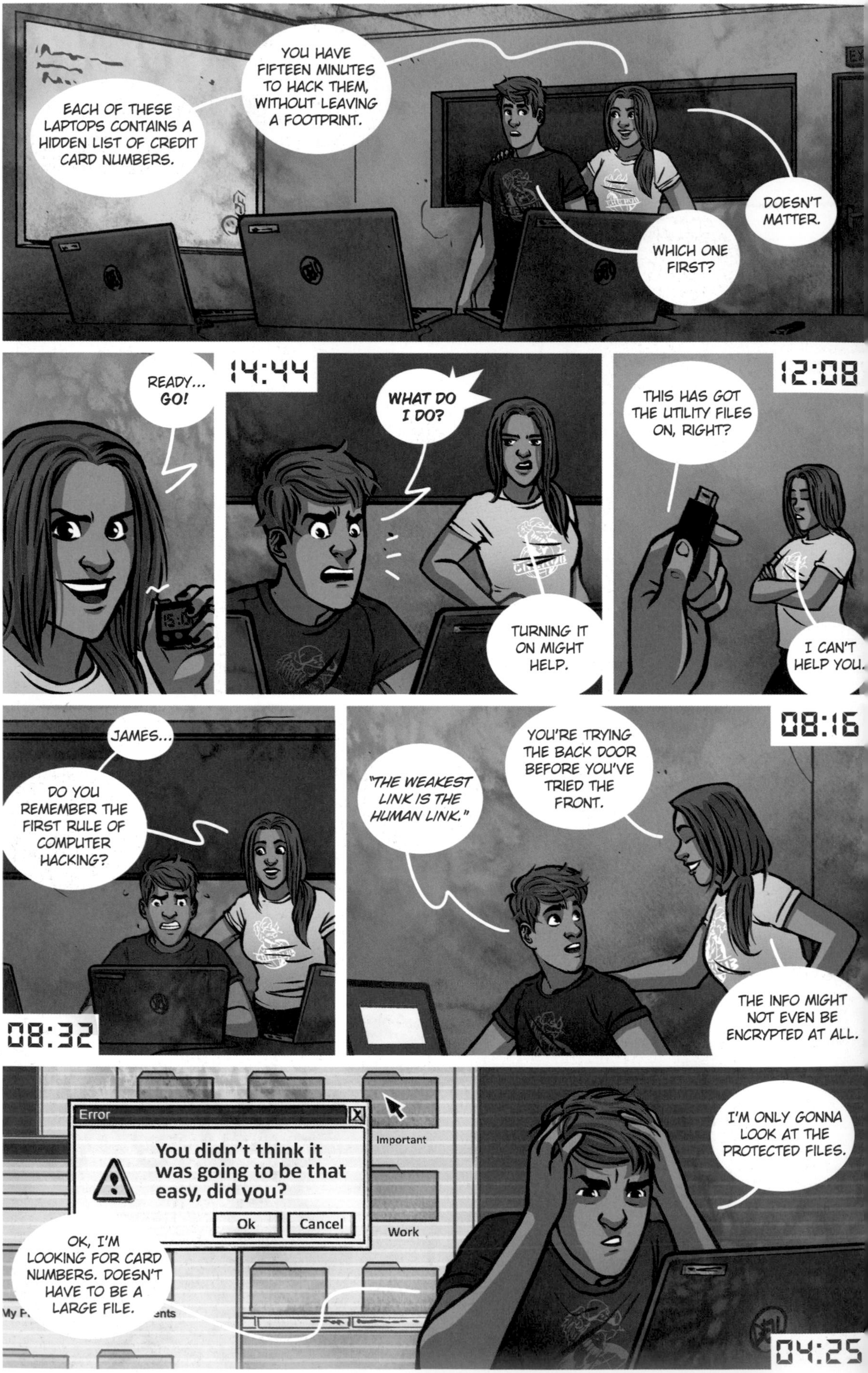
EACH OF THESE LAPTOPS CONTAINS A HIDDEN LIST OF CREDIT CARD NUMBERS.
YOU HAVE FIFTEEN MINUTES TO HACK THEM, WITHOUT LEAVING A FOOTPRINT.
WHICH ONE FIRST?
DOESN'T MATTER.
READY... GO!
14:44
WHAT DO I DO?
TURNING IT ON MIGHT HELP.
12:08
THIS HAS GOT THE UTILITY FILES ON, RIGHT?
I CAN'T HELP YOU.
JAMES...
DO YOU REMEMBER THE FIRST RULE OF COMPUTER HACKING?
08:32
08:16
"THE WEAKEST LINK IS THE HUMAN LINK."
YOU'RE TRYING THE BACK DOOR BEFORE YOU'VE TRIED THE FRONT.
THE INFO MIGHT NOT EVEN BE ENCRYPTED AT ALL.
Error
You didn't think it was going to be that easy, did you?
Ok
Cancel
Important
Work
OK, I'M LOOKING FOR CARD NUMBERS. DOESN'T HAVE TO BE A LARGE FILE.
I'M ONLY GONNA LOOK AT THE PROTECTED FILES.
04:25

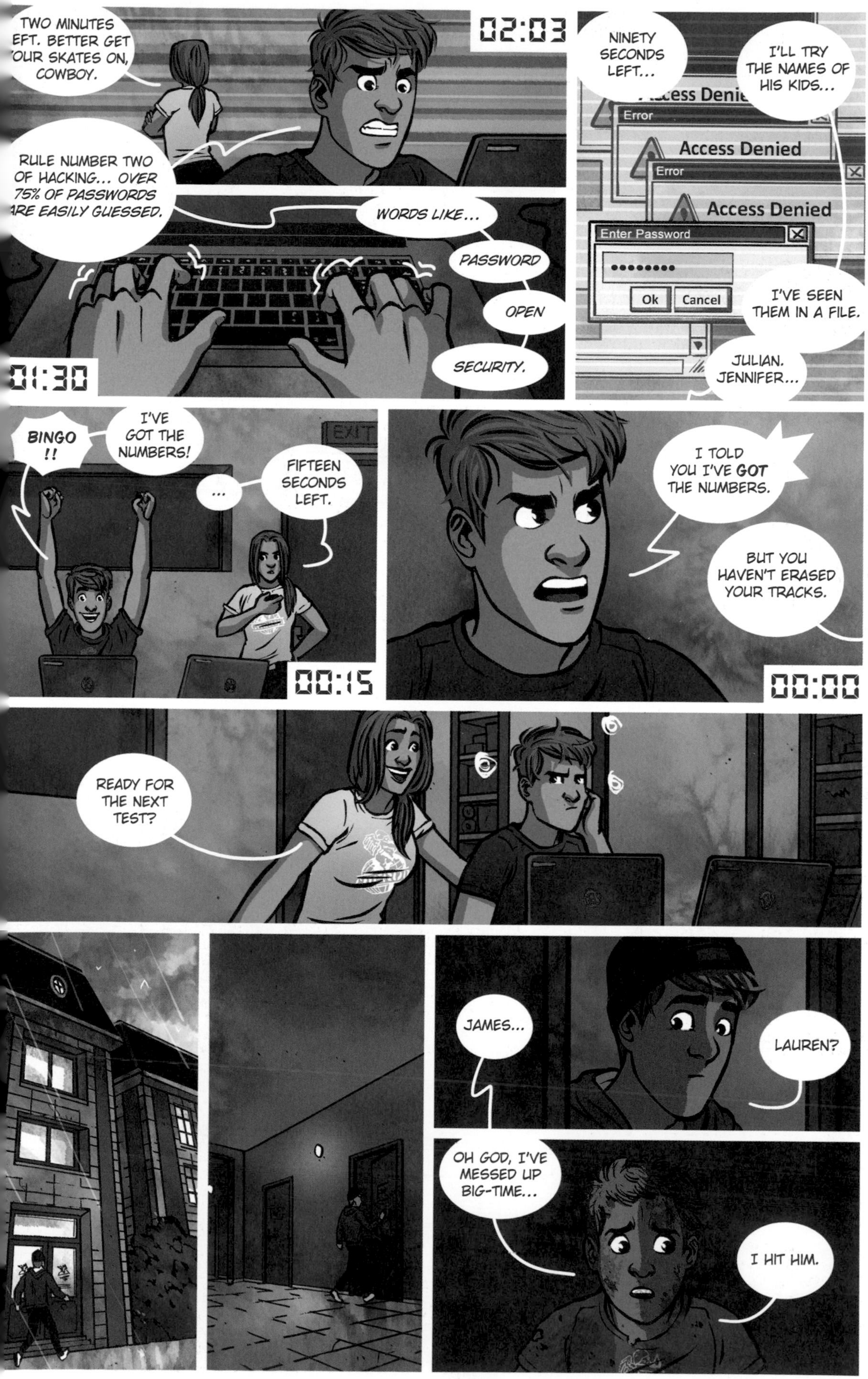

TWO MINUTES LEFT. BETTER GET YOUR SKATES ON, COWBOY.
02:03
RULE NUMBER TWO OF HACKING... OVER 75% OF PASSWORDS ARE EASILY GUESSED.
WORDS LIKE...
PASSWORD
OPEN
SECURITY.
01:30
NINETY SECONDS LEFT...
I'LL TRY THE NAMES OF HIS KIDS...
Access Denied
Error
Access Denied
Error
Access Denied
Enter Password
Ok
Cancel
I'VE SEEN THEM IN A FILE.
JULIAN. JENNIFER...
BINGO !!
I'VE GOT THE NUMBERS!
EXIT
...
FIFTEEN SECONDS LEFT.
00:15
I TOLD YOU I'VE **GOT** THE NUMBERS.
BUT YOU HAVEN'T ERASED YOUR TRACKS.
00:00
READY FOR THE NEXT TEST?
JAMES...
LAUREN?
OH GOD, I'VE MESSED UP BIG-TIME...
I HIT HIM.

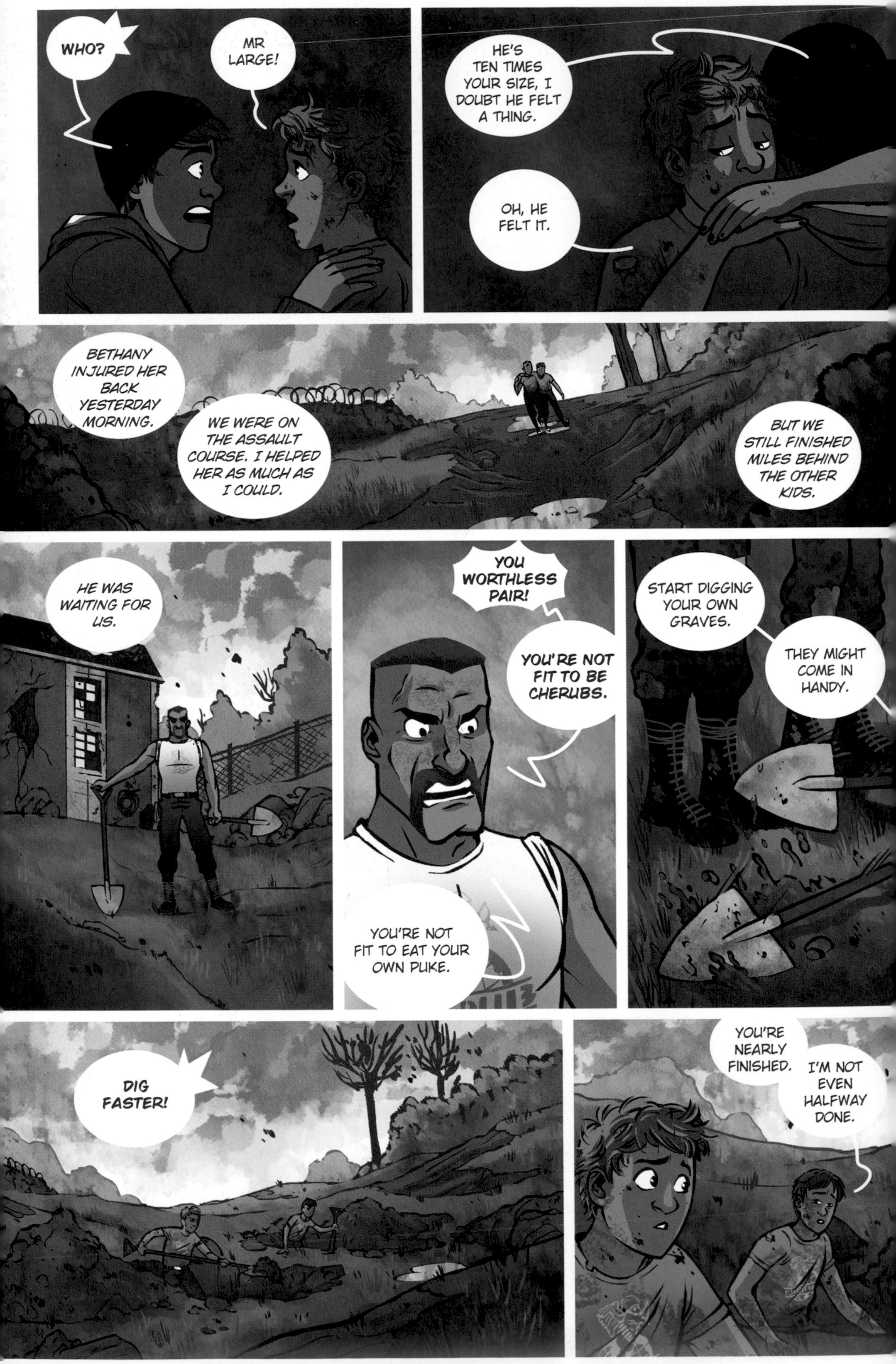
WHO?
MR LARGE!
HE'S TEN TIMES YOUR SIZE, I DOUBT HE FELT A THING.
OH, HE FELT IT.
BETHANY INJURED HER BACK YESTERDAY MORNING.
WE WERE ON THE ASSAULT COURSE. I HELPED HER AS MUCH AS I COULD.
BUT WE STILL FINISHED MILES BEHIND THE OTHER KIDS.
HE WAS WAITING FOR US.
YOU WORTHLESS PAIR!
YOU'RE NOT FIT TO BE CHERUBS.
YOU'RE NOT FIT TO EAT YOUR OWN PUKE.
START DIGGING YOUR OWN GRAVES.
THEY MIGHT COME IN HANDY.
DIG FASTER!
YOU'RE NEARLY FINISHED.
I'M NOT EVEN HALFWAY DONE.

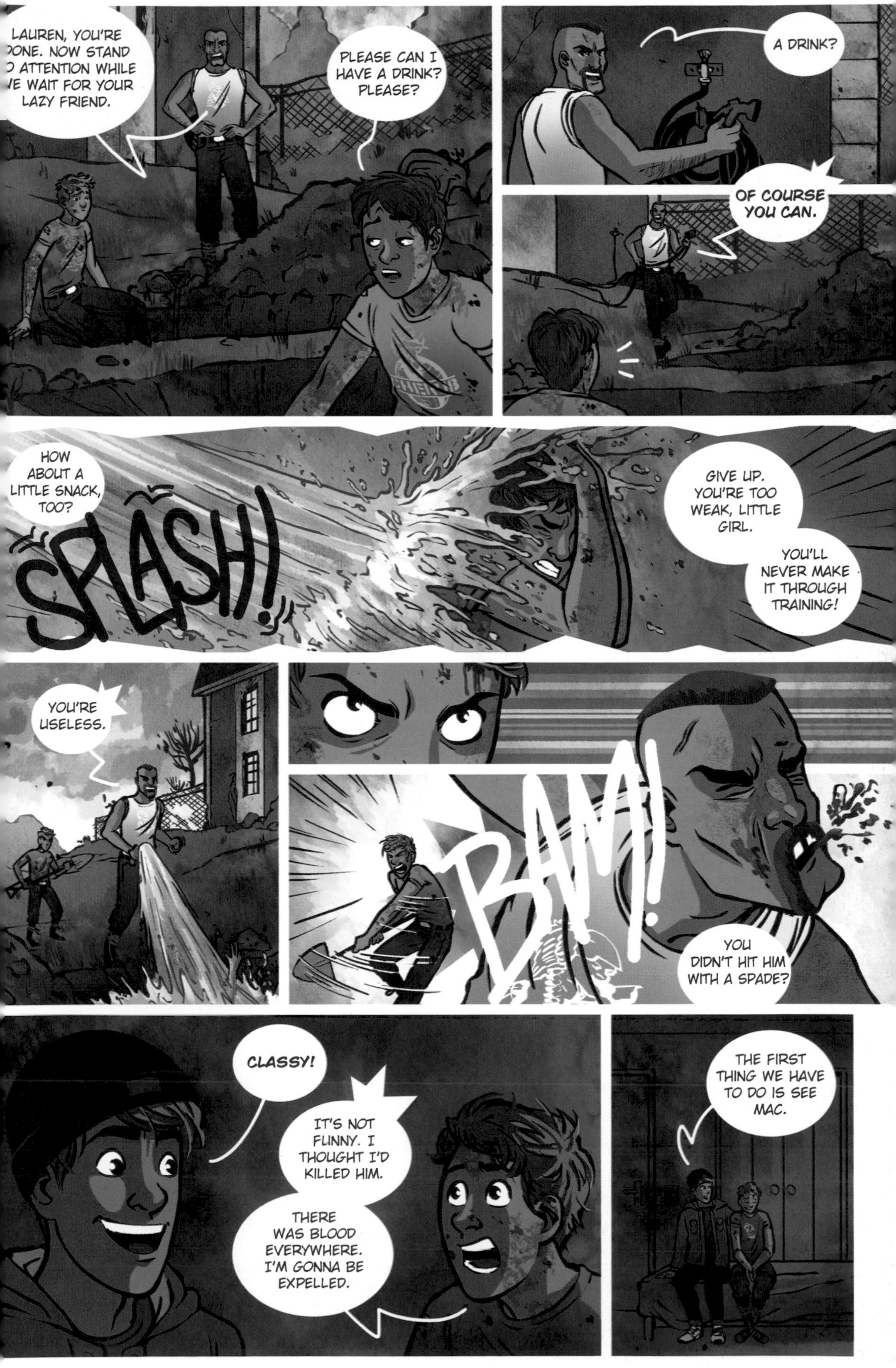
LAUREN, YOU'RE DONE. NOW STAND TO ATTENTION WHILE WE WAIT FOR YOUR LAZY FRIEND.
PLEASE CAN I HAVE A DRINK? PLEASE?
A DRINK?
OF COURSE YOU CAN.
HOW ABOUT A LITTLE SNACK, TOO?
SPLASH!
GIVE UP. YOU'RE TOO WEAK, LITTLE GIRL.
YOU'LL NEVER MAKE IT THROUGH TRAINING!
YOU'RE USELESS.
BAM!
YOU DIDN'T HIT HIM WITH A SPADE?
CLASSY!
IT'S NOT FUNNY. I THOUGHT I'D KILLED HIM.
THERE WAS BLOOD EVERYWHERE. I'M GONNA BE EXPELLED.
THE FIRST THING WE HAVE TO DO IS SEE MAC.

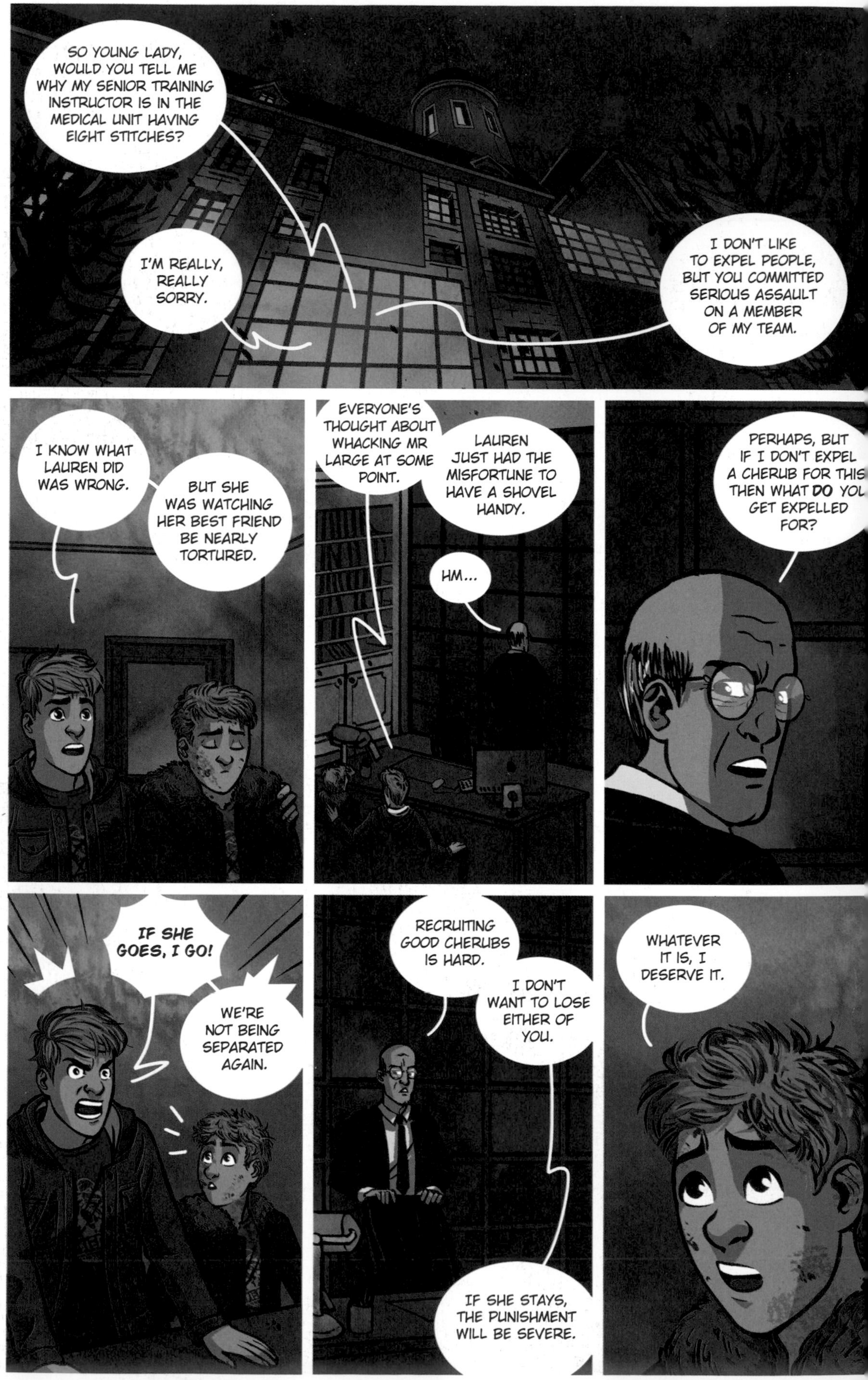
SO YOUNG LADY, WOULD YOU TELL ME WHY MY SENIOR TRAINING INSTRUCTOR IS IN THE MEDICAL UNIT HAVING EIGHT STITCHES?
I'M REALLY, REALLY SORRY.
I DON'T LIKE TO EXPEL PEOPLE, BUT YOU COMMITTED SERIOUS ASSAULT ON A MEMBER OF MY TEAM.
I KNOW WHAT LAUREN DID WAS WRONG.
BUT SHE WAS WATCHING HER BEST FRIEND BE NEARLY TORTURED.
EVERYONE'S THOUGHT ABOUT WHACKING MR LARGE AT SOME POINT.
LAUREN JUST HAD THE MISFORTUNE TO HAVE A SHOVEL HANDY.
HM...
PERHAPS, BUT IF I DON'T EXPEL A CHERUB FOR THIS THEN WHAT DO YOU GET EXPELLED FOR?
IF SHE GOES, I GO!
WE'RE NOT BEING SEPARATED AGAIN.
RECRUITING GOOD CHERUBS IS HARD.
I DON'T WANT TO LOSE EITHER OF YOU.
IF SHE STAYS, THE PUNISHMENT WILL BE SEVERE.
WHATEVER IT IS, I DESERVE IT.

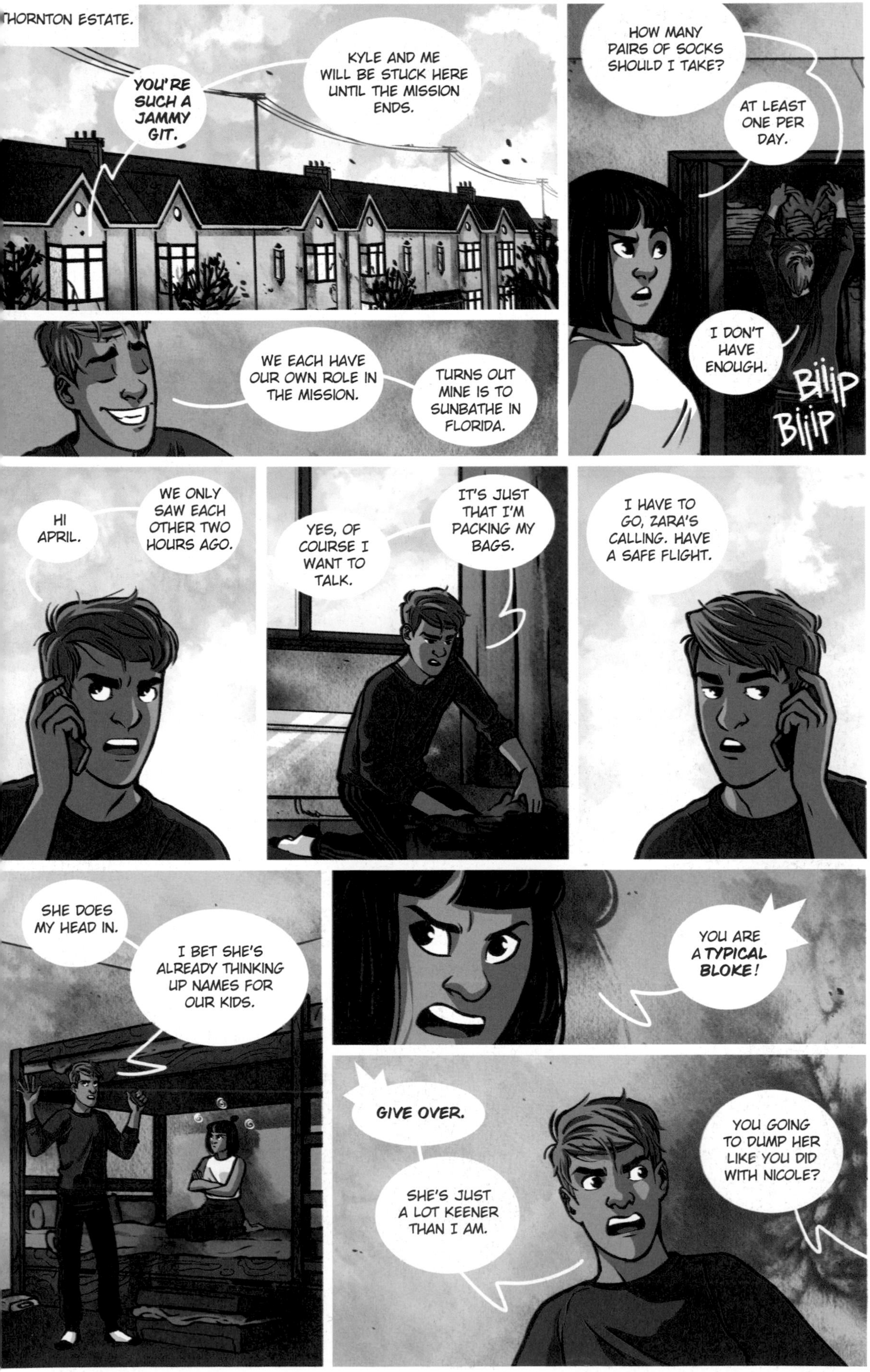
THORNTON ESTATE.
KYLE AND ME WILL BE STUCK HERE UNTIL THE MISSION ENDS.
YOU'RE SUCH A JAMMY GIT.
HOW MANY PAIRS OF SOCKS SHOULD I TAKE?
AT LEAST ONE PER DAY.
WE EACH HAVE OUR OWN ROLE IN THE MISSION.
TURNS OUT MINE IS TO SUNBATHE IN FLORIDA.
I DON'T HAVE ENOUGH.
BIIIP BIIIP
HI APRIL.
WE ONLY SAW EACH OTHER TWO HOURS AGO.
YES, OF COURSE I WANT TO TALK.
IT'S JUST THAT I'M PACKING MY BAGS.
I HAVE TO GO, ZARA'S CALLING. HAVE A SAFE FLIGHT.
SHE DOES MY HEAD IN.
I BET SHE'S ALREADY THINKING UP NAMES FOR OUR KIDS.
YOU ARE A **TYPICAL BLOKE**!
GIVE OVER.
SHE'S JUST A LOT KEENER THAN I AM.
YOU GOING TO DUMP HER LIKE YOU DID WITH NICOLE?

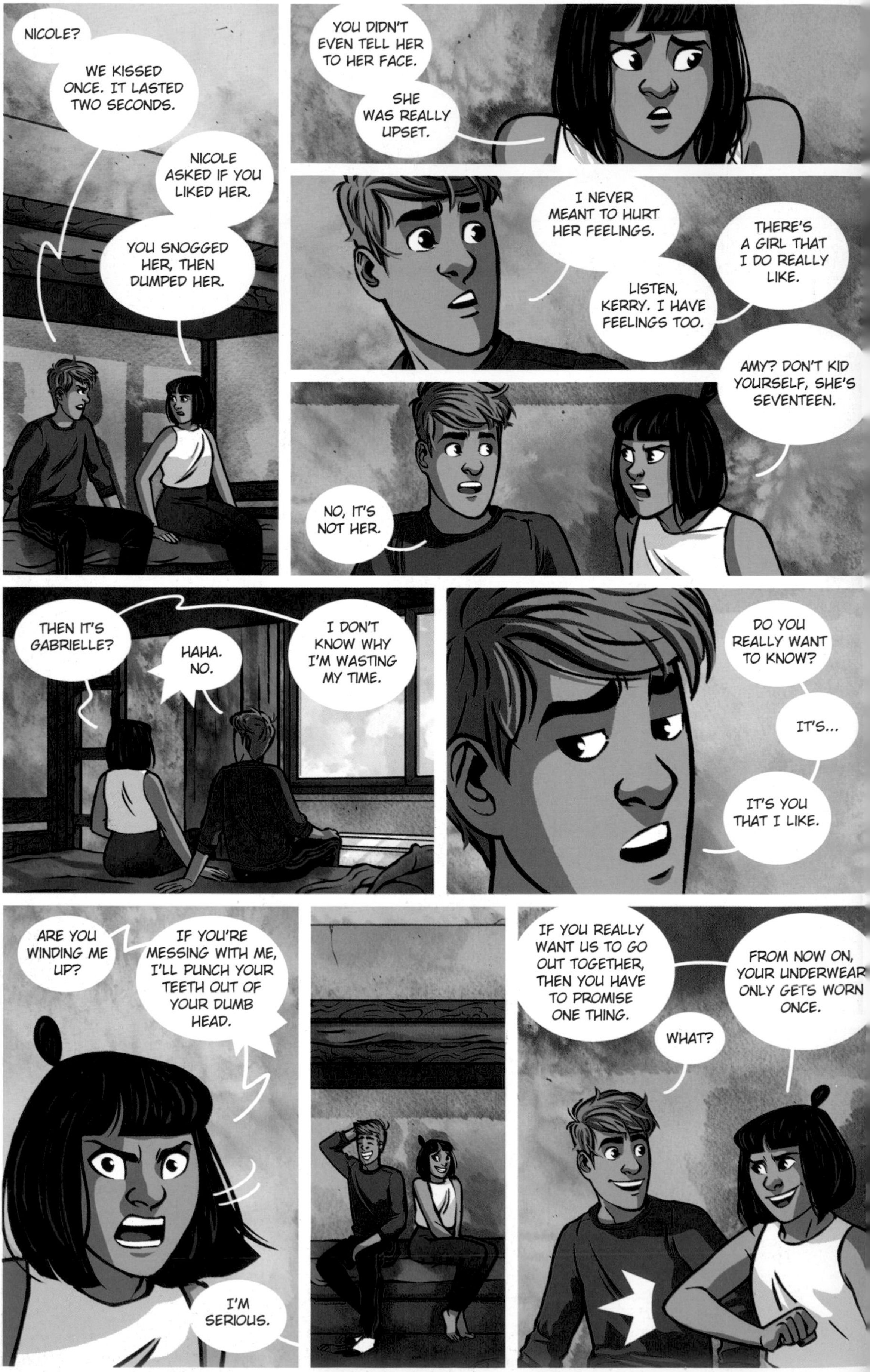
NICOLE?
WE KISSED ONCE. IT LASTED TWO SECONDS.
NICOLE ASKED IF YOU LIKED HER.
YOU SNOGGED HER, THEN DUMPED HER.
YOU DIDN'T EVEN TELL HER TO HER FACE.
SHE WAS REALLY UPSET.
I NEVER MEANT TO HURT HER FEELINGS.
LISTEN, KERRY. I HAVE FEELINGS TOO.
THERE'S A GIRL THAT I DO REALLY LIKE.
AMY? DON'T KID YOURSELF, SHE'S SEVENTEEN.
NO, IT'S NOT HER.
THEN IT'S GABRIELLE?
HAHA. NO.
I DON'T KNOW WHY I'M WASTING MY TIME.
DO YOU REALLY WANT TO KNOW?
IT'S...
IT'S YOU THAT I LIKE.
ARE YOU WINDING ME UP?
IF YOU'RE MESSING WITH ME, I'LL PUNCH YOUR TEETH OUT OF YOUR DUMB HEAD.
I'M SERIOUS.
IF YOU REALLY WANT US TO GO OUT TOGETHER, THEN YOU HAVE TO PROMISE ONE THING.
WHAT?
FROM NOW ON, YOUR UNDERWEAR ONLY GETS WORN ONCE.

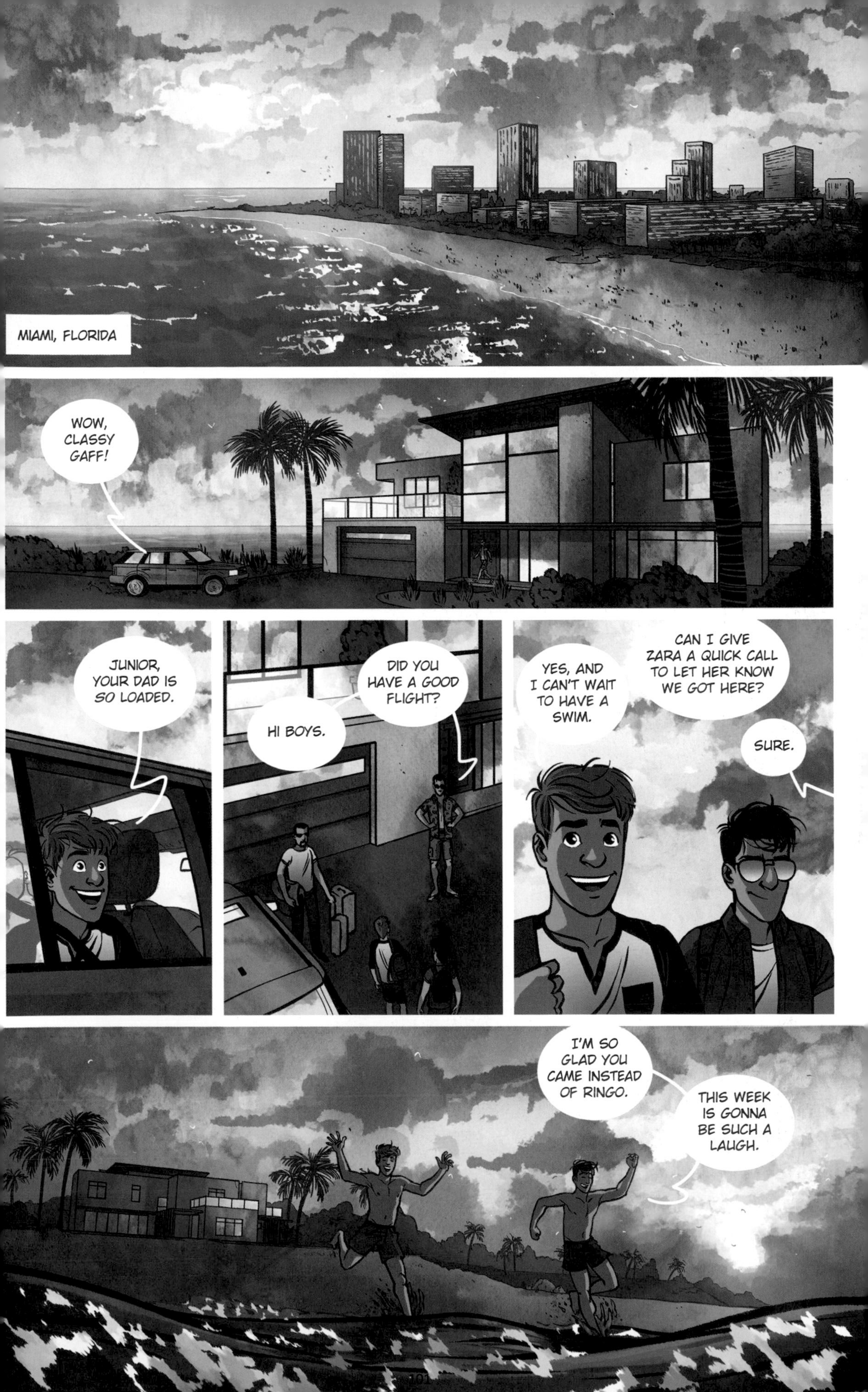

MIAMI, FLORIDA
WOW, CLASSY GAFF!
JUNIOR, YOUR DAD IS SO LOADED.
HI BOYS.
DID YOU HAVE A GOOD FLIGHT?
YES, AND I CAN'T WAIT TO HAVE A SWIM.
CAN I GIVE ZARA A QUICK CALL TO LET HER KNOW WE GOT HERE?
SURE.
I'M SO GLAD YOU CAME INSTEAD OF RINGO.
THIS WEEK IS GONNA BE SUCH A LAUGH.

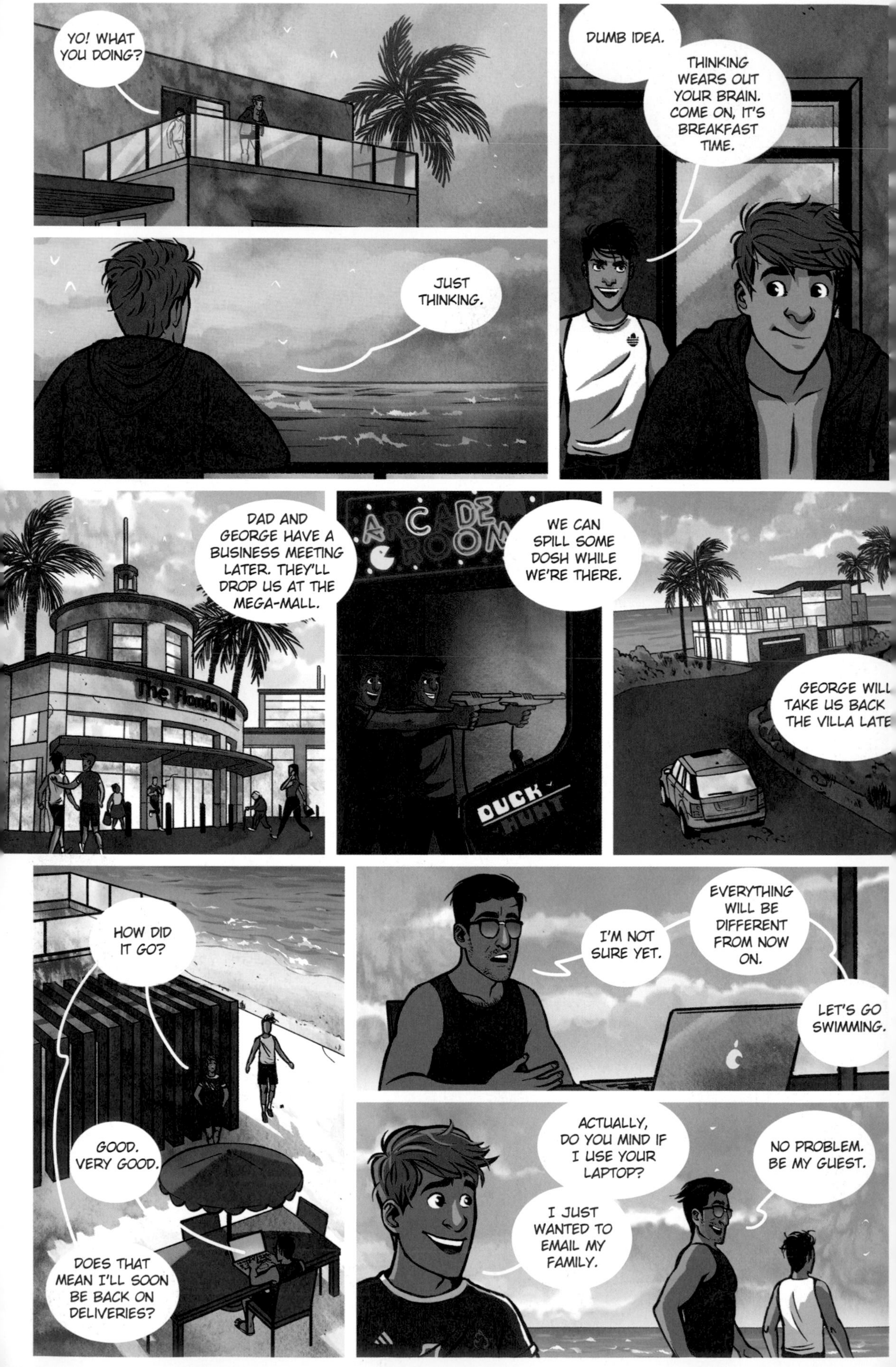
YO! WHAT YOU DOING?
JUST THINKING.
DUMB IDEA.
THINKING WEARS OUT YOUR BRAIN. COME ON, IT'S BREAKFAST TIME.
DAD AND GEORGE HAVE A BUSINESS MEETING LATER. THEY'LL DROP US AT THE MEGA-MALL.
The Florida Mall
ARCADE ROOM
WE CAN SPILL SOME DOSH WHILE WE'RE THERE.
DUCK HUNT
GEORGE WILL TAKE US BACK THE VILLA LATE
HOW DID IT GO?
GOOD. VERY GOOD.
DOES THAT MEAN I'LL SOON BE BACK ON DELIVERIES?
I'M NOT SURE YET.
EVERYTHING WILL BE DIFFERENT FROM NOW ON.
LET'S GO SWIMMING.
ACTUALLY, DO YOU MIND IF I USE YOUR LAPTOP?
I JUST WANTED TO EMAIL MY FAMILY.
NO PROBLEM. BE MY GUEST.

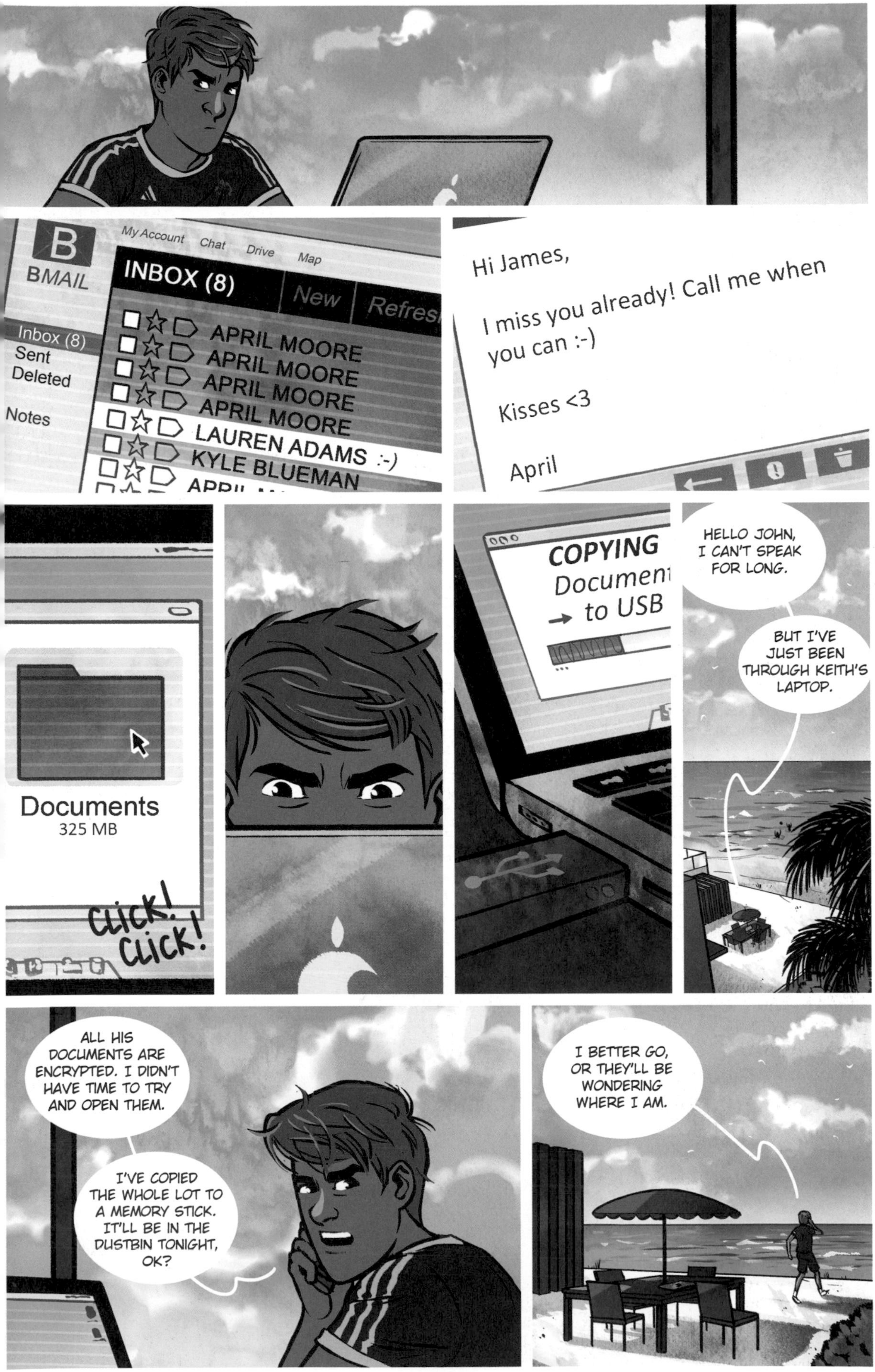
My Account
Chat
Drive
Map
BMAIL
INBOX (8)
New
Inbox (8)
Sent
Deleted
Notes
APRIL MOORE
APRIL MOORE
APRIL MOORE
APRIL MOORE
LAUREN ADAMS :-)
KYLE BLUEMAN
Hi James,
I miss you already! Call me when you can :-)
Kisses <3
April
Documents
325 MB
CLICK! CLICK!
COPYING
to USB
HELLO JOHN, I CAN'T SPEAK FOR LONG.
BUT I'VE JUST BEEN THROUGH KEITH'S LAPTOP.
ALL HIS DOCUMENTS ARE ENCRYPTED. I DIDN'T HAVE TIME TO TRY AND OPEN THEM.
I'VE COPIED THE WHOLE LOT TO A MEMORY STICK. IT'LL BE IN THE DUSTBIN TONIGHT, OK?
I BETTER GO, OR THEY'LL BE WONDERING WHERE I AM.

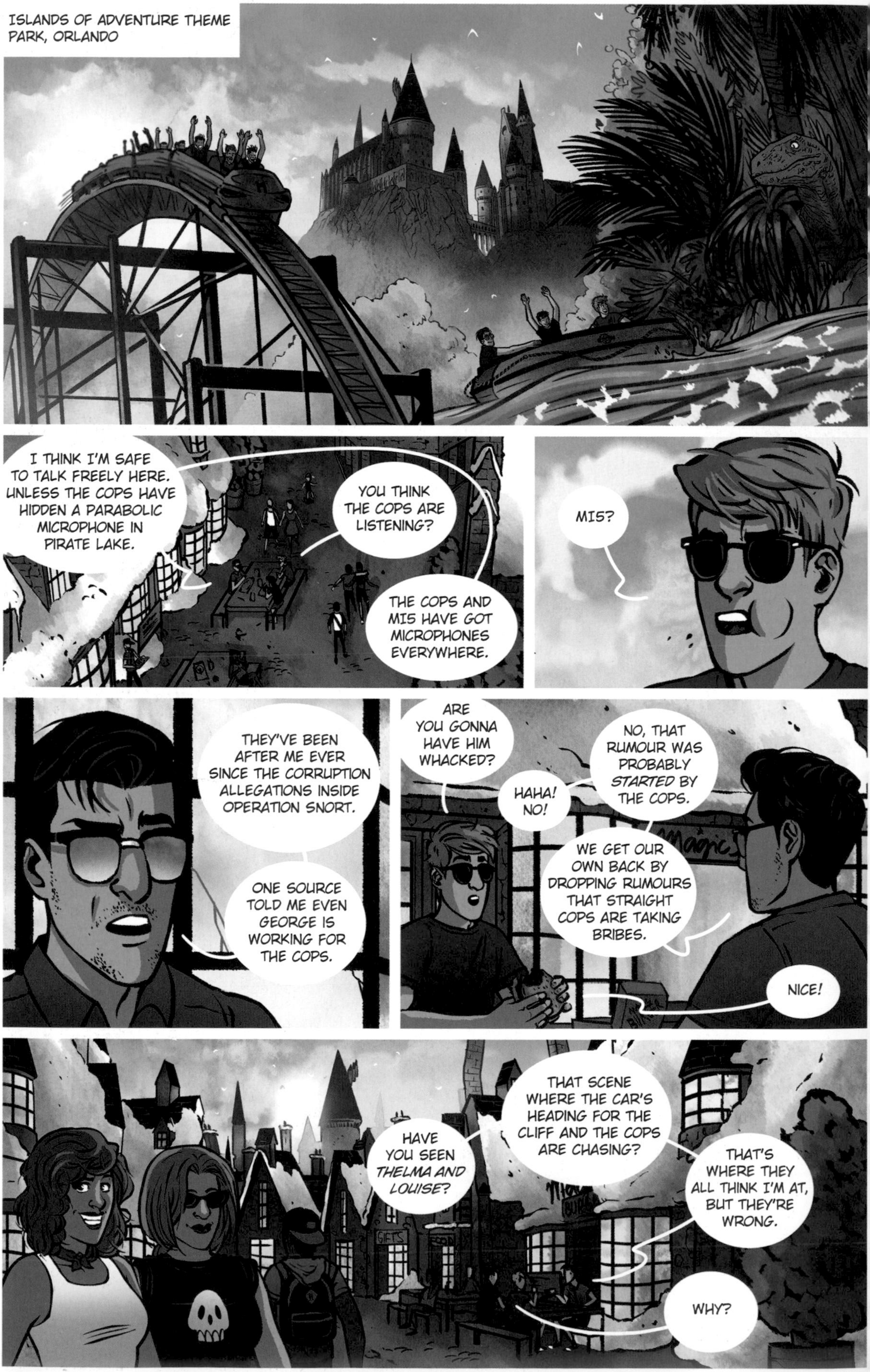
ISLANDS OF ADVENTURE THEME PARK, ORLANDO
I THINK I'M SAFE TO TALK FREELY HERE. UNLESS THE COPS HAVE HIDDEN A PARABOLIC MICROPHONE IN PIRATE LAKE.
YOU THINK THE COPS ARE LISTENING?
THE COPS AND MI5 HAVE GOT MICROPHONES EVERYWHERE.
MI5?
THEY'VE BEEN AFTER ME EVER SINCE THE CORRUPTION ALLEGATIONS INSIDE OPERATION SNORT.
ONE SOURCE TOLD ME EVEN GEORGE IS WORKING FOR THE COPS.
ARE YOU GONNA HAVE HIM WHACKED?
HAHA! NO!
NO, THAT RUMOUR WAS PROBABLY *STARTED* BY THE COPS.
WE GET OUR OWN BACK BY DROPPING RUMOURS THAT STRAIGHT COPS ARE TAKING BRIBES.
NICE!
HAVE YOU SEEN *THELMA AND LOUISE*?
THAT SCENE WHERE THE CAR'S HEADING FOR THE CLIFF AND THE COPS ARE CHASING?
THAT'S WHERE THEY ALL THINK I'M AT, BUT THEY'RE WRONG.
WHY?

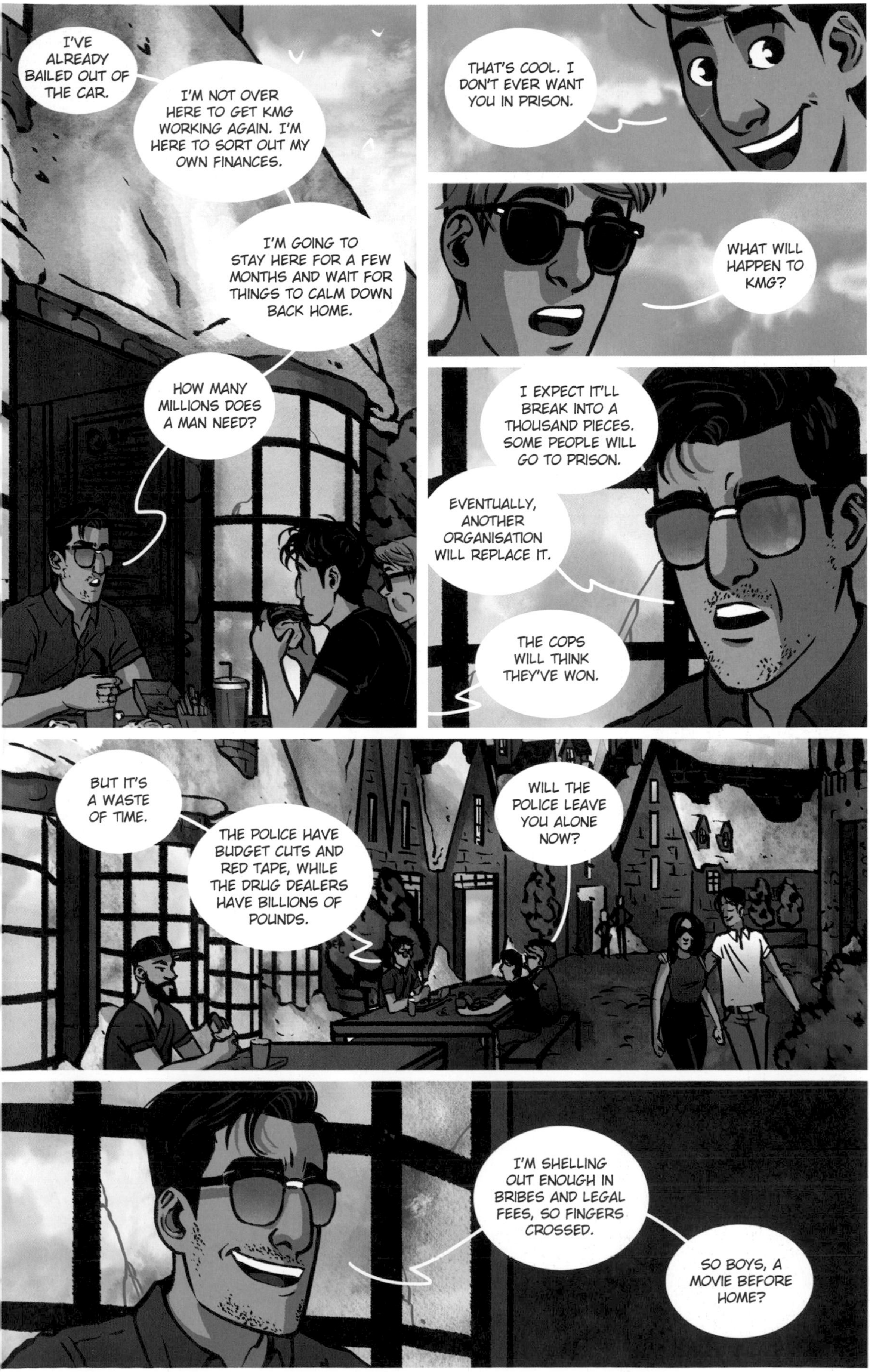
I'VE ALREADY BAILED OUT OF THE CAR.
I'M NOT OVER HERE TO GET KMG WORKING AGAIN. I'M HERE TO SORT OUT MY OWN FINANCES.
I'M GOING TO STAY HERE FOR A FEW MONTHS AND WAIT FOR THINGS TO CALM DOWN BACK HOME.
HOW MANY MILLIONS DOES A MAN NEED?
THAT'S COOL. I DON'T EVER WANT YOU IN PRISON.
WHAT WILL HAPPEN TO KMG?
I EXPECT IT'LL BREAK INTO A THOUSAND PIECES. SOME PEOPLE WILL GO TO PRISON.
EVENTUALLY, ANOTHER ORGANISATION WILL REPLACE IT.
THE COPS WILL THINK THEY'VE WON.
BUT IT'S A WASTE OF TIME.
THE POLICE HAVE BUDGET CUTS AND RED TAPE, WHILE THE DRUG DEALERS HAVE BILLIONS OF POUNDS.
WILL THE POLICE LEAVE YOU ALONE NOW?
I'M SHELLING OUT ENOUGH IN BRIBES AND LEGAL FEES, SO FINGERS CROSSED.
SO BOYS, A MOVIE BEFORE HOME?

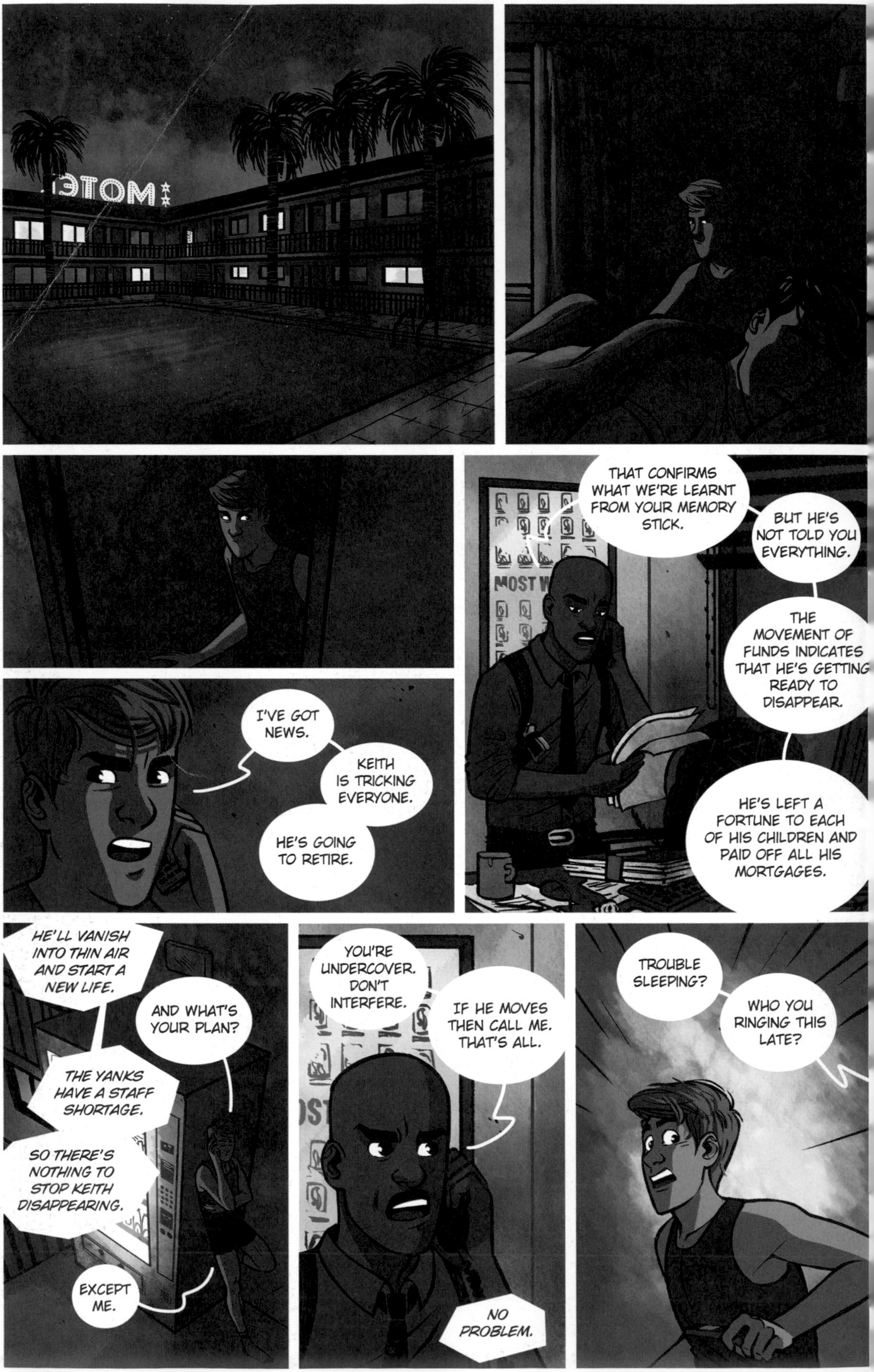
I'VE GOT NEWS.
KEITH IS TRICKING EVERYONE.
HE'S GOING TO RETIRE.
THAT CONFIRMS WHAT WE'RE LEARNT FROM YOUR MEMORY STICK.
BUT HE'S NOT TOLD YOU EVERYTHING.
THE MOVEMENT OF FUNDS INDICATES THAT HE'S GETTING READY TO DISAPPEAR.
HE'S LEFT A FORTUNE TO EACH OF HIS CHILDREN AND PAID OFF ALL HIS MORTGAGES.
HE'LL VANISH INTO THIN AIR AND START A NEW LIFE.
AND WHAT'S YOUR PLAN?
THE YANKS HAVE A STAFF SHORTAGE.
SO THERE'S NOTHING TO STOP KEITH DISAPPEARING.
EXCEPT ME.
YOU'RE UNDERCOVER. DON'T INTERFERE.
IF HE MOVES THEN CALL ME. THAT'S ALL.
NO PROBLEM.
TROUBLE SLEEPING?
WHO YOU RINGING THIS LATE?

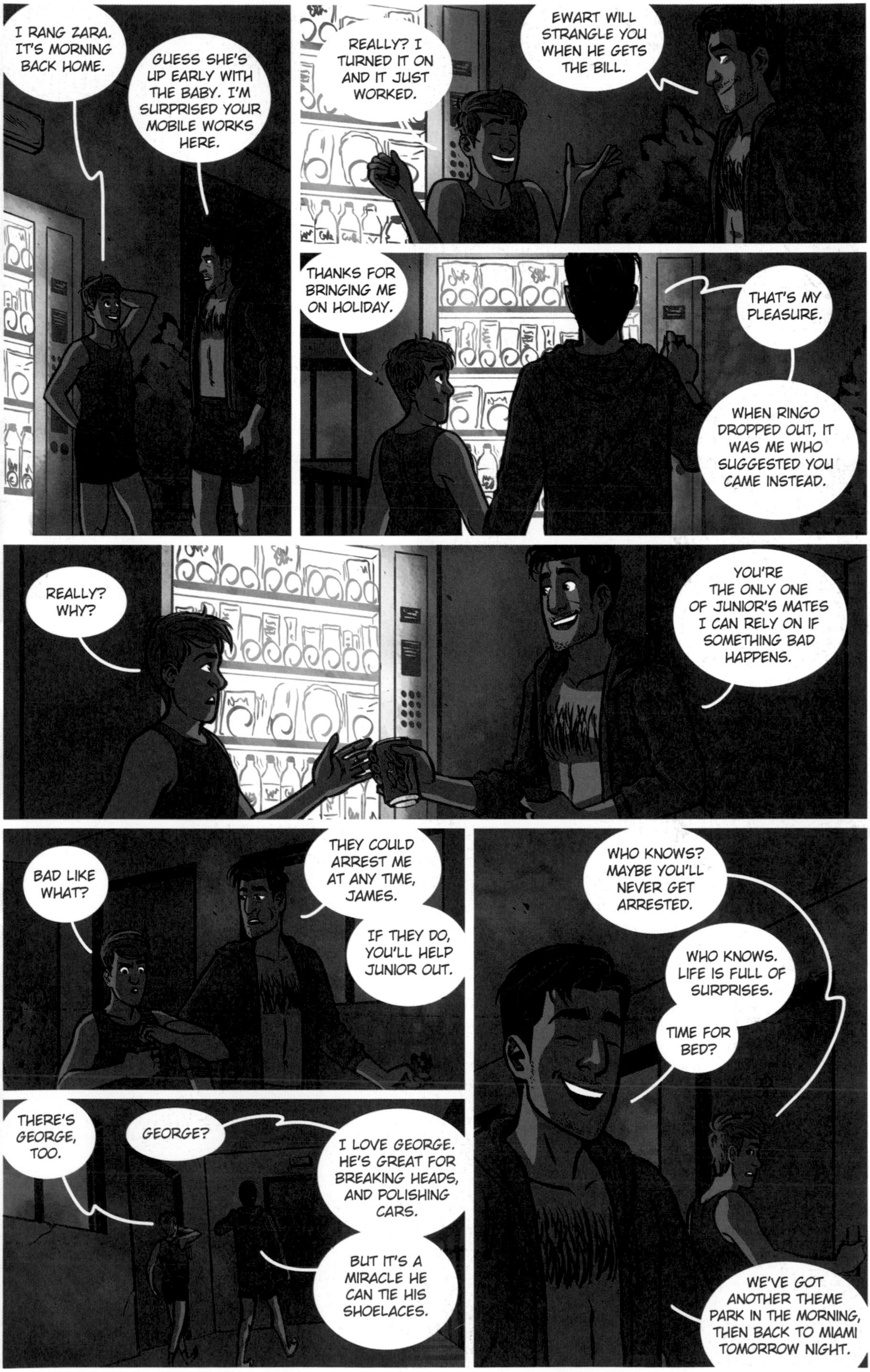
I RANG ZARA. IT'S MORNING BACK HOME.
GUESS SHE'S UP EARLY WITH THE BABY. I'M SURPRISED YOUR MOBILE WORKS HERE.
REALLY? I TURNED IT ON AND IT JUST WORKED.
EWART WILL STRANGLE YOU WHEN HE GETS THE BILL.
THANKS FOR BRINGING ME ON HOLIDAY.
THAT'S MY PLEASURE.
WHEN RINGO DROPPED OUT, IT WAS ME WHO SUGGESTED YOU CAME INSTEAD.
REALLY? WHY?
YOU'RE THE ONLY ONE OF JUNIOR'S MATES I CAN RELY ON IF SOMETHING BAD HAPPENS.
BAD LIKE WHAT?
THEY COULD ARREST ME AT ANY TIME, JAMES.
IF THEY DO, YOU'LL HELP JUNIOR OUT.
THERE'S GEORGE, TOO.
GEORGE?
I LOVE GEORGE. HE'S GREAT FOR BREAKING HEADS, AND POLISHING CARS.
BUT IT'S A MIRACLE HE CAN TIE HIS SHOELACES.
WHO KNOWS? MAYBE YOU'LL NEVER GET ARRESTED.
WHO KNOWS. LIFE IS FULL OF SURPRISES.
TIME FOR BED?
WE'VE GOT ANOTHER THEME PARK IN THE MORNING, THEN BACK TO MIAMI TOMORROW NIGHT.

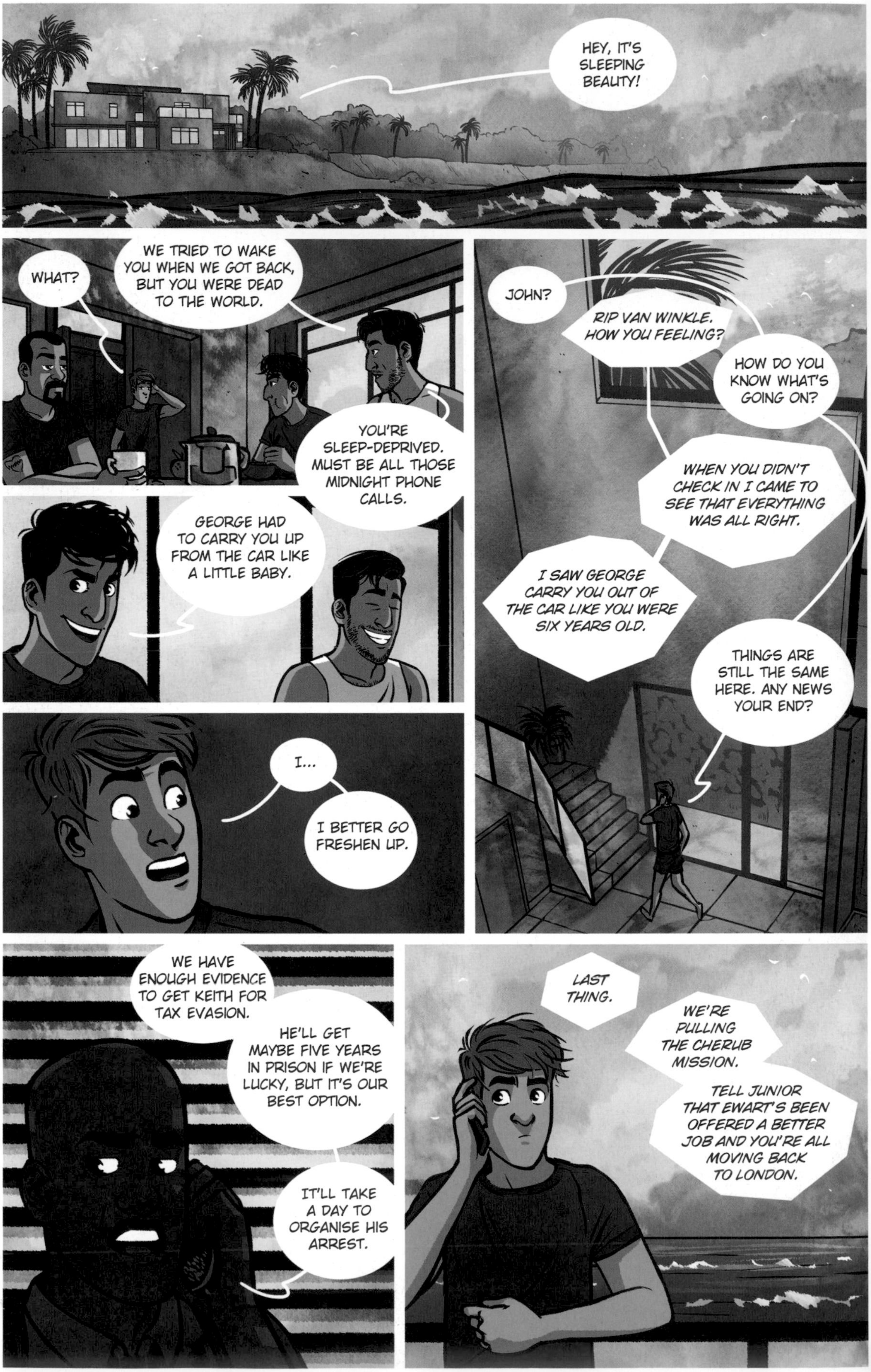
HEY, IT'S SLEEPING BEAUTY!
WHAT?
WE TRIED TO WAKE YOU WHEN WE GOT BACK, BUT YOU WERE DEAD TO THE WORLD.
YOU'RE SLEEP-DEPRIVED. MUST BE ALL THOSE MIDNIGHT PHONE CALLS.
GEORGE HAD TO CARRY YOU UP FROM THE CAR LIKE A LITTLE BABY.
I...
I BETTER GO FRESHEN UP.
JOHN?
RIP VAN WINKLE. HOW YOU FEELING?
HOW DO YOU KNOW WHAT'S GOING ON?
WHEN YOU DIDN'T CHECK IN I CAME TO SEE THAT EVERYTHING WAS ALL RIGHT.
I SAW GEORGE CARRY YOU OUT OF THE CAR LIKE YOU WERE SIX YEARS OLD.
THINGS ARE STILL THE SAME HERE. ANY NEWS YOUR END?
WE HAVE ENOUGH EVIDENCE TO GET KEITH FOR TAX EVASION.
HE'LL GET MAYBE FIVE YEARS IN PRISON IF WE'RE LUCKY, BUT IT'S OUR BEST OPTION.
IT'LL TAKE A DAY TO ORGANISE HIS ARREST.
LAST THING.
WE'RE PULLING THE CHERUB MISSION.
TELL JUNIOR THAT EWART'S BEEN OFFERED A BETTER JOB AND YOU'RE ALL MOVING BACK TO LONDON.

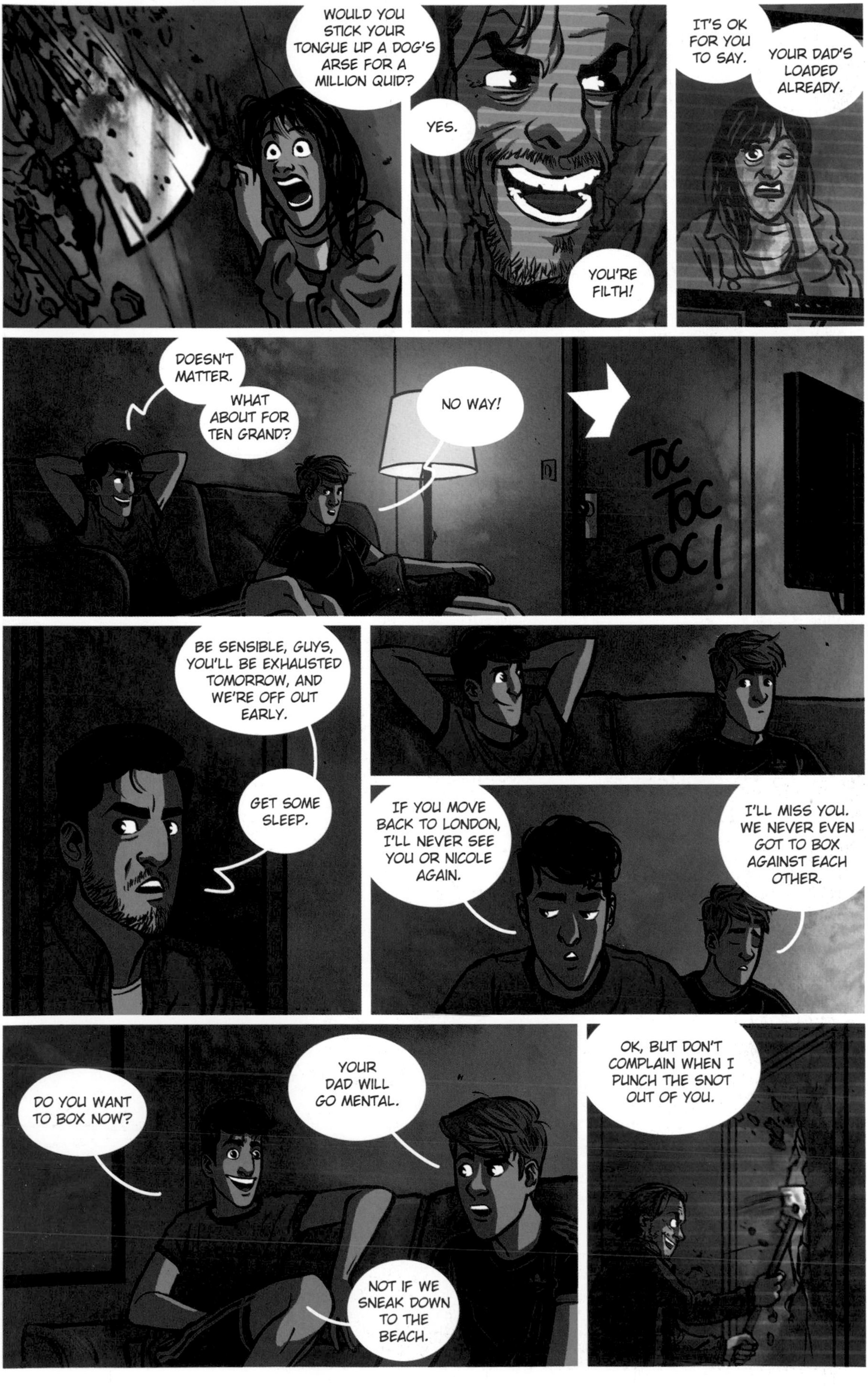
WOULD YOU STICK YOUR TONGUE UP A DOG'S ARSE FOR A MILLION QUID?
YES.
YOU'RE FILTH!
IT'S OK FOR YOU TO SAY.
YOUR DAD'S LOADED ALREADY.
DOESN'T MATTER.
WHAT ABOUT FOR TEN GRAND?
NO WAY!
TOC TOC TOC!
BE SENSIBLE, GUYS, YOU'LL BE EXHAUSTED TOMORROW, AND WE'RE OFF OUT EARLY.
GET SOME SLEEP.
IF YOU MOVE BACK TO LONDON, I'LL NEVER SEE YOU OR NICOLE AGAIN.
I'LL MISS YOU. WE NEVER EVEN GOT TO BOX AGAINST EACH OTHER.
DO YOU WANT TO BOX NOW?
YOUR DAD WILL GO MENTAL.
NOT IF WE SNEAK DOWN TO THE BEACH.
OK, BUT DON'T COMPLAIN WHEN I PUNCH THE SNOT OUT OF YOU.

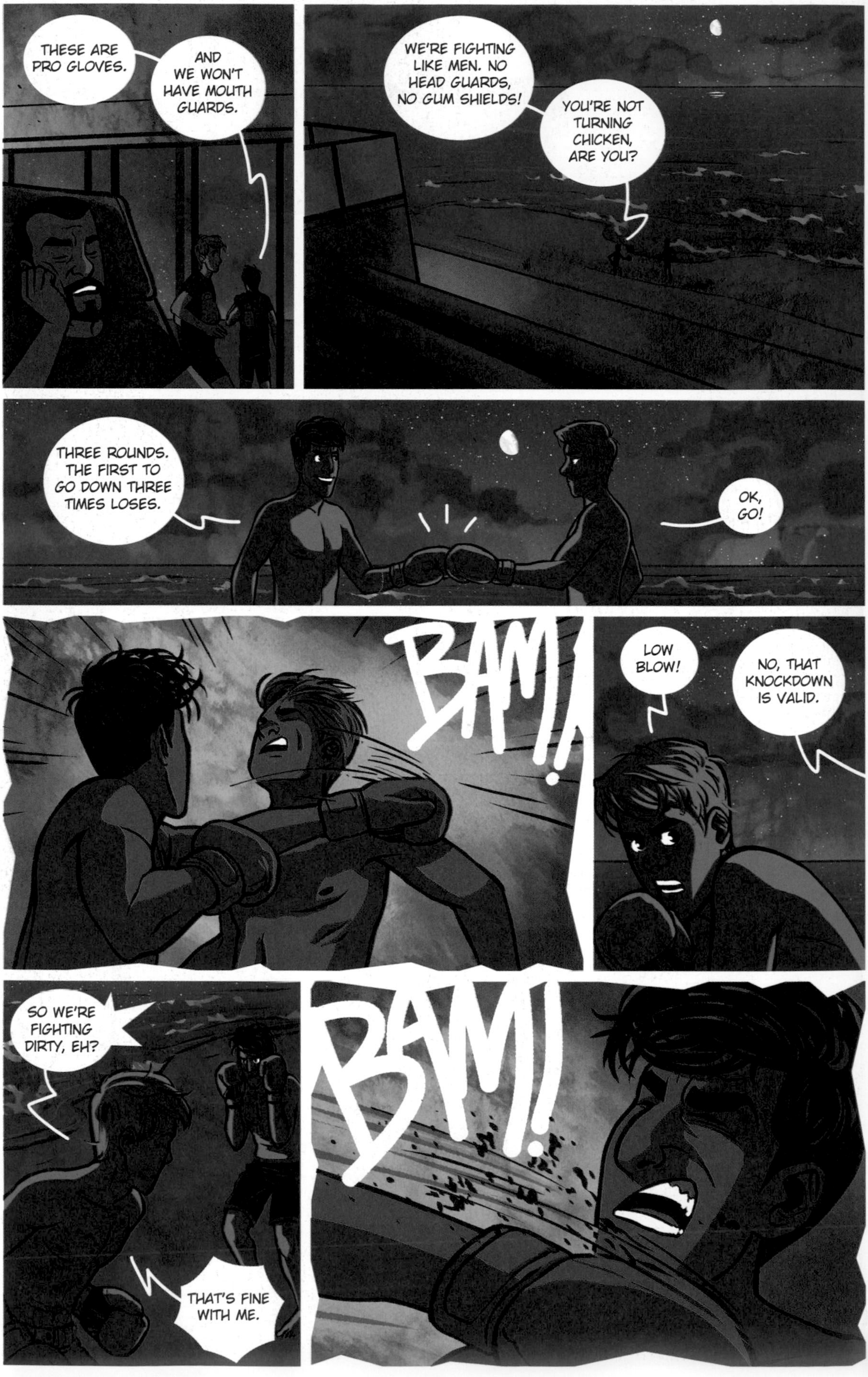
THESE ARE PRO GLOVES.
AND WE WON'T HAVE MOUTH GUARDS.
WE'RE FIGHTING LIKE MEN. NO HEAD GUARDS, NO GUM SHIELDS!
YOU'RE NOT TURNING CHICKEN, ARE YOU?
THREE ROUNDS. THE FIRST TO GO DOWN THREE TIMES LOSES.
OK, GO!
BAM!
LOW BLOW!
NO, THAT KNOCKDOWN IS VALID.
SO WE'RE FIGHTING DIRTY, EH?
THAT'S FINE WITH ME.
BAM!

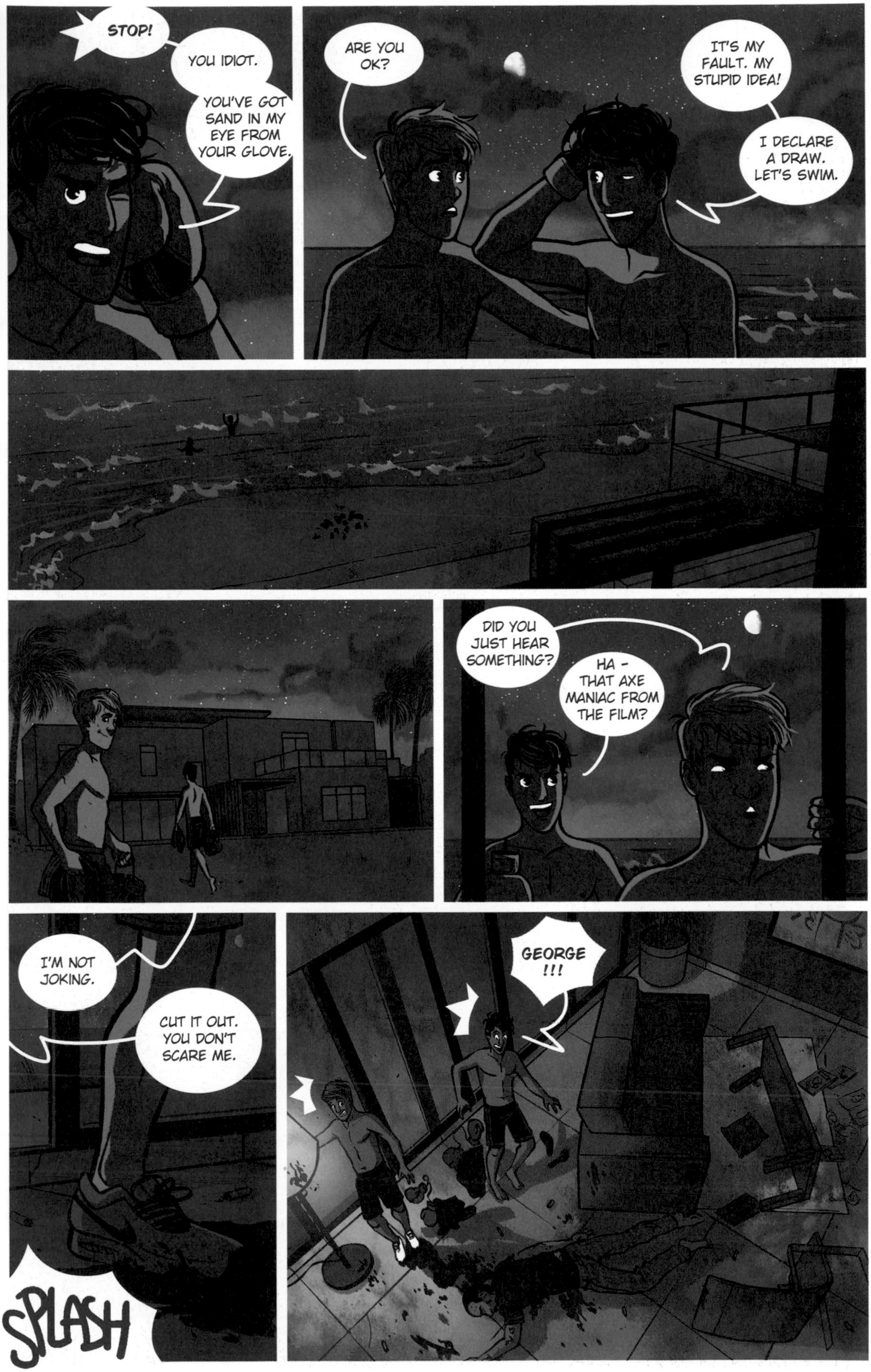
STOP!
YOU IDIOT.
YOU'VE GOT SAND IN MY EYE FROM YOUR GLOVE.
ARE YOU OK?
IT'S MY FAULT. MY STUPID IDEA!
I DECLARE A DRAW. LET'S SWIM.
DID YOU JUST HEAR SOMETHING?
HA - THAT AXE MANIAC FROM THE FILM?
I'M NOT JOKING.
CUT IT OUT. YOU DON'T SCARE ME.
SPLASH
GEORGE !!!

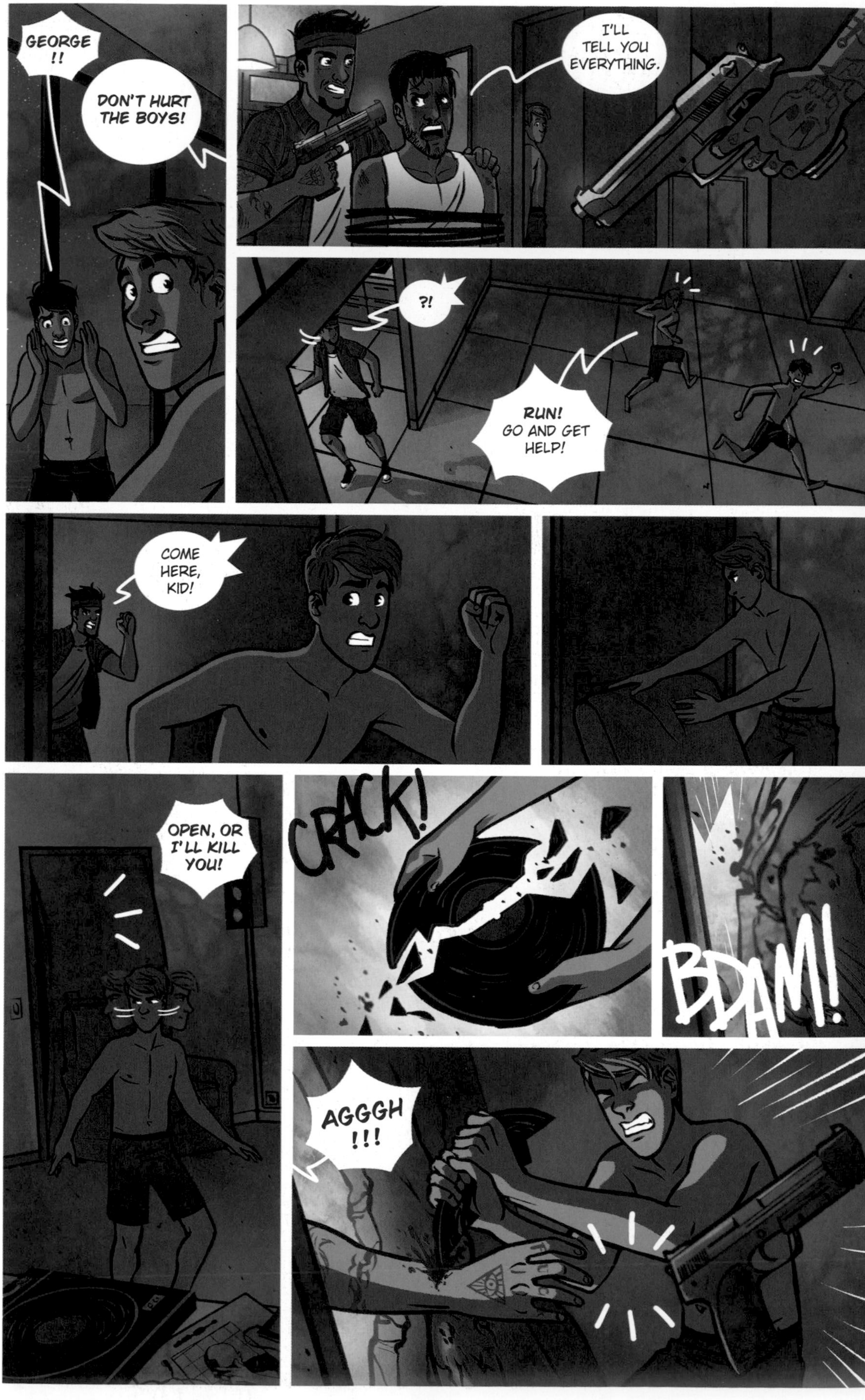
GEORGE !!
DON'T HURT THE BOYS!
I'LL TELL YOU EVERYTHING.
?!
RUN! GO AND GET HELP!
COME HERE, KID!
OPEN, OR I'LL KILL YOU!
CRACK!
BDAM!
AGGGH !!!

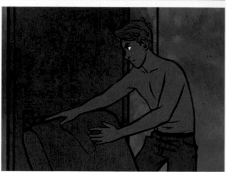

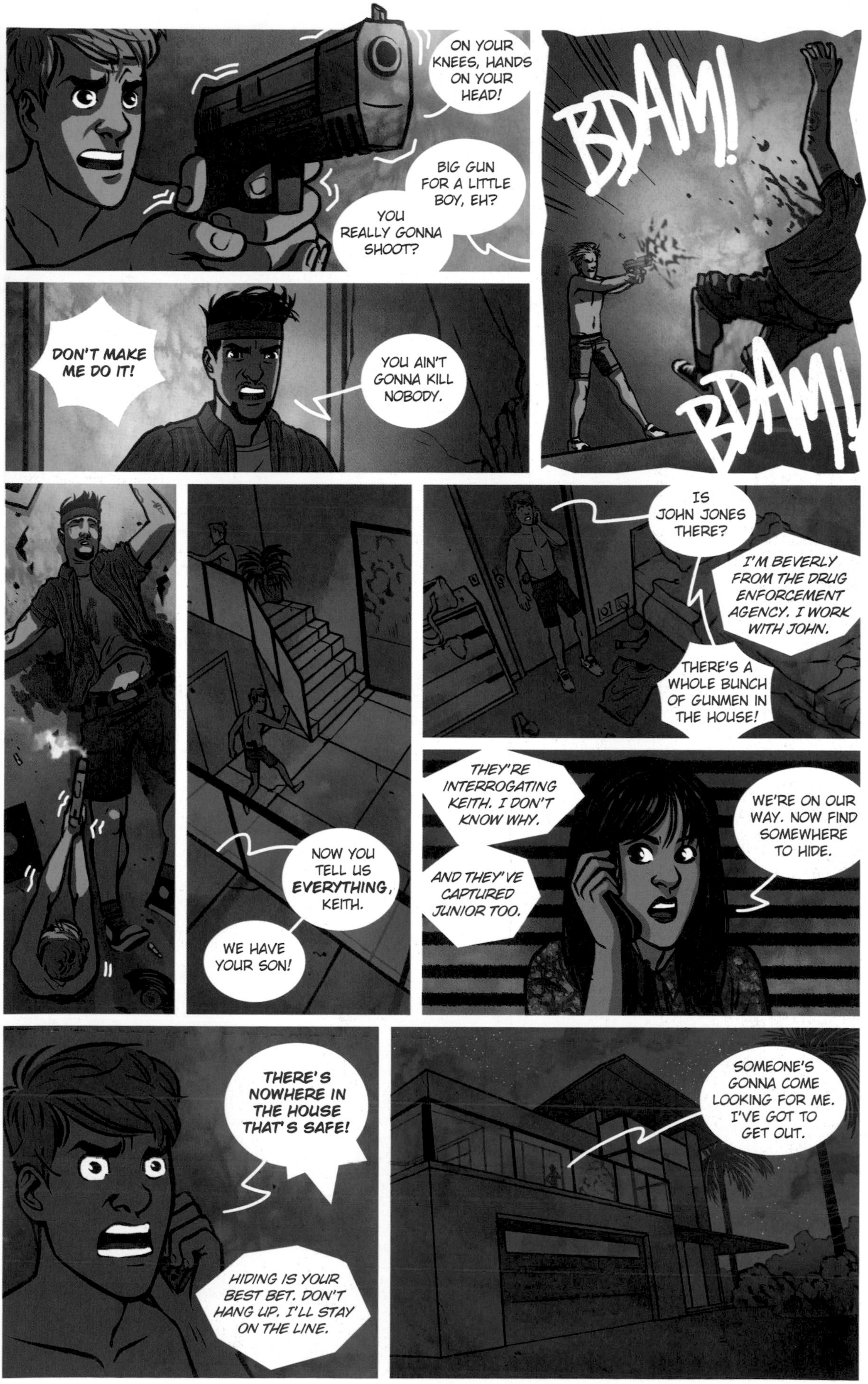
ON YOUR KNEES, HANDS ON YOUR HEAD!
BIG GUN FOR A LITTLE BOY, EH?
YOU REALLY GONNA SHOOT?
DON'T MAKE ME DO IT!
YOU AIN'T GONNA KILL NOBODY.
BDAM!
BDAM!
NOW YOU TELL US EVERYTHING, KEITH.
WE HAVE YOUR SON!
IS JOHN JONES THERE?
I'M BEVERLY FROM THE DRUG ENFORCEMENT AGENCY. I WORK WITH JOHN.
THERE'S A WHOLE BUNCH OF GUNMEN IN THE HOUSE!
THEY'RE INTERROGATING KEITH. I DON'T KNOW WHY.
AND THEY'VE CAPTURED JUNIOR TOO.
WE'RE ON OUR WAY. NOW FIND SOMEWHERE TO HIDE.
THERE'S NOWHERE IN THE HOUSE THAT'S SAFE!
HIDING IS YOUR BEST BET. DON'T HANG UP. I'LL STAY ON THE LINE.
SOMEONE'S GONNA COME LOOKING FOR ME. I'VE GOT TO GET OUT.

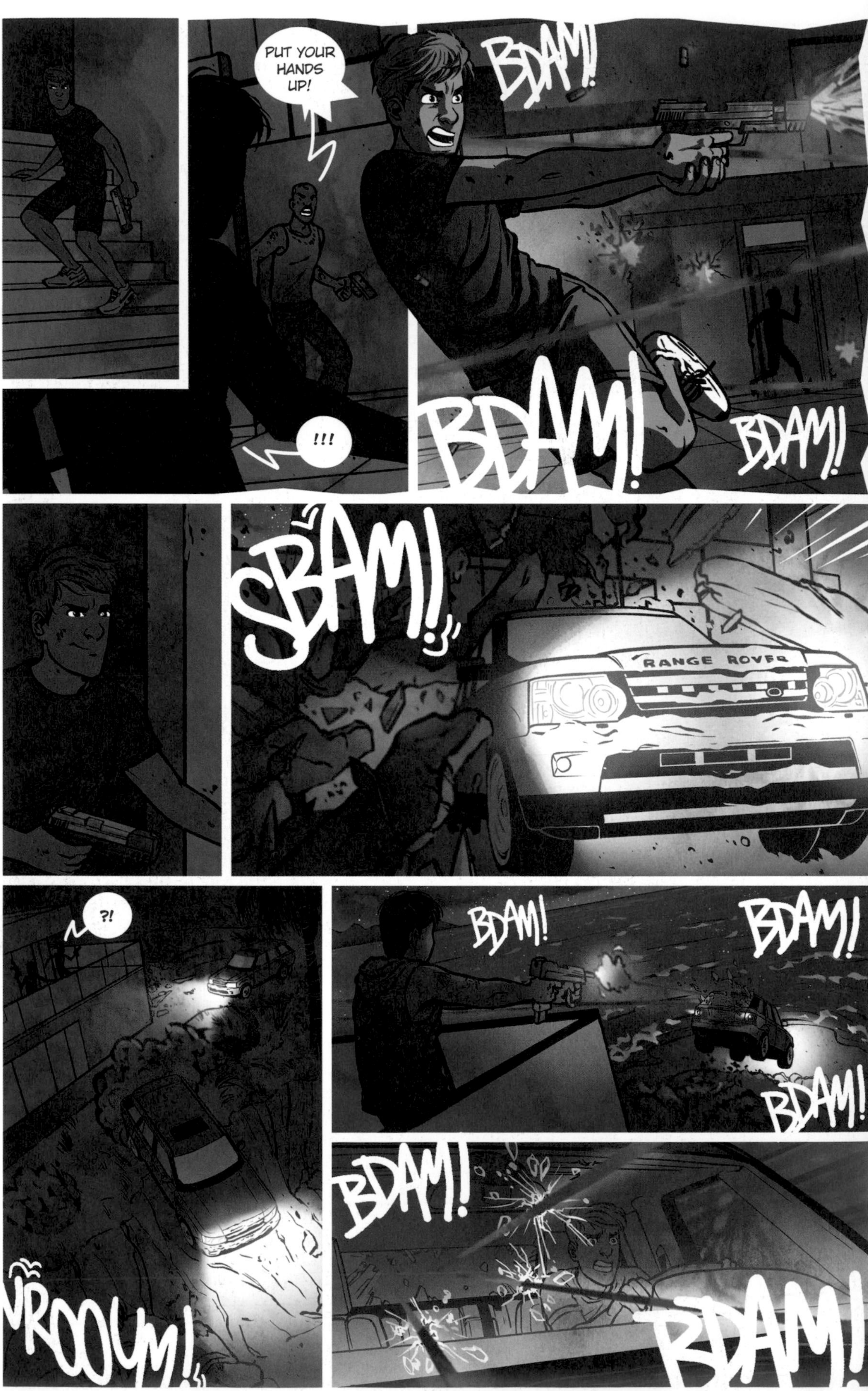
PUT YOUR HANDS UP!
BDAM!
BDAM!
BDAM!
!!!
SBAM!
?!
VROOYM!
BDAM!
BDAM!
BDAM!
BDAM!
BDAM!
RANGE ROVER

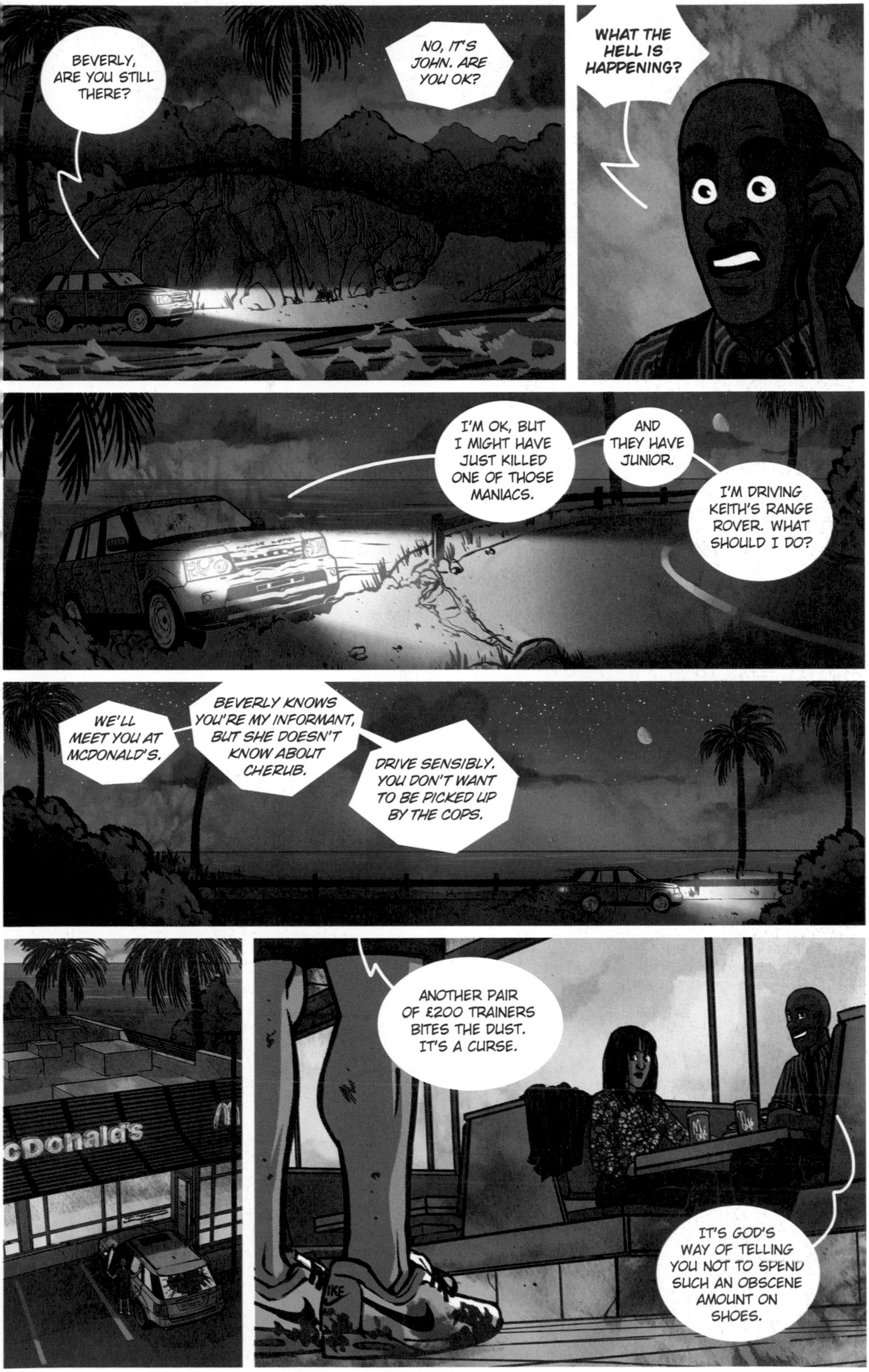

BEVERLY, ARE YOU STILL THERE?
NO, IT'S JOHN. ARE YOU OK?
WHAT THE HELL IS HAPPENING?
I'M OK, BUT I MIGHT HAVE JUST KILLED ONE OF THOSE MANIACS.
AND THEY HAVE JUNIOR.
I'M DRIVING KEITH'S RANGE ROVER. WHAT SHOULD I DO?
WE'LL MEET YOU AT MCDONALD'S.
BEVERLY KNOWS YOU'RE MY INFORMANT, BUT SHE DOESN'T KNOW ABOUT CHERUB.
DRIVE SENSIBLY. YOU DON'T WANT TO BE PICKED UP BY THE COPS.
McDonald's
ANOTHER PAIR OF £200 TRAINERS BITES THE DUST. IT'S A CURSE.
IT'S GOD'S WAY OF TELLING YOU NOT TO SPEND SUCH AN OBSCENE AMOUNT ON SHOES.

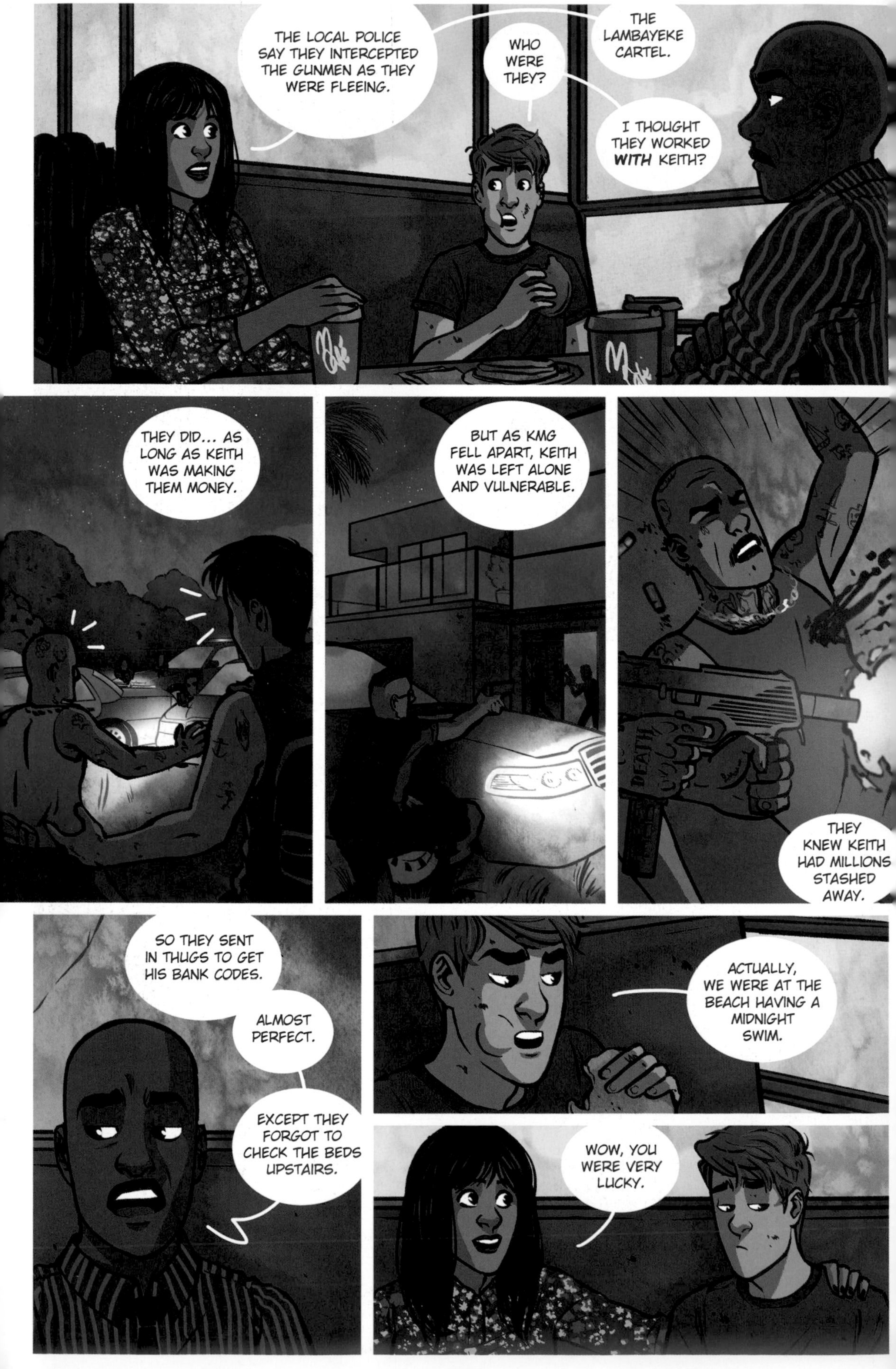
THE LOCAL POLICE SAY THEY INTERCEPTED THE GUNMEN AS THEY WERE FLEEING.
WHO WERE THEY?
THE LAMBAYEKE CARTEL.
I THOUGHT THEY WORKED WITH KEITH?
THEY DID... AS LONG AS KEITH WAS MAKING THEM MONEY.
BUT AS KMG FELL APART, KEITH WAS LEFT ALONE AND VULNERABLE.
DEATH
THEY KNEW KEITH HAD MILLIONS STASHED AWAY.
SO THEY SENT IN THUGS TO GET HIS BANK CODES.
ALMOST PERFECT.
EXCEPT THEY FORGOT TO CHECK THE BEDS UPSTAIRS.
ACTUALLY, WE WERE AT THE BEACH HAVING A MIDNIGHT SWIM.
WOW, YOU WERE VERY LUCKY.

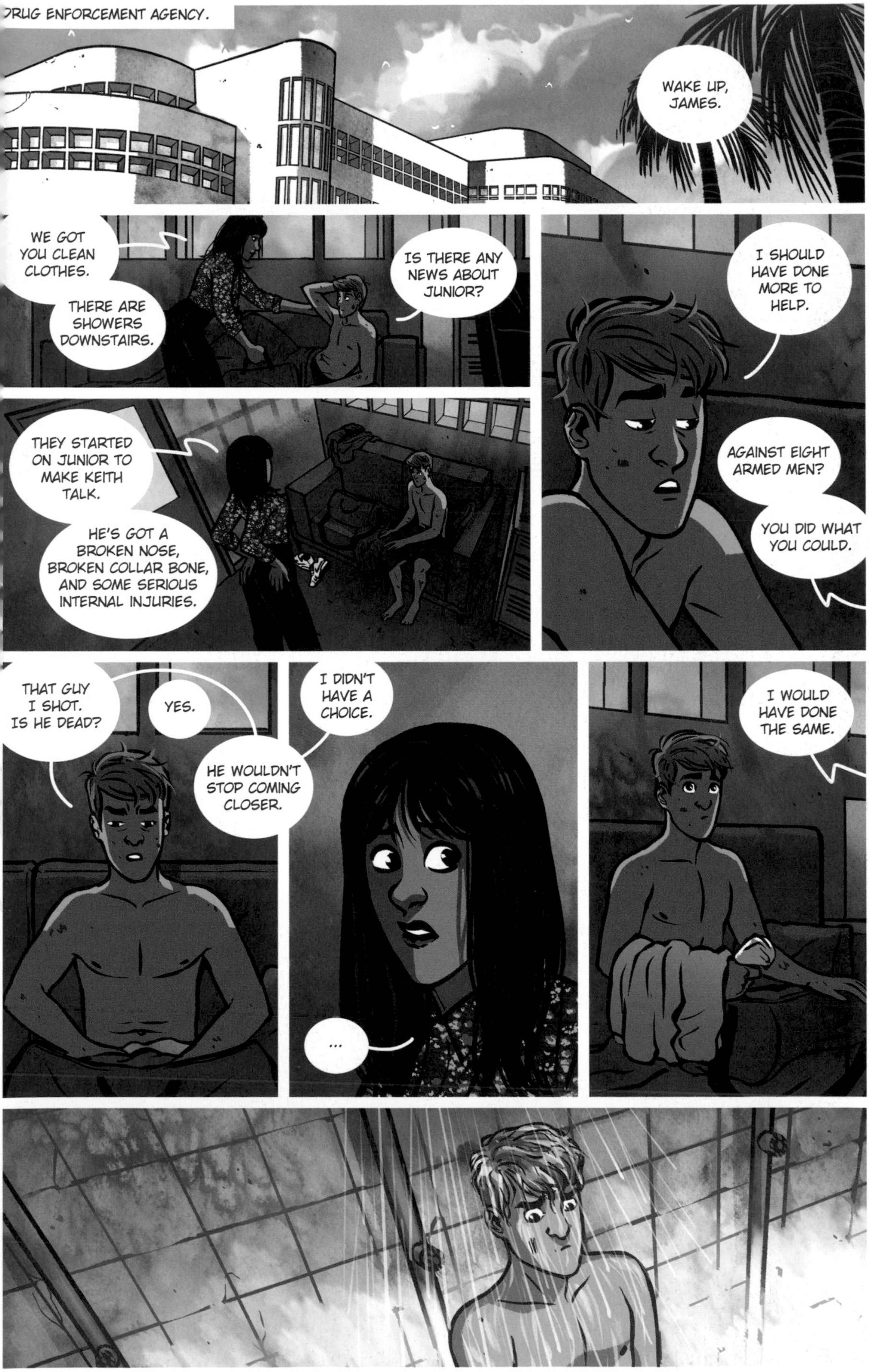
DRUG ENFORCEMENT AGENCY.
WAKE UP, JAMES.
WE GOT YOU CLEAN CLOTHES.
THERE ARE SHOWERS DOWNSTAIRS.
IS THERE ANY NEWS ABOUT JUNIOR?
THEY STARTED ON JUNIOR TO MAKE KEITH TALK.
HE'S GOT A BROKEN NOSE, BROKEN COLLAR BONE, AND SOME SERIOUS INTERNAL INJURIES.
I SHOULD HAVE DONE MORE TO HELP.
AGAINST EIGHT ARMED MEN?
YOU DID WHAT YOU COULD.
THAT GUY I SHOT. IS HE DEAD?
YES.
HE WOULDN'T STOP COMING CLOSER.
I DIDN'T HAVE A CHOICE.
...
I WOULD HAVE DONE THE SAME.

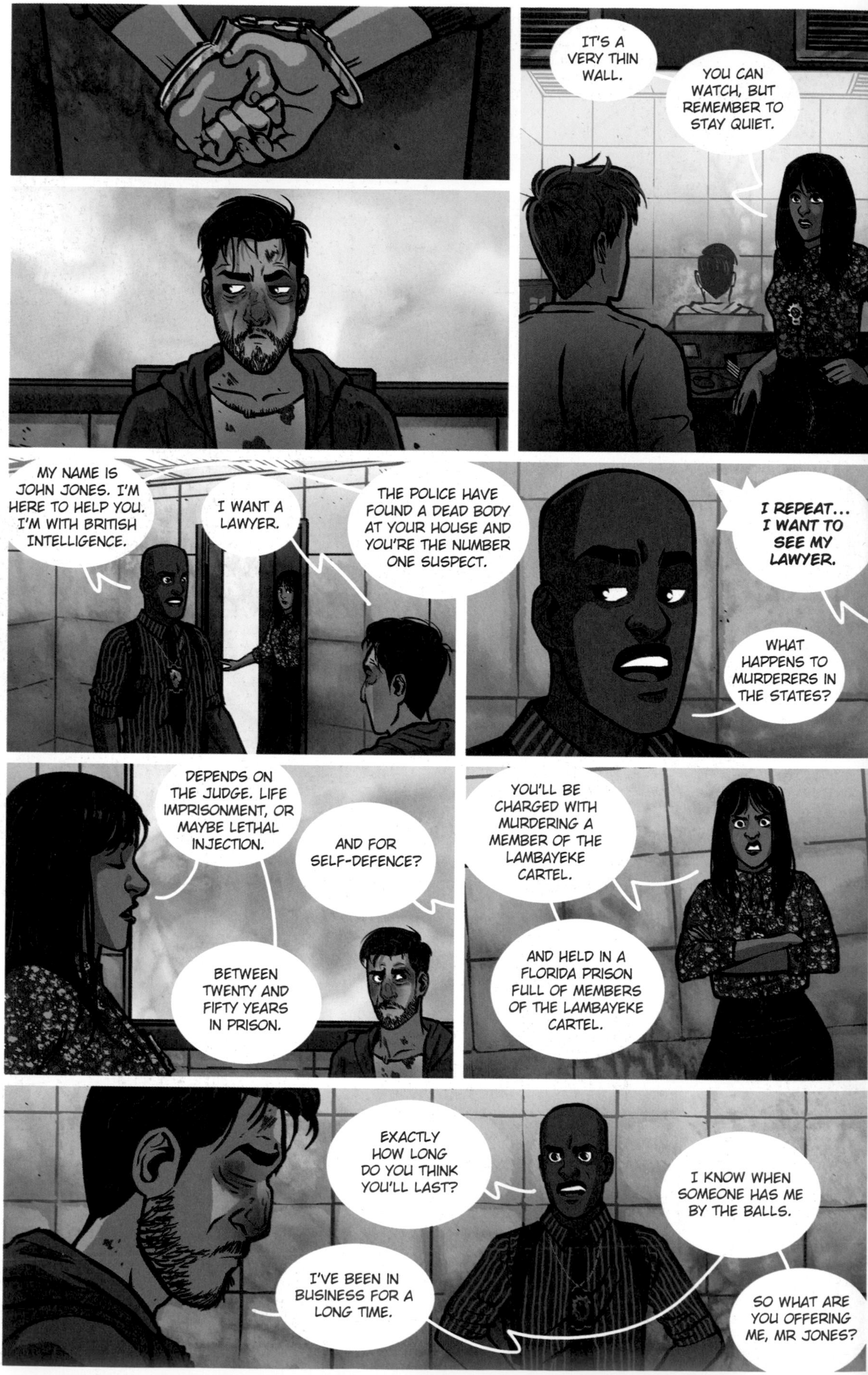
IT'S A VERY THIN WALL.
YOU CAN WATCH, BUT REMEMBER TO STAY QUIET.
MY NAME IS JOHN JONES. I'M HERE TO HELP YOU. I'M WITH BRITISH INTELLIGENCE.
I WANT A LAWYER.
THE POLICE HAVE FOUND A DEAD BODY AT YOUR HOUSE AND YOU'RE THE NUMBER ONE SUSPECT.
I REPEAT... I WANT TO SEE MY LAWYER.
WHAT HAPPENS TO MURDERERS IN THE STATES?
DEPENDS ON THE JUDGE. LIFE IMPRISONMENT, OR MAYBE LETHAL INJECTION.
AND FOR SELF-DEFENCE?
BETWEEN TWENTY AND FIFTY YEARS IN PRISON.
YOU'LL BE CHARGED WITH MURDERING A MEMBER OF THE LAMBAYEKE CARTEL.
AND HELD IN A FLORIDA PRISON FULL OF MEMBERS OF THE LAMBAYEKE CARTEL.
EXACTLY HOW LONG DO YOU THINK YOU'LL LAST?
I'VE BEEN IN BUSINESS FOR A LONG TIME.
I KNOW WHEN SOMEONE HAS ME BY THE BALLS.
SO WHAT ARE YOU OFFERING ME, MR JONES?

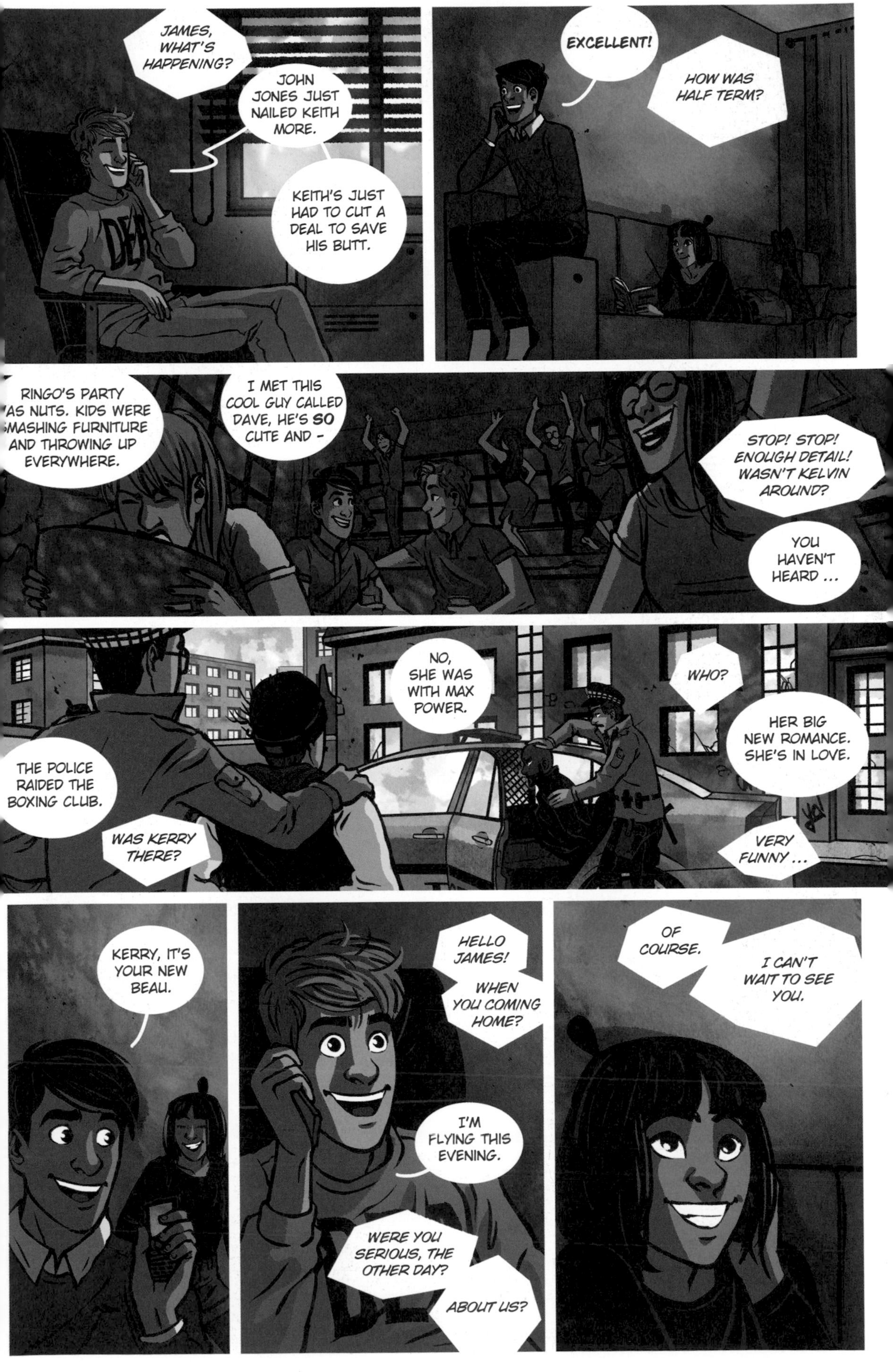
JAMES, WHAT'S HAPPENING?
JOHN JONES JUST NAILED KEITH MORE.
KEITH'S JUST HAD TO CUT A DEAL TO SAVE HIS BUTT.
EXCELLENT!
HOW WAS HALF TERM?
RINGO'S PARTY AS NUTS. KIDS WERE MASHING FURNITURE AND THROWING UP EVERYWHERE.
I MET THIS COOL GUY CALLED DAVE, HE'S SO CUTE AND –
STOP! STOP! ENOUGH DETAIL! WASN'T KELVIN AROUND?
YOU HAVEN'T HEARD ...
THE POLICE RAIDED THE BOXING CLUB.
WAS KERRY THERE?
NO, SHE WAS WITH MAX POWER.
WHO?
HER BIG NEW ROMANCE. SHE'S IN LOVE.
VERY FUNNY ...
KERRY, IT'S YOUR NEW BEAU.
HELLO JAMES!
WHEN YOU COMING HOME?
I'M FLYING THIS EVENING.
WERE YOU SERIOUS, THE OTHER DAY?
ABOUT US?
OF COURSE.
I CAN'T WAIT TO SEE YOU.

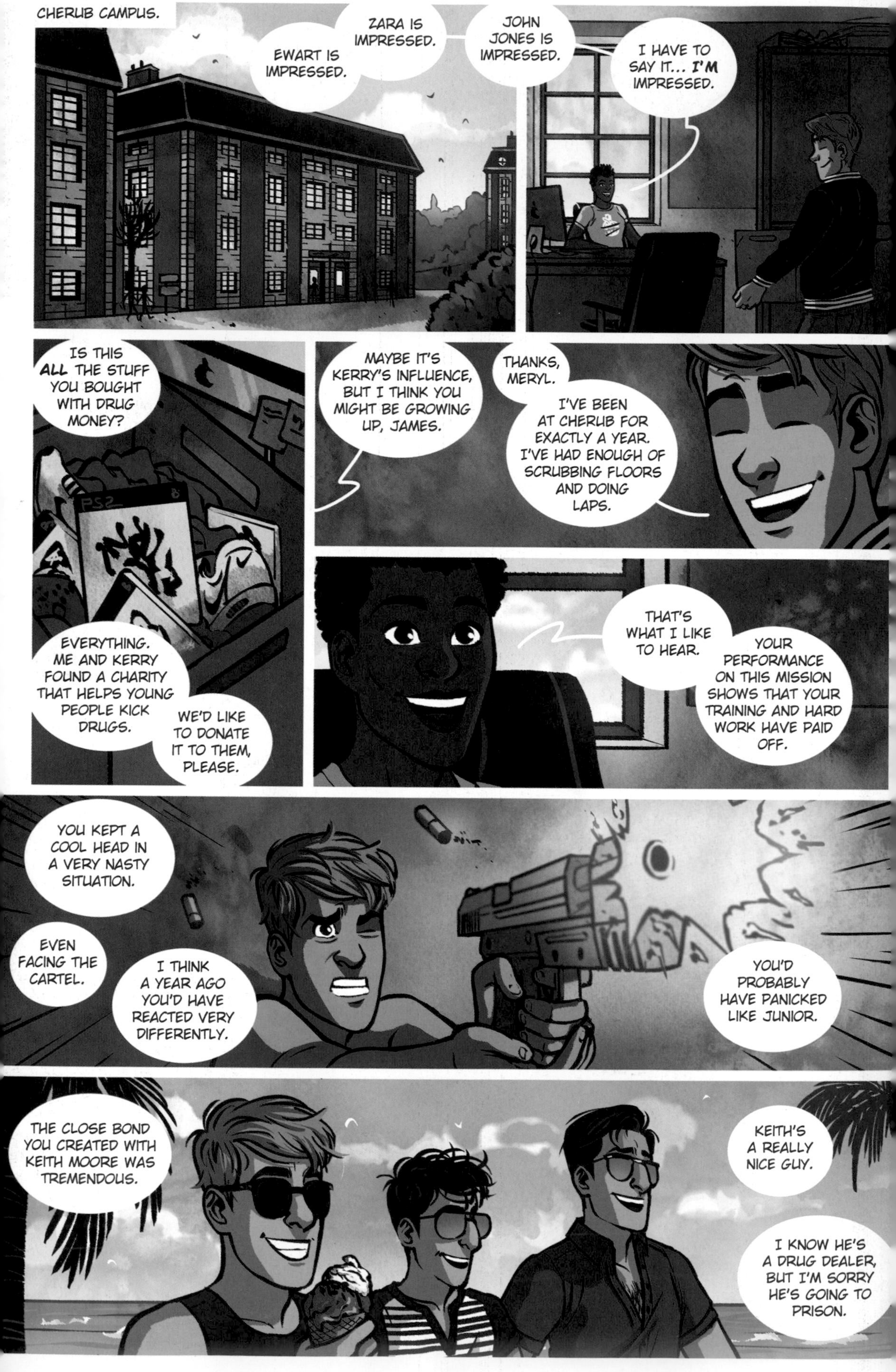
CHERUB CAMPUS.
EWART IS IMPRESSED.
ZARA IS IMPRESSED.
JOHN JONES IS IMPRESSED.
I HAVE TO SAY IT... I'M IMPRESSED.
IS THIS ALL THE STUFF YOU BOUGHT WITH DRUG MONEY?
EVERYTHING. ME AND KERRY FOUND A CHARITY THAT HELPS YOUNG PEOPLE KICK DRUGS.
WE'D LIKE TO DONATE IT TO THEM, PLEASE.
PS2
MAYBE IT'S KERRY'S INFLUENCE, BUT I THINK YOU MIGHT BE GROWING UP, JAMES.
THANKS, MERYL.
I'VE BEEN AT CHERUB FOR EXACTLY A YEAR. I'VE HAD ENOUGH OF SCRUBBING FLOORS AND DOING LAPS.
THAT'S WHAT I LIKE TO HEAR.
YOUR PERFORMANCE ON THIS MISSION SHOWS THAT YOUR TRAINING AND HARD WORK HAVE PAID OFF.
YOU KEPT A COOL HEAD IN A VERY NASTY SITUATION.
EVEN FACING THE CARTEL.
I THINK A YEAR AGO YOU'D HAVE REACTED VERY DIFFERENTLY.
YOU'D PROBABLY HAVE PANICKED LIKE JUNIOR.
THE CLOSE BOND YOU CREATED WITH KEITH MOORE WAS TREMENDOUS.
KEITH'S A REALLY NICE GUY.
I KNOW HE'S A DRUG DEALER, BUT I'M SORRY HE'S GOING TO PRISON.

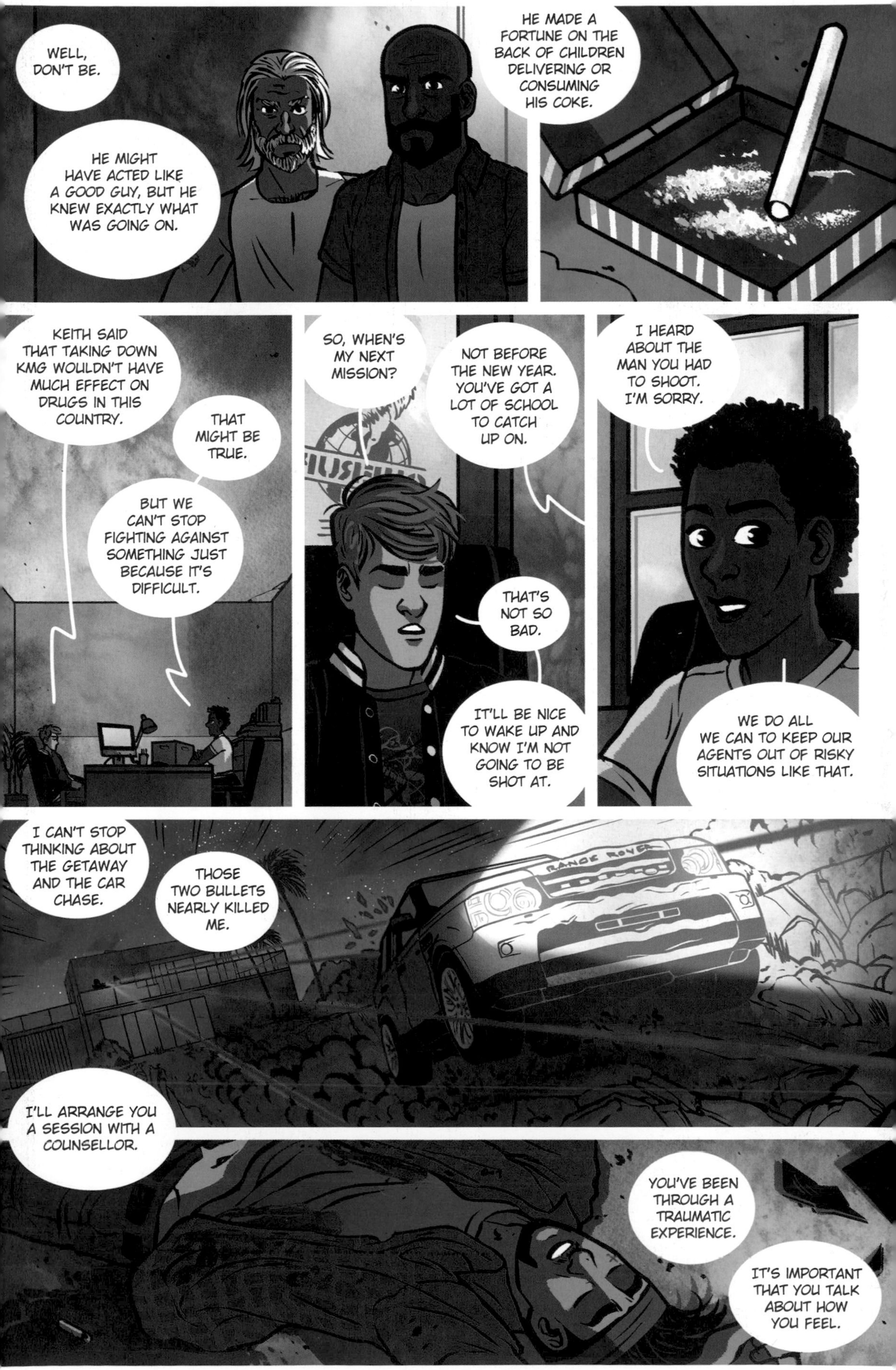
WELL, DON'T BE.
HE MIGHT HAVE ACTED LIKE A GOOD GUY, BUT HE KNEW EXACTLY WHAT WAS GOING ON.
HE MADE A FORTUNE ON THE BACK OF CHILDREN DELIVERING OR CONSUMING HIS COKE.
KEITH SAID THAT TAKING DOWN KMG WOULDN'T HAVE MUCH EFFECT ON DRUGS IN THIS COUNTRY.
THAT MIGHT BE TRUE.
BUT WE CAN'T STOP FIGHTING AGAINST SOMETHING JUST BECAUSE IT'S DIFFICULT.
SO, WHEN'S MY NEXT MISSION?
NOT BEFORE THE NEW YEAR. YOU'VE GOT A LOT OF SCHOOL TO CATCH UP ON.
THAT'S NOT SO BAD.
IT'LL BE NICE TO WAKE UP AND KNOW I'M NOT GOING TO BE SHOT AT.
I HEARD ABOUT THE MAN YOU HAD TO SHOOT. I'M SORRY.
WE DO ALL WE CAN TO KEEP OUR AGENTS OUT OF RISKY SITUATIONS LIKE THAT.
I CAN'T STOP THINKING ABOUT THE GETAWAY AND THE CAR CHASE.
THOSE TWO BULLETS NEARLY KILLED ME.
RANGE ROVER
I'LL ARRANGE YOU A SESSION WITH A COUNSELLOR.
YOU'VE BEEN THROUGH A TRAUMATIC EXPERIENCE.
IT'S IMPORTANT THAT YOU TALK ABOUT HOW YOU FEEL.

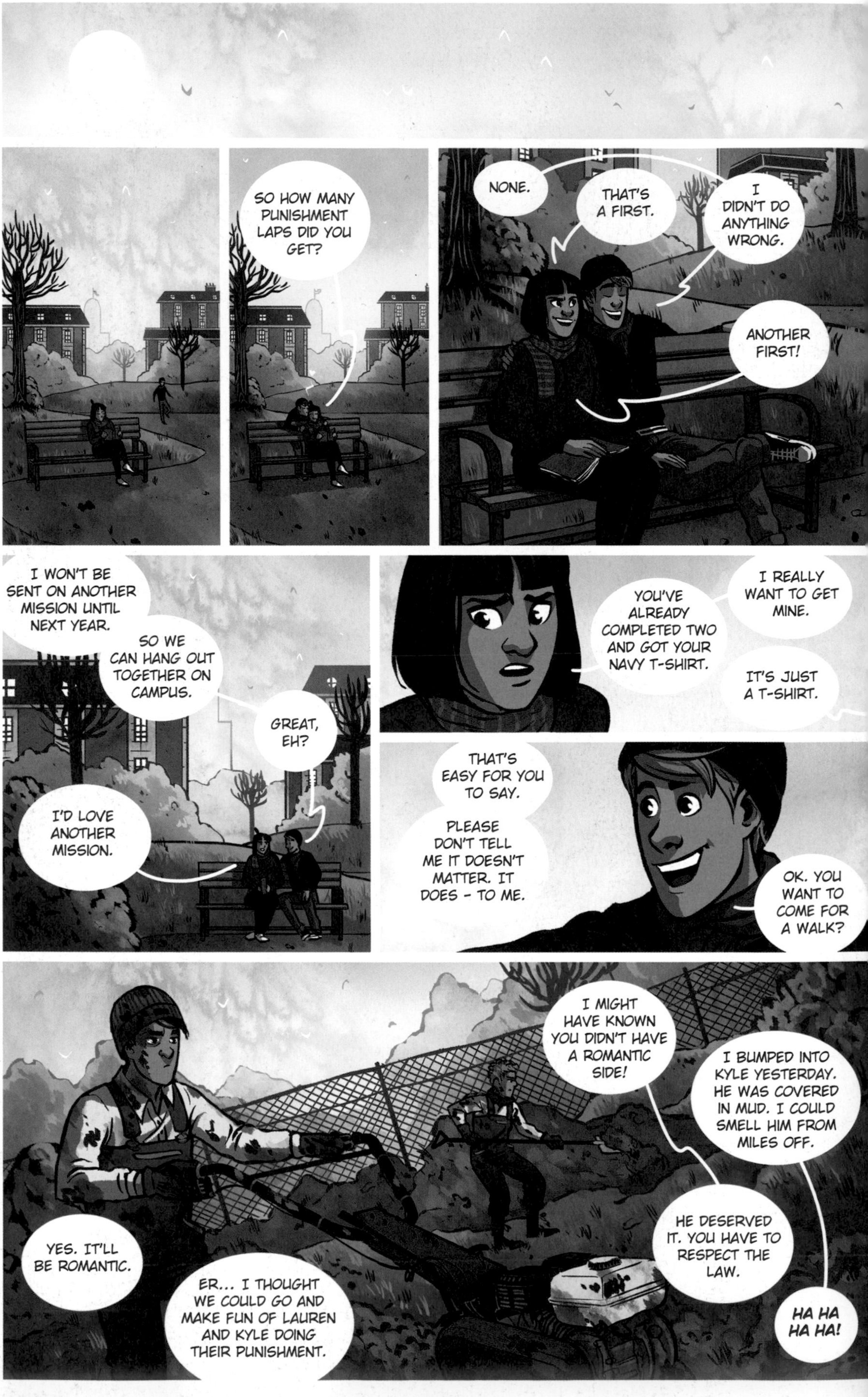
SO HOW MANY PUNISHMENT LAPS DID YOU GET?
NONE.
THAT'S A FIRST.
I DIDN'T DO ANYTHING WRONG.
ANOTHER FIRST!
I WON'T BE SENT ON ANOTHER MISSION UNTIL NEXT YEAR.
SO WE CAN HANG OUT TOGETHER ON CAMPUS.
GREAT, EH?
I'D LOVE ANOTHER MISSION.
YOU'VE ALREADY COMPLETED TWO AND GOT YOUR NAVY T-SHIRT.
I REALLY WANT TO GET MINE.
IT'S JUST A T-SHIRT.
THAT'S EASY FOR YOU TO SAY.
PLEASE DON'T TELL ME IT DOESN'T MATTER. IT DOES - TO ME.
OK. YOU WANT TO COME FOR A WALK?
YES. IT'LL BE ROMANTIC.
ER... I THOUGHT WE COULD GO AND MAKE FUN OF LAUREN AND KYLE DOING THEIR PUNISHMENT.
I MIGHT HAVE KNOWN YOU DIDN'T HAVE A ROMANTIC SIDE!
I BUMPED INTO KYLE YESTERDAY. HE WAS COVERED IN MUD. I COULD SMELL HIM FROM MILES OFF.
HE DESERVED IT. YOU HAVE TO RESPECT THE LAW.
HA HA HA HA!

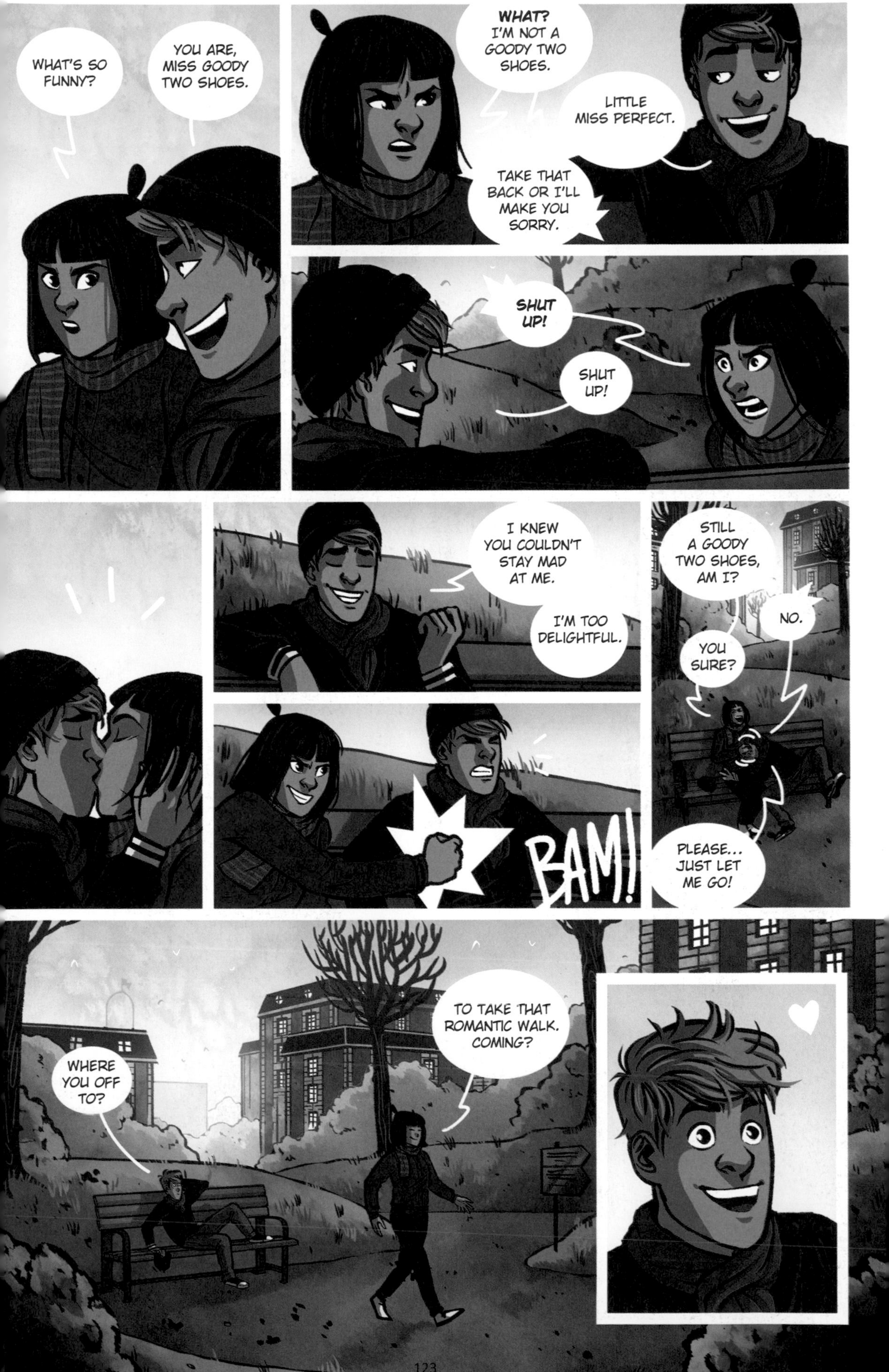
WHAT'S SO FUNNY?
YOU ARE, MISS GOODY TWO SHOES.
WHAT? I'M NOT A GOODY TWO SHOES.
LITTLE MISS PERFECT.
TAKE THAT BACK OR I'LL MAKE YOU SORRY.
SHUT UP!
SHUT UP!
I KNEW YOU COULDN'T STAY MAD AT ME.
I'M TOO DELIGHTFUL.
BAM!
STILL A GOODY TWO SHOES, AM I?
NO.
YOU SURE?
PLEASE... JUST LET ME GO!
WHERE YOU OFF TO?
TO TAKE THAT ROMANTIC WALK. COMING?

KELVIN HOLMES WAS SENTENCED TO THREE YEARS' CUSTODY FOR SUPPLYING DRUGS. MOST OF THE YOUNG DELIVERY RIDERS GOT SHORT YOUTH SENTENCES.

NICOLE EDDISON NOW LIVES WITH TWO RETIRED CHERUBS ON A FARM IN SHROPSHIRE. SHE HAS A BOYFRIEND CALLED JAMES.

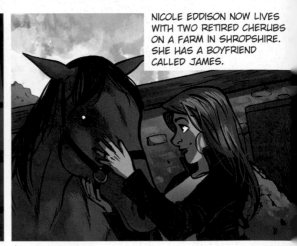

JUNIOR MOORE MADE A FULL RECOVERY FROM HIS INJURIES AND FLEW BACK TO BRITAIN. SHORTLY AFTERWARDS, HIS MOTHER SENT HIM TO A BOARDING SCHOOL THAT SPECIALISES IN DIFFICULT BOYS.

JOHN JONES LEFT MI5 AFTER NINETEEN YEARS OF SERVICE AND ACCEPTED A JOB AS A CHERUB MISSION CONTROLLER.

KEITH MOORE RECEIVED A SENTENCE OF EIGHTEEN YEARS IN PRISON. THE POLICE SEIZED 12 MILLION POUNDS OF KEITH'S FORTUNE, BUT BELIEVE MILLIONS REMAIN HIDDEN IN SECRET BANK ACCOUNTS. HE REMAINS BITTER ABOUT THE LAMBAYEKE CARTEL'S BETRAYAL.

KYLE BAKER AND LAUREN ADAMS SPENT TWO MONTHS CLEANING OUT THE DITCHES BEHIND CHERUB CAMPUS.

KERRY CHANG WAS SENT ON A LONG-TERM MISSION IN HONG KONG. SHE EXCHANGES DAILY EMAILS WITH JAMES.

JAMES ADAMS USED HIS TIME ON CAMPUS TO CATCH UP ON SCHOOLWORK. HE IS STUDYING FOR EXAMS AND NARROWLY FAILED HIS SECOND-DAN BLACK BELT. HE'S LOOKING FORWARD TO BEING GIVEN A NEW MISSION IN THE SPRING. JAMES NOW CONSIDERS CHERUB HIS HOME.

Bestselling series by Robert Muchamore!

The prequel to the bestselling CHERUB series
HB
HENDERSON'S BOYS
THE ESCAPE
Robert Muchamore

'Pacy writing, punchy dialogue and a gripping plot, it's got it all.'
Daily Express

CHERUB
THE RECRUIT
Robert Muchamore
#1 International Bestselling Author

'My son could never see the point of reading a book until he read *The Recruit*. I want to thank you from the bottom of my heart for igniting the fire.' Donna

NO.1 BESTSELLING AUTHOR OF CHERUB
ROBERT MUCHAMORE
ROCK
WAR

'These are the best books ever!'
Jack, 12

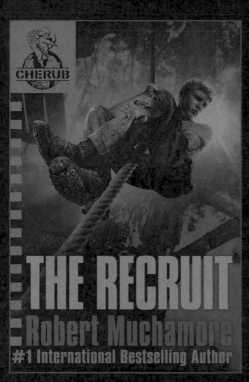

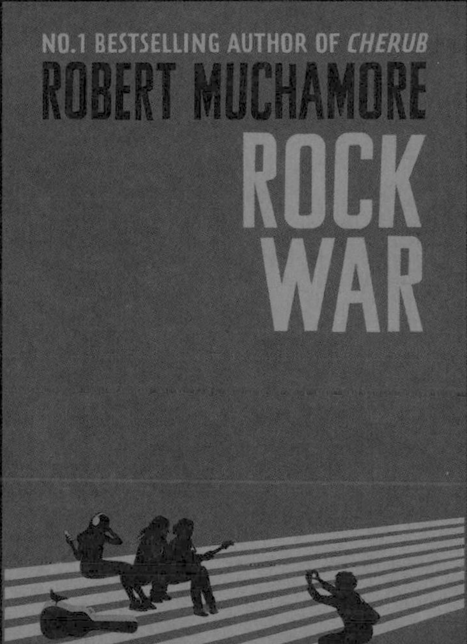